*with me in seattle* book 1

# Come Away
## with me

## KRISTEN PROBY

D0851887

x

JAN    2019

This book is dedicated to my mom, *Gail Holien*. Thank you for giving me the love of reading a good love story and for being the best woman I know. I love you, Mom.

# *books by*
# KRISTEN PROBY

WITH ME IN SEATTLE SERIES:
Come Away With Me
Under The Mistletoe With Me
Fight With Me
Play With Me
Rock With Me
Safe With Me
Tied With Me
Breathe With Me
Forever With Me

LOVE UNDER THE BIG SKY SERIES,
available through Pocket Books:
Loving Cara
Seducing Lauren
Falling for Jillian

THE BOUDREAUX SERIES:
Easy Love
Easy for Keeps: 1001 Dark Nights Novella

Easy Charm

Easy Melody

Easy Kisses

THE FUSION SERIES:

Listen to Me

Close to You

Blush For Me ~ Coming Soon

# one

The light this morning is perfect. I hold my Canon to my face and press the shutter. *Click.* The Puget Sound is covered in color. Pinks, yellows, blues. And for once the wind is almost still. Waves gently lap against the concrete barrier at my feet, and I'm lost in the beauty before me.

*Click.*

I turn to my left and see a young couple walking along the sidewalk. Seattle's Alki Beach is pretty much deserted, aside from a few die-hards, or early morning insomniacs, like me. The young couple are walking away from me, hand in hand, smiling at each other, and I point my lens at them and *click*. I zoom in on their sneaker-clad feet and locked hands and shoot some more, my photographer's eye appreciating their intimate moment on the beach.

I inhale the salty air and stare out at the sound once again as a red-sailed boat gently glides out on the water. The early morning sunshine is just barely beginning to sparkle around it, and I raise my camera again to capture the moment.

"What the fuck are you doing?"

I twirl at the sound of the angry voice and gaze into blue eyes that reflect the bright morning water. They are surrounded by a very, very pissed-off face.

Not merely angry. Livid.

"Excuse me?" I squeak, finding my voice.

"Why can't you all just leave me the fuck alone?" The handsome—really handsome—stranger in front of me is shaking in rage, and I instinctively step back, frowning and beginning to get pissed right back at him. *What the fuck are you doing?*

"I wasn't bothering you," I respond, happy that my voice is stronger with my anger, and retreat back another step. Clearly, Mr. Beautiful Blue Eyes and Sexy Greek God Face is a loony tune. Unfortunately, he follows my backward motion, and I feel the panic start to take hold in my gut.

"I have had it with you following me. Do you think I don't notice? Give me the camera." He extends a long-fingered hand, and my mouth drops open. I pull my camera into my chest and wrap my arms around it protectively.

"No." My voice is amazingly calm, and I want to look around for a means of escape, but I can't stop looking into his angry, sea-colored eyes.

He swallows and narrows his eyes, breathing hard.

"Give me the fucking camera, and I won't press charges for harassment. I just want the photos." He's lowered his voice, but it's no less menacing.

"You can't have my photos!" Who the hell is this guy? I turn to run, and he grabs my arm, whipping me around to face him once again, grabbing for my camera. I start to scream, not believing that I'm being mugged practically outside my front door. Then he lets go of me and braces his hands on his knees, bending at the waist, shaking his head, and I notice that his hands are shaking.

Holy hell.

I take another step back, ready to run, but with his head still down, he holds up his hand and says, "Wait."

I should run. Fast. Call the police and have this whack-job arrested for assault, but I don't move. My breathing starts to calm, and my panic recedes, and for some reason, I don't think he's going to harm me.

Yeah, I'm sure the Green River Killer's victims didn't think he'd harm them either.

"Uh, are you okay?" My voice is breathy, and I realize I'm still clutching my camera to my chest almost painfully. I relax my hands and start to lower them when his head snaps back up.

"Do not take my fucking picture." His voice is low and measured, controlled, but he's still shaking and breathing like he's just run a marathon.

"Okay, okay. I'm not going to. I'm putting the lens cap back on." I do as I say, not taking my eyes from his face, and he watches my hands carefully.

Geez.

He takes a deep breath and shakes his head, and I get a good look at the rest of him. Wow. Beautiful face, chiseled, stubbled jaw and those deep, clear blue eyes. He's got messy, golden-blond hair. He's tall, much taller than my five-foot-six, lean and broad-shouldered. He's wearing blue jeans and a black T-shirt, and both hug that lean body in all the right places.

Damn. He'd look fantastic naked. Ironically, I'd love to get him in front of my camera.

He looks me in the eye again, and he looks vaguely familiar. I feel like I should know him from somewhere, but the fleeting recognition is gone when he speaks.

"I'm going to need you to give me the camera, please."

Is he serious? He's still going to mug me?

I let out a short laugh and finally break eye contact, looking up to the now blue sky and shake my head. I close my eyes then look back over to him, and he's staring at me intently.

I find myself smiling as I say, "You are so not getting this camera."

He tilts his head to the side and narrows his eyes again. Muscles low in my belly clench at his sexy stare, and I silently castigate myself. No getting turned on by your sexy early morning mugger!

"You are not getting this camera. Who the hell do you think you are?" Now my voice is rising, and I pat myself on the back.

"You know who I am."

His response throws me, and I narrow my eyes, staring back at him again, and get the strange feeling once more that I should know him, but I shake my head in frustration.

"No, I don't."

He raises an eyebrow, puts his hands on his lean hips, and he smiles, showing off a perfect line of teeth. The smile doesn't reach his eyes.

"Come on, honey, let's not play this game. Either give me that camera, or delete the photos, and we can get on our way."

Why does he want my photos? Suddenly it occurs to me that he must think I've been taking pictures of him.

"I don't have any photos of you on here, *honey*," I reply.

His eyes narrow again, and his smile slips away. He doesn't believe me.

I take a step toward him. I stare deeply into his widening blue gaze and speak very clearly. "I. Don't. Have. Any. Photos. Of. You. On. My. Camera. I'm not a portrait photographer." I feel my cheeks flush, and I look down for a moment.

"What were you taking photos of?" His voice is level now, and he looks confused.

"The water, the boats." I gesture out toward the sound.

"I saw you point your camera toward me when I was sitting on that bench." He points to the bench behind me. It's near where I shot the photos of the couple holding hands. I pull my camera in front of me again. He tenses up, but I ignore him, turn on the camera and start flipping through my images until I find the ones he's afraid are of him. I walk over to him and stand next to him, my arm almost touching his, and I feel the heat from his sexy body. I make myself ignore it.

"Here, these are the photos I took." I point the screen toward him and start to page through them, showing him all of the images. "Would you like to see the others I took as well?"

"Yes," he whispers.

I continue to show him the images of the water, the sky, the boats, the mountains. I can't help but smell his clean scent as he intently looks at the photos, scrutinizing each one while pulling his lower lip through his thumb and forefinger. His brow is furrowed.

Sweet Jesus, he smells good.

I've taken over two hundred photos this morning, so it takes a few minutes to page through each one. When I'm finished, he looks up into my eyes, and I see his embarrassment, and I'm not sure, but he looks almost sad.

My heart gives a flip as he smiles, a true full-blown, no-holds-barred smile, wiping away the sadness, and shakes his head slowly. He could melt glaciers with that smile. End wars. Resolve the national debt crisis.

"I'm sorry."

"So you should be." I turn the camera off and start to walk away from him.

"Hey, I'm really sorry."

"You must be awfully full of yourself if you think that everyone with a camera is taking your picture." I continue walking, and of course he's caught up with me, matching my stride.

Why is he still here?

He clears his throat. "Can I ask your name?"

"No," I respond.

"Um, why?" He sounds confused.

Hell, I'm confused.

"I don't give my name out to my muggers."

"Muggers?" He stops midstride and pulls me to a stop beside him, his hand on my elbow. I look down at his hand and, raising my eyes back to his, pin him with a glare.

"Let go of me." He does immediately.

"I'm not a mugger."

"You tried to steal my camera. What do you call it?" I start walking again, realizing I'm heading in the opposite direction of my house. Shit.

"Look, I'm not a mugger. Stop for a minute, will you?" He stops again, rubs his face with his hands and looks at me. I face him, put my hands on my jean-clad hips, my camera hanging harmlessly around my neck, and glare at him.

"I don't know who you are," I say in my best no-nonsense voice.

"Clearly," he responds, and a smile tickles his lips, and I can't help but feel my stomach clench, hoping he gives me that big grin again. My not knowing him seems to make him happy, but it's pissing me off.

Should I know him?

"Why are you smiling?" I find myself smiling back at him.

He looks me up and down, taking in my dark hair, currently tied up in a haphazard bun, casual red T-shirt that hugs my breasts, jeans, curvy hips and thighs, and returns his deep blue gaze to mine. His smile widens, and I lose my breath.

Wow.

"I'm Luke." He holds his hand out for me to shake, and I look at it, still not fully trusting him, then back up to him. He raises a brow, almost as a challenge, and I find myself putting my small hand in his big, strong one and clasping it firmly.

"Natalie."

"Natalie," he says my name slowly, looks down at my mouth, and I bite my lower lip. He inhales sharply and looks back into my eyes.

Fuck, he's beautiful. I pull my hand out of his grasp and look down, not knowing what else to say, and still confused as to why I'm still standing here with him.

"I . . . I have to go," I stammer, suddenly nervous. "It was . . . interesting meeting you, Luke." I start to walk around him toward my house, and he steps in front of me.

"Wait, don't go." He runs a hand through his already messy golden hair. "I'm really sorry about all this. Let me make it up to you. Breakfast?"

He frowns slightly, like he didn't mean to say that, and then looks at me hopefully.

Say no, Nat. Go home. Go back to bed. Mmm . . . bed with Luke . . . Sweaty bodies, tangled sheets, his head between my legs, my body writhing as I come . . .

Stop!

I shake my head, trying to push the fantasy aside, and find myself saying, "No, thanks. I should go."

"Husband waiting at home?" he asks, glancing at my ringless finger.

"Uh, no."

"Boyfriend?"

I give him a small smile. "No."

His face relaxes. "Girlfriend?"

I can't stop the laugh that comes. "No."

"Good." He's giving me that big smile again, and I want desperately to say yes to this beautiful stranger, but my common sense kicks in, and I remind myself that this is not safe, I don't know him, and as swoon-worthy as he is, he's still a stranger.

I, of all people, know about stranger danger.

So I ignore the clenching between my legs, give him another small smile, and I say as politely and as forcefully as I can, "Thanks anyway. Have a good day, Luke."

Of course, politely and forcefully sounds all whispery from me right now.

Crap.

I hear him murmur, "Have a good day, Natalie," as I walk briskly away.

I WALK HOME quickly, feeling Luke's eyes on my Kardashian-esque backside until I turn the corner toward my house. Why didn't I wear a longer shirt? My heart is thumping, and I just want to be safe inside, safe from sexy-smiled muggers. My body hasn't responded to a man like this in a long time, and while I admit it feels nice, Luke is just entirely too . . . Wow.

I close and lock my front door then follow my nose to the kitchen. Jules is making breakfast!

"Hey, Nat, get any good photos this morning?" Much to my delight, my BFF is flipping pancakes, and I smell bacon crisping in the oven. My stomach growls as I place my camera on the breakfast bar and pull up a stool.

"Yeah, it was a good morning," I reply. I wonder if I should bring up Luke. Jules tends to be on the romantic side, and she'll most likely have us married off by the end of the conversation, but she is the one person I confide in about everything, so why not? "I got some good shots. Almost got mugged . . . pretty standard morning."

I smile to myself as Jules twirls around, dropping a pancake on my tile floor, gasping.

"What? Are you okay?"

"I'm fine." I let out a snort. "Some guy was pissed that I might have taken his picture." I describe my encounter to her, and she smiles sweetly when I'm finished.

"Sounds like he likes you, friend."

I snort. "Whatever. He's just some random guy."

Jules rolls her eyes and turns back to the pancakes. "He might just be some random guy, but if he's as hot as you say he is, you should have gone to breakfast with him."

I scowl at her. "Gone out to breakfast with the hot mugger?" I ask incredulously.

"Oh, don't be dramatic." Jules flips the bacon in the oven then ladles more pancake batter onto the griddle. "It sounds like he was really nice."

"Yes, when he wasn't trying to steal my obscenely expensive camera, he was a perfect gentleman."

Jules laughs, and I can't help but smile in return. "What do you have going on today?" she asks.

Pleased with the change in conversation, I walk around the breakfast bar and start loading a plate with delicious food. "I have a session at noon, and I need to make some deliveries this afternoon. I really need to try to get in a nap this morning."

"Couldn't sleep again?" Jules asks.

I shake my head. Sleep never comes easily for me.

I reclaim my stool and take a bite of bacon. Jules is next to me. "How about you?"

"Well, since it's Tuesday, I guess I'll go to work today." Jules is a very successful investment banker in downtown Seattle. I couldn't be more proud of my longtime best friend. She's beyond smart and beautiful. She's the whole package. .

"We gotta make a living." I devour the delicious pancakes on my plate, then rinse both our plates and load the dishwasher.

"I can do that." Jules starts to come into the kitchen, but I wave her back.

"No, you cooked. I got this. Go to work."

"Thanks! Have a fun session." She wiggles her eyebrows at me and heads for the garage.

"Have a good day at the office, dear!" I call after her, and we both giggle.

I climb the stairs to my bedroom and strip naked. I really need some sleep. My clients pay me very well to give them a fun, beautiful photo session, and I need to be well rested.

My room is large, with floor-to-ceiling windows. This is the one room of the house that has any pink in it. I love my soft pink duvet and fluffy pink pillows. My bed frame is simple, but the headboard is an old barn door that I nailed to the wall to give the room a rustic feel.

I fall into my king-size bed, the soft sheets hugging my naked body, and gaze out the window to the ocean view. I love this house. I never want to move. Ever. This view alone is priceless. The sapphire-blue water outside calms me, and as my eyes get heavy, I think of deep blue eyes and a killer smile and slip into sleep.

## two

I'm out and about, delivering framed photos of flowers and beach scenes to the restaurants and shops along Alki Beach.

"Hi, Mrs. Henderson!" I smile at the gray-haired, plump woman behind the counter in Gifts Galore, one of my favorite trinket shops. I happily note that my work is hanging behind the cash register. There are shelves and shelves of beachy knickknacks, jewelry, and other artwork. It's a fun place to wander around in.

"Hello, Natalie! I see you have a delivery for me!" She smiles and comes around the counter, pulling me into a big hug.

"I do. I hope you can use them."

"Oh yes, I'm just about out of the others you brought in last week. You've become quite the popular young artist." Mrs. Henderson starts looking through my work, oohing and aahing, and I feel the pride in my chest as she tells me that she'll take all I've brought her today.

We chat at the counter while she writes me a check for last week's sales, and I turn to leave, but stumble into a very firm chest.

"Oh, excuse me . . ." I take a step back and look up.

"Hello, Natalie." Luke's staring down at me, a smile tickling his lips. He looks a bit surprised, happy, and just . . . Oh my.

"Hello, Luke." My voice sounds breathy again, and I mentally wince.

Mrs. Henderson heads to the back of her store to check on a customer, leaving Luke and I alone. I stare down at my sandals, reminding myself I need a pedicure.

What am I supposed to say?

"So, you're an artist." Luke glances over at my framed photos still stacked on the counter.

"Yes." I follow his gaze. "I sell my work in the local shops."

He grins, and I feel that pull again in my gut.

"What are you doing in here?" I ask "This doesn't seem like your kind of store."

"I'm looking for a gift for my sister for her birthday." He starts shuffling through my frames. "These would be perfect. She just bought a new condo. Which ones would you suggest?" He glances back at me, and I have no choice but to join him at the counter and lean close to him as we look through the twenty-plus photos together.

"Does she prefer flowers or scenery?" I ask.

"Er." He swallows. Am I having some kind of effect on him? I lean a little closer to him, pretending to inspect the photos on the counter and hear him catch his breath. "Probably flowers."

"I'd go with these." I smile to myself, enjoying his nearness now that I don't feel threatened by him, and select four photos of flowers, all different kinds and colors, and arrange them in a square for him to see.

"Perfect." His smile lights up his face, and I can't help but smile back. "You're very talented."

His compliment takes me back for a second, and I feel my cheeks flush. "Thank you."

Luke pays Mrs. Henderson, and then follows me as I head out of the store to my car.

"Where are you headed?" he asks as he catches up to me.

"Well, that was my last delivery, so I'll be heading home."

"Or," he says nonchalantly, "I could take you out for coffee."

My stomach tightens excitedly. He's still interested! Am I? He could be an ax murderer. Or worse.

"Happy hour?" he continues.

I smile and look away from him, still striding toward my car.

"Dinner? Can I buy you an ice cream cone?" He runs his free hand through his messy hair, and I mentally hug myself.

Somewhere public should be safe, so before I can put too much more thought into it, I hear myself saying, "Let's go get a drink. There's a bar one block over that has a good happy hour."

"Lead the way!" Damn, I would do just about anything for that grin.

"Don't you want to take your sister's photos to your car?"

"I walked." He shrugs.

"Here, stow them in my car." I open the trunk of my Lexus SUV and pull the door up for him.

"Nice car," he says, surprised. His eyebrows are raised as he gazes at me.

"Thanks." I flip the lever for the door to close and lock the car again as we continue down the sidewalk.

Luke pulls his aviator sunglasses from the neck of his soft white T-shirt and puts them on, looking around him as though he's making sure no one is watching him, and I frown. Is he embarrassed to be seen with me? If so, why did he ask me out?

I'm still puzzling over this as he holds the door to my favorite Irish pub open for me, and we walk into the cool bar.

"Hi! Welcome to the Celtic Swell." A young server smiles at both of us, paying special attention to Luke, and I mentally roll my eyes. "It's a beautiful day out there," she continues. "Would y'all like to sit inside or outside?"

I glance up at Luke, and without pausing or asking me what I'd prefer, he says, "Inside."

"Sure thing. Follow me, handsome." She winks at Luke, ignoring me completely, and leads us to a booth near the back of the bar.

We are seated, and Miss Flirty points out the happy hour menu displayed on the table, smiles broadly at Luke again, and then leaves us alone.

"Are you embarrassed to be out with me?" I am determined to get to the bottom of this.

Luke gasps, takes off his sunglasses, revealing his wide blue eyes, and looks horrified. The knots in my stomach slowly release.

"No! No, Natalie, not at all. In fact, I'm thrilled to spend time with you." He looks so sincere. "Why do you ask?"

"Well . . ." I gratefully sip the water the waitress has set down before me. "You just seem . . ."

"What?"

"Quiet all of a sudden." It's the best I can come up with. Damn, why does he make me so nervous?

"I'm happy to be here, with you. I just . . ." He shakes his head, runs a hand through that beautiful hair. "I am a private man, Natalie." He exhales quickly and closes his eyes, like he's struggling through some difficult internal debate, before turning his bright blue gaze back to mine.

"It's okay." I hold my hands up in front of me as if in surrender. "I was just checking. No worries."

I smile reassuringly and grab the happy hour menu before he can say any more. His change in mood and the reasons behind it are none of my business. We're just out for a drink. Let's keep it light.

He smiles at me, and I'm rescued from having to start small talk by Flirty Waitress taking our orders.

Luke raises an eyebrow in my direction. "What would the lady like?"

"A margarita on the rocks, no salt, extra lime." My eyebrows climb when the waitress' cheeks redden and the only acknowledgment to my statement is her scribbling ferociously on her notepad. Luke is hot, I can't blame her for paying attention to him, yet something primal in me wants to scratch her pretty brown eyes out.

And he's not even *mine*.

Luke chuckles. "Make it two."

"You bet. Anything else?" she asks Luke, pointedly ignoring me, and I smile to myself as Luke hardly spares her a glance before muttering, "No, thanks."

"I deserve a margarita after the day I've had." I sip my water.

"And what kind of day was that?" Luke leans forward, and I love that he genuinely looks interested.

"Well." I sit back, look up at the ceiling like I'm deep in thought. "Let's see. I couldn't sleep much last night, so I decided to take an early morning walk to get some work done. At which point, I was almost mugged." I look back at him and give him a sarcastic look of horror. Luke laughs, a full-out belly laugh, and my own belly clenches down again. Holy Jesus, he's so beautiful!

"And then . . . ?"

"And then, after I made my very daring escape"—I smile at him, and he is grinning from ear to ear, his chin resting in his palm—"I went home, had breakfast with my roommate, then took a short nap."

"I would have loved to see that." His eyes have narrowed, and I feel myself blush.

"Loved to see me have breakfast with my roommate?"

"No, smart-ass, loved to see you nap."

"I'm sure it's not that exciting." I thank the waitress for my drink and take a long sip. Oh, that's good.

"And when you woke up?"

"You really want to know about my whole day?"

"Yes, please." Luke sips his drink, and I watch his lips pucker over his straw. .

"Um . . ." I clear my throat, and Luke grins again, enjoying my re-action to him. "I had a photo session at noon. It wrapped around two. Then I made some deliveries around the neighborhood and ran into this handsome mugger I know, whom I am now enjoying a drink with."

"I like that last part the best."

Oh.

"And what did you do today, sir?" I rest my elbows on the table, happy to have turned the attention back to him.

"Coincidentally, I couldn't sleep well last night either, so I got up early to take a walk and enjoy the water." He pauses to take a sip.

"Mmm hmm . . ."

"Then I made an ass of myself with this incredibly sexy and beauti-ful woman that I ran into."

I gasp and bite my lip. Sexy and beautiful? Wow.

Luke's eyes narrow on my lips.

"Did she forgive you for being an ass?" My voice sounds breathy.

"I'm not sure. I hope so."

"Then what did you do?"

"I walked home to do some reading."

"What kind of reading?" Mmm, this margarita is delicious.

Luke frowns a bit then shrugs. "Just some reading for work."

"Oh? What do you do?" I motion to Miss Flirty for a refill, raise my eyebrow at Luke and signal for his refill as well at his nod.

"Why do you want to know?" He whispers this and suddenly looks ashen.

What the fuck? Is he really a serial killer? A spy? Is he unemployed and looking for a sugar mama? I dismiss that last thought. He wouldn't be able to live in this neighborhood if he were unemployed.

"Well, now I'm intrigued." I lean forward. He looks so uncomfortable, I decide to put him out of his misery. "But it's really none of my business. So, you read, and then?"

Luke visibly relaxes, and I can't help but be more than a bit disappointed that he won't tell me what he does for a living.

"I also took a nap."

I grin and look him up and down. "To be a fly on the wall."

Oh, I almost forgot how much fun it is to flirt!

He laughs, and it tickles me, making me laugh, too.

"Then I went shopping for my sister's birthday gift and found the perfect thing."

"Oh? And what was that?" I tilt my head to the side, enjoying this flirty game, sipping my delicious drink.

"Well, there's this brilliant local artist that takes beautiful photos, and I was lucky enough to find some of her work." He almost looks proud, and it gives me a warm, happy glow.

"That's great." I don't know what else to say.

"So, you had a photo session today?"

Whoa . . . change of topic.

"Yes." I think I need another margarita if this conversation is about to take the turn I think it is. I signal to Miss Flirty and, without asking, order him one, too.

He raises an eyebrow. "I didn't think you did portrait photography."

"Why did you think that?" I ask with a frown.

"Because you said so this morning during our most unusual meeting."

"Oh, that's right. I don't do traditional portrait photography." I clear my throat and look around the bar, anywhere but at him, praying he doesn't ask his next question, and grimace when he asks anyway.

"What kind of portrait photography do you do?" He looks confused.

I take a deep breath. Crap.

"Well, it varies. Depends on the client." I'm nervous again. I don't tell many people about this side of my photography business. I find that most people are too judgmental, and it's honestly no one's business but mine and my clients'.

"Look at me." His voice is low and serious, and he's not playful anymore. Shit.

I look into his eyes and swallow.

"You can tell me, Natalie."

Oh, he's so . . . sexy. And nice. Is that possible?

"Perhaps one day I will. When you tell me what you do for a living." I smirk and kick him under the table, and his mood immediately lifts.

"So there's going to be a 'one day'?"

Oh, I hope so! "If you play your cards right."

"Sassy little thing, aren't you?"

"You have no idea, Luke."

"I'd like to learn, Natalie." And there is that serious face again, making me squirm.

"You're quite the charmer, aren't you?"

Luke grins his wide, gorgeous grin. I smirk again and finish my third drink. My head is getting fuzzy, and I know I'd better stop with the alcohol.

"Another drink." Luke starts to call for Miss Flirty, but I shake my head.

"I'd better go back to water."

"Of course. More water for my lady friend and I, please." The overly friendly waitress saunters away, deliberately swaying her hips, hoping to get Luke's attention, but he's staring at me, ignoring her.

"What kind of movies do you like?"

Huh? Is he asking me out to the movies?

"I don't watch a lot of movies."

He tilts that beautiful head to the side and looks at me like I just told him that pigs fly. "Really?"

"I don't have a lot of time for it."

"Who's your favorite actor?" He smiles, and I feel like this is some sort of test, but I haven't been given the study notes.

"I don't even know who's popular right now." I sit back into the booth seat and purse my lips, thinking about it. "When I was a teenager, I loved Robert Redford." I shrug.

Luke looks like he's been kicked in the stomach, and I'm suddenly embarrassed. Then that beautiful face transforms into his smile, and his eyes soften as they take me in. "Why? Isn't he a little old for you?"

I giggle. "Yes. But I saw *The Way We Were* with him and Barbra Streisand when I was fifteen and fell in love with Hubbell. He was dreamy. I don't pay a lot of attention to movies. There's too much drivel out there."

Luke laughs. "Drivel?"

"Yes! If I see a trailer for one more stupid vampire movie, I'm going to kill myself."

He frowns again, looks around the bar and back to me, his eyes narrowed and apprehensive.

"What? What did I say?"

"Nothing. You're just very unexpected. What are you, twenty-three?"

Why does he want to know my age?

"Twenty-five. You?"

"Twenty-eight."

"So, you're old then." I giggle.

"You have a great laugh." His eyes are shining with happiness, and I mentally hug myself again, forgetting to be nervous, and I realize I'm just really enjoying him. He's just so easy to talk to.

I check my watch and gasp at the time. We've been sitting here for three hours!

"I should go." I smile up at him. "We've been here a long time."

"Time flies when you're with someone beautiful." He leans over and grabs my hand, and I am so caught up in his spell right now. My eyes focus on his lips, and he licks them, making me squirm. Before I know it, he retracts his hand, and I'm left feeling frustrated and missing the warmth of his touch.

"Right back at you." I put my sassy smile back on my face and reach for the check.

"Oh no. That's mine." Luke pulls the check from my fingers and digs out his wallet.

"I'm happy to pay for my own drinks."

He glares at me, and I'm stunned that he looks genuinely mad. Whoa.

"No."

"Okay. Thank you."

His smile is back as he says, "You're most welcome."

Luke settles the bill, and we head back out onto the sidewalk. He hastily puts his sunglasses back on and is visibly aware of who's around us. My heart flips as he takes my hand, and we start to walk toward my car.

The sun is just starting to set, and I look out over the gorgeous sound, the blue water, the boats and the mountains, and long for my camera. I glance up at Luke, and his jaw is tense. He's looking down, and we're walking briskly.

"Hey, slow down." I tug on his hand a bit and deliberately slow my steps. "Are you in a hurry to be rid of me?"

"No, not at all." He looks around us again, then grins down at me, slowing his pace.

"It's going to be a great sunset. Wanna walk along the water? I promise, no camera." I hold my free hand up to show him it's empty.

Luke smirks, and then looks around once more, and I follow his gaze. There are a lot of people out and about enjoying the beautiful day on Alki Beach. Luke shakes his head and looks forlorn for a moment.

We stop by my car, and I think he's looking down at me, but it's hard to tell through his dark glasses.

"I don't like crowds, Natalie. It's kind of a phobia." He shakes his head again, runs his hand through that sexy hair and releases my hand, putting his hands on his hips.

"It's no problem." I feel sorry for him in that moment and want to comfort him. I've never wanted to comfort any man before, ever. I've never had soft feelings toward a man. They've always just been a pleasant diversion, or my worst nightmare. Confusingly, I find myself reaching up and cupping his face in my palm to soothe him.

"Hey," I say softly. "Don't sweat it, Luke."

He leans into my touch and exhales, puts his hand over mine, then clasps it and kisses my knuckles.

Oh my.

"Come on." I deliberately interrupt this lovely moment, needing just a little space. "I'll drive you home."

Luke's jaw drops open.

"I'm not going to make you walk home, carrying these brilliantly genius photos, through the crowds. Hop in."

He flashes me his sexy, face-splitting smile and hops into the passenger seat.

Oh, Natalie, what are you getting yourself into?

# three

Luke's home is a very short drive along the coast, and it strikes me that his place is less than a quarter mile from mine. He directs me to pull into a gated driveway. I can see only a single-lane drive ahead of me. There is no house in view.

"The code is 112774," he directs me.

"Wow, you trust me with the code to your gate?" I am trying to keep the banter between us light to mask my nervousness of going to his house. Will he even invite me inside?

"You'd be amazed at what I'd trust you with, Natalie." I glance back at him and catch his frown. "In fact, so would I."

I ignore his comment and pull through the gate, winding to the left, and gasp at the beautiful modern home before me. It's not huge, it's simple, but the view of the sound is breathtaking, and the white home itself is newer, with clean lines, tons of large windows, beautiful purple and blue hydrangeas lining the front of the house, and pruned shrubs lining the driveway.

"Wow, Luke, this is beautiful."

"Thank you." The pride is back in his voice, and it's evident that he loves his home. I smile at him, completely understanding the feeling.

I park so the passenger side is facing the front door and don't make a move to take my seat belt off. Luke has already jumped out and, to my surprise, walks around the front of my car to my door and opens it.

"Please, come in." He holds a hand out to me, but I pause.

"I should go . . ."

"I'd really love for you to come inside." He gives me that charming grin, and I feel myself softening. "Let me show you the view. Maybe make you dinner. That's all, I swear." His eyes shine with mischief, and I just can't resist him.

I don't want to resist him.

"I'm not keeping you from anything?"

"Nope, I'm a free man, Natalie. Come on."

I shut off the car and take his hand. Wow. The electricity from his touch is still there, and my eyes widen as they find his. His smile is gone, and he's staring intently into my eyes. He pulls my hand up to his lips, then closes my door behind me and leads me up to his door without letting go of me, as if I could run away at any minute.

I can't help but appreciate the way his jeans hang on his hips, molding around his very fine ass. His white T-shirt is untucked and hugs the muscles of his shoulders and arms just perfectly. I want to hug him from behind and sink my nose into his back, inhale his scent, and kiss him there between his defined shoulder blades.

It should seriously be illegal to be that beautiful. He clearly takes very good care of himself. Suddenly, I feel out of my league. He is a ten, and I'm lucky if I hit a seven after I've been buffed and polished at my favorite salon. Not to mention, I have hips and an ass and a bit of a belly bulge that no matter how many sit-ups or yoga exercises I do, it just won't go away. I know I'm not fat, but I'm not supermodel thin like Jules, either.

And, until today, that never bothered me.

Luke unlocks the door and turns to me, and the look in his eyes tells me that he's not looking at my flaws. He seems to be just fine with what he sees, and hope starts to spread through me.

"Welcome, Natalie. Make yourself at home." I follow him inside and can't stop the face-splitting smile that comes at the sight of his magnificent home. The great room is large, with double-height ceilings and pale khaki-colored walls. The back wall is all glass, and the view is of the Puget Sound. The furniture is big, in blues and white and a touch of green. I could curl up in his love seat and stare outside all day.

I wander through the room, my sandals echoing on the dark

hardwood floors, and gaze out the windows for a few moments. The sun is hanging low, just above the mountains, reflecting on the choppy blue water, and pretty white sailboats are coasting along gracefully. I turn to see Luke still on the other side of the room watching me, his arms crossed in front of him. I wish I could read his mind.

"What?" I ask and mirror his stance, crossing my arms in front of me, pushing my cleavage up a bit, exposing it through the V-neck of my red T-shirt.

"You are so beautiful, Natalie."

Oh.

I drop my arms and open my mouth to speak, but nothing comes out, so I just shake my head and look to my right at his very lovely kitchen.

"You have a great kitchen."

"Yes." It's a simple agreement, and Luke is on the move, slowly walking toward me. There's no humor in his eyes now. It's hunger. Hunger for me.

I couldn't move if I wanted to.

"Do you like to cook?" My voice is higher than normal, and the nervousness is back, but this nervousness is not fear. I'm definitely not afraid of him. I'm a bit intimidated by him.

"Yes," he says again, and as he approaches me, he raises his long-fingered hand to run the backs of his fingers down my cheek. I swallow hard and hold his blue gaze.

"You don't want to talk about your kitchen?" I whisper.

"No," he whispers back.

"Oh." I look down at his mouth and back up into his blue eyes. "What do you want to talk about?"

"I don't want to talk, Natalie." Since when has whispering been so sexy? My thighs tighten, and I'm suddenly wet and hot and panting.

Luke grasps my face between both of his hands, still gazing intently into my eyes, as if he's trying to convey some kind of deep message, or perhaps he's asking my permission? I slightly tilt my head back, and he oh so slowly lowers his lips to mine. He rests them there for what feels like minutes, chastely kissing me, loosely resting his soft lips on mine. I reach my hands up and grab his forearms, and he groans as he takes the kiss deeper, persuading my lips open and tickling my tongue with his.

Oh God, he smells so good, and his expert lips are a drug that I just can't resist. He nibbles at the sides of my mouth, nibbles my lower lip then invades my mouth again. He pulls the hair tie out of my hair, spilling my long, chestnut hair around my shoulders, and plunges his hands in it.

"You. Are. So. Beautiful." He murmurs against my mouth, each word between his sweet kisses, and I am completely intoxicated. I run my hands up over his shoulders and twist his hair in my fingers and hold on for dear life.

Oh, this man can kiss!

He slows the kiss down again, gently cupping my face in his hands, and leaves sweet kisses on my jaw, cheeks, my nose, then plants his lips on my forehead and takes a deep, deep breath. I run my hands back down his shoulders—holy shit, is he toned!—over his sexy arms and hold on to his forearms, and I am more than just a little dizzy.

And I don't want him to stop.

As my blurry sight clears, Luke leans back, still cupping my face, and smiles gently down at me. "I've wanted to do that all day."

Where is that music coming from? I realize my phone is ringing inside my purse, still slung across my body, and I break our intimate contact to rummage through and find it. Maroon 5 is whaling on about being at a payphone, and Luke's smile breaks into a big grin as I answer the call.

"Hi, Jules." I mouth *roommate* at him at his raised eyebrow.

"Nat! You haven't answered my texts. Are you okay?" She sounds annoyed, and I roll my eyes.

"I'm fine. Sorry, I didn't see your texts. My phone has been in my bag, I must not have heard it." I take another step back from Luke, trying to clear my head, and he rests his hands on those lean hips.

"Do you have dinner plans?"

"Dinner?"

Luke leans in and whispers in my free ear, "I'm making you dinner." He winks at me—winks!—and then walks around me toward the kitchen, leaving me to my call.

"Um, yeah, I have dinner plans." I wince, knowing that I'm about to get the Jules Third Degree.

"Oh?" I know her expertly plucked brows are raised. I so do not want to have this conversation with Luke in earshot. I hear Adele start to sing and turn to see Luke has paused by a sound system, fiddling with his iPhone.

"Yeah, something just came up. Why? What's going on?" Luke is now in the kitchen, rummaging around in his fridge, and I have a great view of his jean-clad ass. Holy crap.

"I was going to invite you to go to dinner with some of my coworkers, but if you have plans, I'll just see you tonight." There is a pause. "Is it the mugger?"

I gasp. Leave it to Jules! "Maybe."

"Awesome! Have fun, be safe, take pictures if you can. Toodles!" She's hung up, and I can't help but laugh at her. Oh, to have my friend's carefree attitude.

"So, that was your roommate?" Luke asks as he pours us both a glass of white wine. I take a sip and am pleasantly surprised by its fruity sweetness.

"Yeah, she was checking up on me." I sit at the lightly colored granite breakfast bar and page through my texts. I have three, all from Jules.

*Hey, Nat, wanna go to dinner tonight?*

*Nat? Turn your phone on!*

*Natalie, I'm making reservations . . . dinner?*

Oops. I lay my iPhone on the counter top and take another swallow of wine. Luke's watching me.

"Sorry, that was rude." I smile apologetically. "She was worried when I didn't respond to her texts."

Luke shakes his head. "You are definitely not rude, Natalie. So, how do you feel about Alfredo sauce?"

I grin at his flirty tone. "I have a long-standing love affair with Alfredo sauce."

"Really?" He chuckles and tucks a strand of my now messy hair behind my ear. "Lucky Alfredo sauce."

He turns again and starts pulling out pots and pans and ingredients from his pantry and fridge. He's so . . . competent in the kitchen.

When he whips back around to start making order of his chaos, he sees me watching him and gives me a half smile. "What are you thinking?"

"You're very competent in the kitchen."

"Why, thank you." He bows grandly and makes me laugh.

"Who taught you to cook?"

"My mom." He puts a pot of water on to boil and starts grating cheese.

"What can I do to help?"

"Sit there and be beautiful."

I blush. "Really, I want to help."

"Okay, you grate this cheese, and I'll get the chicken going."

I happily come around the island and take over the cheese grating, watching Luke move about his kitchen with ease. Soon, the room smells of grilling chicken, making my mouth water. Luke moves up behind me and puts his arms around me, checking the cheese status, without actually touching me.

My skin is on fire. Touch me! Hold me! But he doesn't. Before I know it, he's moved away, and my body is almost quivering with need.

I don't remember ever feeling this physical pull toward a man before. It's a little scary, but it's a lot of fun.

"Okay, I think we're almost ready to dish up. Can you strain this pasta?" I gladly assist him as he finishes the sauce, and my stomach growls.

Mmm . . . a sexy man who can cook!

Luke pulls down plates, silverware and napkins. "Let's eat outside, enjoy the view."

"Great idea." I smile as we dish up, grab our wine and head out to the deck off the great room. The outside eating space is spectacular. Warm tones of reds and browns, the table seats six, and there is a huge stainless steel grill with outdoor kitchen counters, fridge and sink.

We sit, and my nerves from our earlier delicious kiss are gone, and I'm just plain hungry.

"Hungry?" he asks, reading my mind.

"Starving!"

"Dig in."

I take a bite and close my eyes. "Mmm . . . s'really good."

I cover my mouth with my napkin and laugh.

Luke's eyes dance, and he smirks, taking a drink of his wine. "I'm glad you like it."

"So"—I scoop up another bite—"your mom taught you to cook?"

"Yeah, she always said that all of her children needed to be able to feed themselves after we left the nest."

I watch him stab some chicken with his fork. "How many siblings do you have?"

"I have one brother and one sister."

"Older, younger?" I ask. God, this man can cook.

"Older sister, younger brother."

"And what do they do?"

"Samantha, my sister, is an editor for *Seattle Magazine*." Luke's eyes are full of pride. "Mark is wasting his college education as a fisherman in Alaska."

"I take it you don't approve?" I raise my brow at him as I take a sip of wine.

"Well, he's young. I guess it's good he sows his wild oats now." Luke shrugs.

"Your parents?" I like hearing him talk about his family. He clearly loves them very much.

"They live in Redmond. Dad works for Microsoft, and Mom is a homemaker." He glances down at my empty plate.

"It was delicious, thank you." I lean back in my chair and stretch out my legs.

"You're very welcome." He looks so young with his shy smile. "Would you like some more?"

"Oh no, I'm full." I pat my belly and gaze out at the water. "This is a fantastic view."

"Yes, it is."

I look over at him, and he's gazing at me. My cheeks warm. "You're very complimentary."

"You're easy to compliment."

I smirk.

He tilts his head to the side and picks my hand up in his, bringing it to his mouth. This is the first time he's touched me since that thigh-clenching kiss, and I sigh at the heat of his touch.

"You are quite beautiful, Natalie. Why don't you believe that?"

I'm stupefied. No one has ever called me out on my insecurities because I've never shown them to anyone. I shrug. "I'm happy you think so."

He frowns at my answer but doesn't press me. "I do."

"I wish I had my camera." I don't realize I've said this out loud, and I feel him tense beside me.

"Why?" His voice is cold, and looking into his eyes, I see they're arctic.

"Because of this view." I gesture out to the water. "This would make a wonderful image."

He relaxes beside me. "Maybe one day you'll be able to capture it."

"There's that 'one day' again." I grin at him, and he grins back.

"One day." He says again, and I can't help but feel a little giddy inside. I shiver a bit as a breeze rolls through his patio. The sun has set, and the sky is all purple and orange, and it's cooling off.

"Are you cold?" he asks.

"No, I'm good."

"Really?"

"I'm a tiny bit cold, but I don't want to go inside."

"I'll be back." With that, he stands and gathers our dirty plates.

"Hey, I'll clean up. You cooked."

"Nonsense. You're my guest, Natalie. Besides, I have a housekeeper who will do most of it in the morning. Sit. Stay." He pins me with a serious gaze, then heads inside.

He's so bossy. I think I like it. No one has ever had the audacity to be bossy with me before. It's fun.

I hear the iPod change from Adele to something soft and bluesy, and a few moments later, he's back with a plush green blanket and my iPhone.

"The light was blinking on your phone. I thought you might want to check it." He hands it to me, but before I can look at it, he holds his hand out to me. "Come with me."

"Where are we going?"

"Just over there." He points to a soft love seat closer to the edge of the patio. I take his hand, and he leads me over and I sit, sinking into the cushions. He sits beside me and covers us both in the blanket. His arm is draped around me.

"This is quick." I look into his blue gaze, unsure if being in his arms like this, this quickly is altogether safe, yet I want to be here.

"We're just admiring a pretty view, Natalie." He pulls me closer to him, runs his hand down my side, and I lean on his shoulder. I remember my phone in my hand and pull it out from under the blanket to read it, not bothering to hide it from Luke.

*Hey, gorgeous, plans tonight?*

It's my friend Grant, and while we haven't had sex in a while, sometimes, if we're drunk or lonely, we indulge. I haven't heard from him in weeks, and of course it has to be now, as I'm curled up in this sexy man's arms, that he texts me.

Crap, crap, crap. Luke tenses beside me, and I cringe but hit Reply, still not pulling it out of his eyesight. I have nothing to hide.

*Yeah, I have plans. Sorry.*

Luke doesn't relax beside me, and I know he's mad. Shit.

Grant responds almost immediately.

*Tomorrow?*

*Sorry, Grant, not interested.*

*Okay, bye, Nat.*

I put my phone in my pocket and just lean my head back on Luke's shoulder, not saying anything. What can I say? He lets out a sigh and tightens his hold on me, not saying anything for a long time. Finally, I glance up at him.

"Are you okay?"

"Why wouldn't I be?"

"Um, I don't know. Just checking." The last two words are whispered. He seems mad at me, but I didn't do anything wrong. I told the guy to take a hike!

Suddenly, he shimmies and pulls his iPhone out of his pocket. "What's your phone number?"

My wide gaze finds his, and he raises a brow. I rattle it off to him, and he punches it into his phone. "What's your last name?"

"Conner." He finishes programming my name and number into his phone, and I close my eyes and inhale his clean scent while he continues to fiddle with his gadget.

My phone buzzes in my pocket.

# *four*

I retrieve my phone from my pocket and pull it out of the blanket.

"Oh my, look at that, I have a text! Whoever could it be?" I bat my eyelashes at him and smile sweetly.

Luke laughs. "Maybe you should check it."

"Oh! Good idea." I chuckle and slide the arrow at the bottom of the screen, waking the phone up and open the text from a phone number I don't recognize. I want to squeal like a schoolgirl, but simply smile and open the message.

*Hey, Natalie, save this number. You're going to be seeing it a lot.—Luke Williams*

I grin at him and save the number and his name to my phone.

"So." The smile leaves his face, and he's serious again.

I pull back, out of his grasp, and turn my body toward him, my leg tucked under the opposite knee, mentally preparing myself for a serious conversation.

"So?"

"So." He gazes at me almost warily, and I feel a moment of alarm. "Who's Grant?"

"Just a friend." I shrug.

He raises an eyebrow. "That wasn't just a friendly text, Natalie. I am a man. I know the difference."

I cringe and look back out over the darkening water.

"Look at me." His voice is sharp, and I whip my eyes back to his.

"He is just a friend, Luke. Yes, there has been a physical relationship there in the past, but it's been awhile."

"How long is awhile?"

"Months."

"How many months?"

"Since last fall."

"Is there anyone else?"

"Why is this any of your business?"

"Because you're the first woman I've brought into my home, and all I can think about is getting your beautiful body naked and fucking you senseless. I need to know if there is any competition. I don't share, Natalie." His eyes are on fire, his beautiful lips parted as he breathes heavily, and his hands are in fists.

I open my mouth to speak and close it again. Holy Jesus, he wants to fuck me. Well, back at you, bossy man.

"Saying that you don't share implies that I'm already yours, Luke."

"Aren't you?" he whispers.

This is too much. I've known the man less than twenty-four hours, and he wants to stake a claim! Part of me is yelling, *Yes!* But that damn reasonable side rears her ugly head and shakes her head adamantly. *No!*

I stand abruptly, untangling myself from the blanket.

"Look, Luke . . ." He's suddenly at my side, his strong hand on my chin trapping my gaze in his.

"Answer my question, please." His touch is gentle, but his gaze is raw, and it pulls at me in a way I've never known.

"There is no one," I whisper.

"Thank Christ." And his lips are on mine, but instead of the passionate fervor I'm craving, his lips are gentle and tender, as though he's memorizing my mouth with his lips. He lets go of my chin and wraps my hair in his hand, while the other curls around my lower back, and he pulls me to him, my front against his, and I moan low in my throat. His chest and stomach are hard muscle. I wrap my arms around him and hold him to me, my hands clasping on to his back.

Bravely, I close my teeth over his lower lip and suck him gently into my mouth. His eyes fly open, meeting mine, and he plunges his tongue in my mouth, sliding it along mine in a beautiful rhythm. Our breathing is ragged, and my hands just can't stop moving up and down his back, feeling the hard muscles flex as he moves against me.

Both of his hands slide down to my backside, and he clenches it tightly while nibbling from the side of my mouth down my neck.

"Oh my." I lean my forehead against him, and I feel him smile against my neck.

"You have a great ass, Nat." He pulls me more tightly against him, and I feel his erection against my stomach. I run my own hands down to his derriere.

"Back at you, Luke." My voice is breathy, and he pulls back, his eyes a bit glassy with want and desire, and I know they mirror my own.

Fuck, I want this man.

Our arms are still wrapped around each other, clasping each other's bottoms. I give him another squeeze and run my fingers lightly up under his shirt to his bare skin and smile as he gasps. His beautiful blue eyes are watching mine, and I push my finger between the elastic of his boxers and his skin and run it along to the front of his jeans.

Suddenly, his hands are on mine, and he stills me, not taking his eyes from me. He brings both my hands up to his lips and kisses each finger, then steps back and lets go. The cold air around us is a slap to the face, and I frown in confusion and frustration and feel the sting of rejection.

What the hell?

"Why did you stop?" I hear the hurt in my voice, and I clear my throat.

"Nat, I definitely don't want to stop . . ."

I step toward him, but he backs up and raises his hands in surrender.

"Luke . . ."

"Natalie, let's slow down a bit."

Isn't this what men want?

"If you've changed your mind about me . . ." He's back in front of me before I finish the sentence. His hands are cupping my face, and he's making me look him in the eye, and the raw emotion is still there.

"Listen to me, Natalie. I have not changed my mind. I want you.

You are beautiful and smart and sexy as fuck, but I don't want to take this too fast."

"I'm so confused." I close my eyes and shake my head.

"Hey." I look back into his eyes, and he smiles at me, running his fingertips down my cheek. "Slow."

"I don't know slow, Luke."

He frowns and whispers, "I don't either, so we'll learn together."

I'm so frustrated. My body is craving him, but his words intoxicate me.

"So, no sex? At all?" I sound like a child whose candy has been taken away.

"Not tonight," he says with a smile. He takes a deep breath, kisses my forehead, and takes my hand. I grab the blanket, and we go back inside. His music is still playing.

He takes the blanket from my hands and throws it on the long blue couch to my right. "Would you like a tour?"

I'm still frowning over the no-sex comment, but the idea of seeing the rest of his home perks up my mood, and I nod.

He laces his fingers through mine. "Thank you for joining our tour today, Miss Conner. We are delighted to have you with us."

I laugh at his tour-guide voice and relax a bit. He does have a way of making me laugh.

"You've seen the kitchen."

"I love the kitchen."

He smiles and pulls me down a hallway pointing out a powder room and a spare bedroom. At the end of the hall is another closed door, but he waves it off and says, "Just storage for now."

He leads me back to the great room and up a flight of stairs to a large loft area that he's using as a TV room, with more plush furniture. The flat-screen mounted to the wall is huge, and I can't help but laugh.

"What's so funny?" He looks at the TV, and I snicker.

"Boys and their big TVs."

He chuckles and leads me through to another spare bedroom and bathroom. On the opposite side of the loft, with more floor-to-ceiling windows showing off the view, is the master suite. It's huge, with large-scale white furniture and green, blue and khaki accents. It's incredibly peaceful.

His master bath is beautiful, with a large egg-shaped tub separate from the shower that could be a room all on its own.

I gasp in delight when he shows me the walk-in closet.

"Women and their closets." He's laughing at me, and I can't help but join him.

"This, my friend, is a fantastic closet."

"Yes, it is." He agrees and squeezes my hand, then leads me back through the bedroom and down the stairs to the great room.

I'm suddenly uncomfortable, and before I can change my mind, I pull gently on his hand and wrap my arms around his waist, linking my fingers together at the small of his back and drawing him into a big hug. His arms fold around my shoulders, and he kisses my hair, inhaling my scent.

"Thanks for dinner," I murmur into his chest.

"Anytime."

"Thanks for the tour."

I feel his smile against my head. "Anytime."

"Thanks for your phone number."

He chuckles and pulls back. "I recommend you use it."

"I will." I pull out of his arms and grab my purse. It's time to go home and think about this sweet, sexy man. I certainly can't think when I'm with him.

He walks behind me out to my car, pulls his photos out of the back and takes them inside, then returns to me to open my door.

"Let me know that you get home safely." The shadows from his house lights are playing across his face, the light reflecting in his gorgeous eyes.

"Okay, bossy man." I chuckle up at him.

"Bossy?" He purses his lips like he's giving it some thought, then smirks. "Maybe a little bossy."

He leans down and touches me, just with his lips, running them lightly over mine. "Good night, beautiful."

"Good night." Swoon! Geez, he's just so yummy. I'm thankful that I have enough wits about me to climb into my car and get my seat belt on. He walks back to his doorstep and waves me off as I pull down his driveway.

Holy shit.

I SLING MY purse on the hallway table by my front door, throw my keys in the key bowl and dig for my phone. I heard it ping when I was driving home, and I know exactly who it's from.

"Nat, is that you?" I hear Jules' stilettos click smartly on the hard-wood between the living room and the foyer.

"Yeah, I'm home."

*Thank you for today. Please let me know when you get home.—Luke*

I smile and want to jump up and down in giddiness.

"Well, I guess it went well?" Jules has her hands on her hips, and her blond head tilted with a smile across that gorgeous face of hers. She's still in her cranberry-colored dress and heels from work, her long hair pulled back from her face.

"Oh yeah, it went well."

"So, not so much a mugger, huh?"

"No." I giggle. "He's really nice. And, oh my God, Jules, he's hot." I worry my lip between my teeth, but she reads my mind.

"He's not out of your league, Nat."

I frown at her. "I wasn't going to say that."

She rolls her eyes at me. "You were thinking it. You're hot, too, Nat. Enjoy him. He's lucky you're interested. We both know that doesn't happen often."

"Yes, that's what worries me, too."

I tell her about having happy hour, and how he seemed uncom-fortable out and about with me, but when we were at his house, he was much more relaxed. I tell her about the best kiss on record, and the sunset.

Jules listens patiently, doesn't interrupt, or get all giggly or jumpy like she always does. She simply smiles at me, and before I know it, she's pulled me in for a big hug.

"You deserve a good guy, Natalie. Don't run from it. Enjoy it. Really."

I lean into her and suddenly feel like crying, which is mortifying. "I don't even know when I'll see him again."

She pulls back and grins. "Oh, I have a feeling it won't be long. Sounds like he's smitten." There's the Jules I know!

I smirk and kick my shoes off. "I'm going up to bed. It's been an eventful day."

"Okay, good night, sweetie." She briefly hugs me again and heads back to the living room and whatever she was doing before I came home.

I run upstairs and straight into my bathroom. I take my makeup off and brush my teeth and stare at myself in the mirror for a moment. I touch my lips. They're still sensitive from Luke's kisses. My cheeks have a glow, as do my green eyes. My dark hair, which he pulled out of my bun, is all disheveled and kinda sexy.

Remembering his comments about my ass, I turn and peer at it, giving it a good study. I've always considered my butt to be too big, too round and prominent. Yeah, I definitely have a round butt. I guess Luke likes round butts. I smile to myself, strip naked, turn out the lights and jump into bed to text him back.

*No, thank YOU for today. I had a good time, despite almost being mugged. I'm home and safely tucked in bed.—Nat.*

I smile, happy with my flirty response, and lie back on my pillows. A few seconds later, there is a ping.

*Glad to hear you are safe. What are your plans for tomorrow?*

Oh my! I quickly hit reply.

*No sessions tomorrow, thinking about going to take some photos at Snoqualmie Falls. What are your plans?*

I glare at my phone until I see his response.

*What time shall I pick you up? :)*

Pretty sure of himself, isn't he? I can't help but laugh and turn on my side while considering my response.

*Will it be safe? I will have my camera with me, and I know how that angers you.* I chuckle to myself, thinking I'm quite witty, when suddenly my phone starts to ring, and it's him.

"Hi."

"I thought you'd already forgiven me for this morning." He sounds frustrated. What the . . . ?

"I was kind of being a smart-ass, Luke. I'm sorry, I guess texting is not a great way to flirt." I close my eyes.

He takes a deep breath. "No, I'm sorry. Would you mind if I join you tomorrow?" Gosh, he has a sexy voice, and he sounds hopeful. Who am I to say no?

"I would love the company. Shall we say ten a.m.?"

"That works for me." He sounds relieved, and I get the giddy feeling in my chest again.

"I'll text you my address."

"Okay." He sighs. "So, you're in bed?"

Oh, now it's gonna get good! I smile and lie on my back. "Yes. You?"

"I am, too."

"We had a long day." I'm picturing him in that huge, gorgeous bed of his, naked and lying under the covers, and my mouth is suddenly dry.

"Yes, we did." I hear rustling as he moves in the bed.

"I hope you sleep better tonight."

"Me, too." I hear the smile in his voice.

"Why were you having a hard time sleeping last night?"

There is a long pause, and it's perfectly quiet, and I wonder if I've lost the call.

"Luke?"

"I'm here." He sighs again, then says, "I just don't require a lot of sleep. How about you? Why up so early today?"

I'm not entirely satisfied with his answer but let it go.

"I've suffered from insomnia for a couple years now. I usually only get a few hours of sleep here and there."

"That sucks," he breathes.

"Yeah, but I can take advantage of the early morning light."

"You're something of a workaholic, aren't you, Natalie?" I think he's laughing at me!

"No, I just enjoy what I do."

"And what are you wearing to bed tonight?" Geez! Change of subject!

"Good night, Luke." My smile is in my voice.

"Sweet dreams, Natalie. See you in the morning."

He hangs up, and less than ten seconds later there is a text.

*Can't wait to see you in the morning, and to one day see what you wear to bed.*

Oh, I definitely hit the nail on the head when I said he was a charmer.

*There's that mention of 'one day' again! I'm also looking forward to tomorrow. Sleep well tonight, Handsome, you're going to need it. :) xoxo*

For the first time in over two years, I actually fall to sleep quickly, have calm dreams, and wake with the sun.

*five*

Fuck! I'm late!

Luke's going to be here to get me any minute, and I'm still running around the house, grabbing my camera equipment, purse, and sandals. I'm pulling my hair up in a ponytail when the doorbell rings.

Shit!

"Hey!" I smile as I open the door, then my mouth drops at the delicious sight of him. His dark blond hair is still wet from his shower and all disheveled in that way he has. He's wearing a simple gray T-shirt, his sunglasses tucked in the collar, and khaki cargo shorts.

Yum.

His impossibly blue eyes shine as he smiles down at me. "Hi, beautiful. You look fantastic in red."

I feel my cheeks heat. I love this red sleeveless top and decided to wear the denim shorts that fit my rear just so. Just for him.

"Ready?"

"Almost." I step back to let him in and close the door behind him. "I'm running a bit late. Busy morning, but I'm almost ready."

"Couldn't sleep again?" He frowns down at me.

"The opposite, actually. Slept too well, was almost late for yoga, and had to run a couple errands." I pick up my camera bag and grab my purse off the table by the door. I hate feeling scattered!

Luke grabs my camera bag from me, slings it over his shoulder, and I grin up at him in thanks. "How about you? Sleep better?"

"Much, thank you."

"I'd show you around, but I'd love to get on the road. Rain check?"

"Absolutely, let's go."

I whistle when I see Luke's sporty little Lexus convertible parked in my driveway. He deposits my camera bag in the tiny back seat then opens my door for me with a huge, cat-ate-the-canary grin on his handsome face.

"Nice car."

"I figured it would be a good day for a drive with the top down."

"Sounds good to me." The leather seat is low and soft, and I can't help but be just a little impressed. He has good taste.

Before long we're zipping down the freeway through Seattle and heading out of town on Interstate 90. This car can move! The sun is warm, the wind feels great, and Luke cranks up some Maroon 5. There is no need for idle chitchat. We're just enjoying each other's company, and I find myself relaxing back into the seat and enjoying the lush, green scenery on our way to the falls.

It's obvious Luke knows where Snoqualmie Falls is, and as we get closer, he turns down the music, then rests his hand on my left thigh. Just that touch alone makes my libido sit up and take notice, and I take a deep breath to calm my erratic heart.

"You've clearly been here before."

Luke smiles at me. "Yeah, my parents used to bring us here when we were kids for picnics and stuff."

"Do you mind if I leave my camera bag in the car? I'll just take my camera."

"No problem, I'll close the top." Luke patiently waits for me to gather what I need out of my bag, then closes the top of the car, locks it, and we're off, hiking down the covered bridge that leads to the hotel and the falls access where tourists can ooh and aah over the beautiful water.

I sling the camera strap over my neck and check the settings as I walk.

"How long have you been a photographer?" Luke asks. He's intently watching me adjust the settings.

"All my life, actually. My dad bought me a digital camera when I was about ten, and I never wanted to do anything else." The memory brings a smile to my face, and I look up at him.

"He must be very proud of you," he murmurs.

The pain is swift and hard. "He's gone."

"Gone?"

"My mom and dad were killed almost three years ago." Shit, I didn't mean to say that!

"Damn, Nat, I'm sorry." Luke stops walking and pulls me into his arms, holding me tight, my camera squished between us, and I'm mortified to feel tears prick the backs of my eyes. I do not want this day to turn sad.

"I'm okay." I put my hands flat against his hard chest and look up into his face. "I'm okay. Let's not get sad today."

Luke's frowning down at me, his eyes full of compassion and, to my relief, void of pity. I don't want him to feel sorry for me.

"Hey, I'm okay. Really." I cup his cheek in my hand, and he turns and places a kiss in my palm.

"Okay." He releases me, and we resume our journey to the falls. It doesn't take long, as it's not far from the road.

I glance over at him, and he's still brooding, a small frown on his face. "Luke, cheer up. You didn't say anything wrong. I'm happy you're here."

He looks me in the eye again and gives me a half smile. I relax a little, happy that the mood is lifting, and pick up my camera as we turn the bend to see the falls.

"I'm so glad there isn't anyone else here today." I'm trying to change the subject.

"I'm surprised there aren't," he replies.

"Well, summer's almost over, and it's the middle of the week, so I figured we'd have the place mostly to ourselves." I start snapping photos.

Luke steps back and watches me work. I move up and down the path, getting different angles, stopping to adjust my settings, and take shots of flowers and spider webs and other things that catch my eye. The trees are just beginning to change color, so I aim my camera up and take photos of those, too.

"Ready to move on?" I glance back at him. "I hope I'm not boring you."

He shakes his head. His arms are crossed in front of him, and he's leaning on a fence. He looks relaxed, but his eyes are watching me intently.

"Nothing about watching you is boring, Natalie."

Oh.

He unfolds himself and takes my hand, kissing my knuckles, before leading me farther down the dirt path to get shots at the base of the falls. He again backs away and leaves me to my work. I feel his eyes on me as I move, and I smile to myself.

After about twenty minutes, I'm satisfied with the shots I've captured. "Okay, I think that's a wrap."

I turn to find his eyes have widened in surprise.

"What?"

He shakes his head. "You're done so soon?"

"Well"—I check my camera—"I've taken almost four hundred photos. I think I'll have some good shots out of these."

"I'm sure they'll be beautiful."

I grin and put the lens cap on my lens, careful not to point it at him, and let my camera fall down to my hip. I don't understand why he doesn't like to have his photo taken, but I can respect it. I wish I could talk him into posing for me. He'd be a treat to capture.

"What are you thinking?" he asks as we climb the trail back to the car. He's beside me, his hand on my lower back.

"Why don't you like to have your picture taken?" His eyes meet mine, then he quickly looks away. He shrugs nonchalantly, but I can see he's hiding something.

"Look at me," I say softly, smiling.

His wide blue eyes meet mine, and he's got that *where is she going with this?* expression.

"You can tell me."

We've stopped on the trail, facing each other, and because of the uneven ground, I'm almost at eye level with him. I rest my hands on his shoulders. Luke's eyes widen further, and he swallows, and it looks like he's going to confess something. My stomach clenches. Talk to me!

Suddenly, he shakes his head and closes his eyes briefly.

"I just don't."

I frown up at him, but he shakes his head again and whispers, "It's just part of my phobia of being in crowds. Stupid, I know."

I want to probe him further, but he takes my hands off his shoulders, links his fingers with mine, and snakes our arms around my back, pulling me close. He rubs his nose back and forth over my own, his blue eyes intense.

"I've been thinking about kissing you all day."

"Less thinking and more doing." I'm surprised by my sassy response, or that I'm able to respond at all with my heart beating as fast as it is.

Luke smiles against my lips and sweeps me up in a hot, all-consuming kiss. He releases my hands and finds my ass like he did the night before, pulling me against him. I grasp his face in my hands, holding him close, and just like that I'm lost in him. He's so good with his mouth! He nibbles my lips, and his tongue makes gentle and patient love to mine. I groan and push my hands up into his hair, hanging on for dear life.

"Excuse us!"

I glance behind me to see a group of hikers trying to get around us on the trail. Oops! Luke laughs and pulls me out of the way so they can make their way down the path.

"I guess we got caught," Luke whispers in my ear, tucking a strand of hair behind it, and kisses my cheek.

"I guess so." I giggle breathlessly, and we resume our hike to his sexy car.

"YOU BROUGHT FOOD?" I can't hide the surprise in my voice as

Luke pulls a small cooler and blanket out of the back of the car. I stow my camera and lean my hip against the car.

He gives me a shy smile. "Yeah, I packed a picnic lunch. I know a nice little spot up that trail there to relax for a bit. I hope that's okay? You said you didn't have any sessions today."

"Sounds good to me, I'm starving."

"Good. Come." He takes my hand and leads me into the woods on another dirt trail. The trees and ferns are lush and dense around us, not letting much sunlight in. After we walk for a few minutes, the path opens up to a clearing. There's a beautiful meadow with tall, green grass. A tall, lush oak tree stands in the middle, it's large, green branches providing plenty of shade.

"Oh, it's beautiful!" I let go of his hand and move quickly through the grass to the majestic tree and stare up into its branches. "This tree has to be two hundred years old."

I glance over to Luke, a huge smile on my face. He's standing near me, the cooler and blanket at his feet, his hands in his pockets.

"I'm glad you like it."

I look up again. "Luke, I love it."

I help him spread the big, green blanket we snuggled up in last night in the shade of the tree.

"Get comfy."

I kick my sandals off and sit on the soft blanket, my legs stretched out in front of me and lean back on my hands. Luke also kicks his shoes off—mmm, naked feet—and kneels on the blanket, opening the cooler.

He pulls out a fruit salad, sub sandwiches, and hummus and crackers. My stomach growls, and we both laugh.

"Did you make all this?"

He passes me a sandwich, and I dig in. Mmm . . .

"Yeah, I threw it together this morning." He passes me the fruit and pops a cracker full of hummus in his mouth. "I love a woman who likes to eat."

I stop chewing and look up at him, frowning, remembering my thighs and round butt. "What do you mean?"

"Just what I said. I like a woman who enjoys food." He shrugs and frowns at my expression. "What did you think I meant?"

Shit. "I don't know." I eat a strawberry.

His eyes narrow. "Don't tell me you have body issues."

"Don't be ridiculous."

"Natalie, you're beautiful. You have no reason to be self-conscious."

"Did you not just see how I devoured that sandwich? I'm not self-conscious." Stop talking about this.

He shakes his head.

"This is delicious." I smile sweetly.

He doesn't look like he's buying my change of subject, but he lets it go and starts packing the leftovers back into the cooler.

I lie on my back and take a deep, satisfied breath. Oh, this is nice. Warm late-summer day, good food, sexy man . . . Yes, it's a really good day. Suddenly, Luke is pulling my feet into his lap, and he starts to rub.

Make that a glorious day.

"Oh my. You cook and give foot rubs. I must be hallucinating." I hear him chuckle.

"Hey, what's this?" He runs his thumb just above the arch on the inside of my right foot.

Oh, that. "A tattoo."

He tickles my foot, and I squirm and giggle.

"Obviously, smart-ass. What does it say?"

"One Step at a Time," I reply, and sigh as he continues to work magic on the sole of my foot.

"In what language?"

"Italian."

His finger traces the letters, and I push up on my elbows and watch him. When his eyes meet mine, they're on fire, and the muscles low, low in my stomach clench.

"It's sexy." He grins.

"Thanks." I grin back.

"Do you have any more?" He cocks his head and reaches for my other foot.

"Yes."

His eyes shoot to mine again, and they narrow. "Where?"

"Various places."

"I don't see any others." His eyes skim up my bare legs, my arms, my chest.

"The one on my foot is the only one visible with my clothes on, and that's only when I'm barefoot," I whisper. Oh, this is fun!

He releases my foot.

"Hey! I was enjoying that foot rub."

He grabs my ankles and parts my legs, then crawls up my body on his hands and knees until his nose is almost touching mine.

"I want to know where your other tattoos are, Natalie."

I bite my lip and shake my head. Who can form words with his body so close?

"You're not going to tell me?" He leans in and lightly kisses the corner of my mouth.

Again, I shake my head no.

"Maybe I'll just have to find them."

## six

He kisses the other side of my mouth, his eyes not leaving mine. I nod, slowly.

Luke grins as he pushes me back down against the blanket and covers my body with his. Holy Moses, he feels so good! His long, muscular body seems to fit perfectly against my soft curves. He presses one leg between mine, and I can feel his impressive erection against my hip.

I push my hand under his shirt to caress his bare skin, up and down his ribs. His skin is so smooth and tight over sculpted muscles.

While he continues to make me crazy with that talented mouth of his, he runs his hand from my hip up over my shirt to my breast, and I can't help but bow up off the ground, pressing my breast into his hand. My nipple is hard, straining against my bra and shirt, and he runs his thumb over it.

"Open your eyes." I gaze up into his perfect blue eyes, gazing at me with passion and hunger. My breath catches, and I run my fingertips down his cheek.

"You are so sexy, Natalie. I just can't seem to stop touching you."

"I love you touching me."

"You do?" He caresses my face, pushing errant strands of hair off my cheek.

"Yes," I whisper.

"Your skin is so soft," he murmurs, his fingers still on my cheek. "I love your curvy body."

My eyes widen.

"Don't frown." He kisses me between my eyebrows, as if he's smoothing the frown from my face.

"I'm not so sure about my curvy body." It's a whispered admission that I've never made before, and frankly, I've never felt this vulnerable.

His blue gaze meets mine again, and each word is staccato: "You. Are. Beautiful."

I close my eyes, but he tips my chin, forcing me to look at him again.

"Thank you."

His lips find mine, gently now, lingering and caressing my mouth as if we have all the time in the world. I shift my hips and grind myself against his thigh, and he groans low in his throat.

My blood is on fire. I've never wanted a man like I want Luke. I want to consume him. I want him fast and hard, and I want him to take all day. I love how tender he is with me.

He sits up, pulling me with him and grabs the hem of my shirt. "I want to see you." He's breathless and needy, and in this moment I'd do anything he asked.

I lift my hands above my head, but before he can pull my shirt off, I feel drops of water on my face. I glance up and realize the sky has clouded over, and it's starting to rain, the water seeping through the branches of our oak tree.

"I'm getting wet," I whisper against his mouth.

He grins, his eyes laughing at me. "I hope so."

I can't help but laugh at him, and I wrap my arms around his neck. "That, too, but we're about to get rained on."

"Damn it," Luke murmurs, kissing me chastely. He runs a hand down my back, from my neck to my ass, and I think I purr.

"We should go." I raise an eyebrow at him.

"Don't think I'm not going to discover your tattoo secrets."

"Whatever happened to taking this slow?" My breathing is starting to calm, but my heart is still beating fast. Oh, what this man does to me!

"I think I've changed my mind." He's perfectly serious.

Thank God!

"And why is that?" I run my hands through his hair, completely happy on his lap, with his arms tight around me.

"Because I can't keep my hands off of you. I don't know what you're doing to me, but I'm under some kind of spell." He gives himself a shake and looks around us at the darkening sky.

"The rain is getting heavy. Let's head back." He lets me go, and we gather our things, jogging into the woods and to the car. By the time we get there, we're wet and laughing like kids.

"I don't want to get your leather seats wet!"

"Don't worry about it. Just get in!" He opens the door for me. "I don't want you sick, baby."

Baby? Baby! Am I okay with him calling me baby? He guides me into the seat, slams the door and runs to the driver side. He looks over at me, his hair and shirt soaked, breathing hard, his beautiful blue eyes full of humor.

Oh yes. I'm fine with it.

"Let's get you home and dry." He starts the car and pulls out of the parking lot, toward the freeway.

"So, tell me more about yourself." Luke merges onto the freeway and glances over at me.

"What do you want to know?" I ask.

"Favorite music?"

"Maroon 5," I respond easily.

"Favorite movie?" he asks with a grin.

"Hmm . . . we've had this conversation." I laugh. "I still like *The Way We Were.*"

"Ah yes, you're a Robert Redford fan." He kisses my hand, and I sigh.

"I am."

"First boyfriend?" His eyes turn nervously to mine again, and I freeze. How do I answer this question?

"You know, I don't do this." I turn in the seat to face him.

He glances at me, then back at the road. "Do what?"

I shrug, trying to find the words and wondering why I feel the need to explain myself.

"Hey." He links his fingers with mine and kisses my hand before resting them both in his lap. "What is it?"

"I don't usually spend much time with men. I don't make out. I don't share meals. I don't spend time playing the twenty questions game. I just . . . don't." This is coming out so wrong!

He gazes at me again, surprised.

"Okay, what do you do with men?" He squirms in his seat, and I think he's mad.

"I fuck them." There. It's out there.

"What?" Oh yeah . . . I think he's really mad.

"Luke, I don't date." Oh, how do I explain this? I have never wanted to date anyone before. Before him.

"Are you brushing me off?" His voice is incredulous, and he lets go of my hand.

"No!" I close my eyes and shake my head. "Before I met you, I mean. I just don't want you to think that I'm promiscuous or that I go out with guys into the woods after knowing them for less than two days."

"But you fuck them," he snarls.

"Well, I used to." I turn back in the seat and stare out the windshield. "Before my parents died . . ."

He grabs my hand again, and I whip my head back to him, surprised.

"Go on."

"Before they died, when I was in college, I didn't think much of myself. And, therefore, neither did anyone else. I didn't date as a choice, Luke. But sex was something I understood. I've never wanted to feel anything else for a man." I swallow hard and close my eyes in shame.

"Did something happen to you to make you feel like that?" His voice is dead calm. Too calm.

"Umm . . ." I've never told anyone this. Except Jules.

"Look, Nat, I feel something here, too, and you can bet your sweet, beautiful ass that I'm going to make love to you tonight. I'm not going to fuck you. So I think it's pretty important that we're honest with each other now. No surprises." His handsome face is so sincere, and sweet.

"Last night you said you wanted to fuck me."

"I did. I do. And I will. But not tonight."

"Oh," I breathe.

"Yeah. So, what happened, baby?"

I pull my hand out of his and twist my fingers in my lap. Luke changes lanes, and I try to gather my thoughts. Oh, this hurts.

"When I was seventeen, I dated a guy for a few months who I thought was pretty nice. I was a virgin, which he would tease me about, but I didn't care. I was only seventeen, for Christ sake.

"Well, long story short, he took things too far one night. We were at my house. My parents were at some party, and we were alone, and he . . ." I stop talking and look out the window, not seeing the buildings and trees, swamped in shame.

"He raped me."

Luke inhales sharply, his face contorted in anger. "Motherfucker."

"That's not even the worst part." I laugh mirthlessly with the memory.

"This isn't fucking funny." He's glaring at me now, and my face sobers.

"Trust me, I know." I swallow. "You're very sweary."

"You haven't heard sweary yet. What happened next?"

"My parents came home." It's a whispered confession. Again, Luke inhales loudly.

"My dad almost killed him. The cops were called. He was punished. His dad was a senator, so along with the legal crap, my parents sued his parents and won. My dad was a very high-profile lawyer. I have quite a large trust fund from the lawsuit, which will never be touched by me. I don't need it. My parents made sure I was very well taken care of, and I don't want it anyway."

He doesn't say anything for a long time. He just drives and seems completely lost in thought.

"So," I interrupt the silence, "that's why I had so many issues with guys in college. It took a few years of counseling and my parents' deaths to wake me up and pull me out of some destructive behavior."

"Tattoos?" he asks.

"No, ironically, the tattoos had nothing to do with my past, and everything to do with healing."

He still won't look at me. Fuck, it was too soon!

"Hey." I grab his hand in mine. "I know that was a lot to dump on you, and we just met. If you'd rather just drop me off at home and cut our losses, I understand."

"No, Natalie, you're not getting rid of me that easily." He squeezes my fingers in his, and the relief I feel is incredible.

"You seem a little quiet."

"I don't honestly know what to say." He frowns and glances at me.

"I just . . ." I pause to collect my thoughts. "I feel this heading somewhere intimate, and I thought you should know." The last two words are a whisper.

"You've never dated anyone, ever?"

I shake my head.

"Honey, we have a lot of catching up to do." His voice is tender again, and I feel hope slowly spread through me.

"We do?"

"Oh yeah. I have one question, though."

"Okay."

"Where is that fucker?"

"I don't know. Why?"

"Because I'm going to kill him."

I can't believe he just said that! I chuckle softly. "No need. I'm sure he's a miserable man, Luke."

"He should be in hell."

"He will be." I grasp his hand tighter with mine. "Trust me, he's not an issue anymore. My dad saved me."

"Thank God." He kisses my knuckles, and I feel him start to relax beside me.

Wow, I told him the worst, and he still wants to see me? How did I get so lucky?

Luke pulls up in front of my house and turns off the car. He opens my door for me and lifts my camera bag out of the back, following me to the house. I unlock the door and motion for him to come inside.

"Jules!" I call out for my roommate, but the house feels empty.

"I don't think she's here." I smile at him and take my bag from him, setting it on the floor and my purse on the table. I take his keys from him and lay them on the table as well.

"Can I show you around?" I suddenly feel shy.

"Sure, after you."

I grasp his hand in mine. "Thank you for joining our tour today, Mr. Williams, we're delighted to have you with us."

Luke laughs, a full-on belly laugh, and I feel my shyness melt away. "Oh, I do love your sense of humor, Natalie."

I pick my camera bag back up off the floor, and he raises a brow. "I'll show you the studio and put this away too."

He nods, and I lead him through my house.

"I see you have a great view, too." He motions to the floor-to-ceiling windows off the great room, and I smile.

"I do. This is obviously the living, dining and kitchen." I glance at the reds and browns of our couches, dark wood dining furniture, and the simple elegance of the kitchen.

"Great kitchen." He winks down at me.

"Yes," I reply, and he chuckles. "But I don't cook much. Jules does a lot of the cooking."

"I'd love to cook for you here." His gaze is bright.

"I'd like that." I feel my cheeks heat. "Okay, let's go out to the studio, then I'll show you around upstairs."

"Out?"

"Yeah, I converted the guesthouse into a studio. It's my favorite part of the house. Come on."

I lead him out the sliding glass doors, across the backyard to the studio. I pause at the door and look up at him speculatively.

"What is it?" he asks, curiosity written across his face.

"Don't freak out on me, okay?"

"Why would I freak out?"

"Well, I told you I don't do traditional portraiture." I bite my lip.

"Baby, after our conversation earlier and the way I feel about you right now, I guarantee I will not freak out."

I watch his face and see that he means it and turn to unlock the door.

Here goes nothing.

I walk in ahead of him and put my bag on the floor. I switch on the lights, and Luke follows me inside. He stops just inside the threshold, his jaw dropped, his eyes wide, taking in my studio.

I turn and look with him. There is a king-size bed in one corner with white sheets draped over the canopy, ready for tomorrow's session. There are more floor-to-ceiling windows—perfect lighting!—across the room. I have racks of lingerie, corsets, boas, shoes, and other props. But what he seems to be focused on are the canvas photos hanging around the room.

He walks over to one and gazes at the couple in the throes of passion. It's in black and white, a side view of a couple lying on my king-size bed. The man is on top, braced over her, his mouth on her breast. Her head is thrown back, her mouth open, her leg wrapped around his hip, and her foot resting on the back of his thigh.

It's an erotic, intimate photo, and one of my favorites.

Luke turns in a circle, taking in all of the art on my walls, some of women or men in provocative poses, most of couples in different sexual positions. Finally, his eyes find mine.

"This is what I do," I whisper.

"Natalie"—he swallows and looks at my favorite photo again—"this is incredible."

"Really?"

He nods, his eyes wide. "Yeah, it's amazing. Sexy as hell. How did you get into this?"

I can't stop the smile on my face. "In college. Girls wanted me to take boudoir photos of them for their boyfriends, so I set up a makeshift studio in my apartment and started the business there."

"And the couples?"

"That sort of evolved. Most of them are return customers. The boyfriends or husbands loved the photos of their girls, and they wanted intimate photos of them as a couple."

"It's not porn." I just want that clarified and watch his face.

He frowns. "Baby, this is art. It's definitely not porn."

I smile, relieved. "There's a bedroom that I use to store props and furniture in for various shoots, and I use the kitchen to store refreshments for the clients. Sometimes, the girls like to have photos taken in there, too. It's fun."

He walks over to me, cups my cheek in his palm and kisses me softly. "You're amazingly talented."

Wow.

"Thank you. And for the record, I don't ever have sex in here. Ever."

His eyes dance with mischief. "Is that a challenge?"

"No, it's a fact."

"Why?"

"Because these aren't my memories. They're my clients'."

"So, you don't bring men in here?"

"Just you, handsome." I smile shyly.

"Good to know."

"Actually," I continue, looking him square in his bright blue eyes. "I've never invited a man to my home before."

His eyes widen, and he inhales deeply. "Your bed?"

"Just me."

"That's about to change." He grasps my hand and pulls me out of the studio, slamming the door behind us, leading me back into the house.

"Where is your bedroom?"

# seven

Holy hell, he's a man on a mission.

Luke is dragging me through the house, breathing hard, his eyes feral.

"Your bedroom?" he repeats, and I point up the stairs, unable to articulate words.

I don't remember my own name! And he hasn't even touched me.

Wow.

As he pulls me up the stairs, I get a great view of his tight ass, and my stomach clenches.

"To the right," I finally find my voice, and he pulls me into my bedroom, shuts and locks the door, and pulls me to him.

There's still plenty of light coming in the windows off the blue waters of the sound, and for just a moment I stand with his arms around my waist, my hands on his broad shoulders, and drink in the sight of his beautiful face.

"You're so handsome," I whisper.

He grins at me and leans down to nuzzle my neck, gently walking me backward to the bed. Thank God I made it this morning!

I'm expecting him to push me back onto the bed, but instead he steps back from me, not touching me at all, and his burning eyes run up and down my body, finally landing on my eyes.

"Are you sure about this?"

What? "Are you having doubts?"

"Hell, no, I just want to make sure this is what you want, baby. If you say no, that's fine, but please, God, don't say no."

Oh wow. He's giving me control, and I don't know if it's because of what I told him in the car, or if he's just being chivalrous, and frankly, I don't care. This is my choice.

*He* is my choice.

Staring him square in the eye, I say with a surprisingly sure voice, "Luke, please get us naked and make love to me."

He smiles, that huge, heart-stopping smile, and whips his T-shirt over his head.

Whoa!

He's all lean muscle and broad shoulders. His stomach is sculpted, with those incredibly sexy lines that run down the hips and to his cock. His arms are muscular . . . he's just so . . . *strong*.

I raise my hand to touch him, but he shakes his head, still smiling. "If you touch me, this will go much faster than either of us wants."

Oh. "We have all night."

"And we'll be taking advantage of it, baby, trust me. But this first time is going to be special."

I start to take my shirt off, and he stops me. "I'd like to do that."

"Well, then, hurry up!" I hear the whine in my voice but can't stop it, and I can't help but laugh with him.

"My pleasure." He shucks his shorts and underwear in one fast movement, and suddenly I'm getting a front-row view of Luke in all his glory.

He is simply a Greek god. His body is perfect in every way.

And he wants me!

He walks to me and grabs the hem of my shirt, pulling it over my head. He runs his fingers under my bra straps and leans in to nibble on my neck, just under my earlobe.

"Luke," I murmur.

"Easy, baby." He reaches behind me, deftly unclasps my bra and peels it down my arms. He makes quick work of my shorts and panties, pushing his hands between the fabric and my ass, cupping it, then slowly gliding them down my legs.

Oh, he's good with his hands!

He stands back up and lifts me, and suddenly I'm cradled in his arms. I wrap my arms around his neck, and he kisses my lips softly as he lowers me onto the bed.

"Sweet Jesus, you're beautiful, Nat." He whispers this against my throat, and I can do nothing but close my eyes and grip the blanket beneath me.

"Let's find those tattoos."

I smile as he kisses and licks his way down to my breasts, then gasp as he tugs one nipple firmly into his mouth and laves it with his expert tongue. Lightning shoots straight to my groin, and my hips start to shimmy of their own accord. I moan his name and twist his soft blond hair in my fingers.

"Hush, baby." He runs his hand down the opposite breast and tweaks it with his thumb.

"Oh God!"

My body's response to him is overwhelming.

I feel him smile against my skin, and he moves down, suddenly rolling me onto my right side. "What have we here?"

"Perhaps another tattoo?" My voice cracks as he runs his hand from my left hip to my shoulder.

"What does it say, baby?"

It's script, as are all of my tats, that runs up my ribs, but I'm too busy trying to remember to breathe to talk.

"Natalie, what does it say?" He kisses each letter gently, arms wrapped around my hips, braced on his elbows.

"It says, Be happy for this moment." I groan and continue. "This moment is your life."

"In what language?" His finger is rubbing it now. Oh wow.

"Sanskrit."

"Mmm . . . turn onto your stomach."

I oblige and groan as he kisses my shoulder, over to my spine and starts working his way down, down, down.

"God, your mouth feels good," I groan, and I feel him smile against my sensitive skin.

"And this?" He nibbles between my shoulder blades.

"It's Greek."

"What does it say, beautiful?" Oh God, his hands are just every-where. My skin is on fire, and he wants me to talk?

"Love deeply."

"You're so fucking sexy, Nat."

"You're making me feel pretty fucking sexy, Luke."

He nibbles his way down to my lower back.

"No tramp stamp?" I hear his smile.

"Hell, no," I respond.

He plants open-mouth, wet kisses on my left buttock, then my right, and then I hear his breath catch.

"Christ, baby."

He nibbles my upper thigh, just under my right buttock, and I about come up off the bed.

"Easy. What's this one?"

I smile. "A tattoo."

"Oh, you are a smart-ass." He slaps me on the ass, hard, and I gasp.

"Ah!" I look back at him in shock, my eyes wide, and he grins.

"What does it say?" He raises an eyebrow, daring me to make a sassy retort, and I swallow.

Holy fuck, no one's ever spanked me before. It's . . . *hot.*

"Happiness Is A Journey," I whisper. "In French."

He groans and kisses it tenderly. I lie back down, flat on the bed and enjoy the nibbles and kisses Luke leaves up and down my legs. He stops and gives the arch of my right foot extra special attention again, making me grin and want to clench my legs closed at the same time.

Suddenly, he flips me onto my back, and he raises my left foot up, bending my knee, and kisses my ankle, slowly moving up my leg. He is a wonder to watch as he worships my skin.

His eyes narrow when he catches sight of my belly button piercing, but then they darken when he sees my freshly waxed pubis.

"Oh, honey, what's this?"

I start to respond with my witty tattoo retort, but it's caught in my throat when he bends that sexy blond head over and ever so gently rains tiny kisses over the one word scripted on my pubis.

"It says Forgive, in Italian."

He gives it one last wet kiss then climbs up my torso, kisses the silver heart in my belly, then up my sternum, until he's bracing himself on his elbows on either side of my head and smoothes my hair off my face. His blue eyes shine with need, his mouth open as he pants, and I've never felt so wanted, so needed, by anyone in my life.

"Do you have any idea how amazing you are?" He rubs his nose against mine and licks the seam of my lips lightly.

My ragged breath catches. "Not half as amazing as you make me feel."

"Oh my God, baby, I want you." I feel his amazing erection against me, and I tilt my hips up in invitation.

"Yes." I nibble his lower lip.

He reaches down between us and gently rests a finger against my clitoris. I arch up and gasp as I feel it all the way to my toes.

His mouth is hungrily on mine now, kissing me hard and deep, and suddenly I feel that fantastic finger slip lower to the lips of my opening, and he growls against my lips.

"Fuck, you're so wet."

"I so want you."

He slips his finger in and out of me, and then he adds another, and I think I'm going to die from the sensations zinging around my body.

I grip his ass in my hands and tilt my pelvis up in invitation. "Now."

"Hold on."

What the fuck? Hold on?!

Suddenly, he dives over the side of the bed to snag his shorts and pulls a foil packet out of his back pocket. I smile as he tears it open, his eyes locked on mine, and he rolls it down his cock.

He leans over me again, poised at my entrance. I run my fingers up his spine to his gorgeous hair and lift my legs up, tilting my pelvis again. He rubs his nose over mine and slowly, oh so damned slowly, eases into me.

"Oh my," I breathe, as he closes his eyes tightly and leans his forehead against mine.

"Natalie," he whispers raggedly.

He pushes into me, all the way, and stops. When I start to move my hips, he stops me, staring down at me again.

"Just wait."

I just want to move. I want him to pound in and out of me, to make me explode around him, and he looks so calm.

I squeeze my muscles around him, just once, and that's it.

"Fuck," he whispers, and he starts to move in and out, gaining momentum. I'm meeting him with my hips, and we establish a delicious rhythm. His lips are on mine again, sliding and tangling with mine, and his hands are cupping my head, tangled in my hair.

I run my nails down his back, and he pulls a hand down to my breast, then to my hip, and finally farther down to hook my knee around his arm, opening me wider, and I feel myself start to tighten, as all of the hair on my body stands up on end, and I bury my face in his neck.

"Yes, baby, let go."

And I do, convulsing around him.

"Oh, Luke!"

Suddenly, I feel him stiffen and push into me twice more, and he empties himself into me.

"Natalie!"

MY BREATHING IS starting to calm, and my vision clears, and I am cradling Luke against my chest. I run my fingers through his soft blond hair and gaze down at him as he catches his breath.

"I'm sorry, I'm heavy. I'll move in about an hour." Luke doesn't move but smiles.

I yank on his hair, then lean down and kiss his forehead.

"You're fine," I whisper and continue to pet his hair.

"Just fine?" He frowns playfully and pushes up off of me, breaking our precious connection. He discards the condom and lies down next to me, pulling me into his arms.

"Okay, you're better than fine."

"How are you?" he asks, serious now.

"I'm . . ." I search for the word. "Fantastic."

"Yes, you are." He kisses me lightly. "So, why the different languages?"

I shrug and look away, but he pulls my chin back toward him.

"I don't want anyone to know what they say unless I tell them."

"Who has been so lucky, Miss Conner?" He raises an eyebrow.

"You," I whisper.

"And?"

"You."

He gasps. "Really?"

"Yes."

He runs the backs of his fingers down my cheek, then his thumb across my bottom lip, and I bite it.

"Oh, you want to get rough, do you?"

"Maybe later."

"What do you want to do, baby?" Oh, he's so sweet.

"I think I need a shower." I grin up at him and sit up, shimmy off the bed and turn back to him.

"I do love your ass, Nat."

I laugh, turn and wiggle it for him, then saunter toward the bathroom.

"You'd better join me before I use all the hot water!"

# eight

**W**ho is this woman, and what has she done with me?

I can't believe how at ease I feel with Luke, especially naked. I've never, ever just walked around in the nude like it's no big thing. My clients do it all the time, and I admire their confidence, but that's just not me.

Until today.

Until him.

*I do love your ass, Nat.* The words he uttered before he clamored out of bed to join me in the shower still make me smile. He loves my full ass, my body art, my curves.

He seems to especially love my curves.

I glance up at him in the shower and smile. Oh, he's pretty. He's scrubbing his hair, and I can't help but pour some body wash in my hands and start washing his back.

"Mmm . . ." he growls, and leans his head back in the spray to rinse his hair.

"How often do you work out?" I ask.

"Just about every day." He turns, pouring the fragrant soap into his own hands. "Turn around."

"How about you?" he asks as he starts massaging my shoulders.

"What was the question?" I murmur.

He chuckles. "How often do you work out?"

"I do yoga three or four times a week when I can fit it in. My work is pretty physical, too. That's it." I shrug.

"It's working for you." His voice is sincere, and I glance back at him and smile.

"Back at you."

He rhythmically circles his hands over my back and down to my bottom, and then steps around me so my back is in the water and starts massaging my front.

"You have great hands," I whisper and brace myself on his hips.

"You have great skin," he responds. His hands run over my breasts and tight nipples, suds running down my torso. He eases one hand down my belly and finds my clitoris with a finger. He backs me up against the wall and pulls my earlobe between his teeth.

"Ah!"

"I would love to make love to you here, baby, but there's no condom dispenser in the shower." I feel him grin and look up into his bright blue eyes.

Before he can slip a finger inside me, I grab his hand and bring it up to my lips, pulling his finger into my mouth, sucking it hard. His pupils dilate, and he bites his lip.

"I have a better idea."

With that, I run my hands down his chest, over his abdomen and to his hips. I sink down to my knees and am at eye level with his impressive, very hard cock. I wrap my hand around it, moving up and down, looking up into his eyes.

"Shit, baby." He closes his eyes and leans both hands against the wall of the shower, and seeing the pleasure on his beautiful face empowers me.

I lean in and lick around the rim of the head, then take him in my mouth and suck hard.

"Fuck!"

Oh yes!

I push and pull him in and out of my mouth, my teeth sheathed behind my lips. I'm sucking and licking, swirling around the tip as I pull up. He starts to rock his hips against me, and I take him deeper and deeper, feeling the tip at the back of my mouth.

"Oh shit, Nat. Stop, baby, I'm gonna come."

But I don't want to stop, so I don't. I continue the torment, reveling in making him crazy. He grabs hold of the bun on top of my head and growls as he comes, and I swallow quickly.

He's panting, his forehead leaning against the tile. As he catches his breath, he looks down at me, his eyes molten blue, and pulls me to my feet, kissing me long and hard.

Oh my.

"Come on, let's get out of the water." He pulls away, turns off the water and hands me a fluffy towel.

"Are you hungry?" I ask.

"Starving." He grins wickedly, and I laugh at him, wrapping the towel around me as I walk around him and into my bedroom. I spy his gray T-shirt on the floor and scoop it up. I drop the towel and pull the shirt over my head. Mmm . . . it smells like him.

No panties. I giggle at my audacity and turn to find Luke standing in the doorway, a towel around his hips and his eyes on me.

"That's some show, Nat."

"Glad you liked it," I reply with a smile. "Come on, we'll find something to eat in the kitchen."

I wait for him to pull on his shorts—no underwear!—and we head downstairs.

Luke sits on a bar stool and watches me move about the kitchen.

"I have no idea what we have," I say shyly. "This is Jules' domain. Hmm . . . Caesar salad?"

I hold the bowl up out of the fridge, and he nods. I dish it out for both of us, and then walk around and sit next to him.

"So you don't cook at all?" he asks.

I grimace. "I can, I choose not to. Jules has always lived with me, and she loves to cook, so it works for us."

At the mention of her name, I hear the front door open. "Nat?" she calls.

"I'm in the kitchen," I call back.

"Do you have company?"

I frown. "Yeah."

"Okay, going to bed. See you tomorrow." I hear her shoes click up the stairs.

Luke raises a brow and looks at me. I shrug.

"Maybe she had a bad day," he says.

"Maybe." I frown but shrug it off. I'll ask her about it tomorrow. I figured she would have been curious to get a peek at Luke, but seeing as we're both half naked, I'm relieved. I don't really want anyone to see Luke without his shirt on.

I clear the few dishes we have and stack them in the dishwasher, then turn back and lean my elbows on the counter.

"Will you stay with me tonight?" I ask.

Luke's eyes widen, and he smiles. He doesn't say anything. He just stands and comes around the breakfast bar to me. Without touching me, he leans in and gently lays his lips on mine.

Geez, where did I find this guy?

"I'd love to stay tonight," he whispers against my lips. Oh, there's that sexy whispering thing he does so well.

"Okay, good," I whisper back.

Suddenly, he turns his back to me and says, "Jump on."

"What?"

"Jump on my back, we're going upstairs." He reaches his arms back like he's going to catch me, and I laugh as I jump up onto his back, wrap my arms around his neck and hitch my legs up around his hips.

I lean down and pull his earlobe between my teeth, and he takes off for the stairs, effortlessly climbing them, and we are both laughing like crazy when he stops next to the bed and pulls the covers back.

I squeal as he unceremoniously drops me on the bed.

"You know," he says, his face suddenly very serious, as he sprawls out beside me on his side.

"What?" I ask sarcastically.

He runs his fingertip along the neckline of his T-shirt. "You never did ask me if you could borrow my shirt."

"I didn't?" I widen my eyes and bite my lip.

He shakes his head. "No, you didn't. Very rude of you."

"I'm so sorry. How can I ever make it up to you?" I try to look contrite.

"I don't know. I'm very offended." He still looks so serious, and I want to break out into laughter, but I'm enjoying our game too much.

"Can I buy you a new one?" I ask.

"Well, I'm really very fond of that one."

"Oh," I bite my lip again and push him onto his back. "Can I take a picture of it and give it to you?"

I unfasten his shorts, and he raises his hips so I can pull them down his legs, his erection springing free. I pull a condom out of the pocket and discard them onto the floor.

"No," he whispers. "It's just not the same."

"Hmm . . ." I roll the condom onto his cock and straddle his hips. I look down at him, narrowing my eyes like I'm thinking very hard, trying to solve this problem.

"Well"—I cross my arms and grip the hem of his soft gray shirt, pulling it over my head—"I guess I'd better return it then."

I hand him the shirt, but he throws it on the floor and sits up so we're nose-to-nose. He grasps my ass in his hands and lifts me over his cock, and I slide down onto him.

"Fuck, baby, you're so wet."

"That little game turned me on."

He growls and kisses me, guiding me up and down with his hands on my rear. I plant my hands on his shoulders and push, and he lies back on the bed. I lean down and kiss him tenderly, my hips still moving, his hands still on my butt.

Then I sit up and start to really move, reveling in how deep he feels, clenching around him. He runs his hands up my stomach to cup my breasts and tease my nipples with his thumbs.

"Ah!" I throw my head back and grind down on him harder, faster, and feel myself tightening, and I'm going to come already.

"Come for me, baby." His hands are gripping my hips, pushing me down onto him harder and harder, and I explode around him.

Before I've had a chance to come down to earth, Luke has moved out from under me, pushing me onto my stomach. He's lying on my back, his chest hair tickling my shoulder blades. He kisses the back of my neck and then over my tattoo. He parts my legs with one of his and then he's inside me again.

"Oh God!"

"Oh, baby, you feel so good." He's braced himself on his fists on either side of me and is pushing into me over and over, hitting that sweet spot on the front side of my vagina, sending little glittery sparks of yumminess all through me. I feel myself being pushed to the edge again, and I cry out Luke's name as I come, my orgasm gripping my body and wringing me dry.

He cries out my name as he finds his own release and collapses on top of me.

"Wow," I mumble into the pillows, and I feel his smile against my back.

"What was that?"

"Wow," I say again, not moving my head.

He bites my shoulder, and I yelp, pushing him off me. He chuckles as he discards the condom and wraps us in the blanket, pulling me into his arms, his front to my back.

"I'm sorry, miss, I didn't hear you."

"I said, 'That was just so-so.' "

He lets out a full belly laugh and hugs me close.

"Is this the wrong time to tell you that I'm on birth control?" I turn in his arms as I say this to see his reaction.

"What?" His eyes narrow, and now he looks pissed. Shit!

"Well, yeah, I am. Why are you mad?" I back up a few inches to look in his face.

"I thought you said it's been almost a year since you were with anyone."

"It has been."

He raises an eyebrow.

"Women don't go on and off birth control just because they're in a physical relationship." I roll my eyes. "It would mess with our hormones too much."

"Oh." He frowns again and then looks at my tattoos.

"I've been tested each year at my physical. I'm perfectly healthy." I smile.

"So, I could have had you in the shower?"

I laugh and nod but then stop and eye him speculatively. "Well . . ."

"I also get physicals regularly, haven't had a partner in about the same amount of time as you, and am healthy as can be."

"Then, yes." Oh, I so do not want to think about him being with other women. No, no, no.

"Well, shit, I think we need another shower."

I laugh and snuggle back into his arms, resting my head on his chest. "Tomorrow. I'm sleepy."

"Maybe we'll solve each other's insomnia."

"It's worth a try." I yawn and kiss his chest.

"Go to sleep, baby."

I WAKE IN the morning to bright sunlight and a heavy arm draped over me. I've never slept with anyone before, so this is new. And amazingly comfortable.

Luke is asleep on my pillow. He looks so young and relaxed. He needs to shave, and his hair is messy, as usual. I want to run my fingers through it, but nature calls, so I carefully slide out from under his arm and head into the bathroom.

When I tiptoe back into the bedroom, Luke is still fast asleep, but he's turned to his other side, wrapping his body around the covers so a naked arm, leg, buttock and back are all exposed.

Holy sweet baby Jesus, he is a sight to behold!

I just can't help myself. What self-respecting woman could have this in her bed and not touch?

Not me.

I climb back onto the bed and run the palm of my hand from the heel of his foot, up over his toned calf and hamstrings, over his tight derriere and up his back, then run my fingers through his hair. I nibble his neck and across his shoulders. I kiss his spine and make my way down to the base of his back where two very sexy little dimples live, right above his ass.

I hear him groan and grin.

I run my fingernails down his ass to his thighs and kiss my way up his side over his ribs.

He slowly shifts and turns onto his back, and I kiss up his body, nipping a nipple and resting my hand on the sexy V at his hips. I look up into sleepy, amused blue eyes.

"Good morning, handsome."

"Well, good morning, beautiful."

Suddenly, I'm flat on my back and Luke has laced his fingers in mine and pulls both my hands above my head. He kisses my neck and my chin and moves his hands down my arms to cup my head in his hands.

"How are you this morning?" he whispers against my mouth and rubs his nose back and forth on mine.

"I'm good."

"Just good?" He kisses my jaw, and I sigh.

"What were you going for?" I ask and tilt my head, giving him better access.

"Amazing," he whispers.

I smile and run my hands down his back. "That works, too."

He leans up to look down at me again, and I cup his cheek in my hand.

"How are you?" I ask.

"I've never been better."

My eyes widen at his serious reply. "Wow, I was just looking for good."

"Oh, honey, I surpassed good yesterday morning."

"You are quite charming."

He smiles down at me. "You are quite beautiful in the morning."

I snort at him and start to brush him off, but he holds my chin firm.

"You." Kiss. "Are." Kiss. "Beautiful." Kiss.

Holy shit.

"You aren't so bad yourself." I smile against his mouth.

"I want you, baby," he murmurs.

"I can tell." I grind my hips up against his erection, and he gasps.

"Jesus, you've got me horny like a teenager, Nat. What the fuck are you doing to me?" His blue eyes gaze into mine, and he moves his hips, the tip of his cock resting against me, and I tilt my pelvis, welcoming him inside me.

"Ah!" I grasp his shoulders as he pushes deeply inside me. He buries his face in my neck, gently sucking and kissing me. His thrusts become faster and harder, and our breathing is harsh.

"Oh, baby . . . I've never . . . Fuck, you feel good."

I cup his bottom in my hands and squeeze, pulling him in deeper.

"Come with me, baby." He's breathing raggedly, and I can feel him falling over the edge, and he takes me with him.

"Oh yes!" I cry and convulse around him.

Minutes later, after our breathing and bodies have calmed, he raises his head and kisses me gently. He eases out of me, and I find I'm a bit sore, but I don't mind.

"I'll be back." He gets up and goes into the restroom.

I sit up and stretch lazily. Oh, yes, I'm sore. Clearly, these muscles haven't been used in a while. I hug myself, then get up and throw on a T-shirt and yoga pants.

"You got dressed." I laugh at Luke's pouty face as he comes out of the bathroom. He wraps me in his arms and hugs me tight, and I sigh. Wow, is this just too good to be true?

"I'm going to go make some coffee. Meet me downstairs?" I stroke his cheek with my hand.

"Sure, I'll be right behind you."

# nine

"Well, good morning, sunshine!" I greet Jules as I saunter into the kitchen. She's just back from a run, her blond hair pulled back in a ponytail, dressed like me in a white T-shirt and black yoga pants. She puts the coffee grounds back in the freezer and smiles over at me.

"Good morning, yourself. Did he leave?"

"No, he'll be down in a minute. We're having coffee."

"You invited him over." It's not a question.

"Yes."

"And let him stay."

"Yes."

Her blue eyes are sharp. "A little against your usual M.O."

"I know." I sigh and take three mugs out of the cabinet. "He's different, Jules. I don't know where this is going, but I want to find out."

She pats me on the shoulder and smiles. "I'm happy for you, sweetie."

I hear Luke walk in behind me, and Jules' eyes bulge. I know, he's hot!

I turn and smile at him.

"Luke, this is my best friend, Jules. Jules, this is . . ."

"Luke Williams!" Her voice is shrill, and now she's smiling, her hands in fists. She's practically jumping up and down.

"Ohmygod! Ohmygod! Ohmygod! Luke Williams is in our kitchen!" She shoves my shoulder and does a little circle happy dance.

What the fuck?

I look back at Luke, and he's gone perfectly still. He's completely pale. He swallows hard and looks at me but doesn't touch me.

Jules has stopped her happy dance. "You didn't tell me you were all gooey over Luke Freaking Williams!"

"I take it you know him?" I ask, my voice a whisper.

What am I missing?

Jules stops, her jaw drops, and her eyes widen.

"Of course I know *of* him. Nat, that's Luke Williams."

"I'm aware," I reply, but my face is flushed, and I'm starting to feel like everyone is in on some big joke and I'm the butt of it.

"No, Nat . . ."

Luke finds his voice. "Natalie, I can explain."

He reaches for me, but I move out of his grasp and round the breakfast bar to put space between us.

"Explain what?"

"Natalie." Jules swallows and looks at him, gets an irritatingly swoony smile on her face, then looks back at me. "This Luke Williams is famous."

"What?" I narrow my eyes and look at him again, and it suddenly all makes sense.

*Don't fucking take my picture.*

*Why won't you all just leave me alone?*

*I don't like crowds.*

"From the *Nightwalker* movies, Nat," Jules whispers.

Luke hasn't said anything, and he's no longer looking at me. His hands are on his hips, and he's hanging his head.

"You lied to me." I hate how broken my voice sounds.

His head whips up, and he pins me with those beautiful blue eyes. "No, I didn't."

"I asked you, more than once, what you do for a living, and you kept brushing me off." Oh, this hurts.

"I just . . ." He runs his hands through his hair. "Natalie, what I feel for you . . ."

"Stop." I hold my hand up. "You said yesterday in the car, no surprises."

He swallows.

"God, I feel so stupid." I close my eyes and want to lay my head on the bar and cry.

"No, baby . . ." He starts to move toward me, but I back away again, making him stop.

"No, you listen, *baby*." The rage is kicking in, and I'm starting to shake with it. "I trusted you with things that I've never trusted with anyone else. And the whole time you were lying to me."

"It's not like that . . ."

"Natalie . . ." Jules steps forward, but I pin her in her place with a glare.

"So, I was a joke. 'Let's see how far I can get with this girl before she figures out who I am'? Well, you fucked her, Luke. Good for you."

"No!" He comes around the bar, ignoring my warnings of staying back and grasps my shoulders in his hands. His eyes are glacial, his face taut, as if he's in pain.

"No, Natalie. Nothing about us is a joke. And I did not fuck you, I made love to you."

I'm just so embarrassed. "Everyone in the country knows who you are, Luke."

"Not everyone," he replies.

"You're right. Apparently, I'm the only one who isn't bright enough to recognize you." I pull out of his grasp and back away. He drops his arms to his sides.

"Natalie," Jules tries again. "Why would you know who he is? You never saw his movies."

"His face is on millions of T-shirts, Jules! There are action figures in his likeness."

Luke grimaces and turns away.

"Girls of all ages squeal just the way you did five minutes ago and lose their fucking minds! It's my fucking job to know faces! God, I'm an idiot." I'm so embarrassed, I just want to run. I want him gone. I want him to hold me and tell me it's not true.

What the fuck would he ever want with me? He can have anyone in the world. Literally.

"Nat . . ." Luke reaches out for me, but I pull away, ignoring the pain in his voice.

"Just go."

"No, I don't want to leave." His beautiful face is in agony, mirroring mine.

I fold my arms around myself to keep from reaching out to him. "I don't want you here. I can't be with someone who lies to me." Oh, just go.

"I didn't lie! Natalie, that's not my life anymore. Let's talk about this."

I've heard enough, and I just need to get away from him. "I have a session in an hour, I need a shower, and I want you gone by the time I come out."

"You're overreacting!" His voice is manic, his eyes pleading with me.

"Get the fuck out of my house!" I scream at him, hot tears falling down my face.

"Natalie, don't do this . . ."

I turn and run up the stairs, through my room and into the bathroom, locking myself inside. I lean against the door and slide to the floor, my body convulsing as huge sobs rack my body.

"Natalie, open the door."

Fuck, he followed me.

"Just go away." There's no strength left in my voice. I just want him to go.

"I'm not going away, goddammit! Open the fucking door!"

"No!" I stand and lean my forehead on the door, my hands in fists and braced on the cool white wood.

"Natalie, so help me God, if you don't open this door, I'll break it down. Come out here and look at me." His voice sounds ragged and close to mine. And he's really pissed. But so am I! I don't respond, and suddenly Luke hits the wall to the left of the door.

"OPEN THE MOTHERFUCKING DOOR!"

I still don't respond. Hot tears are rolling down my face.

"Fine, Nat, if you want to act like a child, fine. I don't need this." I hear him stomp out of my room and down the stairs.

How did I get myself in this mess? How did I not recognize him? His hair is longer, and it's been a good five years since the last movie came out, so his body has filled out more, and he's older, but how could I not recognize that beautiful face?

Suddenly, I'm reminded of our talk when we had drinks at the pub. *If I see a trailer for one more stupid vampire movie, I'm going to kill myself.*

Oh God. Could this be any more humiliating?

Luke starred in three vampire movies that not only did well, but became such a huge sensation that you couldn't go anywhere without seeing news about the stars or merchandise of all kinds.

And I've just spent the past forty-eight hours falling in love with a man who is not only completely out of my league, but I don't even play the same sport.

Why didn't he tell me? Why did he let me tell him all of my secrets, while he didn't tell me any of his?

I sulk over to the tub and turn on the water. I have to pull myself together for my session. I cringe. Today's client is a couple, and I'm going to have to take intimate photos of them, encourage them to love each other, be romantic.

Shit.

I shower quickly, but let the water spray on my face for a few extra seconds. I'm going to look horrible with red, puffy eyes.

After I'm dry and dressed, I blow my hair dry and secure it back in a bun. I examine my face. Yep, red, puffy eyes. I don't bother with makeup and pray that my eyes calm down in the next thirty minutes. I just have to get through this session, then I can ball up in my bed and cry for days if I want to. Just two hours to get through and not think of Luke.

I poke my head out of the bathroom, but the bedroom is empty. Thank goodness. The wall next to the door where Luke hit it is unscarred. He didn't hit it that hard. I go into the spare bedroom and peek out the front-facing window. Luke's car is gone from the driveway.

He left.

Downstairs, Jules is still in the kitchen, a coffee mug in hand, tears in her eyes.

"Natalie, I'm so sorry."

I hold my hands up in surrender. "It's not your fault. I can't talk about this right now, Jules. I have a session in a few minutes."

"He's a wreck, Nat."

"Just stop."

"You have to talk to him."

"Stop! Jules, I can't talk about this." My voice catches, and I take a deep breath, willing the tears to stay at bay.

"Okay, we'll talk after the session then."

"Don't you have work?" I ask.

"I called out. I'm going to be here with you." She gives me a small smile.

"I love you, Jules." I turn to leave, but a thought occurs to me. "Do me a favor?"

"Of course. What is it, sweetie?"

"Strip my bed and wash all the bedding?" I couldn't stand to have to smell him later when I'm wallowing in self-pity.

"Sure."

IT WAS THE worst session of my life. I was scattered, sad, and edgy. The couple were great. They were very much in love, sexy, and I know that I got some great shots, but I feel badly that it wasn't the fun session I usually provide, so I'll refund the session fee. It's the least I can do.

I change into khaki shorts and a blue tank top, thanking the Lord above for my best friend when I see my bed has been stripped, washed and remade. My muscles have been reminding me all morning of last night's activities, and with every turn and stretch, my heart breaks just a little more.

Downstairs, I grab my iPhone to check messages and return calls, snag a tall glass of sweet tea from the fridge and join Jules on the back patio.

"How did it go?" she asks.

"It sucked." I shrug and sink into a red plushy chaise lounge.

"Sorry."

"I'll refund their money, but I think they'll still be happy with the photos." I turn my phone on and take a deep breath.

"Are you sure you want to check that?" Jules asks from the chaise beside me. Her eyes are closed, and she's drinking in the sunshine.

"I have to see if any clients called. I'll ignore him." I refuse to say his name out loud.

I have seven missed calls, five voice mails and three texts waiting for me.

There is absolutely nothing waiting for me from Luke, and I can't help but be disappointed. He said he didn't need this, so does that mean that we're over, just like that? Most likely, yes. Luke Williams can have anyone. Why would he want me?

I turn the phone off, slam it on the table beside my drink and pull my knees up to my chin, rest my forehead, and let the tears come full force.

"Oh, honey, don't cry." Jules climbs on my chaise with me and wraps her arms around me.

"I just feel so foolish," I mutter into her shoulder.

"You really didn't know who he is?"

"No. He looks a little different now," I reply defensively.

"Yeah, he does. He's aged well." Her smile is in her voice, and I can't help but agree.

"He has." I sigh. "Of course, now I see it. I should have known as soon as he mugged me at the beach."

"Maybe you were just too surprised."

"I guess, but what excuse do I have after that? I spent almost two solid days with the man, Jules."

"Hey, stop beating yourself up. You have been enjoying a sweet, sexy man for two days. There's no crime in that."

"I told him so much. I told him about Mom and Dad, the rape, everything. I even showed him my studio."

Jules looks down at me with wide eyes. "And you had sex in your own bed."

"Don't remind me."

"How did he react to all of it?"

I sit up and take a sip of tea. "He seemed sad for me that Mom and Dad are gone. The rape infuriated him, and he wants to kill that slimeball. He was really cool about the studio and said that it was sexy and I'm talented."

"Well, that all sounds encouraging."

"And last night was just . . ." How do I describe it? "Amazing and wonderful. He loves my curves, and when he touches me, just . . . wow." I can't stop the smile on my lips, and Jules smiles back.

"You made it with Luke Williams."

And my smile is gone.

"I'm sorry, but give me five minutes to gush. Is he as hot naked in real life as he is in the movies?"

"He was naked in the movie?" I squeak.

"From behind, yeah. It's my favorite part."

Oh, I definitely don't like it that all of America has seen Luke's ass. "I think his ass is better in person," I reply.

"Oh, you're killing me!" Jules sounds fifteen, and I giggle. "You know, he hasn't had a new movie since the last *Nightwalker* five years ago."

"Why?"

"I don't know." Jules shrugs and climbs back onto her chaise, taking a sip of my tea. "Rumor had it that some crazed fan broke into his house and hurt herself."

I gasp. "Was he hurt?"

"No, I don't think so. I don't think he was home. But who knows how much of the television tabloid stuff is true? I heard he just left LA and stopped acting. I had no idea he'd moved here."

"He's from here," I tell her. "His family lives around here."

"Oh, cool." Jules looks at me speculatively. "Are you sure you're done with him, Nat? You should have seen him after you ran out this morning."

"What did he do?"

"Well, he has quite a potty mouth, but then, so do you. He paced and swore, and I tried to stop him from running after you, because I knew that wasn't going to be the way to smooth things over."

"No, I didn't want to see him."

"He was a mess. He's mad about you. I think you should get to know him, the real him, better and give it a chance." I frown at her. "Besides, I've never seen you act this way about a man before. Don't give up on this yet."

"He lied to me, and you know how I feel about that!"

"Oh, Natalie, think. Have you stopped to think that maybe it was a nice change for him to be around someone who didn't want anything from him? Who didn't recognize him and squeal and ask him stupid questions? He was just a normal guy hanging out with a normal girl. I wouldn't want to ruin that, either."

I think hard about what Jules is saying, and yes, it makes sense.

"He still should have told me, at least yesterday." I am now sulking, and I don't care.

"You're right. Let him apologize. Maybe you'll get some good gifts out of the deal. Jewelry? Wine? Flowers?" She laughs when I stick my tongue out at her.

"Not today."

"Don't play games with him, Nat."

I scowl. "I'm not playing anything. He hurt my feelings. I just want to hang out with my best friend and do girl stuff today. Besides, when he stormed out of my room, he said he didn't need this, so I'm assuming he's no longer interested."

"Oh, he's interested." She waves the thought away with a flick of her wrist. "Wanna go shopping?" she asks hopefully.

"No. Ironically, I want to go to the movies. But nothing with Luke

Williams in it."

"Okay, there's nothing with his name on it there anyway. I think we deserve extra butter on our popcorn."

"And no diet soda. And because you recognized him before I did, you're buying."

Jules pouts as we gather our things and get in the car, headed to the movies where I can lose myself in someone else's story for a few hours and spend time with the one person in this world whom I trust completely.

# Ten

It's late when Jules and I get home. The high-paced action/adventure film we caught—with Vin Diesel, no less—was exactly what I needed to escape reality for a few hours. And I ended up giving in to Jules to go shopping afterward. How can I, Natalie Conner, pass up new shoes? They are my vice.

"Those red Louboutins you found are to die for," Jules says as we're pulling bags out of the back of my Lexus.

"I know. I love them. I don't know when I'll get to wear them, but I couldn't resist them." I reach for the bag of shoes, and we head for the front door.

We stop abruptly when we see what's waiting on our doorstep. Dozens of bouquets of roses, in all different shapes, sizes and colors, are covering the porch, the front steps, every surface possible. The aroma is amazing. There must be fifty-dozen roses here, minimum.

"Oh, Natalie." Jules' eyes are wide, and her face gets all gooey, taking it all in.

I can't help but get just a little gooey with her.

"Wow." It's all I can say, and I'm just so relieved. Maybe it's not over? We walk up the steps, careful not to knock anything over, and I see an envelope taped to the door with my name written on it.

"Here!" Jules pulls it off and hands it to me. It's too dark to see well, so we step inside and drop our bags. Jules starts hauling bouquets in.

"Where should I put these?"

"Um . . . I don't know. Just put them throughout the house."

Her smile is huge. "He gets mad props for this, girl."

"Yeah, he does." I feel my own wide smile and stare down at the envelope and then carefully rip it open.

*Dear Natalie,*

*There is a rose here for every time I thought of you today. I wish you would talk to me and let me explain why I didn't tell you who I am, and I'm so deeply sorry that you had to find out from your friend. I have a lot of explaining to do, and I hope you give me a chance to make it up to you.*

*Please call me when you're ready to talk.*

*Yours,*

*Luke*

Oh, yes, he's charming. I tuck the note in my pocket and help Jules bring all of the flowers inside, scattering them all over the house. It looks like there's either going to be a funeral or a wedding in my living room in the morning, and it makes me giggle.

"See?" Jules smirks. "I told you he's crazy about you."

"Or just crazy," I reply, laughing.

"You'd better call him and thank him."

"Yes, Mom." I roll my eyes at her. We lock up after the final bouquet has been brought in and fussed over. "Here, take some of these up to your room."

"Don't have to tell me twice!" Jules tucks a bouquet under each arm and heads upstairs with her shopping conquests.

I grab my phone, which has stayed turned off all day, my new shoes, and a gorgeous arrangement of perfect long-stemmed red roses with pearls tucked into the petals, and go up to my room. I kick my sandals off, set the vase on my bedside table, and put the new shoes in their new home in the closet. Going back to the flowers, I can't help but fuss over them and bury my nose in a soft, fragrant bloom. I notice another note, tucked in the stems, and pull it out, sitting on the bed as I read.

*These reminded me of your gorgeous long legs and delicious red lips. And one day, I'd love to see you dressed in nothing but pearls.*

Oh my. Is this what it feels like to be romanced? I wouldn't know, but I think I like it. And it occurs to me that he's been romancing me all along. The delicious dinner at his house, cuddling on his deck watching the sunset, our amazing picnic lunch yesterday. He was right when he said that he made love to me last night. Sex has never been that intimate for me.

But he did lie, even if it was by omission, and that's a deal breaker for me.

I decide to give him a chance to explain. I'll go to his house tomorrow and hear him out. I already miss him. His touch, his smile, his belly laugh, the feel of that soft blond hair in my fingers. I desperately want something good to happen with this man, and maybe that's what scares me most of all, even more than his celebrity status and the fact that he could have any skinny little glamorous woman on the planet.

If things go too much further, he could hurt me.

But the thought of not seeing him again makes my chest ache.

I pull my phone and the letter from the front door out of my pocket. I fire up the phone and impatiently wait for it to wake up.

Three missed calls, two voice mails and two texts. Nothing from Luke.

Both voice mails are from clients, so I save those and remind myself to call them and the four from this morning back tomorrow.

I scroll down to Luke's number and hit Call.

He answers on the first ring.

"Hi," he says softly.

"Hi," I murmur, my eyes closing at the sound of his voice. "Thank you for the beautiful flowers."

"Do you like them?" I hear his smile.

"They are amazing. And bountiful." I can't help but chuckle.

"I thought of you a lot today."

"Apparently so."

"Natalie, I'm so sorry . . ."

"No, Luke," I interrupt him, the agony in his voice my undoing. "I'm sorry, too. I may have overreacted just a bit."

"No, I understand. I should have said something yesterday."

"Yeah, you should have." I sigh. "I don't want to talk about this over the phone. Are you busy tomorrow morning?"

"You want to see me tomorrow?"

I hear the excitement in his voice, and I melt even more. "Well, I was thinking I could come over to your place, and we could talk."

"Yes. Come now."

I laugh and turn on my side on the bed, feeling my stomach start to settle for the first time since this morning. "I'm tired and don't think I'm up for a long conversation tonight."

"What did you do today?" he asks.

"Jules and I did some shopping." Should I tell him about the movie?

"What did you buy?"

God, I love his sexy voice. "Shoes."

"You like shoes?"

"I'm a woman. I am desperately, irrevocably in love with shoes."

"What do the new shoes look like?"

"Red stiletto Louboutins." I grin as I think about my sexy new shoes.

He whistles. "Wow."

"Yes, they are wow." I laugh.

Suddenly, it's quiet, and I think I've lost the call. "Luke?"

"Yeah, sorry, I was just imagining you wearing nothing but those shoes and pearls."

"Wow," I murmur.

"Yes, it was wow." His voice is low, and I hear his grin, and I just want to touch him.

"What else did you do today?" he asks, interrupting my thoughts.

"Well, ironically enough, we went to the movies."

I hear him gasp. "I thought you didn't watch many movies."

"I don't, but I had a rough morning and wanted to forget for a little while, so we overdosed on popcorn and soda and a bare-chested Vin Diesel."

"Was it good?"

"A bare-chested Vin Diesel is always good," I reply haughtily.

"You wound me, Natalie."

"A bare-chested Luke is better," I whisper.

"That's better," he whispers back.

"I like it when you whisper."

"You do? Why?"

"It's hot."

"Really?"

"Very hot." Oh, I love this flirtiness that we have.

"I'll remember that."

I suddenly wish I'd taken him up on his offer to go to his house now, so before I can make an ass of myself and beg, I end the call.

"Nine o'clock tomorrow?" I ask.

"I'll have breakfast waiting," he murmurs.

"Good night."

"Good night, beautiful," he whispers.

I WAKE TO an incessant doorbell. I glance at the alarm clock. Who the hell is ringing my doorbell at seven-thirty in the damn morning? I fumble around for yoga pants and a shirt and grumpily trudge down the stairs.

Standing at my door is a young blond girl, maybe sixteen, holding a Starbucks to-go mug and a single red rose.

"Are you Natalie?" she asks with a smile.

"Yes."

"These are for you." She's excited as she pushes the coffee and flower toward me.

"Uh, thanks." I take them from her, pushing the rose against my nose.

"There's a note, too." She holds it out to me and claps her hands. "This is the most romantic thing I've ever seen in my life!"

I laugh at her excitement and open my door wider so she can see the dozens of bouquets of roses in the living room. Her eyes about pop out of her pretty little head.

"Holy shit! Wow. You're so lucky. Bye!" She waves and is off.

I take a sip of the coffee—oh God, that's good. How did he know white mochas are my favorite?—and open the note.

*Good morning, gorgeous. Just a little something to start your day off right. Can't wait to see you. Luke*

Holy Moses, he's just so sweet.

Jules comes down the stairs yawning. "Who was at the door?"

"Does Starbucks deliver?" I ask.

"Uh, I wish." She eyes my coffee and the rose.

"A girl just delivered these."

"Jesus, this is starting to get sickening." Jules heads for the kitchen, and I laugh, following her.

"I'm going to see him this morning."

"Good. I don't want the details." She starts making her own coffee. "Wait. You're the only one getting laid. Yes, I do want details. And pictures."

I grin and bury my nose in the rose again. "I'm not going to sleep with him. We're just going to talk."

"Right."

"We are."

"Okay. Let me know how that works out for you." She sets the coffee to drip, then smiles over at me. "I'm glad you're giving him a chance."

"Just because he's *the* Luke Williams?"

"No, because he's a good guy who finally treats you the way you deserve to be treated."

"What am I getting myself into?"

"Something fun." She shrugs. "Stop overthinking it and enjoy it."

"Okay. I'm going to shower and head over to his place for breakfast."

"Be safe." She calls after me.

"I always am," I call back.

I STAND AT Luke's door and pause before ringing the bell. Am I over-dressed? I glance down at my yellow sundress and strappy black sandals. Summer is hanging on with a vengeance, and it's going to be warm to-day. Maybe I should have worn shorts.

Maybe I should stop procrastinating and ring the damn doorbell.

A few seconds later, Luke opens the door, and before I can say a word, he wraps me in his arms and kisses me with a need I've never felt before. He runs one hand down to the small of my back, pulling me against him. His other hand cups the side of my head while his mouth moves deftly over mine, back and forth, his tongue pushing into my mouth to dance and move against my own.

Oh God, I missed him! It's only been twenty-four hours, but it feels like I haven't seen him in days. I run my hands up his back, under his shirt, feeling his smooth skin, and moan against his mouth.

He slows the kiss, gently touching my lips with his, and when I open my eyes, he rests his forehead on mine.

"Do you always answer the door like this?" I whisper.

"Oh God, Natalie, I was afraid I wouldn't see you again." His voice is raspy with anguish, and I grasp his face in my hands, imploring him to look me in the eye.

"I'm here."

"Thank God." He steps back, and I let my eyes slide over him. His body does amazing things to a white button-down shirt, sleeves rolled to the elbows, and jeans. He's barefoot. His hair is messy and sexy and is begging for my fingers.

"You look fantastic. Come in, make yourself at home." The smell coming from the kitchen is amazing, and my stomach growls.

"You're cooking?" I ask, glancing back at him.

"I promised you breakfast."

"You already sent me coffee, which was delicious and unexpected. Thank you." I lean up and kiss him chastely on the mouth.

"You're welcome." He smiles. "I hope you like French toast, bacon, fruit and coffee."

"Perfect."

"It's all set up outside."

I follow him out onto his magnificent deck, and he motions for me to go ahead of him. Was I really here just a few nights ago? It feels like a long time ago, so much has happened since then.

The table is covered with a white cloth. The food is on warming plates, under silver, domed lids. There is coffee and juice, but the red roses are what catch my eye. Three dozen, in three separate bouquets, are set in even distances down the table.

Tears come to my eyes as I feel Luke's hands on my shoulders from behind me. He's gone to so much trouble! Even after the way I spoke to him yesterday.

I turn in his arms and look up into his intense, beautiful blue eyes. "Thank you, so much."

"It's my pleasure, honey. I told you in the car, we have a lot of catching up to do. Get used to it."

I don't know what to say. He pulls me in for a hug and kisses my forehead.

"Come on, let's eat. I'm starving."

We sit in the same seats we sat in the other night. He uncovers our plates, and I breathe the delicious scents in appreciatively.

"Smells fantastic." I pour warm syrup over my French toast and take a bite of bacon. "Mmm . . . bacon."

He laughs and takes a bite of his own bacon. "I do love watching you eat, baby."

"Why?" I ask with my mouth full of the soft, delicious toast.

"Because you're so honest about it. Like everything you do, I guess. I love it that you enjoy food."

"Clearly. Have you seen the size of my ass?"

His eyes blaze as he glares at me over his coffee mug. "Don't ever put yourself down like that around me again, Natalie."

I frown and look down at my plate.

"I don't know how many times I have to tell you or show you how beautiful I think you are for you to get it through your head."

"Luke . . ."

He reaches out with his long fingers and grasps my chin, tilting my face back up to meet my eyes.

"Look at me. There is nothing for you to be uncomfortable about when it comes to your body. Eat whatever you want. I love watching you eat. I'd love to work out with you, just because I love watching you move. Your curves are beautiful, and I can't wait to get my hands on them again."

"Okay."

What else am I supposed to say to that?

"Are you trying to send the florists' kids to college?" I ask, trying to distract him.

# eleven

L uke laughs at my quip, and I relax a little. I really need to watch what I say around him about my body. I've never been so self-conscious with other men, but that's probably because I didn't really care what they thought of me. They could take me or leave me.

I want Luke to take me.

"Thank you for breakfast." I pick up my coffee and lean back in my chair, admiring the view of the water and the boats sailing across it.

"You're welcome." He stands and holds his hand out for me to take. "Come, let's get more comfortable and have that talk."

Wow, I'm not going to have to drag it out of him! This is good. I take his hand and abandon my coffee, but grab the orange juice, and follow him over to the plush love seat. I sit facing him and wait for him to start.

Luke sits on the edge of the sofa and runs his fingers through his hair. He's agitated, probably nervous. I don't really know what to say to put him at ease. And I desperately want him to start talking.

"Hey," I say and link my fingers with his. "It's okay. Tell me whatever you're comfortable telling me, and we'll go from there."

His eyes are worried, his brow furrowed, as he leans back and kisses my knuckles.

"First of all, I didn't mean to lie to you." He looks me square in the eye. "I should have been honest with you the night you were here, but frankly, I just got so caught up in you. You make me forget my own name sometimes."

So he has that problem, too, huh?

"Obviously, the morning we met I thought you were taking photos of me. That doesn't happen often anymore, but every once in a while it does, and I panic."

"I won't ever take your picture without your permission."

He squeezes my hand and gives me a sad smile.

"Thank you," he murmurs. He takes a deep breath and continues. "A few years ago things were pretty crazy. The paparazzi can be merciless, and sometimes the fans are worse. I've never been great in crowds, no idea why, but being literally chased down the street by hundreds of people on a regular basis pushed it into a full-blown phobia. Every moment of my life was documented for five years."

He turns toward me, his eyes wide and haunted. "I couldn't have had a girlfriend if I had wanted one. There was never a moment to myself."

"I thought I read something about you being with the co-star . . . Meredith Something or other."

He shakes his head with frustration. "That was all fabricated for the sake of the films. For the publicity. The studio owns you when you're in big-budget films, Nat. They dictate who you're with, what you do, where you go. I was too young to truly understand what that meant.

"Meredith is nice, but she was never my girlfriend, and that's just another example of how ruthless the paparazzi are. They can twist anything around until they get the story they want, rather than the boring truth." He swallows and frowns, and then his beautiful blue eyes find mine again.

"If you have questions about my past, you need to ask me. Don't go looking around online for answers."

Geez. "Okay."

"This is important. It could make us or break us, and I refuse to lose you over something that is no longer a part of my life."

"Is stuff still printed about you?" I ask.

"Sometimes. Not often anymore. Thank God."

"Have you really not made a movie in five years?"

"I haven't acted in one in five years," he replies.

"Why?"

He runs his hand through his hair again. "Because not all money is good money."

"What does that mean?"

"I made a lot of money from those films, Nat. I still do, thanks to merchandising, and my accountant and lawyers. And I could still be making a lot of money acting in films, but at what cost? So I can be hounded and have my life ruled?"

"What about actors like Matt Damon and Ben Affleck? They seem to lead fairly private lives," I remind him.

He nods. "Yes, they do, but they're also a bit older now and aren't starring in romantic comedies geared toward young women. They aren't great fodder for the rags anymore."

"So no movie business at all?" I ask, wanting to know more. He still hasn't told me what he does now.

"I didn't say that."

Oh. "Okay."

"I produce now, help movies get made. I'm not an actor anymore."

"So does that mean that you have to be gone for long periods of time?" I keep the panic out of my voice, but my blood runs cold. I don't want him gone most of the time!

"No, I do most of my work from home." He kisses my hand again. "I go to L.A. or New York for a few days here and there, but that's it. I also work with other producers who are able to do most of the hands-on work."

"Oh." Wow, he really does live in a completely different world from mine. "I have a question."

"Shoot."

"Jules said yesterday that she'd heard that someone hurt themselves in your house."

Luke goes pale, and his eyes suddenly look bleak.

"Yeah. I was in New York doing publicity for the last movie." He swallows. "A young girl, a fan, broke into my house. She lit it on fire."

I gasp. "Oh my God."

"That would have been bad enough, but she did a really bad job of it and got caught in the house and ended up dying in there."

"Holy shit, Luke."

"That's when I knew I was done. It's too crazy, and I'm just not made for it. Other actors manage okay in that world, but it's not worth people's lives to me."

"She was obviously a messed-up girl, honey."

His eyes dart to mine. "That's the first time you've called me anything other than my name."

I smile shyly and shrug.

"Yeah, she was messed up. It didn't make it right."

"Do you miss it?"

"I miss the work. Acting is fun, and I like to think I was good at it. Being on set was a lot of fun, and I learned a lot. But I don't miss the rest of it."

"Okay, so here's the million-dollar question. Why didn't you just tell me?"

"At first I didn't believe you when you said you didn't know who I am." He smiles sadly at me. "That rarely happens. And then when it became obvious that it was true, it was just such a breath of fresh air to be normal."

"You're not normal, Luke, and I mean that in a good way."

He smirks. "You know what I mean. You didn't become a fifteen-year-old like Jules did yesterday. You seemed to like me, not a character in a movie."

"I've never seen your movies," I state matter-of-factly.

"I love that." His voice is completely honest.

"But were you ever going to tell me? I was going to find out sooner or later. That's what I'm struggling with, Luke. That's why I freaked out on you yesterday. I confided things to you that I just don't share with anyone. Even Jules doesn't know about my tattoos."

His eyes smolder at the mention of my tattoos, but I press on.

"Clearly, after our conversation in the car, you should know that I have trust issues with men. All men. I don't keep men in my life."

"I'm hoping that's about to change," he whispers.

"This wasn't a great start to convince me to make any changes."

"Natalie, think about the rest of the time we've been together. I'm still the same man I was before we were in your kitchen yesterday morning. I still like to cook. I think your work is sexy. I can't keep my hands off you. I'm just a man."

"I know."

"You do?"

"Yes. I'm not an idiot. But you know me better than anyone, after less than a week, and I can't help but feel a little foolish. Yesterday was really embarrassing for me."

"It was embarrassing for me, too."

"Well, I'm glad that's over."

"What?"

"My first embarrassing moment in front of you."

He smiles, but it's fleeting. He gets serious again. "Can we start over?"

"No."

His face falls. "So it's over?"

"No, I don't want to start over because that would mean erasing everything we've had, and honestly, aside from yesterday, the past few days have been really good." I bite my lip and gaze over at him.

His impossibly beautiful face breaks into a heart-stopping smile. God, he just looks so . . . joyful. I can't help but match it.

"Natalie, these have been the best few days of my life, and I mean that."

"Wow."

Finally, he pulls me onto his lap and into his arms. I bury my face in his neck, wrap my arms around him and hold on, inhaling his sexy scent, planting soft kisses on his cheek.

I lean back and take his face in my hands, gazing deeply into his eyes. "Just don't ever act with me."

"Baby, you don't have to worry about that."

Suddenly he's kissing me, and we're on the move. He stands with me in his arms and heads inside the house. He's carrying me like I weigh nothing, and it's so . . . hot.

"Where are we going?" I ask against his lips.

"My bed."

Oh.

"We didn't clean up after breakfast."

"Later."

"We could get naked on the deck," I suggest and bite his earlobe.

He growls. "No, my bed." We're moving up the stairs. "I'm getting you naked and plan to spend about a week in bed with you."

I can't help but laugh. "I have clients on Monday."

"Okay, but today and tomorrow you're all mine."

"Yours?" I raise an eyebrow at him.

"Mine." He repeats and stands me gently at the side of his bed. He grabs the hem of my dress and pulls it over my head. "Sweet Jesus, you're not wearing any underwear."

I grin. "Nope."

"This whole time, you've been sitting six inches from me with no fucking underwear?"

"Yep." I laugh and start unbuttoning his shirt. His eyes watch mine intently, and I pop the buttons, one by one. I push the shirt over his shoulders, and he lets it fall to the floor.

Next, I push my finger between the elastic of his boxers and his skin, the way I did the other night when he stopped me. His eyes flash with need, and he makes no move to stop me this time. I smile and run my tongue along my lower lip. I glide my fingers along his stomach to his fly and open his jeans. I pull the soft denim and gray boxers slowly over his lean hips and down his legs. He steps out of them and kicks them aside.

"There, you've caught up to me," I murmur and gaze back up into his heated blue eyes.

He doesn't touch me, which is making me mad with longing. I want those skilled hands on me!

"I love it when you look at me like that," he murmurs and moves toward me.

I back up, the backs of my legs meeting the edge of the bed.

"How am I looking at you?"

"Your beautiful green eyes are looking at me like you just can't wait until I touch you."

"I can't."

"Lie back on the bed, baby."

I do as he asks and gaze up at him, enjoying the view that is Luke. All of the blood in my body has pooled between my legs, and I'm panting. All without him actually touching me.

"What are you doing to me?" I ask, surprised that I spoke the words aloud.

He grins and climbs onto the bed, straddles my legs, his hands planted on either side of my shoulders. He's still not actually touching me. He lowers his head and sweeps his lips across mine. Once, then twice.

"I'm seducing you."

"You're good at it." He smiles against my lips. I grasp his hips, but he pulls back, out of my reach. "Hey!"

"Grab on to the headboard."

"I want to touch you."

He lightly kisses me again. "Trust me, baby. Hold on to the headboard."

I reach above me and grab on to the white wooden headboard.

"Keep your hands there, okay?"

"Okay."

He smiles and kisses my lips once more, then my chin. I close my eyes and tilt my head back, giving him access to my neck. He takes advantage and licks all the way down to my collarbone.

He lowers his body down onto mine as he moves down my body. He clasps one breast in his hand, worrying my sensitive nipple between his fingers while he sucks the other one in his mouth, and it's a direct hit to my groin.

"Oh shit." I bow up off the bed, my body zinging in sensation. He blows softly on the nipple and moves to the other one to pay the same respects.

"So beautiful," he mutters against my breast. "I love your breasts. You fill my hands perfectly."

"Can I move my hands now?" I breathe.

"No way. Keep them where they are."

"I want to touch you."

"You will, but don't move yet."

I groan in frustration, and he starts kissing down my torso again. He laves my belly piercing with his tongue. "This is so hot."

"I was thinking about taking it out."

"Please don't, I love it."

"Okay," I say shyly.

He grins and moves farther down, his hands running down my sides to my hips. Suddenly, he grips the insides of my thighs and pushes them wide apart. He rubs his nose over the tattoo on my pubis and moans.

"Who did you have to forgive, baby?"

I gasp and stare down at him with wide eyes. His eyes meet mine, and I'm mortified to feel tears prick at the backs of my eyes.

"Myself," I whisper.

"Oh, baby." He kisses my tattoo sweetly, his fingers moving up my inner thighs to my center. He runs one finger down my cleft, from my clitoris to my anus, and I cry out.

"Argh!" Ohmygod!

"Honey, you are so wet." His tongue follows his finger, and my hips convulse. He holds my thighs firmly against the bed, spread wide open for him.

"So sweet." He runs that glorious tongue back up to my lips and then presses it inside me, kissing me intimately as if he were kissing my face, his nose pressed against my clitoris.

"Holy shit!" I cry and feel him smile against me. His hands move around to cup my ass and lift me, and he presses his face into me farther, and he's taking no prisoners. He rubs his nose back and forth over my clitoris as his tongue moves around and around inside me, and I am almost afraid of my orgasm. I come fast and hard, pulling myself with my hands still clenched on the headboard off the bed, calling out Luke's name, or I think that's what I'm saying anyway.

I may be speaking in tongues.

He continues the sweet torture until the last tremble moves through me, then he kisses his way up my body, stopping to pay special attention to each breast, and finally lying over me, resting his pelvis on mine, his elbows on each side of my shoulders. His hard shaft is lying against my very wet center, and when I roll my hips to wrap my legs around him, I feel it slide up and down.

Luke's eyes clench shut. "Oh God, Nat, you feel so good."

"So do you." I pull myself up and kiss his lips, tasting him and me.

He moves his hips now, sliding that deliciously large and hard cock up and down my folds, but not slipping inside me yet. The tip keeps bumping up against my clitoris, shooting sparks of sensation through me.

"Let me touch you," I beg.

"God, yes, touch me."

Hallelujah!

I grip his hair in my hands and pull his face to mine. He kisses me voraciously, and while what he's doing against my center feels so fantastic, I just want him in me.

"Luke," I breathe against his mouth.

"What do you need, baby?"

"You. In. Me. Now." Each word is staccato between kisses. He groans deep in his throat and finally slips inside me.

Hard.

Oh sweet Jesus!

"Ah!" He's pounding into me, over and over, each thrust harder than the last. His breath is ragged and broken. I reach down and grab his ass, pulling him harder.

"Oh, Natalie, come with me, baby." His words, his voice, are my undoing, and I explode around him. I am just sensation, as he pushes inside me to the hilt, grinding and grinding, moving back and forth, as he empties himself into me.

I run my fingers up his spine and push them gently through his damp hair as he shudders over me, whispering my name like a prayer.

## twelve

I love his hair. It's just the right length for me to run my fingers through the softness, over and over. Luke sighs in contentment, his cheek resting against my sternum, and I cradle him in my arms. We stay this way for a long while, in companionable silence.

When his breathing slows, and I think he's gone to sleep, he raises his head, kisses my chest where his cheek has been, and our eyes meet.

"Stay with me this weekend."

"I thought we'd already established that," I reply.

"Damn right." He kisses me quickly then rolls off me and strolls into the bathroom. Yes, he has a fine derriere.

"I have a question," I call to him in the bathroom.

"Shoot," he calls back.

"Did you have a butt double in your movie?" I pull my dress over my head and begin finger-combing my hair, tying it back in a ponytail.

"Uh . . ." I hear water running in the sink, and he pokes his head out the door. "No."

"Oh." How do I feel about this?

"I thought you didn't see the movies." He flashes his half smile at me. Swoon!

"I didn't. That was a particularly favorite scene of Jules'," I explain.

"Ah." He disappears back into the bathroom for a few minutes then reappears in fresh red boxers—drool!—and pulls on his discarded jeans and white button-down shirt.

"I don't know how I feel about that," I murmur as I watch him dress.

"Why?"

"I don't think I like it that everyone in the free world has seen your ass."

He pulls me off the bed and against his solid chest, linking his hands at my lower back.

"Why, Natalie, are you jealous?"

"Of about a hundred million girls ogling you?" I raise an eyebrow. "What's to be jealous of?"

"Absolutely nothing." He gently sweeps his lips over mine in that way he has that makes my knees all weak. "Your hands and eyes are the only ones I want on my ass, baby."

"Okay," I whisper against his mouth. "If I'm going to stay here this weekend"—I step back out of his arms and grasp his hands in mine—"I need to run home and grab a few things. I hadn't planned on a weekend vacation."

"Let's go do that now, then come back here."

"You want to spend all weekend here at the house?"

"Most of it, yes." He brings my hands to his lips. "We can hang out here today, do whatever you want. Let me cook for you and take care of you."

My jaw drops. I'm unable to articulate words.

"And tomorrow, I want you to go to my parents' house with me for dinner."

"What?"

"They do a family thing every Sunday, and I think my brother's in town for the weekend."

"I can't meet your family!" I pull my hands out of his and wrap my arms around my stomach. Meet his family!

"Why not?"

"You've known me less than a week!"

"So?"

"So? So! Luke . . ."

He quickly grabs my hands again and smiles lazily down into my panicked eyes. "It's just some burgers on the grill, Nat. It's no biggie. I want you to meet my family."

"Aren't we moving kind of fast?"

He scowls and looks down at our hands then back into my eyes. "You're staying the weekend with me. Part of my weekend is spending an afternoon with my family. I want you to come."

He wants me to meet his family! I just can't quite wrap my head around this. But he looks so hopeful, and I must admit, part of me is very curious to meet his parents and see where he grew up.

"Okay, I'll come."

His eyes light up with boyish excitement. "You will?"

"Yes, I can't seem to resist your charms," I mutter sarcastically.

"Come on." He slaps my ass and ushers me toward the stairs. "Let's go get your stuff before I rip that dress off you again."

I AM SITTING at Luke's dining room table editing photos. We spent an hour or so gathering my clothes, necessities and my computer, camera and memory cards from my house, then spent another half hour cleaning up our breakfast.

Things would have progressed faster had we not been too busy touching, kissing and stealing glances at each other the whole time.

Suddenly, Katy Perry's song *Teenage Dream* makes a whole lot of sense.

I gaze across the brightly lit living space to Luke's couch, where he's lounging casually, his bare feet crossed at the ankle, a stack of movie scripts on the ottoman. He's got one of the scripts open on his lap, and he's biting his thumbnail as he reads.

Visions of me straddling his lap and throwing the script over the back of the couch make me smile, but I turn back to the image on my computer screen.

I'm editing the photos I took while Luke and I were at the falls the other day. There are about twenty-five of them that are my favorites, and I'll print and frame them, offering them for sale around town.

As I close the file containing the falls photos, I sense Luke get up and head for the kitchen.

"Would you like something to drink?"

"Just some water, thanks." I smile at him and open the next file of photos to edit. These will be much more fun.

The couple I photographed yesterday fills my screen. Luke steps behind me and sets my water on the table.

"Wow."

I look up and grin. "They're good-looking, aren't they?"

"They are. They need to loosen up a bit."

I laugh. "The first twenty images get tossed out of every shoot. It takes at least that long for the client to relax."

I page through about twenty photos and stop.

"See? They don't even know I'm there anymore." The blond woman is in a black barely there teddy. The dark man is sitting on the bed, legs crossed, and she's straddling his lap, arms around his neck and fingers in his hair, kissing him.

"Yeah, much better." He starts to rub my shoulders as he watches me work. "When did you take these?" he asks.

"Yesterday." I lean into his hands and moan. He's amazing with his hands.

"After our fight." It isn't a question.

"Yeah. Oh God, don't stop doing that."

He kisses my head, and I feel him smile. "I prefer hearing those words come out of that sexy mouth of yours when you're naked."

I laugh and lean my head back, looking up at him upside down.

"Later. I have to finish these. The client's already getting a refund, and I want them to have their pictures as soon as possible."

"Why are they getting a refund? Nat, they're fantastic."

"Because it wasn't my usual fun session. I feel bad."

"I'm sorry." He kisses my head again.

"Don't be. They'll be happy with the shots and with getting their money back. Give me an hour."

"Okay, take your time, baby." He goes back to reading his script, running his hands through his unruly hair, and I can't help but grin, enjoying our easy camaraderie.

I put the finishing touches on the last sexy photo of my too-good-looking clients and grin in satisfaction. Despite my horrible mood yesterday, I rocked these pictures.

"Okay, come look."

Luke rises gracefully from the couch and stands behind me again. I page through each finished image, proud of how they turned out.

"They are amazing." He kisses my cheek gently, and I smile wide, glowing in his praise.

"Thank you. I hope they like them."

"They'd be idiots not to. Are you finished for today?"

"Yep, that's all of them. I'm all caught up until my session Monday." I close my computer down and stand up, stretching.

"How is the reading coming?" I ask, gesturing to his stack of scripts.

"Tedious. It's all been crap so far today."

"No blockbusters in that pile?" I run my hand down his cheek, unable to keep myself from touching him.

"Definitely not." He turns and places a kiss in my palm, and I feel my blood start to hum.

"I'm sorry I've been a boring companion this afternoon." I smooth both of my hands up over his shoulders and around his neck, pulling him in close, and kiss his chin.

"There is nothing boring about you, baby." He turns his head, giving me access to his throat, and I place chaste kisses down to his collarbone. "Although, now that we're both done with work . . ."

"Yes?" My fingers are in his hair now, pulling his lips down to mine.

"We could do something a little more energetic."

"What did you have in mind?" I love the way his hands feel against the small of my back as he pulls me closer to him.

"Are you still naked under this dress?"

"I don't know," I say innocently, and widen my eyes. "Maybe you should check."

"It's a tough job, baby." He gathers the skirt with his fingers, hiking it up around my hips, and cups my bare bottom in his hands.

"I love your ass." He's nibbling my lips and kneading my butt rhythmically. Mmm . . . feels so good. He slides one hand down between my legs and slips a finger inside me from behind, and I arch against him.

"Oh, Luke . . ."

"You're so ready for me, honey."

"I kept picturing myself attacking you on the couch while you were reading."

"You did?" His smile is delighted, and he continues to torture me with his finger.

"Yeah, it got me hot."

"Fuck, Natalie, looking at you gets me hot."

"Come here." I lead him back to the couch and motion for him to sit. He complies and gazes up at me with bright blue, lustful eyes.

Instead of straddling him, I kneel between his knees and reach for the clasp on his jeans.

"You're wearing too many clothes." My voice is breathy.

I open his jeans, and he lifts his hips so I can pull them down and discard them. His erection springs free, hard and ready for me.

I lick my lips.

Even his cock is pretty, which is a thought I never thought I'd have. It's large, and hard, nestled in a small patch of curly blond hair. No manscaping here, but he doesn't need to.

I run my hands up his thighs and grip him in both hands. He sucks breath in through his teeth, his jaw clenched, and his eyes are on fire.

My hands start to move up and down, and I lean down and brush the very tip with my tongue, tasting the bead of liquid at the end.

"Shit, baby."

He pulls my hair free from my ponytail and pushes his fingers through it, and I get bolder with my mouth, moving faster and pulling him in deeper, rubbing my tongue up and down the impressive length of him. My left hand moves lower and cups his balls, and he goes mad.

"Enough!" He grips me beneath my arms and pulls me on top of him so that I straddle his lap, and pushes into me swiftly, and I'm so thankful for my lack of panties beneath this dress.

"Ah!"

"I. Need. You." Our eyes meet, his hands on my hips, moving me up and down in a punishing, sweet rhythm, pushing so far inside me that it's just almost painful. I pull my dress over my head, and Luke's lips find a nipple, pulling it relentlessly into his mouth, and suckling.

I am gripping the back of the couch above his head, and I lean back, giving him unfettered access to my breasts, and surrender to the tightening of my womb, the flexing of my thighs, and I explode around him, my body singing in sensation.

Luke pulls me down on him, hard, and empties himself into me. "Oh yes, baby!"

WE ARE STRETCHED out on the couch, lying side by side. Luke is tracing the letters up my ribs with his fingertip.

"It's for my parents," I whisper.

"Why this phrase?" he whispers in response.

"Because it's important to remember to be in the moment. It can be over so fast."

"And why on your left side?"

"Because it's close to my heart."

He kisses my forehead and runs his fingers up and down my back, soothing me.

"Can I ask a question about them?" God, when he whispers like that, he can ask me anything he wants!

"Of course."

"What happened to them?"

I sigh and kiss his chin. "They were killed in a plane crash about three years ago. My dad used to fly, and he had a small plane that they would use for weekend trips."

"That's an expensive hobby."

"Yeah, he could afford it." I take a deep breath and look up into Luke's relaxed eyes. "I think I mentioned the other day that he was a high-profile lawyer."

"Yeah."

"Well, he was good at it. He did very well, and when they died together, I was the only beneficiary."

"Hey, I wasn't asking you about your financial situation." He grazes my cheek with the backs of his fingers.

"I know." I shrug. "Anyway, they were going down to Mexico for the weekend. I was supposed to go with them."

Luke's arms tighten around me, and I run my fingers through his chest hair.

"I decided at the last minute to stay home because I had finals at school the following week."

"I'm so sorry." He's resting his lips on my forehead now, and I'm curled into him, absorbing his strength, his heat. "They must have been amazing people."

"Why do you say that?" I lean back and search his blue eyes.

"Because you're amazing, baby."

Geez, charming doesn't even begin to describe this man.

"They were amazing," I whisper. "I know that my dad always wanted me to be something grander than a photographer, like a doctor, or a lawyer, or go into finance, something that would make a lot of money. But you know what?"

"What?"

"Neither of them even batted an eye when I said I was going to take pictures for a living. They just loved me. They just wanted me to be happy.

"My dad's job was ruthless and demanding, and he could be a complete asshole in the courtroom. I went and watched him once, and I didn't even recognize him. He almost scared me.

"But when he was home, he was so gentle. He was a big man, tall, with big hands. And he always smelled like fabric softener and coffee. And even when I was grown, he would let me curl up in his lap and hold me."

Luke swallows hard.

"What?" I ask.

"You don't have anyone to take care of you anymore."

"I've been taking care of myself for a long time, honey. Even when my parents were still here."

He briefly closes his eyes and clenches his jaw, as if he's angry, or frustrated. What did I say?

He leans in and sweeps his lips across mine, slipping me beneath him, and gently, tenderly, makes love to me.

# thirteen

I wake alone on the couch. A light blanket covers me, and I'm still naked from Luke's lovemaking. My skin feels sensitive and warm under the blanket. I could curl up and sleep here all night.

Wow. I've never had gentle, sweet, loving sex before, and I must admit, there's a lot to be said for it.

I sit up and stretch, looking around the great room. It's dark outside now, surprising me. How long was I asleep? Heavenly aromas are coming from the kitchen, but Luke's not in it. I stand and wrap the blanket around me and go to find him.

As I stroll toward the kitchen, I can hear Luke talking and look out on the deck. He's sitting on the love seat, talking on the phone. I turn to go upstairs and have a shower to give him privacy, but then I hear my name, and I can't help but stop to hear what he's saying.

"You'll like her."

Must be his family?

"No, Samantha, it's not like that. She's different. I wouldn't be bringing her to Mom and Dad's if that were the case. Look, I just wanted to give you a heads up that I'm bringing her with me tomorrow. I've already talked to Mom, and she's excited to meet her. Do not play the overprotective big sister tomorrow. Please."

I can't help but smile.

"I'm serious, Sam. Be nice. I love you, too. See you tomorrow."

He ends the call and runs his hands through his hair, standing to come inside and sees me inside the doorway. I give him a small smile, taking in his disheveled handsomeness in his faded jeans and white shirt.

"Overprotective sister, huh?"

"You have no idea."

"I can hold my own, Mr. Williams." He joins me inside, and I open the blanket so he can slide his arms around my waist, and I wrap the blanket around his back.

"I know, but she can be ruthless. Sam and I have always been particularly close because we're less than two years apart in age. She has a history of thinking she needs to protect me, so just don't be surprised if she's a little cool toward you tomorrow."

"She's never liked your girlfriends in the past?"

"She's never met anyone from my past."

"What do you mean?"

"I've never introduced anyone to my family before."

"Why me?"

He leans down and kisses me in that gentle way he has, and I sigh. "Because you didn't know who I am. And you have gotten under my skin. I don't think I'll ever have enough of you."

"I'd like to know you better," I whisper, intentionally missing his point.

"Ditto, baby."

"You know me better than anyone."

"There's still a lot to learn." He brushes my hair off my face, and I grasp his wrist so I can kiss his palm.

"How long was I asleep?"

"Just about an hour."

"It smells good in here." He grins down at me.

"Stir-fry okay for dinner?"

"Mmm . . . sounds great. Do I have time to take a quick shower first?"

"Sure, baby. You go shower, and I'll get dinner ready." He pulls out of the blanket and releases me.

"I could get used to being spoiled like this," I quip.

I turn from him and head for the stairway when I hear him mumble, "I'm counting on it."

THE DRIVE TO Luke's parents' house is fairly short. It's a rainy Sunday afternoon, so we're in Luke's black Mercedes SUV. How many cars does he have? I look to my left and take a deep breath, trying to fight down the nerves. My stomach is in knots.

I'm flat-out terrified of meeting his parents.

This weekend has been wonderful. After dinner last night, we cuddled on the couch and watched old comedies from the eighties and laughed all night. Then he took me to bed and made sweet love to me like he had on the couch.

Wow, he can be so tender. I can't help but remember when he slapped my ass the first time we made love, and I wonder when he's going to do that again.

Variety is the spice of life, after all. Perhaps we'll play when we get back to his place later.

He looks so beautiful, sitting here in his black T-shirt and another pair of faded blue jeans. His strong hands are on the wheel, and I shiver as I think of how they feel on me.

"Are you cold?" He reaches for the climate controls on the dash, but I stop his hand.

"No, I'm not cold."

He glances at me, and then does a double take, raising an eyebrow.

"I love your hands," I say as I twine my fingers with his. He raises them to his lips and kisses my wrist.

"They're just hands." He gives me a wicked smile, and my stomach clenches.

"They do crazy things to me," I whisper.

"Behave, or I'll pull this car over and fuck you."

I gasp at his words. This is a completely different attitude from last night, and frankly, it's hot. Desire pools in my groin, and I smile as I decide to play with him a little.

"Don't make promises you can't keep."

"Oh, honey, trust me, that's a promise I can definitely keep."

I pick at an imaginary piece of lint on my red sundress. I'm wearing a soft blue denim jacket over it because of the weather and brown peep-toe sandals.

"Prove it."

He whips his head toward me and narrows his eyes. "Excuse me?"

"You heard me," I whisper and pull the hem of my dress up around the tops of my thighs, thrumming my fingers against my already sensitive flesh.

"You want to fuck in the car on the way to meet my parents?" His voice is incredulous, but his eyes are on fire, and his breathing is shallow.

"Yes, please."

He takes the next exit off the freeway and parks behind a strip mall. It's heavily lined with dense trees, and there is no traffic behind the long building. He parks at the far end and shuts the car off and pulls me over the console and into his lap. One hand dives into my hair and the other under my hemline and cups my ass.

"You are so fucking sexy. I want you all the time."

"I want you, too."

I'm panting and needy, and I want him in me now.

"Straddle me, baby." Luke shifts the seat back with the automatic button, and I lean back against the steering wheel as he unzips his pants, freeing his erection. He cups my ass in both hands, pulls my thong panties to the side and lowers me onto him.

"Fuck, yes, Luke."

"Argh!"

I move up and down violently in the small confines of the car. His hands stay on my ass, guiding me, our eyes locked and mouths open, gasping for air.

"Fuck, I'm gonna come."

"Yes, baby, come for me."

I grind against him once, twice and then explode, milking his cock with my muscles, and I feel him come apart beneath me, emptying into me.

I lean forward, resting my forehead against his as our breathing calms.

"Holy shit, Nat, that was just a little unexpected."

I pull up off of him and climb back over to my seat, straightening my dress.

"It turns me on to watch you drive."

"Well, hell, let's go on lots of road trips, baby."

I laugh and realize that it also helped to calm some of my nerves.

Luke zips himself up, rights his seat and starts the car.

WE ARRIVE AT his parents' home a few moments later, just a few minutes late. I check my hair and makeup in the mirror, noting my bright eyes and rosy cheeks, compliments of a very satisfying bout of car sex.

"Nervous?" he asks me.

"Yes," I admit and offer him a smile.

He leans over the console and takes my chin between his thumb and forefinger and gives me a gentle kiss. "They're going to love you. You have nothing to be nervous about."

"I hope you're right."

"Come on."

He hops out of the car and comes around to open my door for me before leading me up to the entrance of the large, beautiful home.

The house is a white colonial-style home with manicured lawns and beautiful, colorful flower beds.

"Does your mom garden?" I ask.

"Yes, she's passionate about flowers," he responds, and I can't help but smirk. "What?"

"Like her son. My living room could rival her rose garden right now."

He laughs as we approach the door and kisses my hand. "Are you complaining?"

"Not in the least."

The red door opens, and a very small, petite blond woman greets us with a huge smile.

"Oh, darling, you're here!" Luke leans down so she can kiss his cheek and gives her a warm hug.

"Hi, Mom. I'd like you to meet Natalie Conner."

"Natalie, it is such a pleasure. Welcome to our home." She shakes my hand warmly, and I instantly like her.

"Thank you for having me, Mrs. Williams."

"Please, call me Lucy. Come in, you two."

We follow her through the vast foyer, toward the back of the house, which I assume is where the kitchen is. I briefly glimpse a formal living area with white furniture and a large formal dining room. Luke is still holding my hand and kisses my knuckles. I gaze up at him, and he smiles warmly down at me, clearly happy to have me here.

Damn, he's pretty.

"Luke and Natalie are here!" Lucy announces as we enter the eat-in kitchen. The kitchen is homey and large, in brown and bronze tones. The countertops are all dark brown granite, the appliances are stainless steel, and the oven is enormous. Any chef would covet this kitchen. There is a casual dining area, opening up to a family room with a large television and plush, inviting furniture in more shades of brown, copper and bronze.

It's incredible and comfortable.

"Welcome, Natalie." A very tall blond man is busy working in the kitchen. He wipes his hands on a towel and comes around the island toward me. "We're so happy to meet you."

"Nat, this is my dad, Neil."

"I'm delighted to meet you, sir." He shakes my hand firmly, and his kind blue eyes smile at me. Luke is a dead-ringer for his father.

Luke's younger brother, Mark, who also looks like his father and older brother, is helping Neil in the kitchen. "'Sup, Natalie?"

"You must be Mark." I smile at him, and he nods.

"Yep, I'm the best-looking one here, aside from you." He gives me a Cheshire cat smile, and I can't help but laugh. The Williams men are all handsome as sin and charming to boot!

"And this," Luke interrupts, glaring at his little brother, "is my sister, Samantha."

Samantha is sitting on one of the plush couches with an iPad in her lap and a wine glass in her hand. She is simply beautiful and petite like her mother, blond and blue-eyed, with delicate features. But her eyes are shrewd, and she is not smiling or welcoming me into the fold.

"Natalie." She nods at me once, and then goes back to her engrossing piece of technology.

I look up at Luke, but he's staring at Samantha. I can feel the tension in him, and remembering their phone call last night, I squeeze his hand so he looks down at me. Clearly, Samantha is going to be the hardest one to get to know in his family.

I shrug and smile at him, and he smiles back at me, some of the tension leaving his shoulders.

"Natalie, come sit with me at the table so we can chat while the boys cook. Luke, grab an apron, son. I think your dad needs help with the steaks."

"I do not need any help." Neil looks affronted, but I can tell this is a running joke in the family. "I can cook a steak just fine."

Lucy rolls her eyes at him and leads me to the dining table. "Would you like a glass of wine, dear?"

"Yes, please."

We settle at the table with our drinks, and I take a large sip, mentally preparing myself for the interrogation that is about to come.

"So tell me, what do you do, Natalie?"

"I'm a photographer." I glance over at Luke in the kitchen with his father, and my mouth goes just a little dry at the sight of three very handsome, virile men bustling around the kitchen. What is it about a man who can cook?

"Oh, how interesting. What kind of photography do you do?" Lucy leans her elbows on the table and takes a sip of her wine. She's genuinely interested in me, and it makes me relax.

"I mostly do nature photography. I live on Alki Beach, not far from Luke, so I have a lot of opportunities to take photos of the water, the boats and such. And I enjoy taking day trips around the area to take photos of flowers and just pretty things in general." I take another sip of my wine, and Luke catches my eye with a naughty grin. He smirks and goes back to chopping something.

"I'd love to see some of your work. Do you have a website?"

"No, I sell my work in shops around Alki and in downtown Seattle near Pike Place Market."

"I will have to look for it." Lucy smiles at me, and I can't help but lean forward so only she can hear me.

"I have to thank you for something," I whisper.

Her eyes widen in interest, and her grin widens. "What, dear?"

"Thank you for teaching your son how to cook. He's amazing in the kitchen."

She laughs, a full-on belly laugh, and clasps my hand in hers. "Oh, darling, you are welcome."

I glance in the kitchen, and Luke is staring at us open-mouthed. He frowns, and I smile to myself.

"What are you two whispering about?"

"Nothing," Lucy responds innocently. "How is my steak coming along?"

WE'RE ALL SEATED at the table off the kitchen. Neil is at one end, and Lucy is at the other. I'm seated to Neil's right with Luke next to me, and Samantha and Mark are across from us.

The guys prepared rib-eye steaks, roasted baby red potatoes and roasted asparagus with garlic and bacon. Luke refills my wine glass as serving plates are passed around the table.

"So, Natalie"—Neil hands me a basket full of rolls—"are you from around here?"

"Yes, I grew up in Bellevue."

"Oh? That's not far from here. Would I know your parents?"

Luke's fork stops midway between his plate and his mouth at his father's question.

"Dad . . ."

"No, it's okay," I murmur softly and smile at Luke's father.

"My parents passed away a few years ago, but you may have known them. Jack and Leslie Conner."

Neil's eyebrows shoot up. "The lawyer Jack Conner?"

"Yes, sir." I take a bite of steak.

"He did work for us at Microsoft on occasion."

I look up and notice Samantha's brief scowl before she smoothes her face into a perfectly neutral expression and drinks about half the glass of wine in front of her in one gulp. She fills her glass again and drinks some more.

"I'm so sorry to hear about your parents, Natalie," Lucy says softly. "I'd heard of their passing on the news when it happened."

"Thank you." I desperately want to change the subject, but Mark comes to my rescue.

"How did you guys meet?"

I smile smugly at Luke and answer him myself. "Luke tried to mug me one morning."

All eyes go to Luke, and I can't help but laugh. Luke's cheeks flush as he looks over at me.

"You should know my brother doesn't need to mug anyone." Samantha's voice is cold and mocking, and she clearly doesn't find me funny. Mark elbows her.

"She's kidding, Sam." Luke grasps my hand under the table, and I resume eating with my left hand, content to keep my right one snuggled in his.

"I was taking photos down at the beach one morning, and he mistakenly thought I was taking photos of him, so he approached me. Quite angrily, really."

Lucy gives her son a knowing look and glances back at me. "How did you react, Natalie?"

"I was angry. I thought I was being mugged for my camera."

"You thought Luke Williams was trying to mug you?" Samantha's voice is incredulous.

"I didn't know who he was." I shrug and take a sip of wine.

"Right." She snorts.

"Samantha . . ." Luke's warning is unheeded by his now tipsy sister.

"Anyway," I continue, "we ended up running into each other later that same day when he was out buying a gift for your birthday."

"Which I'm now reconsidering based on your behavior," Luke adds.

"So you mean to tell me that you don't know what my brother does for a living?" Her face is openly hostile now.

"Samantha, what in the world is wrong with you?" Lucy's face is flushed, and she's clearly embarrassed by her daughter's performance.

"Of course, now I know what Luke does for a living, Samantha," I respond before Samantha can. "But I didn't recognize him at first, no."

"So you're not just fucking my brother because he's a rich movie star?"

Holy fuck.

# fourteen

"Samantha!"

"What the hell!"

"Oh my God!"

The Williams family all start yelling at Luke's sister in unison, but she remains firm, her eyes blazing at me. Amazingly, I take a deep breath and find a Zen-like calm that is very *un-me*.

I grip Luke's thigh when he starts to come out of his chair in fury.

"Samantha, what the hell is wrong with you?"

"Luke, stop."

"No, Nat, I will not have you spoken to like that, least of all by my own family!"

"Hey." I grip his thigh again, and I feel all eyes on me as I look up him.

I turn my gaze back to his sister, and I know my eyes betray my outer calm. I'm just so pissed.

"First of all, and I mean no disrespect to your family, Luke, how dare you say such a thing about your brother?"

Samantha gasps, and I continue, "Not only are you intimating that I'm a whore, but you're also insinuating that your brother has the intelligence of a mud fence to be with a woman who would take advantage of him because of his celebrity or his money, and be perfectly okay with that.

"I don't need or want Luke's money. Not that it's any of your business, but I do just fine, thank you. I've never seen his movies, but I don't doubt that he's very talented. What I do know is that he's amazingly smart. He is honestly the kindest man I've ever met, and he is beautiful, inside and out. I will not tolerate anyone speaking about him like that, Ms. Williams."

I scoot my chair away from the table and stand.

"Natalie." Luke grabs for my hand, and I squeeze it reassuringly.

"Is there a restroom nearby where I can regroup?" I ask Lucy.

"Of course, dear, down the hall to the left."

I look down at Luke and then throw caution to the wind and lean down to kiss his lips. "I'll be back."

As I walk, more calmly than I feel, down the hall, I hear the table erupt in anger at Luke's sister. Good. She deserves everything she's about to get.

I find the bathroom and lock myself inside. Leaning my hands on the vanity, I hang my head, trying to keep the shaking at bay. I know it's from the adrenaline, but I can't make it stop.

Maybe I should have kept my big mouth shut, but she just made me so mad! I don't know what her problem is with me, but she's been openly hostile all night. And the last comment just pushed me over the edge.

I'm sure his parents now hate me for verbally castigating their daughter at the dinner table. Although, they seemed to be more shocked than anything when it was happening, and Mark had a wide grin on his face as I walked away from the table.

Oh, how am I going to go back out there and face them?

I take five deep breaths. The shaking starts to subside, and I don't know how long I've been locked in the bathroom. I open the door and start the journey back to the table.

Before I can turn the corner, I hear Lucy's soft voice. "Honey, she obviously loves you."

I stop in my tracks and listen.

"Mom . . ." Luke starts to speak, but Lucy interrupts him.

"I know, it's none of our business, but it's pretty clear how she feels about you, honey. Why else would she defend you like that?"

"She's a keeper." This is Mark's voice, I think.

I decide to stop eavesdropping and walk into the room, noticing that Samantha is no longer at the table.

Luke stands and quickly walks to me, wrapping me in his strong arms. "Are you okay?"

"I'm fine." I pull back and smile up at him, then turn to his family. "I'm so sorry for the way I spoke to your daughter . . ."

Neil holds up a hand to stop my speech. "No, Natalie, we are sorry for her behavior. Please, come finish your meal. Samantha won't be rejoining us."

I look up into Luke's eyes, and he looks nervous and unsure, his eyes searching mine.

"Okay."

"You're sure you're okay?" he murmurs.

"Yes, let's finish dinner." We sit back in our places and continue eating.

"This is really delicious." I smile at Neil, and he grins back at me.

"I'm glad you like it."

"I love a man who can cook." I grin at Lucy, who beams back at me, and settle in to enjoy the rest of our evening.

LUKE IS QUIET on the way back to his place after dinner. He's biting his thumbnail, which tells me that he's thinking. He's not touched me since we left, and I can't help but start to feel a little apprehensive.

"Are you okay?" I ask, breaking the silence.

He glances over at me and frowns. "Of course."

"Okay. Good." I clasp my hands in my lap and stare at the lights from the city in the distance out my window. As we pull up to his house, the silence is deafening. He opens my door for me and escorts me up his front steps to usher me inside. He turns on a light as I walk to the kitchen and lay my purse on the breakfast bar.

I turn to look at him and am surprised to find that he's not in the room. Where did he go?

I frown as unease starts to unfurl through my stomach. Oh my

God, I really screwed up. He must be mad at me for the way I spoke to his sister at dinner. Where is he?

Maybe he wants me to leave, and he's giving me space to pack my things.

I climb the stairs and head for his bedroom, willing myself not to cry until I get home. I'll just pack my things and get the hell out of here. Then I can fall apart.

Just before I cross the threshold into his bedroom, my phone pings in my pocket. I pull it out, and I have a text.

From Luke.

*Natalie, would you please join me in my bathroom?*

Huh?

I walk through the bedroom and to the entrance to the bathroom and stop in my tracks.

He has drawn a bath in that huge egg-shaped tub of his, and the scent of lavender is hanging in the air. There are candles lit on the vanity and the side of the tub. Luke is standing next to the tub wearing only his jeans, the top button undone.

Finally, I find my voice, but all I can say is, "Hi."

"Hi."

"I thought you were mad at me."

"Why?" He walks over to me and grips my chin in his thumb and forefinger, tilting my head back so I can look him in the eye.

"Because you've been so quiet since we left your parents' house."

"I've just been thinking." His fingers caress my cheek, and he tenderly kisses my forehead.

"About?" I whisper.

"Let's get in the bath." Oh! I want him to keep talking.

"I'm overdressed for a bath."

"So you are, baby." He peels my jacket off my shoulders and down my arms and sets it on a nearby chair. He pulls my dress over my head and gently folds it and places it over the jacket.

"Step out of your shoes."

I comply, unable to take my eyes from his. He wraps his arms around me and leans down to kiss my shoulder, while unclasping my bra and pulling it down my arms. As he steps back, I hook my thong in my thumbs and push it off my hips, letting it drop to the floor. I stand before him and flush with pleasure at the way his eyes go glassy with desire as he runs them up and down my nakedness.

"You're overdressed, too," I whisper, and my stomach clenches as I see his pupils dilate.

"So I am." He unzips the jeans and pulls them and his boxers off in one smooth motion, leaving him gloriously naked before me.

"Come." He holds his hand out to me so he can help me step into the water. I sink down and sigh as the hot water envelops me.

"Aren't you going to join me?"

"Yes." He steps in and sits facing me, his legs on either side of mine, and leans against the opposite side.

"This is nice." It's the truth. The water is soothing after the difficult encounter with his sister, and he's naked, which makes everything nice.

"It is."

"You're very monosyllabic tonight, you know."

He grins at me almost shyly. "I'm sorry. I have a lot going through my head."

"Spill it."

He shakes his head.

"Oh, no, you don't. What's going on in that handsome head of yours, Williams?"

"I'm really sorry about the way my sister treated you tonight."

Oh.

"I'm just sorry for the way I reacted, Luke. I'm sorry that I made you uncomfortable and for speaking that way to your family."

"No, don't apologize. She was way out of line. I had a bad feeling that she'd act like that, that's why I called her last night."

"Luke." I pick up one of his feet and start to rub. His eyes widen and then he closes them and leans his head against the tub with a groan. "I don't have siblings, but I can understand wanting to protect someone I love. What I don't understand is, why the blatant hostility? I don't get it."

"Well, something you said tonight hit a little too close to home," he murmurs, then opens his eyes and sighs, looking everywhere but at me.

"What?"

"The part about me being stupid enough to be with someone I know is using me because I'm rich and famous."

I gasp and drop his foot. Oh my God, this is mortifying. "I don't understand."

He takes my right foot in his hands and rubs his thumb over my tattoo, frowning.

"My last relationship was with a woman who was with me for all those reasons."

"Oh." I do not want to hear this.

"Yeah."

"How long ago?"

"I broke it off over a year ago."

"I thought you said that you've never introduced anyone to your family." I lean my head back on the tub. I just can't look at him when I'm feeling jealous and nervous and unsure.

"I haven't. They never met her. They knew of her, more so after the fact."

I'm staring at the ceiling, listening to him, trying to find that Zen-like calm I found at his parents' dining room table.

"Why?" My voice is calmer than I feel.

"Because she went to the tabloids and said that she was pregnant when I decided to break our engagement."

"What the fuck?" My head snaps up, and I hold his gaze. "You're a father?"

"No!" He tightly closes his eyes and shakes his head in frustration. "She sold the lie to the tabloids to get back at me for breaking up with her."

"You were going to marry her?" I feel like I've been kicked in the stomach.

"Yes." He's watching me warily, no doubt gauging my reaction to all of this.

"And you never introduced her to your family?"

"She never had much interest in meeting them. Whenever I'd arrange it, something would come up." He shrugs.

"And you didn't find that odd?"

"I do now."

"Why did you break it off?"

"Because she wasn't right for me."

"That's a lame answer."

"It's the truth." He shrugs and then sighs. "I guess I finally realized that had I not been famous or wealthy, she wouldn't have given me the time of day. She didn't like it that I'd stopped acting and hoped that the producing thing was just a phase and I'd miss being the center of attention. She wanted to be a celebrity wife, and that wasn't something I was interested in."

"Do you still talk to her?"

"No."

I lean my head back again and look at my now wrinkled fingers. The water is starting to cool. Time flies when you're trying to hold a calm conversation about your lover's ex-fiancée.

"I guess that explains a lot."

"Nat . . ."

"Hold on." I hold my hand up to stop him. "Give me a minute."

"Okay." He frowns and continues to rub my foot.

Why do I feel so betrayed all over again? And then it hits me.

"I must have looked pretty stupid to your family when I didn't know about your ex-fiancée."

He abruptly leans forward and pulls me onto his lap, ignoring the water sloshing onto the floor, and wraps his arms around me.

"You were magnificent tonight. I didn't know if I should be proud or emasculated at the way you jumped to my defense like that."

"You should have warned me."

"I know."

I run my fingers through his hair and sigh. "We still have so much to learn about each other."

"We'll get there, baby."

"It made me crazy when your sister was talking about you like that."

He shakes his head and laughs ruefully. "Ironically, she was talking about you, baby."

"I know, but in doing so she made it about you, and I couldn't stand it."

"No one has ever jumped to my defense like that. You were so calm and sure of yourself, and so pissed off. Your green eyes were on fire, and you just looked so beautiful. I wanted to fuck you right there at the table."

"Luke Williams!" I pull back and stare at him, shocked.

"It's true. You turned me on, big time."

"I don't think that would have been appropriate with your parents sitting at that same table."

"I don't think I would have cared if the pope and Elvis were sitting at that table."

I laugh and snuggle up against him again.

"Oh, baby, what am I going to do with you?"

"Anything you want."

"Come on." He stands me up out of the water, and then climbs to his feet behind me. I can't get over how strong he is. He moves me around like I'm nothing at all.

He slings a towel around his hips and grabs another soft, white, fluffy towel off the towel warmer and wraps it around me. He pulls me against him and kisses me deeply, passionately, before letting go so he can dry my body.

Oh my.

He runs the towel up and down me, soaking up the extra moisture. I can't resist leaning forward and kissing his sternum, and I hear his quick inhale.

When I'm dry, I take the towel from around his waist and return the favor, enjoying the intoxicating sight of his muscular physique.

"There, all dry," I whisper.

"Thank Christ." He pulls me to him, his hands in my hair, and kisses me deeply. I wrap my arms around him and drag my nails down his back.

"God, baby, you'll unman here in the bathroom."

"Good." I scrape his back again, and he growls against my neck. He abruptly spins me and plants my hands on the vanity facing the wide mirror over the sinks. I look up and am taken aback by the sexy sight that is Luke standing behind me, about six inches taller than I am, all golden hair and bronze body, leaning down to kiss my bare shoulders. He cups the back of my neck in his hand and smoothes it down my spine, hovering for a moment over my tattoo, watching his own hand's progression, and his breathing increases. He pulls my hips back so I'm bent over, and I just can't stop watching his beautiful, expressive face as he touches me.

Finally, he runs a single finger down my bottom and slips it inside me.

"Oh, Luke."

"Baby, you're so ready." I feel him position the head of his cock on my lips and slowly, oh so slowly, push inside me. His eyes meet mine in the mirror as he pushes farther until he's buried completely in my folds.

"Spank me." Fuck! Did I just say that?

"What?" He stops, his hands on my hips, and he's gaping at me in the mirror.

"Spank me."

"You like it rough, baby?" He grins quizzically at me.

"Not until I met you." His face changes from curiosity to pure possession in a matter of seconds, and I can't help but clench around him.

"Fuck, Natalie." He raises his right hand and brings it down on my buttock.

"Yes!" I circle my hips, and he starts moving in and out of me, holding my hips. I'm backing up against him, and we find our rhythm. Finally, he raises his hand again and slaps my ass, and it's so fucking hot!

"Again?" he asks breathlessly.

"Yes."

He obliges, and I feel the tension beginning low in my belly. My legs clench, and I tighten around him, my orgasm ripping through me.

"Oh, baby, yes."

I watch in fascination as Luke tightly closes his eyes and grips my hips harder, his own orgasm pushing through him and explodes inside me.

He runs that beautiful hand down my back again, his breathing still choppy, and smiles at me in the mirror. "I had no idea you like it rough."

"It's a newly acquired taste."

He slips out of me and leans down to kiss the tattoo on my upper thigh, below my buttock, and I gasp.

"I think this is the sexiest tattoo you have."

"You do?"

"Mmm hmm." He's tracing it with his finger, and chills run up my back.

"Why?"

"Well, it looks fucking sexy."

"I'm glad you like it." I grin down at him, still through the mirror.

"I love them all," he says earnestly, and I can't help but fall just a little in love with his honest face.

"I want you happy, Nat."

"Oh." I turn at his words, and he stands up, wrapping his arms around my shoulders and pulling me into a big hug.

"I don't know what to do with these feelings I'm having for you," I whisper against his chest.

"We're just going to take this one day at a time, baby." He pulls back and gives me his tender kiss.

"Okay, I can do that."

"Good, let's get some sleep." He picks me up in his arms and heads for the bed.

"You know, I can walk." I laugh and press my face in his neck.

"No need, I have you."

"I love how strong you are."

"Do you now?"

"Yes. Speaking of, I have to get up early tomorrow for yoga, and then I have a session at eleven."

"Okay. Want me to pick you up for lunch?" He pulls the duvet back and lays me down on the bed, climbing in behind me, and pulls me into his arms.

"Aren't you sick of me?"

"Are you sick of me?" He pulls me around so he can see my face.

"Well, no."

"I want to see you for lunch tomorrow. Please."

"Okay," I mumble and curl up in his arms to sleep.

# fifteen

There are some days that the work just flows. This is, thankfully, one of those days.

It was tough leaving Luke's bed this morning, but I'm glad I went to yoga to get my blood pumping. I had a relaxed breakfast with Jules, where I filled her in on the weekend events, and I couldn't even be very mad when my eleven o'clock session was late.

Brad is a hot twenty-one-year-old with a lot of model potential. He's got the face and the body, and he's hired me to help him beef up his portfolio. I usually work with women or couples, but Brad is professional and sincerely wants to break into show biz, and I just couldn't turn him away.

Not to mention he's tall, dark and extremely handsome. Not a bad way to spend a few hours out of the day.

We've been having a lot of fun all morning. Brad is easily six-foot-three and completely toned. Not unlike Luke, but I push him to the side of my brain and focus on the job. Where Luke is bronzed and golden, Brad is tanned and dark, with dark hair and eyes and the hint of a five o'clock shadow on his sculpted jaw.

He's stripped down to an impossibly small pair of nude boxer briefs that barely cover the essentials, and he's wrapped from the waist down in a white satin sheet.

"You're good at this, Natalie. It doesn't even feel like work."

"Thank you." I raise the camera to my eye and start clicking. "These sessions should be fun."

"Are you single?" he asks as he gives the camera a sexy half smile.

"Uh, no." I frown at him. "No flirting, Brad."

"Sorry, couldn't resist. I'm in bed, mostly naked, and a beautiful woman is taking my photo."

I laugh and change memory cards. Man, it's hot in here! I take my blue hoodie off, leaving a fitted black tank over my sports bra. I have cropped yoga pants on, but go in the bathroom and change into yoga shorts. I refasten my hair up into a bun and kick off my shoes.

"Okay, Brad, back in bed."

"How can I resist that?" He is such a flirt! He climbs back on the bed and pulls the sheet low over his hips.

"Okay, on your back, one arm over your head. Good, don't move." I climb on the bed and straddle his hips with my feet, standing directly over him.

"This is a great shot." I'm snapping away, so pleased with the images I'm capturing.

"Should I look serious for some?"

"Sure, don't give me that sexy smile. Perfect!" Snap, snap, snap. I walk up his body, focusing down on his face. I almost lose my balance, but he reaches up and clasps his hands around the backs of my calves.

"Whew! Thanks." I giggle and continue to snap head shots while he throws one hand back up over his head, keeping one hand braced on my leg to keep me steady.

"What the fuck is going on?!"

Brad and I both jump, startled at the angry shout coming from my front door.

"Luke! You scared the hell out of me!"

Brad immediately releases my leg, accurately assessing that he may have his moneymaker punched any moment.

"What the fuck, Natalie!"

"Stop yelling at me!" I jump off the bed and stow my camera. "Brad, you can go ahead and get dressed. We're finished here anyway."

Brad rises off the bed, letting the sheet fall, and I avert my eyes. He saunters into the bathroom to get dressed.

"What the hell is your problem?" I hiss at Luke.

"What do you think? You were on a bed with a naked man, and his hands were on you!"

I take a deep breath. "He wasn't naked, Luke. I am not naked."

"Close enough," he mutters.

"Hey, this is why I told you not to freak out on me when I showed you this studio."

"You didn't tell me that you work with young naked men." He's pissed all over again.

"I don't, usually. He's a friend of a friend who needs images for his portfolio. Don't be a jealous ass."

"You led me to believe that you work with women or couples, Natalie."

"Luke, I just told you, this is an exception."

"I don't like it."

"It doesn't matter if you like it."

Luke glares at me like I've grown a second head and runs both hands through his hair.

Brad saunters out of the bathroom, fully dressed in jeans, T-shirt and sneakers. "Thanks again, Natalie. I had a great time."

I smile warmly at him. "Me, too, and you're welcome. I should have them edited for you this week."

"Great. See ya." He leaves, shutting the door behind him.

I turn back to Luke to find his glacial blue eyes narrowed on me. He's royally pissed.

"What, exactly, are you mad about?" I ask as I turn back to the bed and begin stripping the sheets.

"Natalie, I just walked into this studio to find my girlfriend standing in what would only be appropriate as nightwear over a naked guy on a bed, and he's got his hands on her bare leg. What do you think I'm mad about?" His voice has risen several decibels, but I'm stuck like stupid on one word.

"Girlfriend?"

He stops his rant and stares at me. "Yes, girlfriend. I thought after this past weekend that that's where we are."

Oh.

Wow.

"Am I wrong?" His voice is worryingly calm.

"Well, no, I guess I just hadn't thought about it." I finish with the bed and turn to face him again. "Luke, this is my job."

"I don't like it."

"It isn't your place to tell me that I can't do this."

"I didn't say that."

"That's what you're implying. I've done this for years. No one has ever gotten out of hand. Remember, I told you I don't have sex in here, and I don't have sex with clients. Jesus, do you have so little faith in me?"

"No, it's just . . ." He runs his hands through his hair again and paces back and forth. "I wasn't expecting to feel the way I felt when I saw his hand on you."

"How did you feel?" I tilt my head at him, my curiosity piqued.

"Like I wanted to kill him," he growls.

"Oh."

"Nat, think of how you would feel if I had to do a love scene in a movie. It would be work to me, but I'd still have to hold another woman, kiss her . . ."

"Stop right there." I do not want to hear this.

"It's the same thing for me."

Geez.

I take a deep breath and sit on the side of the bed, suddenly weary. "I'm sorry, it didn't occur to me. Honey, I haven't had to explain my actions to another human being in years."

"I know."

"You were jealous."

"Jealous is too tame a word for what I was feeling."

Part of me wants to squeal and do a little happy dance, but I hold it in and gaze at him impassively. "You don't have any reason to be jealous. You're all I see, Luke, even when I'm not with you."

He closes his eyes tightly, as though some great weight has been lifted, and I take him all in. He's wearing another button-down shirt today, in black this time, and black jeans. He looks young and impossibly beautiful.

And I'm his girlfriend!

I stand and move to him, wrapping my arms around his waist. He puts his arms around me, linking his fingers at the small of my back, and we just gaze at each other for a minute.

"Please don't be mad at me," I whisper.

"I'm not."

"You were."

"Yeah, I was." He kisses my forehead. "Don't you have any real clothes in here?"

"Yeah, it got hot in here, so I took them off."

He narrows his eyes again, and they go cold. Shit.

"Don't freak out on me. It happens no matter who I'm photographing. I don't have AC in here."

"Why not?"

"Well, honestly, because a sweaty body is sexy on film."

"Oh." He furrows his brow.

"Hey, stop it. You have nothing to be jealous over, honey." I run my hands down his face, loving the roughness of his stubble against my palms.

"I love it when you call me that." He leans into my touch and closes his eyes.

"You do?"

"Yeah, you usually just call me by my name."

"You're a terms-of-endearment kind of guy, huh?" I stand on my toes and kiss his lips gently, and his eyes warm up.

"Obviously, *baby*."

"I love it when you call me baby."

Now his eyes light up like it's Christmas. "Why?"

"No one ever has before," I whisper.

He sighs and hugs me close. "I forget how inexperienced you are when it comes to relationships."

"Yeah, so cut me some slack. There has to be a learning curve." I pinch his tight butt, and he laughs.

"Okay, okay. Just do me a favor." His face is serious again.

"What?"

"No more single men. Please."

I frown and want to argue with him.

"Please, Natalie. For me."

"What if we have a chaperone?"

"Talk with me before you book another single man, and we'll discuss it. I don't like feeling like this. I'm asking you to respect how I feel."

Well, when he puts it like that.

"Okay, I'll talk with you first." It's a concession, but I can't help but think about what he said about love scenes, and I know I'd go out of my mind with jealousy if I were in that position.

"Did you do any love scenes in your movies?" I ask and search his face.

"Why do you think there was a butt shot?" He grins down at me.

"I don't ever want to see those movies, Luke."

"Fine by me, baby."

"So, I'm your girlfriend, huh?"

"Absolutely." He kisses me deeply, and I grip on to his shoulders, pulling him down to me.

When he pulls back, I can't resist running my fingers through his hair. "Okay, let's go get lunch. Fighting with you makes me hungry."

"You're putting on some decent clothes first."

I LEAVE LUKE with Jules in the kitchen and run upstairs to get dressed. I smirk to myself, remembering the look of apprehension on Luke's face when confronted with Jules, but she was cool as could be, and I'm relieved that her adolescent behavior where he's concerned has subsided.

I throw on a pair of blue jeans that hug my ass, a green top and matching green heels. It may just be lunch, but I never get to wear my heels, and Luke's tall enough that I could wear them all the time.

So I think I just might. He seems to like them.

I brush out my brown hair, leaving it loose so it frames my face, and apply some eyeliner and mascara.

I'm good to go.

I find Luke and Jules still in the kitchen, talking about all things cooking.

"I bake my bacon," Luke is saying. He's standing with his back to me so he doesn't see me enter the room. "That way there's less mess on the stove top."

"I don't care how it's cooked." I wrap my arms around his middle and press my nose between his shoulder blades, breathing him in. He smells of fabric softener and body wash, and his shirt is soft against my face. "As long as it ends up in my mouth," I mumble against him, and I hear him chuckle.

He turns to look at me and grins wide. "You are gorgeous in green. It matches your eyes." He runs his fingers down my face, and I sigh.

"Thank you. Is this better than what I had on earlier?"

"Much. Do you have any more sessions today?"

"I have one tonight around eight."

He frowns. "Why so late?"

"A lot of people work during the day, so I have to schedule evening sessions sometimes. It doesn't happen often because I prefer using the natural daylight rather than my lighting equipment, but sometimes it's necessary."

"Who is it?" He eyes me speculatively, and I sigh.

"Just a girl who wants some pretty photos for her husband for their anniversary."

"Oh, okay."

I run my hand through his hair. "Don't worry, babe. There are no single men on my books right now."

"Can you let me know when there *are*?" Jules pipes in quickly. "All this mushy stuff is reminding me how long it's been since I got laid. Go to lunch. Or get a room."

We say our goodbyes, and he holds the door of the Mercedes SUV open for me so I can climb in. When he's behind the wheel, he leans over the console and kisses me lightly.

"Where are we going?" I ask as he starts the car.

"How does seafood sound?"

"We live in Seattle. I think it's a prerequisite to love seafood to live here."

"Seafood it is, then." He grips my hand in his and smiles over at me. "You look beautiful."

"Thank you." I feel my face flush, and I look down at our joined hands. "You always look beautiful."

He laughs and shakes his head. "It's just genetics."

"What did you do this morning?" I ask, changing the subject.

"I went to the gym and worked out with my trainer."

"You have a trainer?" Of course he does.

"Yeah, he kicks my ass." He grins at me, and I can't help but grin back. "How was yoga?"

"It was great. I love it. Have you ever tried it?"

"Um, no."

"Not manly enough for you?" I roll my eyes.

"It's not that. I just like a rigorous workout."

"Go with me Wednesday morning."

He frowns and eyes me speculatively. "I'll make you a deal."

Uh oh, where is this going?

"What kind of deal?"

"I'll go with you to yoga on Wednesday if you go to the gym with me tomorrow."

I bite my lip and look out my window. I'm afraid of looking like a fool. I don't have the tight, little body that most of the other women have in gyms. Yoga keeps me toned and flexible.

"You don't have to go with me," I whisper.

"Natalie, what did I say?"

"Nothing." I can't look him in the eye. I hate feeling self-conscious, and I'm just now to the point of not feeling that way naked in front of Luke.

"Baby, what's wrong?" He pulls into the parking lot of the

restaurant and cuts the engine, turning toward me in his seat.

"Nothing, I . . ."

"Look at me." His voice is stern, and when my eyes meet his, they're ice blue. "Talk to me."

"No, you get mad at me when I talk about my body. Just leave it alone. We'll work out separately. It's okay."

"Why are you so hard on yourself?" He's bewildered.

"I'm not. Well, not until now," I whisper.

"Stop this. You have nothing to be ashamed of, baby."

"I'm not ashamed. I know you find me attractive, and I love that."

"Then what's the problem?"

"I don't want to make an ass of myself."

"But you want me to go to yoga and try to twist into a pretzel and make an ass of myself?"

Oh. Good point.

I giggle and put my fingers over my mouth.

"Are you laughing at me?" He's smiling again, and the tension in my stomach relaxes.

"I wouldn't dare."

"So, are you going with me to the gym or not?"

"I so wish you'd let me take your picture."

His eyes widen, and he goes very still, and I mentally kick myself. "Why?"

"Because I'd love to take your picture at yoga. This is going to be hilarious!"

He relaxes and laughs as he gets out of the car, coming around to open my door. "Come on, I want to watch you eat."

# sixteen

S alty's sits on a pier on Puget Sound. It offers great views and great
food. The hostess seats us near the windows looking out on the
water, and we are busy reading the menu. I glance up at Luke and
can't help but sigh just a little. He's just so disarmingly handsome. He's
biting that thumbnail as he peruses the menu.

"Can I have your hand, please?" I hold my hand out.

"You can hold my hand anytime, baby." He shoots me a sexy smile
but gives me the wrong hand.

"No, the one you're biting, please."

He extends his hand to me with a frown, and I lean over the table
and kiss the thumbnail. "You're going to make this bleed." I look up into
his sea-blue eyes and am pleased to see that his breathing has changed
and that my touch is turning him on.

"Don't start this here, please." His voice is low and sexy, and my
stomach clenches.

"I don't know what you mean." I widen my eyes innocently. "I'm
just making sure you'll have an appetite for your lunch."

"I'll tell you what I have an appetite for." He grins wolfishly, but
before I can respond, the waitress is at the tableside.

"What can I get you two today? Would you like to start with an appetizer?" She glances up at both of us with a smile, but she freezes when
she sees Luke, and all the blood drains from her face.

"Luke Williams! Oh wow! I'm such a big fan, Luke . . . er . . . sir.
I've seen all of the *Nightwalker* movies, like, forty times. Oh my God,
they are so good. I can't believe you're here! Can I get an autograph?

Can I get a picture?" The words all come out in a rush, and I can't help but sit back and drop my jaw.

Luke glances at me but seems to find his balance quickly and pastes on a dazzling drop-your-panties smile, just for Miss Gushy, but it doesn't reach his eyes, and I know that this is the smile he uses for fans.

It's fascinating.

"I'm sorry, I don't give photographs, but I'm happy to sign something for you."

"Oh great! Here." She shoves her notepad and pen at him.

"What's your name, sugar?" Oh, he is really laying it on thick.

"Hilary. Oh my gosh, wait until my friends find out I met you! They will be so jealous." She's practically jumping up and down, and Luke's smile never falters.

"Well, I'm glad you enjoyed the movies. Here you go." He passes the pad back to her, and she clutches it to her chest, her face all gooey and swoony, and I have to look down to keep from laughing and rolling my eyes at her.

After a few lengthy seconds of her just standing there, staring at him, I decide to rescue him.

"So, um, we'd like to order now, if that's okay with you, Hilary."

She shakes herself out of her trance and blushes but doesn't meet my eyes. "Oh, of course. What can I get you?" She stares expectantly at Luke, and he smirks.

"What would you like, baby?" And my man is back.

"I'll just have the salmon Caesar salad, please, with extra lemon on the side. What kind of white wines do you have?" I am still staring into Luke's eyes and am relieved to see that his eyes are dancing with humor.

"Oh, um . . ." She rattles off the white wine list, and I order a sweet Riesling to go with my salad.

"And what can I get you, Mr. Williams . . . er . . . sir?" Her face is on fire.

"I'll actually have the same as my girlfriend. Sounds delicious."

Girlfriend!

"Okay, let me know if I can get you anything else. Thanks again for the autograph!" And off she goes.

"Are you okay?" I ask when we're alone.

"Yeah, that wasn't so bad. How are you?"

"Amused. I didn't know whether to laugh at her or feel sorry for her."

"Hey, are you saying that I'm not a heartthrob? I'm hurt." He sits back and clutches his chest, right over his heart.

"Oh no, you definitely make my heart throb, along with a few other areas, Mr. Williams . . . er . . . sir."

"You have a sassy mouth, Natalie."

"I'm glad you noticed."

We settle in to enjoy our lunch, but other waitresses and kitchen staff keep stopping by the table to get autographs or gush about how much they loved his movies and ask him why he's not acting anymore. Thankfully, the restaurant isn't terribly busy, so there aren't many customers bothering us.

Finally, when I've lost count of how many employees have come to interrupt our lunch, I excuse myself.

"You okay?" Luke asks me.

"I'm fine. I'll be right back." I give him a bright, reassuring smile, and leave the table.

I find Hilary near the bar. "I need to speak with the manager, please."

"Oh, sure. I'll grab her." She disappears into what I assume is the kitchen and reappears with a tall redhead, about my age, who hasn't managed to make it to our table yet.

"Can I help you, ma'am?" Geez, when did I become a ma'am?

"I hope so. Luke Williams and I are having lunch here, and your staff has been interrupting us to ask him for autographs and to speak with him. I'd really appreciate it if you'd ask them to stop."

She frowns as she listens to my complaint. "I'm sorry, they shouldn't have approached you at all. That's against policy. Can I comp your lunch?"

"It's not about the money. It's about the lack of privacy. I'm sure he's not the first celebrity to come to your restaurant."

"Of course not. I'll take care of it. I apologize on behalf of the staff."

I walk back to our table and overhear Hilary apologize to her boss.

There's a busboy standing next to our table when I return, and I tap him on the shoulder. "Your boss would like to see you."

"Oh! Okay. Thanks for the autograph!" He grins and leaves.

"That won't be happening again," I inform Luke.

"What did you do?"

"I went to management. Other customers are one thing, but it's not appropriate for the staff to interrupt us every five minutes."

"Nat, this is just how it is sometimes."

"Well"—I shrug—"they've had enough of you. This is my lunch date with my boyfriend, and I'm done sharing him."

His eyes light up, and the smile he gives me is even brighter than the drop-your-panties one he gave the waitress, and I melt just a little inside.

"Your boyfriend is enjoying this lunch date with you."

"I'm glad." I smile shyly and take a sip of wine.

The rest of the meal is delicious, and we aren't bothered at all, unless it's to ask if we want more wine or dessert. Hilary places the leather check holder on the table and walks away.

Luke opens it and frowns, then smiles and passes it to me. Instead of a check, there is a note.

*We appreciate your patience and generosity toward our staff. Today's lunch is on the house, and please accept this $250 gift card to join us again, uninterrupted, soon.*

—*The Management*

"Oh my. I guess my chat with the manager worked."

"Looks like a date night is in our future." Luke grins and slips the card in his wallet.

"NATALIE, I HAD such a good time tonight. I know my husband will love these photos." Darla gives me a smile and a hug before leaving the studio.

"He's going to swallow his tongue when he sees these, I guarantee it."

"Maybe we can come in sometime before the holidays and do a couples session. It sounds like a lot of fun." Darla slings her black Coach handbag on her shoulder.

"I would love that! Just let me know when you'd like to set it up. I'll walk you out."

I wave goodbye to Darla and start cleaning up from our boudoir session. Darla was a lot of fun, very pretty and flirty, and she had some great ideas, too. I gather some lingerie that will need to go to the cleaners and push furniture back in place. I'm turning off the bright photography lights when my phone pings.

My heart leaps, and I can't help but hope it's Luke. He dropped me off at home after our lunch date and said he had some work to take care of at home, which was fine, because I needed to do some laundry and work myself.

But I miss him, and the thought of not seeing him until tomorrow morning when I go to the gym with him—which still fills me with dread—is a depressing thought.

*Are you finished with your session, baby?*

I do love it when he calls me baby.

*Just finished, going inside now. What are you doing?*

I lock up the studio and head into the house. Fall is in the air now, and after the sun sets, it's really chilly, so I hug my hoodie around me as I cross the backyard.

Jules left the kitchen light on for me, and I stop at the fridge to grab myself a bottle of water and a handful of grapes before heading up to my bedroom. As I climb the stairs, I hear Adele crooning and wonder briefly if it's coming from Jules' bedroom.

I walk into my own room and stop.

Holy shit.

The music is coming from my room, and there's Luke, sitting on my bed, barefoot, in black basketball shorts and a black T-shirt. He's frowning at his laptop and biting his thumbnail.

"So this is what you're doing."

He smiles and looks up at the sound of my voice. "I hope you don't mind. Jules let me in. I thought I'd just wait for you here."

I walk over to the bed and crawl up next to him, offering him my last grape. "I don't mind. I was just thinking about you."

"Yeah?"

"Yeah."

He closes his computer and sets it on the floor, and when he sits back up, I climb on his lap.

"I was afraid you'd think I was being presumptuous."

I hear the smile in his voice as he kisses my head, and I settle in and nuzzle his chest. It's just so good to see him, to touch him. "You are being presumptuous, but I don't mind."

"I missed you today."

I pull back and run my fingers down his face. "You saw me at lunch."

"So I did. But that was hours ago. I can't seem to get enough of you, baby."

"Are you staying the night?" I ask breathlessly.

"If you'll let me, yes."

"Good."

I reach up and kiss the side of his mouth, his chin, his nose, while running my fingers through his soft hair. His beautiful eyes are watching mine, and he's patiently letting me touch and kiss him. His hands are softly rubbing up and down my back, and desire is lazily unfurling through me.

I grip the hem of his shirt in my hands and lean back so I can pull it up over his head.

"I love your body," I murmur as I run my hands over his shoulders, his chest and down his arms, and his hands tighten on my ass.

"Do you?"

"Hmm . . ." I kiss his neck and nibble up to his ear. "You're fucking hot."

"Jesus, baby, I want you."

I feel powerful and sexy, knowing that I'm making him crazy with my touch, and I just want us both naked. Now. "I'm yours, Luke."

His eyes smolder. "Damn right, you're mine."

He makes quick work of my hoodie, top and bra, and then pushes me back onto the bed so he can strip me out of my pants and underwear. His mouth is all over me now, on my breasts, my neck, my side. My hands are in his hair as he shimmies out of his shorts and boxers, discarding them on the floor.

"Oh, Luke." My blood is thrumming now, and I have to have him inside me.

"Yes, baby, what do you need?"

"You, in me. Now."

He smiles against my stomach and laves my piercing with his tongue. "Not yet."

I groan and move my hips under him.

"Not yet, baby." He stills my hips with his hands and climbs up my torso, leaning on his elbow at my side. He kisses me deeply, slowly, his tongue doing incredibly delicious things to my mouth. His strong hand is stroking up and down my side, and I grasp his face in my hands and return his kiss with equal ardor.

I gasp as his fingers find my nipple and pull relentlessly, sending little zings of pleasure down to my groin. I can't help but resume moving my hips, and I run my hand down his side and around to cup his ass, pulling him to me.

"Fuck, Nat, you're so beautiful." His wicked mouth is making its way down my throat. He runs his hand down my back, over my ass, and hitches my leg up around his hip. He pushes forward and slowly, barely, slips just the tip of his cock inside me.

"Oh God, yes."

"Is this what you want?"

"Yes!" I wrap my arms around him, pulling him to me. Suddenly, he rolls on top of me, and I hitch the other leg around him, and he thrusts into me, all the way. I roll my hips, and he groans, his lips on mine, his elbows at the sides of my head and hands buried in my hair.

I grip his ass in my hands, but he stops abruptly and gazes down at me. His eyes are molten blue, the look on his face absolutely serious and almost reverent.

"What's wrong?" I ask breathlessly.

He shakes his head and closes his eyes as if he's in pain, and a sliver of panic pierces my heart.

"What is it?" I smooth my hand down his cheek.

"I just . . ." He opens his eyes again, pinning me in his intense stare and starts to move his hips once again, pistoning in and out of me like there's more than just desire pushing him.

"You just feel so good, baby."

I groan and move my hips, meeting his, and then he sits back on his heels quickly, taking me with him, not breaking our precious contact. I wrap my arms around his neck and plant my feet beside his hips, and he guides me up and down his shaft, his hands planted firmly on my ass.

I feel the oh-so-familiar tightening of my body as my orgasm nears, and he must feel it, too, because he picks up the pace and pulls me down on him harder.

"Give it to me, baby . . . Come on, beautiful . . . Come for me."

And I shatter around him, completely exhausted.

He pulls me down one more time and erupts beneath me, calling out my name with his release.

LUKE IS WRAPPED around me in my bed, his front pressed against my back. It's warm and comfortable and just . . . safe.

"You've become quite insatiable since I met you, Natalie."

I can't help but laugh. "Yeah, I'm just using you for your body."

"I knew it!" He tickles my ribs, and I squirm in his arms, turning to face him.

"Are you going to kick my ass in the gym tomorrow?" I run my fingertip over his lower lip.

"No, I'd prefer to watch your ass." I giggle and kiss his chin.

"You can do that anytime. You don't need to take me to the gym to do it."

"It'll be fun to work out together."

"Okay."

"Trust me."

"I do, implicitly." The honesty in my voice is absolute. I do trust him, and it fills me with a warmth I've not felt since before my parents died.

Luke kisses my forehead and tucks me in against his chest. "Go to sleep, beautiful girl."

# seventeen

"**W**ake up, baby." Luke is brushing my hair off my face and gently kissing my forehead.

I want him to go away so I can bury myself in the covers and go back to sleep. It's too early!

"No."

"Come on, honey, open those pretty green eyes."

"I don't have to."

He chuckles and kisses my cheek. "Come on, morning girl, wake up. It's time to go get me all hot and bothered at the gym."

I roll onto my side and open one eye, peering at him uncertainly. "You hate me."

"No, baby, just the opposite. Come on, let's get up." He brushes his lips over my cheek and then my lips again, and I sigh.

"Let's stay here and get all hot and bothered, handsome."

"Oh, no, you don't. Come on, up." He slaps my ass and rolls away from me. He's already dressed!

"Oh Jesus, you're a morning person. This could change everything." I sit up and stretch and eye him warily.

"Gonna dump me already?" He smiles delightedly.

"I'm thinking about it." I rub my hands down my face and realize I smell coffee. "Do I smell coffee?"

Luke picks a mug up off the end table and takes a sip. "I brought this up for you, but since you're dumping me, I'll drink it myself."

I lunge up off the bed and dive for the mug in his hand. "Mine!"

"Ah, ah, ah!" He holds it out of my reach. "You hurt my feelings."

His grin betrays him, but I play along, enjoying this game. "I'm so sorry. Can I please have that coffee?"

I bite my lip and gaze up at him innocently through my eyelashes.

He purses his lips and moves his head from side to side as if considering my request.

"Well, maybe. If you kiss me."

I pucker up and lift my face to his, planting my lips on his cheek with a loud smack.

"Now?" I ask.

"Oh, I think you can do better than that. This is really good coffee." He takes another sip and moves quickly away from me as I lunge at him again.

Changing my tactics, I slide my hand in his shorts and grip his growing erection in my hand, rubbing up and down.

"Now?"

His eyes dilate, and he grins wickedly. "I do love the way you think, baby."

He hands me the mug, and I release him, walking toward the bathroom.

"Hey!"

"I'm gonna get you hot and bothered at the gym, not here," I toss over my shoulder and shut the door behind me while Luke laughs.

"Honey," he yells through the door. "You get me hot and bothered everywhere."

LUKE'S GYM IS small and out of the way, which shouldn't surprise me. He's less likely to be recognized here, and I like that it seems to be a no-nonsense kind of place, with upbeat rock pumping through the sound system and no frills. No smoothie bar, no girls meandering about with hardly any clothes on. People come here to work out, not to be seen.

It's so him.

"Where do you want to start?" he asks me as he ushers me ahead of him through the door.

"We're not meeting with your trainer?" I'm relieved that it will just be us today. I don't feel confident enough to work with a trainer. I know that I'm strong and toned, despite my curves, but I don't like strangers touching me or looking at my body.

"Just us today, baby."

"Okay, I think I'll run for a bit."

"Sounds good." He leads me to a line of treadmills, and we choose two machines side by side at the end of the row.

"I brought music." I pull my iPhone and earbuds out of my bra and plug them in my ears.

"What else do you have in there?" He laughs, and I join him. I love his carefree mood today. He's having fun, and it makes me relax. "That's fine. I'm going to watch the news." He points to the flat-screen TV in front of us.

He shows me how to work the treadmill, gets me started, then jumps on his and breaks out into a steady jog.

My mouth goes dry. Sweet Mother of God, this man is amazing. He moves with no effort, and I have to consciously look away before I trip.

I crank up my music—Lady Gaga today—and set my pace with the beat of the music. I've always liked to run. I just never seem to find the time.

I watch the instrument panel in front of me and empty my mind, listening to Ms. Gaga sing about a bad romance. Within minutes, I'm in the zone, and I smile as Kelly Clarkson sings about being stronger.

Yes, I could get used to this.

Before I know it, thirty minutes and about three miles have passed, and I'm sweating like crazy. I slow the belt down to walk for five minutes, then hop off, reaching for my water. I look to my right where Luke was, but he's gone.

I frown and search across the gym, looking for him. I don't immediately see him, so I gather my towel, tuck my phone into my bra and wander out among the free weights.

"Can I help you find something?" I whirl around at the deep voice and then grin.

"Brad! Hey, how's it going?"

"Good."

He pats me on the shoulder, gripping me for just a few seconds longer than polite, and continues to smile widely. "I haven't seen you in here before. Thinking of joining?"

"Oh, I'm here with someone today."

"Cool. Can I get you some water or a fresh towel?"

"You must work here," I mutter drily.

"Oh, yeah, I do. Hey, I can show you how to use some of the weights if you want."

"That won't be necessary." Both Brad and I twirl at the sound of Luke's cold voice.

"Hey." Brad smiles at Luke and holds out his hand. "I didn't introduce myself yesterday. I'm Brad."

Luke shakes his hand and gives him a smile, but it doesn't reach his eyes. "Luke."

Brad's eyes widen, and he swallows. "Holy shit, you're Luke Williams."

Luke's smile doesn't falter. "Yes, I am."

"Well, um . . ." Brad gives me a quizzical glance then smiles back at Luke. "It's nice to meet you. Catch you later, Natalie." He nods at me and disappears among the weights.

"So it seems Brad is more than a friend of a friend." Luke turns to me, his eyes cold and distant.

Shit.

"No, that's exactly what he is."

"Didn't look that way."

"How did it look?" I back away from him and cross my arms across my chest.

"It looked like he was picking you up."

I shake my head adamantly. "He is just a flirty guy, Luke. He was being nice. I was looking around for you."

"I got a phone call. I have to leave, I'm sorry. I have to run home and do some work."

"Fine, let's go."

"Do you have to work today?" He opens my car door for me, and I slide in.

"No," I respond when he's behind the wheel. "I have today off."

"You're welcome to come home with me." How can he go from being pissed off and jealous to sweet and accommodating?

"That's okay, just take me home."

"Are you mad at me?" His voice is soft, and I can't look him in the face.

"Yes. Are you always going to overreact whenever a man speaks to me?"

"He's had his hands on you twice in two days, Natalie. He wasn't just speaking to you."

"But I didn't do anything wrong."

"He wants in your pants, and you didn't do anything to dissuade him."

"Luke, I'm more than capable of saying no. Trust me, that's all I've said all my adult life. Until you." My voice is raised in my frustration. Doesn't he see that I'm mad about him? That I don't want anyone else?

"I will never be okay with another man putting his hands on you. Get used to it." His voice is sharp, and his eyes are so cold.

He pulls up in front of my house, and I jump out without waiting for him to open the door. He leaps out of his side and follows me up to the front porch.

"Go home, Luke. Go work." I shove my key in the lock and turn it, but his large hand covers mine so I can't turn the knob.

"Natalie, don't be mad at me."

"Don't be mad at you? I may be your girlfriend, but I'm not your property."

"I didn't say you are." He backs up as if I've slapped him.

"Brad's just a flirty kid. Trust me, nothing is ever going to happen with him."

His eyes flare at Brad's name again, and I want to kiss him for caring enough to be jealous and smack the shit out of him for being so jealous he's almost blind with it.

I take a deep breath and decide to change tactics.

"Remember yesterday when you compared seeing Brad and me on that bed in the studio with seeing you onscreen in a love scene?"

"Yeah." He runs a hand through his hair and looks thoroughly frustrated.

"Am I supposed to get jealous every time a fan fawns all over you? They all want in your pants. All of them. They fantasize about fucking you and wooing you and about you being their boyfriend. Trust me, those girls have all spent more time thinking about you than I care to think about."

He starts to speak, but then closes his mouth and shakes his head.

"Don't you dare say that it isn't the same thing. A crush is a crush is a crush. Brad has as much a chance of getting in my pants as any one of those pathetic women has of getting into yours."

He exhales loudly. "Well, I guess I can see your point."

"Go work. I'm going to take a shower."

"Are you still mad at me?" He closes the gap between us and grips my hand in his tightly.

"A little. I'll get over it. Go work and call me later."

"Okay." He bends down and runs his lips lightly over mine, then pushes his fingers in my hair and pulls me to him, kissing me deeply, as if his apology is in his kiss, and I can't help but melt against him.

"You make me crazy," I murmur against his lips.

"Ditto, baby. I'll talk to you tonight."

He leaves me on the porch, and I watch him slip into his sleek black SUV. He smiles and waves and pulls out of my driveway.

I've fallen in love with a beautiful, sexy, sweet, jealous control freak.

Shit.

JULES IS IN the kitchen when I go inside. I slam my purse on the breakfast bar and yank the fridge open, looking for a water.

"Well, hello, sunshine," Jules says sarcastically.

"What are you doing here? Aren't you supposed to be at work?"

"I'm working from home. Hey, you're really pissed. What happened?" She plants her hands on her hips and scowls at me, and I immediately feel better.

"He just irritated me at the gym. Luke has a jealous streak."

"Scary jealous or sexy jealous?" Jules asks, her eyebrows raised.

"Stupid jealous." I sigh and fall into the deep cushions of the red couch in the living room. Jules follows and sits in the armchair opposite me, her bare feet propped on the ottoman.

"He's obviously crazy about you." She takes a swig of her own water.

I shrug. "I guess. I'm new to all this, Jules. I don't like being questioned about things I do."

"He's not being a controlling asshole, is he?"

"No, but he does have a bossy streak. Not in a bad way. I know he cares about me. He's really sweet and gentle with me. But, boy, he does not like Brad." I roll my eyes and lean my head back against the cushion.

"Sexy model client Brad?"

"Yeah." I explain about Luke walking in on us in the studio yesterday and running into Brad at the gym today.

"Gee, I wonder why. That kid has it bad for you."

I scowl at her. "He does not! He's just flirty! Don't you start, too."

"You never could recognize when someone was interested in you, Nat."

"Luke has nothing to worry about."

"Oh, I know that." She brushes my words aside with a wave of her hand.

"Why doesn't he?"

"This is new to him, too."

"Whose side are you on?"

"Yours, sweetie. Always yours. Where is he?"

"He went home to work. Someone called while we were working out."

"Maybe you could use a day apart."

"Probably. Hey, what are you really doing here? You've been work-ing from home a lot lately."

Jules frowns and shrugs. "Telecommuting is easy."

"Uh uh. I don't buy it." She's not telling me something. "I know you too well, Julianne Montgomery."

"My new boss is kind of a dick." She shrugs again, but she looks like she might be fighting tears.

Alarmed, I sit on the ottoman, making her lower her feet, and grasp her hands. "Has he hurt you?"

"No, he's just a condescending asshole." She shrugs again, but then breaks down in tears. Holy shit.

"Sweetie, what is it?"

She drops her head in her hands and cries, a hard, sobbing cry.

"I fucked him," she cries through her hands.

"What?" I sit back, my jaw dropped, shocked. Jules has a strict poli-cy: no screwing coworkers.

"The night you first brought Luke home." I remember that night, when Jules went straight upstairs without coming to the kitchen to meet Luke.

"How? Jules, this isn't like you."

"I know." She wipes her eyes and her nose on the back of her hand. "We went out for dinner with some other people from the office, and I had too much to drink."

"Honey, is he trying to ruin things for you at work?"

"No! No, nothing like that." She takes a deep breath, and I hand her a tissue. "It's just so uncomfortable. And it doesn't help that he's freak-ing hot. Almost Luke Williams hot." She smiles at me, and my shoul-ders relax just a little.

"Wow, that's pretty hot."

"I know, right?" She shakes her head and looks sad again. I hate seeing Sad Jules. "And, Nat, you'd be shocked what he's hiding under those business suits he wears to work. Wow. It was the best sex of my damn life."

"Jules, are you hung up on this guy?"

"It doesn't matter even if I am. There is a no-fraternizing policy at our office. We could both be fired." Her eyes well again, and I just feel so helpless.

"What has his reaction been to all this?"

"Well, he was pretty pissed when he woke up the next morning and I was gone."

"Ah, so you did the whole sleep-with-'em-then-bail-when-they're-asleep move." I nod knowingly.

"Yeah. I didn't want to face the ugly morning after."

"Can't blame you there. But if he was pissed you were gone, maybe he really likes you."

"It doesn't matter. It's hopeless."

"But . . ."

"No, don't try to fix this, Nat. It's done. I'll go back to the office eventually. I just need a little time to regroup. I took a few vacation days, and now I'm working from home until I work up the nerve to see him again."

"Okay." I rub her arm soothingly, and then stand. "I'm going up to shower. Let me know if you need me."

"Thanks." She gives me a watery smile. "Oh, Nat?"

"Yeah?"

"Stupid jealous is kinda hot."

# eighteen

*I'm picking you up in an hour. Please dress formally.*

Oh my. I stare at the text and read it again.

I glance at the clock. It's five-thirty, and I'm definitely not anywhere close to being formal or sexy. I don't even know where to start.

This is a job for Jules.

"Jules!" I yell out my bedroom door, mentally thumbing through my closet.

"What?"

"I need to get sexy."

"What?"

I shove my phone in her hands, and she breaks into a huge smile. "Wow, he knows how to woo a girl."

"Jules!" I clasp on to her shoulders and shake her. "Help me. I'm not good at this."

"Come on." She grabs my wrist and drags me into my closet. "The new red Louboutins are a no-brainer." She pulls them off the shelf and hands them to me.

"What am I going to wear with them?" I'm in a panic.

"Don't you have a little black dress?"

"No." I frown. I don't have many dresses at all.

"Everyone has a little black dress, Natalie."

"Not me." I shrug.

"Get in the shower and scrub, shave and loofa. I'll be back."

"That sounds painful." My eyes widen in fear, and Jules smirks at me.

"We're just getting started. Go! Clock's ticking." She jogs back to her room, and I start the shower.

FIFTY MINUTES LATER, I am buffed and polished. Jules has curled my thick chestnut hair and managed to twist it up into some kind of sexy knot thing, with tendrils hanging around my face.

The face is a Julianne masterpiece. She's made my eyes look all smoky and sultry, accentuating the green in them. My cheekbones are defined, and my lips are pouty with a cranberry-red lip stain that is guaranteed to not smudge or come off for eighteen hours, which sounds too good to be true to me, but I'll take it.

My eyes run down the rest of my body in the full-length mirror hanging on the back of my closet door.

I'm hot.

Jules has lent me a to-die-for black dress. The neckline reminds me of something Elizabeth Taylor would have worn, just off the shoulder with a deep V-neck. The back swoops down low across the small of my back. It's sleeveless and gathered at the waist with a thick waistband. The skirt is floaty and soft and flirts just at my knees.

Under the dress is some impressive black underwear and a garter belt with nude stockings. I've never worn stockings before, but they're amazingly comfortable and feel silky and sexy.

My beautiful red stiletto Louboutins are killer with this dress.

Jules walks into the room and lets out a loud wolf whistle.

"Well, don't you clean up well, best friend of mine?"

I laugh and do a turn so she can see the whole effect. "Will I do?"

"Girl, he's going to die of heart failure the minute he sees you. You look amazing." She smiles and hugs me tight.

"Here, this wrap and purse will go with your outfit." She hands me a beautiful red wrap and a handbag that perfectly match the shoes, and I smile in gratitude.

The doorbell rings, and there are now about five million butterflies in my stomach.

"I'll answer. Take your time, make him sweat." She kisses my cheek and hurries down the stairs.

I stare at myself in the mirror for a few more minutes, and then put my things in Jules' red handbag.

Here goes nothing.

Do not fall down the stairs. Do not fall down the stairs.

This is my mantra as I walk down the stairs. I don't think I'm breathing, I'm too nervous. Where is he taking me?

I get to the bottom of the stairs and enter the foyer, and all of my wits completely scatter.

Luke is wearing a black double-breasted suit with a white shirt and a blue tie that perfectly matches his incredible eyes. His messy hair has been tamed somewhat, and it's begging for my fingers. He looks every bit the wealthy, sophisticated movie star, and he's all mine.

His eyes lock on mine, and a slow, delighted grin spreads across his face.

"Natalie, you take my breath away."

"You're not so bad yourself."

Luke closes the gap between us and hands me a bouquet of red roses. "These are for you."

"Thank you," I murmur as I bury my nose in them and breathe them in. "They're lovely."

"We should go. We have reservations." He takes my hand and kisses my knuckles, shooting shivers up my arm.

"Okay."

Jules magically appears from nowhere. "I'll put those in water for you. Have fun, you guys. You both look incredible."

"Thanks, Jules." I hand her the flowers, and Luke ushers me out of the house.

Instead of his Mercedes or the Lexus, there's a black stretch limo parked in my driveway with a sharply dressed driver standing at the open back door.

"Madam." He nods at me, and I smile in return.

Holy shit, Luke's gone all out! Is this how he says he's sorry? If so, we might have to argue more often.

I climb in the back of the spacious limo and slide over so Luke can follow. The inside must seat ten easily. It's all soft black leather seats and some sort of impressive sound system and other gadgets. The privacy glass is up.

Luke slides gracefully next to me and kisses my hand again.

"Luke, this is . . . amazing. Thank you."

"We haven't even gone anywhere yet." He looks so young and happy, and he's clearly excited for what he has planned for us tonight.

"It's already more than you should have done."

"No, it's exactly what you deserve, baby." He leans over and gives me his sweet, tender kiss, the one that makes my insides quiver. "You look gorgeous tonight."

I smile and flush at the compliment. "Thank you."

"Are those the new shoes?"

"Yes." I grin.

"They are wow."

"I know."

He laughs and pours me a glass of champagne as the driver pulls away from the house and heads toward Seattle.

"A toast." He holds his glass in the air, and I mirror him. "To a beautiful woman, who has become very special to me, and who is the most incredible person I've ever known. Thank you for being here with me." He clinks his glass to mine, and I blink back tears as I take a sip of the sweet pink drink.

"You are charming," I murmur and smile shyly at him.

"You are sexy as hell."

"Where are we going?" I take another sip of the champagne. Mmm . . . delicious.

"It's a surprise."

"Will it take awhile to get there?"

"A little while. Why do you ask?"

I take his drink out of his hand and place it next to mine on a small table near the minifridge.

"Because." I hike my skirt up a bit and straddle his lap. His eyes widen in surprise, and his strong hands glide up my stocking-clad legs. "I want to fuck you in this limousine."

"Holy shit, baby, you're wearing stockings."

I smile smugly and nod.

"I had a whole seduction scene planned for later." His breath hitches as I grind my center against his growing erection.

"Trust me, I don't want to ruin your plans." I lean forward and brush my lips over his. "But if you're not inside me in about twenty seconds, I'm not responsible for my actions."

"That's an offer I will never, ever refuse, baby." He slides me back on his knees so he can unfasten his pants, pulling his shirttails out of them and pushing them down around his thighs.

Instead of straddling him, I slip off his lap and onto my knees on the luxuriously carpeted floor. I smooth my hands up his strong thighs and stroke them up and down his cock.

"Holy shit, Nat, you are so fucking hot."

"You make me crazy." I smear the bead of moisture around the tip with my thumb and then put it in my mouth and suck, and his eyes go wide.

"Taste good?"

"Mmm . . . my favorite."

I take him in my mouth, just swirling my tongue around the tip and gliding my hands up and down his impressive length. I feel his fingertips just barely grazing my hairline around my ears, and I know he wants to sink his fingers in my hair but doesn't want to mess it up.

I grip his shaft with my lips firmly and sink down until I feel him against the back of my throat.

"Sweet Jesus, Natalie, stop."

I grin to myself and pull back but then sink down again, loving that I'm making him crazy.

"No, stop, I don't want to come in your mouth." He reaches down and lifts me onto his lap so I'm straddling him again. He reaches between us and pulls my panties to the side, and I rub my folds against him, feeling my wetness spreading over him.

"God, baby, you're so wet."

"You are so sexy, honey. I need you inside me."

He growls and kisses me hard while lifting my ass over him and sinks easily inside me. I grip the back of the seat behind his head and begin riding him, slowly at first, but his hands move me up and down faster and faster.

"Come for me, beautiful." He's kissing my neck and moves one hand between us to graze his thumb over my clitoris, and I'm lost. I shudder and clench down around him, crying out as he pushes up one last, hard time and empties himself into me.

"Fuck, Natalie." His breathing is ragged. I wrap my fingers in his hair and kiss him with all I have, pouring my heart and soul into the kiss, trying to convey the words that I just can't say: that I love him so much.

He tenderly cups my face in his hands and slows the kiss, pulling back so he can look into my eyes, and I see the love reflected back to me. It makes me glow inside, and it makes me want to run as fast as I can in the other direction.

"Thank you for tonight," I whisper.

"Oh, baby, it's just getting started." He gives me a slow, sweet smile and lifts me off of him. I rummage around and find a towel, and we clean up and straighten our clothes.

Settling back into our seats, Luke freshens our champagne and wraps his arm around me.

"I'm sorry about today," he murmurs.

"Me, too." I sigh and lean my head on his shoulder. "Did you get your work done?"

"For the most part. I'll have to make a few calls tomorrow."

"Oh good." He's running his fingertips up and down my bare arm, and I want to purr.

"What did you do today?"

"I hung out with Jules." I take his hand in mine and lace my fingers through his, reveling in how long and lean his hands are. "She's got some stuff going on, so I did the best friend thing."

"Is she okay?" He sounds sincerely concerned, and I can't help but grin. My sweet man.

"She will be. Man troubles."

"Ah. So, what does the best friend thing entail, exactly?" He kisses my forehead.

"Well, a lot of talking, eating ice cream and other things that I'm not allowed to divulge."

"Oh?" He chuckles and kisses my forehead again.

"Yeah, I could tell you, but then I'd have to kill you, and I've grown quite fond of you."

"Is that so?" He leans back so he can look me in the eye, and I nod gravely.

"Yes, very fond of you."

"And what are you most fond of, exactly?" He gives me his sweet smile, and I know that despite our teasing, he wants an honest answer.

"I'm fond of this." I lean up and kiss his lips softly. "You say such sweet things to me and make my body hum with it."

"Happy to hear that, beautiful girl."

I smile and kiss the palm of his hand. "And I enjoy your hands, and how expressive they are and how they feel when they're on me."

"Mmm . . . they love being on you, baby."

I lay my cheek on his chest, just over his heart. "Most of all, I love your heart. How kind you are and how gentle you are with me. Most of the time," I add and smile up at him.

His lips part as he exhales. "Natalie, I don't know what I did to deserve you, but I would do it again, over and over." He runs his knuckles down my cheek and kisses me tenderly as the limo comes to a stop.

"We're here."

Luke climbs out ahead of me and takes my hand to help me out of the impressive car. He pulls me to his side, and my eyes are glued to the enormous chateau before us.

"Oh my."

"This is Chateau Ste. Michelle. We're going to have dinner here tonight."

"I didn't know they had a restaurant." My wide eyes meet his.

"They don't. They do special events. Tonight, for a few hours at least, it's all ours."

I'm struck dumb. He rented out the entire chateau for me?

"Come." He leads me toward the front of the building where an older woman, in her midfifties, is waiting for us.

"Welcome, Mr. Williams and Ms. Conner. I'm Mrs. Davidson. We're delighted to have you. Would you please follow me?" She leads us on a cobblestone path around the side of the chateau. It's lined with old-fashioned streetlights illuminate the whole side of the building.

Luke tucks my hand in his arm and escorts me along behind Mrs. Davidson. As we round the bend behind the house, I gasp at the sight before me.

"Oh, Luke." I feel him grin down at me, watching my reaction to the most beautiful display I've ever seen. The stone path leads us beneath an arbor that is covered in grapevines. The vines are heavy with luscious, purple grapes. There are white twinkling Christmas lights draped over roughly ten two-person tables and wound through the arbor and vines lining the small space. There is soft, bluesy music crooning in the background.

The small table in the center of the stone patio is covered in a white tablecloth. The china is also white, but on one plate sits a single red rose. Luke walks forward and pulls the chair out for me, and I sit.

He picks up the rose, and I look up into his joy-filled eyes. He sniffs the delicate flower before extending it to me.

"For you, beautiful."

"Thank you." I put the bloom against my nose and sniff its sweetness.

Luke sits opposite me at the table.

"Honey, this is wonderful. Thank you." I reach over and grasp his hand in mine, so moved by this devastatingly romantic gesture.

"I'm glad you like it." He grins and gestures to the waiter.

"Sir, madam." The waiter is dressed in a white jacket and black pants and bow tie. He's an older gentleman with white hair and a British accent, and I can't help but fall just a little in love with him.

"Thank you for joining us this evening. We will be serving you three courses, in addition to an appetizer course and, of course, dessert. I hope you're hungry." He winks at me and motions to someone inside the building.

"Here is your appetizer. Chili garlic calamari, paired with our 2009 dry Riesling, and Hawaiian-style chicken skewers, paired with the 2008 Cabinet Riesling."

The plates are set in front of us with glasses of wine.

I meet Luke's eyes over the table. "It looks too pretty to eat."

"Enjoy, baby."

We dig in and enjoy the appetizers. The wines complement each dish perfectly, flooding my mouth with amazing flavors and textures.

Luke reaches over and holds my hand, rubbing his thumb over my knuckles as we finish our wine and wait for the next course.

"Are you having fun?"

"Much more than fun. This is . . . a fairy tale." I feel my cheeks heat, but it's the truth.

"This is a beautiful vineyard. We'll have to come again during the day so you can see the grounds."

"I'd love that."

"May I present your first course?" Our waiter is back and removes our empty plates and wine glasses. "This is our mojito-marinated halibut with mango, avocado and black bean salsa, served with the 2009 Midsummer's White. Enjoy." He backs away, leaving us with the delicious meal.

We're served two more courses of pork tenderloin and New York steak with Yukon gold potatoes and, of course, the perfect wines to accompany them.

I'm feeling very full and just a little lightheaded from all the wine when it's time for dessert to be served.

"Oh my God, Luke, I don't know if there is any room left in this dress for dessert." I sit back and rub my belly, and Luke laughs, his eyes alight with happiness. He's having a really good time and has been light-hearted and complimentary throughout our meal. He's so good at this.

He motions to the waiter, who immediately steps to the tableside. "Yes, sir."

"I think that Ms. Conner and I will share the dessert, please."

"Very good, sir."

"Good plan. Besides, we're going to work all these calories off at yoga tomorrow morning."

"Ah yes, yoga. You're going to make me go, huh?"

"No, I'm not making you."

"We could skip it and stay in bed all day." He winks at me over his wine glass.

"I can't skip it. I'm the instructor."

"I had no idea." He furrows his brow in confusion.

"I only teach three classes a week." I shrug. "Besides, I'm very flexible. You should enjoy the show." I smile smugly into my glass and watch his eyes glass over.

"I wouldn't miss it for the world."

The waiter reappears with our dessert of strawberry crème brûlée tart, on one plate, and two glasses of the Eroica Ice Wine.

He also sets a baby-blue Tiffany necklace-size box in the center of the table, bows to both of us, and walks away.

Oh. My. God.

# nineteen

I stare numbly at the perfect blue box tied with a white bow. What's this?

"It's for you," he murmurs and grips my hand. My eyes find his, and I just don't know what to say.

"You shouldn't have done this." My voice is a whisper.

"You haven't opened it yet," he responds drily, but his eyes are guarded.

I'm sure this is not the response he was expecting. I don't want to hurt his feelings.

He picks up the box and passes it to me. "Open it, baby."

I pull the ribbon off the box, and nestled beneath it on top of the box is a note.

*These remind me of you. Simply beautiful.*
*—Luke*

Oh my.

I smile up at him, and I see his shoulders relax a bit with his grin. He's sitting forward, leaning on the table, waiting in anticipation for me to open the box.

I pull the lid off the box and gasp.

Nestled in Tiffany blue satin is a string of exquisite pearls. They have a platinum clasp, and the pearls are milky white, with an almost iridescent glow that reflects the soft twinkling lights around us. I lift them out of the box, and they are smooth and cool to the touch.

"Luke, they're fabulous."

"Here." He gracefully unfolds his lean body from his chair and comes to stand behind me, taking the strand of beautiful pearls from my hands and unclasping them. He drapes them around my neck, and my fingers immediately touch them as he fastens them. They lay just at my collarbone. He leans down and kisses me gently on the cheek and offers his hand to me as Norah Jones begins crooning about coming away with her.

"Dance with me." His blue eyes are shining with happiness, and I'm so caught up in the romance, so caught up in him, I just can't resist him.

"It would be my pleasure."

He pulls me into his arms and begins whisking me around the patio.

"Thank you for the beautiful pearls," I whisper up to him.

"You are welcome, beautiful. They look perfect on you." As he sways me back and forth in time to the music, he leans down and places his lips gently on mine.

"You're good at this."

He smiles down at me. "The studio made me take lessons."

"I approve."

"I'm happy to hear it." As the song ends, he pulls me closer against his chest and wraps his arms around me, planting his lips gently on my forehead. "Come home with me tonight."

"You'd rather go to your place tonight?"

"Yes. I want you in my bed."

I smile and run my fingers through his soft blond hair, soaking in his beautiful face. His eyes are so blue, his freshly shaven jaw chiseled. I've never loved anyone so much.

"Okay. I'm going to need a few things from my house."

His fingers trace my skin just under the pearls, and a shiver dances down my spine. "Jules already took care of it."

I raise an eyebrow. "Pretty sure of yourself."

"Just hopeful, baby." He kisses my forehead again and cups my face in his hands. His lips find my nose, my cheeks and then settle softly on my lips. It's one of his special, gentle kisses, and I sigh as the muscles deep in my stomach begin to tighten.

"Take me home," I whisper against his lips, and his eyes blink open, burning with desire.

He leads me back to the table, and I see that our things have been gathered up and most likely taken to the car. The waiter appears with my wrap and handbag, and Luke tucks my hand in the crook of his elbow and escorts me back to the car, sliding across the leather seat behind me.

Inside, there is a fresh bottle of champagne and another fresh red rose.

"What is it with you and red roses?"

"You don't like them?" His voice is worried, and he furrows his brow.

"No, I love them. You're just spoiling me." I bury my nose in the blossom and peek up at him through my lashes.

"You look very beautiful right now, in those pearls and black dress and a red rose pressed to your face." He runs his finger down my cheek, and I sigh.

"Thank you."

"Come here." He lifts me effortlessly onto his lap, and I curl into him, burying my face in his neck.

"Tonight was the most magical night of my life, Luke."

I feel his smile as he kisses my forehead. "Mine, too."

"WAKE UP, BABY, we're home." Luke is kissing my forehead and brushing my cheek with his fingers.

"I'm sorry I fell asleep." I sit up and realize I'm still clutching the rose.

"I love holding you while you sleep, baby. Come on, let's go in."

The driver opens Luke's door, and Luke lifts me onto the seat next to him, ushering me out ahead of him. He thanks the driver and escorts me into the house.

My feet are starting to feel the effects of these fantastically beautiful shoes, but I don't want to take them off yet. Luke removes my wrap from my shoulders, skimming his fingers across my skin, and just like that my libido wakes up.

"Are your feet hurting?" He's always so aware of how I might be feeling, and it makes me smile.

"A little, but I'm okay."

He leans down and scoops me into his arms and begins the journey up to his bedroom.

"You do enjoy carrying me," I murmur and kiss his cheek.

"It's for purely selfish reasons."

"Oh? And what are those reasons?" I kiss his cheek again. I love the way his skin feels against my face.

"Well, one, I enjoy having you in my arms. And, two, I don't want you to take those shoes off yet."

He carries me into his bedroom and sets me down on my feet in the middle of the room. He flips a switch on the wall, and the light on the end table illuminates, throwing soft shadows across the room.

"Let me help you out of that dress."

I turn, and he kisses my shoulder as he lowers the zipper down the back and slips the straps down my arms. The dress falls and pools at my feet. He holds my hand, and I step out of it and turn back toward him.

He gasps and steps back from me, not touching me, and I've never felt more beautiful. His eyes are shining with adoration and desire, skimming over my hair and pearls, down to my breasts held firmly in place by a black lace strapless bra. He lowers his gaze over my belly piercing, black lace barely there panties that match the bra, garter belt, stockings and down to my killer red shoes.

Yes, I know I look amazing right now, and it's the most powerful, sexy feeling in the world.

I don't move toward him. I stand where I am, letting him drink me in with his eyes. I slowly reach up and unpin my hair, one thick curl at a time, and let it fall around my shoulders, dropping the pins to the floor.

"You are every fantasy I've ever had come true, Natalie." He swallows hard and flexes his hands in and out of fists, and I know he's dying to touch me.

I smile softly, not wanting to break this spell, and reach behind me to unclasp my bra and let it join the dress and pins on the floor, releasing my breasts. My nipples pucker under his hungry gaze.

"What would you like me to do now?" I whisper.

His eyes focus on mine, just a bit glassy like he's intoxicated, but I know it's not from the wine we've consumed all evening. He closes his eyes briefly, and then starts shedding his clothes, letting them fall unheeded to the floor around him.

Suddenly, he's standing before me, naked. "I'm almost afraid to touch you," he whispers.

"Why?" I cock my head, confused. Touch me! Please, for the love of all that's holy, touch me!

"I'm afraid you're not real."

And just like that I see the vulnerability in his eyes, and I walk to him, raising my hands up his chest, over his shoulders and into his hair. His blue gaze is on mine, and I smile tenderly.

"I'm real, and I'm yours." I push up on my toes and run my lips across his, and he shudders, exhaling deeply.

He reaches down and cups my bottom in his hands and lifts me, wrapping my legs around his waist, and walks us back to the bed. But he doesn't drop me. He wraps his impossibly strong arms around me and lowers me gently, without lifting his lips from mine.

He kisses me madly, voraciously, cupping my face in his hands while he lies over me, bracing himself on his elbows. My hands drift down his back to his butt and back up to his shoulders, over and over. His erection presses against my now wet panties, and he rocks his hips back and forth, sending zings of electricity through me.

"God, I've been fantasizing about this since the day I met you," he mutters as he moves his mouth from mine to my neck.

"About what?"

"You, in pearls and these shoes, wrapped around me."

"How's it working out for you?" I gasp as he rocks against me again, and I tighten my legs around his hips.

He smiles against my neck. "Better than I ever dreamed possible." He rubs his nose along my pearls. "You look so magnificent in these."

"I love them. Thank you."

He leans up on his elbows and pins me with those shining blue eyes, gazing intently into mine. He brushes his thumbs down my cheeks, and I run my fingers through his hair.

"What is it?" I ask, reveling in the intense way he's looking down at me.

"I love you."

The words are strong, firm, with no hesitation. His intense gaze never falters, and I know, undoubtedly, that he means it. My heart stops, tears fall from the corners of my eyes, and I clasp his precious face in my hands as I gaze up at my incredible man.

"I love you, too."

He brushes my tears away with his fingertips, and then leans down and kisses my eyelids.

"Don't cry, baby." His lips graze my cheek and settle back on my lips again, and I'm completely bewildered and lost to him.

"Make love to me, please." I want him more than anything. I want to feel him move through me. I want to see the passion on his face as he erupts inside me.

He smiles tenderly, sits back and hitches my panties in his thumbs. I raise my hips so he can slide them down my legs. He moves back on top of me and smoothes one hand up my leg, over the stockings, and lightly rubs his fingertips over the skin just above where the stockings end.

It's delicious.

That talented hand moves between my legs, and he slips two fingers inside me, his thumb wreaking havoc on my clitoris, and I bow up off the bed.

Oh God, it's just so good.

"Feel it, baby."

Oh, I do. My hips circle, and his fingers push in and out of me in a sensual rhythm. He leans down and kisses me, his tongue invading my mouth with the same rhythm of his fingers. Just as I feel my body quicken and the shudders start, he pulls them out of me.

"No!"

He grins down at me and swiftly fills me, burying himself inside me.

"Oh yes."

"Better?" His eyes burn down into mine, and he starts to move, and I'm overcome with sensation. My body is on fire. My heart is so full of love for this beautiful man. I can't find my voice, so I simply nod and hold on to him, gripping his tight rear, pulling him to me.

"Oh, baby, you're so tight." He clenches his jaw, and I grip him with my most intimate muscles, knowing that he's so close to his own violent explosion, and that I'm going with him.

"Come with me, my love." His eyes fly open and then shut again as he shudders inside me, and my body follows, clenching around him, pulsing with need.

"Oh, Natalie, yes!"

LUKE IS IN his favorite spot, his head resting between my breasts, arms hugging my hips, and our breathing is starting to slow.

I can't believe that I had to wait twenty-five years for a man to truly make sweet, tender love to me.

Well, almost twenty-six years as of Saturday.

I also can't believe that we just let the L-word slip. I hope it wasn't just because it was in the heat of the moment, because of this impossibly romantic night. But as I think back on the look in his eyes as he said those three words, I know that he meant it. Even though we've only known each other for such a short time, and there's still so much to learn.

I also know that my heart has never been so full, and I have never met a man as kind, intelligent and as sweet as he is. I feel safe with him, and I feel beautiful and cherished.

Yes, he has a jealous streak, but don't we all?

"Don't overthink this, baby."

I look down and frown.

"Overthink what?"

"I hear the wheels turning in that gorgeous head of yours." He kisses my sternum, rolls off of me and lies next to me, facing me, bracing his head on his elbow.

"I'm not thinking."

"You're not a good liar." He leans over and kisses my nose and brushes a lock of hair off my cheek.

"I need to take my pearls off." I sit up and turn my back to him and feel him unhinge the clasp.

"Why?" He lays them on the nightstand, and I lie back down.

"I don't want them to snag on something and break in the night." I sigh and glide my hand down his side to his hip.

"I meant it, you know."

I smile and stretch lazily. "I know."

"What time are we getting up in the morning?"

I'm relieved that he's changing the subject. I have a lot to think about. "Class is at nine."

"Then we'd better get some sleep."

"I'm not sleeping in these shoes."

He laughs and sits up, sliding each shoe off my feet and placing them gently on the floor. He then unhooks the stockings from the garter and peels them down my legs.

"You have beautiful legs, baby." He kisses them and pulls the garter off me as well, tossing it on the floor.

He crawls up next to me and covers us in the duvet, scooping me into his arms. I rest my head on his chest and sigh, feeling his lips on my forehead.

"Go to sleep, beautiful."

"Good night," I mumble and drift into an exhausted sleep.

I WAKE SUDDENLY and reach for Luke, but he's not there. The bed is cold and empty.

Where did he go?

I pull on the white dress shirt he was wearing earlier tonight and leave the bedroom. He's not in the loft, so I go downstairs.

It's dark. I don't see him in the living room or kitchen, and I'm about to get really scared when I see movement on the deck.

I walk through the darkness to the open door, unnoticed. He's standing at the railing, bathed in moonlight. He's wearing a dark pair of pajama pants that hang on his sexy hips, and he's topless. He's leaning his elbows on the railing and is looking out on the midnight-blue water that is reflecting the moon.

I wish with all my might that I had my camera.

I walk up behind him and kiss his back, wrapping my arms around his middle. I love holding him like this.

"Did I wake you?" he whispers.

"No, I woke up because you were gone." I kiss him again. "Are you okay?"

"I'm fine, just couldn't sleep." He turns around to face me and leans his hips on the railing, wrapping me in his arms. His face is bathed in moonlight, his eyes gazing intently down at me. "How are you?"

"Lonely. Come back to bed."

"Okay," he whispers and kisses my forehead. "I see you've borrowed my shirt again."

"It's a nasty habit of mine."

"That's okay. You can return it to me upstairs." He scoops me into his arms, and I laugh as he carries me back to the bedroom.

# twenty

I'm surprised to wake before Luke. We have to be at yoga in an hour, but I can't resist lying here and watching him sleep.

The early morning light filters in through his floor-to-ceiling windows. I love his large bedroom with its large-scale furniture. The bed is enormous, the white sheets feel like Egyptian cotton, and they are soft against my skin.

Luke lies on his back, one hand flung over his head. His face is soft in sleep, his morning stubble so sexy along his jaw, and his usually messy hair even messier than usual.

And he loves me!

I saunter into the bathroom to answer nature's call, and when I walk back into the bedroom, I pick up the scattered clothes, shoes and hairpins from last night, a huge grin plastered on my face.

I notice one of my small suitcases is sitting on a chair near the windows, and I make a mental note to thank Jules.

I am happy to find my yoga gear, fresh underwear and other casual clothes and toiletries, including a toothbrush, all new, in the suitcase. I decide to unpack and settle in a bit. If he wants me to move back out, fine. If he wants to move some stuff into my place, that's fine, too.

I add my toothbrush and a stick of deodorant to his vanity and a bottle of body wash and shampoo to the shower. Jules must have gone shopping for all this last night, and I not only mentally thank her, I plan to surprise her with a special treat.

I leave the clothes in the suitcase, but pull on my yoga gear and look back over to the bed.

Luke's still asleep, and we still have plenty of time, so I leave him be and head downstairs to make coffee.

I poke around his kitchen, opening espresso-colored cabinets, and finally locate the coffee and maker, get it set to drip and find some mugs as well. As the coffee perks, I open the French door out to the deck and step out to enjoy the view of the beautiful Puget Sound and take a deep breath of fresh air.

It's a beautiful day. The sky is a brilliant blue, as the morning sun is up fully and shining on the deep blue water. The ferry is gliding gracefully toward Bainbridge Island. Seagulls fly over the water, and the breeze is blowing gently through my hair. It's a glorious day.

"I thought you weren't a morning person."

I spin at the sound of his rough, sexy voice. He enfolds me in his arms and hugs me close.

"Good morning, handsome."

"Good morning, baby."

Leaning my head back, I grin up at him. "I'm making coffee."

"So I smell. Thank you. Why didn't you wake me?" He kisses my forehead and takes a deep breath.

"You looked so peaceful, and we're in no hurry."

"You unpacked."

I lean my head against his chest, avoiding his gaze. "Yeah, I can re-pack if you'd rather I didn't leave my stuff here."

He grips my chin in his fingers and tips my head back, brushing my lips with his in a kiss that makes my toes curl.

"I like having your stuff here. Leave it."

"Okay." I smile shyly at him. "Let's get some coffee."

"ARE YOU READY?" I grin at Luke, who's now dressed in loose, black basketball shorts and a tank top. He looks fantastic.

"As I'll ever be." He looks nervous, and my heart melts.

"You'll be fine. Just remember what I said. Go at your own pace and stretch only as far as is comfortable. I don't want you to get hurt."

"I won't get hurt."

"Okay." I know he thinks this is going to be a piece of cake. I have no doubt that he's in excellent physical condition, but yoga is more physically demanding than most people realize.

I unlock the studio and usher him in. The glass windows are frosted so people walking by can't stop and stare. There are mirrors covering one whole wall with a barre mounted to it for the afternoon ballet class. Yoga mats are rolled up and stacked in a corner. I walk over to the sound system and choose some calming music.

"Okay, let's grab our mats. Clients will start trickling in soon."

"How many people usually attend this class?"

I can sense his unease about being recognized. "Only about eight or ten. It's a small class."

He nods, and we spread out our mats, me in the front of the class by the mirrors and him in front of me. Clients walk in and grab mats, spread all over the studio. No one even pays any attention to Luke, and I see him relax. I smile at him reassuringly, and he winks back at me.

"Okay, everyone, let's get started." For the next hour I lead the class through the series of poses, varying my poses to accommodate both novice and experienced clients. I typically lose myself to the music and the flow of the yoga itself, but I can't help but be distracted by Luke and his strong body. He's more flexible than I gave him credit for, and he's graceful. Watching his toned body move and flex is a delight.

He's watching me, too, with more interest than just to see which pose I'm moving into. When our eyes meet, the heat is unmistakable, and I know I'm turning him on as much as he's turning me on.

I can't wait to get him alone.

I'm in the downward dog pose, and I turn to look out over the class and see that Luke's gaze is on my ass.

I smirk.

Finally, class is over, and I'm so turned on I can hardly see straight. The clients all wave goodbye and shuffle out to get on with their day, and finally Luke and I are left alone. He walks over to the door and flips the lock, and my heart does a big ol' flip in my chest.

"Is there another class in here this morning?" he asks.

"No, not until this afternoon."

"Good."

"What did you think?" I ask.

"I think," he begins, as he walks slowly toward me, "that you are the sexiest woman I've ever seen in my life."

His eyes narrow, and his face is serious.

"Oh." I try to gather my wits. "So, I take it you liked it?"

"I had no idea you could move that gorgeous little body of yours like that."

"I've been doing this for a long time."

"Yeah, I see." He's finally standing less than a foot away from me, and I reach up to run my hand down his face.

"I'm glad you were here. It was a pleasure to watch you move."

He smiles, delighted with me, and cups my hand in his own, leaning in to my touch and closing his eyes for just a few moments. He opens those baby blues, and they are now on fire.

Holy hell, I love it when he looks at me like that.

He backs me up against the mirror and clasps my face in his hands, kissing me as if his life depends on it. I grip his hips and give myself over to his kiss, pouring all my frustration from the past hour into it.

"I want you," he murmurs against my lips.

"I've wanted you for the past hour. I'm surprised I was able to speak during class."

He smiles against my lips. "Let's take these off, shall we?"

He pulls my tank and sports bra over my head and throws them on the ground, then makes quick work of my pants and underwear. I repay the favor, divesting him of his black workout clothes, and he spins me around to face the mirror.

"Put your hands on the bar, baby."

I gladly comply. He kisses my shoulder and wraps his arms around my front, cupping my breasts and worrying the sensitive nipples with his fingers. Watching our reflection sends electricity straight to my groin. His large bronze hands span my chest, cupping my white breasts.

His lips are on my shoulder, his eyes closed, and the look on his face is primal and needy and *oh my*.

"Ah!" I lean my head back against his chest, pushing my breasts into his hands.

"You made me crazy watching you in all those poses, baby. I don't know how I managed to control my hard-on."

I gasp and smile at him in the mirror.

He glides a hand down my side, tracing my tattoo, over my hip, across my buttock and finds my center.

"Fuck, baby, you're so ready for me." His lips are on my neck, nibbling, sending shivers down my spine.

Suddenly, he pulls back on my hips so I'm bent over, bracing my hands on the bar, and he smacks my ass hard before slamming his cock into me.

"Oh God!"

He grips my hair in one hand and my hip in the other and pushes into me, faster and faster, harder and harder, his stormy eyes on mine in the mirror.

Fuck, it feels so good! I push back on him and feel the orgasm rip through me, fast, hard, and I explode around him.

He thrusts twice more and shudders in his own release.

AS WE LEAVE the yoga studio, I get a text from Jules.

*Birthday dinner at the folks' tomorrow night? Bring Luke.*

I frown. How do I bring this up?

"What's wrong?" He ushers me into his car and leans in to kiss me before getting behind the wheel.

"Nothing's wrong."

He raises an eyebrow at me, and I squirm.

"Talk to me, baby."

"Jules' parents have invited us over to their place for dinner tomorrow night."

"Oh? What's the occasion?" He starts the car and pulls out of the lot toward his house.

"My birthday," I whisper and bite my lip.

"What?" He glances over at me, his eyes wide, then back to the road ahead.

"Well, it's not really until Saturday, but they want to do a birthday dinner tomorrow night." I twist my fingers in my lap and gaze down. This is uncomfortable.

"Are you close to her family?"

"Yeah, they pretty much adopted me after my folks passed." This is much easier to talk about. "Her parents are great. She has four older brothers. The oldest, Isaac, and his wife just had a baby. I haven't met her yet."

"So it'll be a family thing."

Oh, what is he thinking? He doesn't look mad, but he doesn't look pleased.

"Yes. Will you go with me?"

"Of course. Sounds fun. But when were you going to tell me your birthday is this weekend?"

Oh.

I shrug and look out the window. "I hadn't really thought about it, honestly. I don't make a big deal out of it."

"Maybe I want to make a big deal out of it." His voice is deceptively soft.

"Don't be mad," I whisper. "It would make me feel stupid to say, 'So, let's go to yoga, and by the way, my birthday is Saturday.'"

"No, that would have been helpful." He pulls up to my house, dropping me off so I can work. He grabs Jules' dress and my shoes out of the back, and we go inside.

"So, I guess we're going to the dinner tomorrow night?"

"Yeah, we are." He hugs me tight.

"Thank you. Do you have much work today?" I ask, trying to distract him.

"Yeah, some. You?"

"I have two sessions, and I have to take Jules' dress to the cleaners."

He frowns deeply. "Jules' dress?"

Crap.

"Yeah, she lent it to me."

"Why?"

"Because I don't have any formal wear." I shrug. "It's no big deal."

"I don't want you to have to borrow clothes." He narrows his eyes and plants his hands on his hips.

"Luke, that's what girls do. We borrow each other's clothes. It's no big deal."

"I want to take you shopping for your birthday."

"No." I shake my head emphatically and walk toward the kitchen.

"Why ever not?"

"You do not need to buy me clothes. I can buy three-thousand-dollar shoes without batting an eye, Luke. I don't need you to clothe me."

"I didn't say you needed me to. I'm your boyfriend, for Christ sake. That's what we do. Let me spoil you."

"You do spoil me." I smile as I remember the flowers, the coffee, dinner last night. "You spoil me in all the ways that matter."

"Nat, I'm very wealthy. I can afford to spend money on you."

"Ditto." I cross my arms over my chest.

"You are so fucking stubborn!" He shakes his head and runs his hand through his hair, and I can't help but be amused.

"Are you smirking?" he asks.

"Kind of. You're funny when you're irritated with me."

He laughs and looks at the ceiling. "God, you're frustrating."

"I know. But I love you."

His eyes soften, and he pulls me into his arms. "I love you, too."

I lean up and kiss him sweetly on the lips, then the corner of his mouth.

"I'm serious, baby. Take my credit card, grab Jules and go shopping. Both of you, on me, for your birthday."

I open my mouth to argue, but Jules breezes into the kitchen. "Okay, don't have to tell me twice. Thanks." She winks at him and grins.

"Hey!" I say. "No way. I mean it."

"Jules, do you have plans tomorrow before dinner at your parents?" Luke is talking to her but looking at me, his jaw set.

I am so going to lose this argument.

"Nope. I happen to have a clear calendar." She smiles.

"Great. Will you please take my girlfriend shopping? And I think the spa is in order, too."

The spa, too? My jaw drops.

"It would be an honor and a pleasure, generous boyfriend-in-law." Jules laughs at her quip, and Luke joins her, and all I can do is look back and forth between them.

"I'm in the goddamn room, people!"

"I know, baby, I'm just planning a little something for your birth-day." He flashes a wolfish smile and winks, and I don't know whether to smack him or really kiss him.

"I like your boyfriend, Nat." Jules smiles at me sweetly, and I know I'm sunk.

"Fine," I mutter.

"Your enthusiasm is inspiring." Luke's eyes are shining in humor.

"We'll go to the spa, but no shopping." I'm really hoping he'll accept the compromise, but I can see by the set of his jaw that there's no use in arguing.

"You will shop. Buy whatever you want. There's no limit on the card."

I shake my head at him. "Talk about stubborn."

He shrugs and kisses me hard, then pulls away abruptly, leaving me off balance.

"Will you come to my place when your sessions are over?"

"Yeah, I'll text you when I'm done." I sigh, resigned to my fate to-morrow. I know that Jules will make me follow Luke's instructions.

Traitor.

"Good. I'll see you later." He kisses me again and rests his forehead on mine. "I love you, beautiful."

And just like that my world is set right again, and in this moment I'd do just about anything he wanted.

"I love you, too, bossy man."

# twenty-one

**"**J**ules, I don't want to spend his money."** I hear the whine in my voice, but I don't care.

"Sweetie, he wants to do something nice for you. It's your birthday."

We are wandering through Neiman Marcus in downtown Seattle. The crowds are light today given that it's the middle of the week. The perfectly coiffed saleswomen are very attentive and overeager to make a midweek commission.

"I feel like a gold digger."

Jules laughs as she pulls a blue blouse off a rack, then quickly dismisses it. "You are no gold digger. Here, try this." She hands me a black blouse, and we continue wandering.

We've already been to the spa this morning. We both had facials, massages, pedicures and manicures and had our bits and pieces freshly waxed. I have to say, it felt fantastic. "The spa was enough. It was generous and relaxing and perfect."

"Nat, stop fighting this. Luke is being incredibly generous and wants—*wants*—us to enjoy ourselves today. I agree that there's no need to go ape-shit crazy, but humor the man and get a few nice things. You'll probably need a few formal dresses if he continues to plan things like the other night, which, by the way, *holy shit*. Plus, you may have to go to a movie premiere or something sometime, and you have to look the part."

Holy shit is right.

I'd never considered that. Does he go to the premieres of the movies he works on now?

Hell.

Two hours, and a few thousand dollars later, we leave the store loaded down with bags and boxes. I can't believe she talked me into all of this. I'm happy that she also managed to snag a few things for herself. Luke would approve.

I have purchased three new evening dresses and the appropriate undergarments for them, a few blouses and jeans, two new pairs of shoes—Manolo Blahniks!—and a new Gucci handbag.

I might chicken out and return it all tomorrow.

Jules also scored a new pair of Louboutins and a handbag. She looks beautiful as we leave the store and head to the car. She's the happiest I've seen her since her tryst with her boss. Smiling, carefree and relaxed.

Three hours at the spa and two hours of spending someone else's money at Neiman's will do that to a girl.

We head back to our house to get ready for the party tonight. I'm really excited to see Jules' family and to meet her new niece, little Sophie.

Luke will be here in an hour.

"Are you going to wear that pretty new red top with the new jeans?" Jules pulls her new Louis Vuitton handbag out of its brown dustcover and makes quick work of moving all her things into it.

"Yeah, I think so. That's an awesome handbag." Aside from shoes, handbags are my weakness, and I can't help but ooh and aah over my pretty new Gucci bag.

"Have I mentioned that I like your boyfriend?" Jules smirks.

"He is an over-the-top guy, that's for sure."

"He really loves you, Nat. I can see it written all over him. He just wants you to be happy."

My heart goes a little gooey at her statement. She's right. And if spoiling me with some new things makes him happy, who am I to complain?

"Did you warn your family about him? I don't want them to go fan crazy on him today."

"Yeah, I did. They've had plenty of time to go fan crazy in private. You know they'll be cool. Besides, I have brothers. They don't care that he's sexy."

"Good point." We smile at each other and then head upstairs to primp for tonight.

"HELLO, GORGEOUS." LUKE pulls me in his arms and kisses me soundly.

"Hello, handsome." I smile up at him and usher him inside the house.

"Are you ladies ready?" He looks delicious in his black jeans and untucked white button-down shirt.

I run my fingers through his soft blond hair. "Yes."

"You look happy." He kisses my cheek and hugs me to him again. "And beautiful in this red blouse."

"It's new." I feel my cheeks flush.

"Yeah? I like it very much."

"Thank you, for everything." I kiss him, cupping his beautiful face in my hands.

"Did you have fun?"

"We had a great time. You spoiled us today. Thank you for including Jules."

"I'm fond of Jules."

"Oh?" I raise an eyebrow.

"She loves you, and she's your best friend."

Damn, he's just so sweet.

"Oh God, please don't be like this all night." Jules walks into the foyer and rolls her eyes.

"Hello to you, too." Luke laughs and kisses my forehead, then releases me.

"Thanks for today, Luke. We had a great time, and I am now the proud owner of this delightful handbag." Jules smiles sweetly.

"It suits you. You're welcome. Shall we go?"

I grab my camera bag and follow Luke out to the car. He raises an eyebrow, glancing at my bag. "Do you think I'm going to a family dinner with a brand new baby without my camera? I'm a girl, Luke."

He smirks and opens my door for me.

Luke and I follow Jules in a separate vehicle to her parents' house. They live in a new subdivision in North Seattle where most of the houses look alike. Well-kept lawns, small front porches with hanging baskets of colorful flowers and kids riding bicycles on the sidewalks. The house is average in size, with a large backyard.

No one, even the Montgomerys themselves, know that I'm the anonymous donor who paid their mortgage off earlier this year.

"This is a nice neighborhood," Luke comments, and I smile at him.

"It is. It suits Jules' parents. They're empty nesters, so the house is the perfect size for them. I'm glad it's a nice day today. We can all sit out in the backyard. Her dad has done a great job landscaping it. You'll love it."

We pull up to the house, and Jules' mom, Gail, comes running out to greet us.

"Oh, my girls are home! Hello, honey." She envelops me in her arms, and I feel tears prick my eyes. This woman is so special to me.

She pulls back and looks at me, her hands still gripping my shoulders. "You look lovely, dear. Happy birthday."

"Thank you, Gail. This is my boyfriend, Luke."

"Mrs. Montgomery." Luke offers his hand, but she also wraps him in a big hug.

"It's so nice to meet you, Luke. Please, call me Gail. Welcome."

His smile is wide and a little bit shy. "Thank you."

"Hi, Mom." Jules hugs her mom tightly.

"Everyone else is here. We're in the backyard. Your dad is grilling, and I'm praying he doesn't burn the house down."

Luke takes my hand, and we wander through the beautifully furnished home, past the state-of-the-art kitchen and out to the backyard. I smile at Luke's gasp.

"I told you," I murmur to him.

The back of the house faces a greenbelt, so there are no neighbors behind them. The yard is just under an acre. Beautiful shrubs and bushes border the tall privacy fence that encloses the yard. Stone paths lined with solar lights lead to different gardens. There is a riot of color from all the flowers, reds and yellows, purples, pinks. Some of the gardens have little benches next to them to sit and enjoy the day.

There are also large fruit trees for shade. Steven Montgomery spends endless hours on this garden, and it shows.

The patio is also large and covered. A huge stainless steel grill occupies the far left corner, smoke billowing out of it. Two round patio tables, with six chairs around each, sit in the middle of the patio, and to the far right is a seating area of two rocking love seats.

"I could spend all day out here," Luke murmurs, and I nod.

I glance at the tables and spot two familiar, but unexpected faces, and whirl around to Luke. "Your parents are here!"

He blushes a bit and shrugs. "Jules asked me if she could invite them, and I thought it would be a good idea. I want our families to get to know each other, Nat."

"Wow." I'm struck dumb. He never stops surprising me.

"Is it okay?"

Is it okay? I love him. His parents are lovely, and yes, I want them to know my family. Jules' family is the only family I have.

"It's great."

He smiles, relieved, and kisses my hand.

I lead Luke over to the tables and begin introducing him to Jules' large family, hugging Lucy and Neil.

"It's so good to see you, darling girl." Lucy holds me extra tight, and I return the embrace.

"Thank you for coming. I'm happy to see you both."

Jules' dad abandons the grill and jogs toward me. "Come here, birthday girl!" He sweeps me up in a big hug and twirls me around in a circle. "You're too thin. I'm going to fatten you up today."

I laugh and kiss his smooth cheek. He's a shorter man, but made of solid muscle like his sons, and balding on top, though he used to be blond like his daughter. He's one of the kindest men I've ever known. "I can't wait. I'm hungry."

"Good. Is this your man?" He turns to Luke and holds out a hand.

"Yes, this is Luke."

"Some kind of fancy movie star, aren't you?" Oh God. He's going to give Luke a hard time. A hush falls over the patio as everyone stops talking to listen to the exchange.

I blush scarlet and start to interrupt, but Luke puts his hand on my elbow and smiles down at me before shaking Steven's hand firmly.

"No, sir, I'm not fancy or a star. Thank you for including me and my family here today."

"Am I going to have to kill you for hurting her?" Steven keeps Luke's hand in his own, narrowing his eyes at him, and I just want to die. Now.

Holy fucking shit.

Luke laughs. "No, sir. Can I help you at the grill?"

"You know your way around a grill?" Steven smiles, and I exhale deeply.

"I do."

"Well, why didn't you say? We're cooking ribs and chicken." And just like that, Steven slaps Luke on the back and leads him over to the grill.

Jules' brothers wander over to introduce themselves to Luke and offer him a beer, and the chatter resumes.

Isaac's wife, Stacy, hugs me tight. "Happy birthday." She's a petite woman with red hair and laughing blue eyes.

"Thank you. You look fantastic! Where's the baby?" My eyes scan the patio until I find Sophie cradled in Jules' arms on one of the rocking love seats.

Stacy and I join her, and I hold my hands out. "Baby. Mine."

Jules laughs. "I just got her."

"I don't care. I've never held her. Hand her over, Montgomery."

Jules passes me little Sophie, and I just melt. She is tiny, less than two weeks old. Her dark hair is long and soft and a little wild in the way baby hair is, and Stacy has put a pretty pink headband on her. She's in a beautiful pink little dress with pink bloomers, and she's barefoot.

I run my hand down her cheek and press my lips to her forehead. She's sleeping, oblivious to the party going on around her.

"Oh, Stacy, I'm in love with her." I smile up at the new mother, and she preens.

"She's such a good baby."

"She's precious." I look down at her again and move her so she's resting on my chest, curled up under my chin. I rub her back and begin to rock and hum. There is just nothing like having a newborn on you.

"You're so sweet," I murmur down to her.

I look up to meet Luke's intense gaze. He's watching me, his look unreadable. What's he thinking?

I smile at him, and one corner of his mouth curls up, and his eyes soften.

I glance to my left and find Lucy's gaze also trained on me thoughtfully. A slow smile spreads across her face, and she winks at me.

Sophie makes a mewling sound, and I look down at her. I grab her pacifier and plug it into her mouth, and she sucks greedily as I run my fingertips down her soft hair.

"Natalie!"

"Huh?"

Jules is laughing. "I asked you if you brought your camera."

"Of course. I'm holding my newest model now. Maybe we can get some family shots after dinner?"

"Absolutely. Now give me back the baby."

"No."

"You're so selfish." Jules scowls at me, and Stacy laughs.

"Yes. Sophie and I are going for a walk." I stand with her and wander down one of the paths to a shady garden.

"Aren't the flowers pretty, Sophie?" I croon to the sleepy baby and rock her back and forth.

"You're good with her." Luke has joined us, and I smile lazily at him.

"I love babies. I never had siblings, so I'm living vicariously through Jules." I shrug and kiss Sophie's head.

He reaches out and runs the back of his finger down Sophie's cheek, and I feel my heart flip. His finger looks so big on her tiny little cheek.

"She's sweet," I murmur.

"You're sweet." He tucks a strand of my hair behind my ear and runs his thumb down my jaw before slipping his hand back in his pocket.

I gaze down at the sleeping baby, and for the first time in my life, I imagine that I might have this one day. A husband and a baby, and when I picture it in my head, it's this man before me by my side.

I've got it bad. Stop this. Get rid of the baby.

"Hey! Dinner's ready, and I want that baby back!" Jules is standing at the edge of the patio yelling toward us, and I smile at Luke.

"I'm gonna have to arm wrestle her later to get this baby back."

Luke laughs and escorts us to the patio for dinner.

THIS HAS BEEN the best birthday dinner of my life. The Montgomerys have seamlessly folded Luke's family into their own, engaging them in lively conversation and enjoying their company. Neil and Lucy seem relaxed and happy, laughing with Steven and Gail, sharing stories about when their children were young.

All of the brothers—Isaac, Will, Caleb and Matt—have teased Luke mercilessly about being a famous actor, asked questions about pretty actresses, and done a lot of talking about football since Will is currently playing with the Seahawks, and they're men.

What is it about boys and football?

Luke has laughed more than I've ever seen him, and I've fallen even more in love with him while watching him with my family. He's been attentive to me, refilling my drink, holding my hand and keeping tabs on where I am all evening. I suspect I would have felt smothered by anyone else, but he makes me feel loved.

Because he loves me.

Baby Sophie has been passed around all evening and is currently lying quietly in Lucy's arms. Lucy is cooing at her.

"Aren't grandkids the best?" Gail smiles softly at her beautiful granddaughter.

"We don't have any yet, but I can't wait." Lucy grins at Gail and then over at Luke, and he squirms in his seat.

I can't help but laugh out loud at him.

"Do you find me funny, baby?" Luke narrows his eyes at me, but I see the humor in them.

"Yes, that was funny."

"Okay, cake time!" Jules comes out of the house carrying a beautiful chocolate cake with twenty-six candles lit on it.

"You're going to burn the house down with that, Jules."

She smirks and sets it in front of me.

"Make a wish," Luke whispers in my ear.

I blow all the candles out in one breath.

Gail cuts the cake and passes it around. It smells heavenly. Gail makes the most delicious cakes.

"Thank you for making my favorite cake, Gail." I lean over and kiss her cheek.

"You're welcome, darling. I love you."

"I love you, too."

"Okay, now presents!" Jules hops up, and I frown.

"No presents. How many times do I have to tell you people? No presents!"

Everyone just laughs at me.

"We don't listen to you, brat." Isaac smirks at me, and I glare at him.

"I don't like you."

"You love me."

"You guys do too much for me already." I glance at Luke nervously. "It embarrasses me when you buy me stuff."

"It's not your birthday unless you have presents." Jules sets a red gift bag in front of me. "Open mine first." She's hopping in her seat in excitement, and my mood lifts.

She's bought me my favorite perfume and a beautiful silver bracelet. "Oh, thank you! I love it!"

"Can I borrow it?" Jules asks.

We all laugh, and I'm relaxed again, enjoying my family.

As usual, they've gone a bit overboard. The brothers all pitched in on a gift card.

"More shopping!" Jules and I exclaim in unison, and we break out into giggles.

Luke laughs next to me and kisses my temple, and I smile shyly at him.

Lucy and Neil give me a very generous gift card to use at the Microsoft Store in Bellevue. Wow.

"Thank you so much."

"Our pleasure, dear." Lucy smiles and kisses Sophie's sweet head.

"Ours next." Gail hands me a purple gift bag with purple paper.

"This party is more than enough!"

"You will not sass us." Steven shakes his finger at me and tries to look stern, but I've heard this before, and I giggle. "I will take you over my knee."

"Yes, sir." I open the bag to find a pair of earrings that I recognize, and I gasp, searching their faces.

They are both smiling tenderly at me.

"These are yours." I look back down at the beautiful diamond drop earrings and run my finger over them. They've been recently cleaned and sparkle in the soft evening light.

"We want you to have them." Gail has tears in her eyes, and I'm about to join her.

"They were your mother's. They should go to Jules." My voice is thick with tears.

"I have plenty of jewelry. They should be yours. Nana loved you." Jules is running her hand down my hair, and I just know that if I move I will cry. I'm so overwhelmed by the love this family has for me.

I shake my head but scoot my chair back and round the table to hug Gail and Steven tightly. Gail dabs at her eyes, and Steven cups my face in his hands and grins at me.

"We love you, baby girl."

"I love you, too. Thank you."

I take my seat and look up into Luke's beautiful face. He smiles and kisses my fingers.

"Last but not least." Luke sets a manila envelope before me.

"No, honey, you've done way too much already." I shake my head and scoot it back across the table toward him.

"Open it," he says, exasperated, and pushes it back toward me.

"Just open it already!" Will yells from across the table, and I glare at him. "I can't take the damn suspense!"

We all laugh, and I open the envelope. I pull out two passports and an itinerary. I read the itinerary and feel the blood leave my face and my jaw drop.

"We're going to Tahiti?!"

The table erupts with whoops and whistles and shouts of joy. The brothers applaud, giving Luke a standing ovation, and he laughs.

"Yes, tomorrow, for a week."

"But, we have work."

"My current project just wrapped, and I'm hoping you'll reschedule your appointments." He's gazing down at me with love shining from his blue eyes.

"Wow. Tahiti?"

He laughs and kisses me, square on the mouth, in front of my whole family.

"Get a room!" Matthew yells.

I clear my throat and look around the patio. "I just want to say," I begin and blink the tears from my eyes, "all the people I love the most in this world are here, and I can't tell you how thankful I am to have you. Thank you for all you've done for me, and not just these gifts, though they are wonderful. I am blessed. Even the boys have their good moments." I smile at them, and they salute me with their drinks and throw winks at me.

I take a deep breath. "Thank you for making me a part of your family. I love you very much."

I look up at Luke and around the patio into each face that is so dear to me.

"Now, give me that baby."

# twenty-two

**"I** enjoyed them." Luke links his fingers with mine and kisses my knuckles as he drives us back toward Alki Beach.

"They enjoyed you, too. Thank you for coming, and inviting your parents. I had a great time." I can't hide my delighted smile.

"I'm glad. Are you excited about our trip?" His grin is wide.

"I have a lot to do tonight to get ready. Maybe I should stay home tonight so I can pack and make calls and stuff."

Luke frowns. "It won't take me long to pack. I can drop you off at home, go pack, and come back to your place." He swallows and glances at me.

"What's wrong?" Why does he suddenly look nervous?

"I don't want you to bail on me."

"Bail on you?"

"Yeah, decide you don't want to go."

Where is this vulnerability coming from? "I do want to go."

"Good." He smiles at me.

I find it doesn't take me long to pack either. A whole week in Tahiti entails a few bikinis, sarongs, pullovers and flip-flops. I also add one nice tank dress, in case we have dinner, and a pair of heels, some shorts and tank tops.

I'll throw my toiletries together in the morning before our nine a.m. flight.

I sit at the kitchen table and begin calling next week's clients to reschedule when I hear Luke come in through the front door.

"Baby?"

"In the kitchen!"

"Hey." He leans down and kisses me sweetly, and I sigh.

"Hi. Gonna make some calls. Make yourself at home."

"Okay." He saunters into the kitchen and grabs a bottle of water out of the fridge.

Half an hour later, all my calls are made, appointments rescheduled, and I'm officially on vacation.

Imagine that!

I have a huge, cat-ate-the-canary grin on my face as I crawl into Luke's lap where he sits on my couch. He's been reading a script.

"Well, hello, happy girl." He nuzzles my neck.

"Hi, obsessively generous boyfriend." He laughs and wraps his arms gently around me.

"I am looking forward to lying on a sandy beach with you, baby."

"Hmm . . . me, too. And snorkeling!"

"You snorkel?" He continues to nuzzle my neck and nips at my ear, and I squirm.

"Yeah, I have. It's been awhile."

"You smell so good. What else do you want to do?"

"Well, for one whole day . . ." I run my fingers through his hair and lean back so I can look at the pretty.

"Yes?"

"I want to stay naked and in bed with you."

"That's going to be my favorite day on this whole vacation." He runs his hand gently up and down my back, and I grin.

"Me, too. Are we staying in one of those huts that sits over the water?"

"Yes."

"Cool. We can skinny-dip."

He laughs delightedly. "Aren't you just the exhibitionist?"

"No, we'll do it at night." I lay my head on his shoulder and sigh deeply, suddenly tired but completely relaxed. "Can I bring my camera?"

"I assumed you would."

"I won't if it makes you uncomfortable." I made sure to be careful not to capture his photo tonight after dinner while I was taking photos of little Sophie and the rest of our families.

"I trust you completely. You can take my picture."

I sit upright in his lap, my jaw dropped and eyes wide. "I can?"

"Well, we're going to want pictures from our vacation, aren't we? Natalie, after everything that we've done, how can I not trust you to take my picture? We should have memories together."

I feel my smile grow, and I'm just so . . . happy. "I'm dying to take your picture, and before you freak out on me . . ."

"I'm not going to freak out on you," he says with a laugh.

"I want to take your photo because it's what I do, and you are so beautiful, Luke. There have been so many moments that I wish I could capture. I would never share any of our images with anyone unless I had your permission, but I want photos of you. I want photos of us together."

"I want photos of us, too."

I hug him tightly and then lay my head on his shoulder again.

"Are you sleepy?" he murmurs as he rhythmically runs his fingers through my hair.

"A little." I gaze up into his beautiful blue eyes. "Thank you."

"Baby, I told you, I enjoy spoiling you."

"No, not that." I shake my head and look down. "Although, yes, thank you for that, too. I just . . ."

"What?" He tilts my chin back up so he can see me.

"I love you."

His eyes flare, and he inhales deeply. "I love you, baby."

"Let's go to bed."

"My pleasure." He lifts me effortlessly in his arms and carries me upstairs.

"IT'S GOING TO be a long flight." My voice is strong, but my stomach is in knots. Luke has hired a driver to take us to the airport, and we are in the back seat. I'm clutching on to his strong hand and worrying my lip with my teeth.

"We'll be fine." He pulls me over into his lap and nuzzles my neck. I recognize the distraction tactic, but it doesn't help.

"Do we have a layover in LA?" I ask.

"No."

"Oh." I frown and catch my breath when his lips graze the sensitive spot below my ear. "I didn't know there were direct flights from Seattle to Tahiti."

"I don't know if there are. A friend of mine is lending us his jet."

"Oh." Holy shit.

"Nat, have you flown since your parents passed?" He tilts my chin and looks into my eyes, and he looks nervous and worried about me.

I cup his cheek in my hand. "No."

"Baby, are you okay with this?" He kisses my palm.

"I'll be fine. It's like ripping off a Band-Aid. I just have to do it."

"If it makes you feel better, I plan to keep you fully occupied for most of the flight. You won't have time to be scared." He grins mischievously at me, and I giggle.

"Promises, promises . . ."

Before long, we arrive at SeaTac. The driver pulls onto the tarmac next to a large private jet. This is much bigger than anything my dad ever flew.

The driver opens our door and then begins transferring our luggage to the beautiful aircraft. Luke speaks with the pilot and co-pilot and the pretty flight attendant, but my ears are buzzing with too much nervousness to hear, or care, what they're saying.

The inside of the cabin is beautiful. It must seat twelve. The seats are large and plush black leather. Luke leads me to two that are side-by-side, and we sit.

"How are you?"

"How do I look?" I whisper.

"Pale and glassy-eyed."

"So, terrified then."

"Yes."

"That's accurate."

Luke buckles my seat belt for me—Geez!—and wraps an arm around me. "I've got you, baby."

"I know. I'll be fine in a little while."

His beautiful blue eyes are heavy with worry, and I pull his head down so I can kiss him. He sweeps his lips across mine in that way he has that makes me quiver inside and runs his fingers through my hair.

"You look beautiful today."

I'm just in blue jeans and a green tank top. I take in his black T-shirt and khaki shorts and grin. "Back at you, handsome."

The pilot's voice comes over the speakers announcing that we're ready for takeoff, what our altitude will be, and how long the flight will be. Thankfully, it should be a fairly smooth flight.

I hear the engines roar to life, and I pull out of Luke's arms so I can clutch his hand. Within seconds, we are racing down the runway and lifting off the ground.

I think I'm going to pass out.

"Breathe, baby."

I pull in a deep breath and let it out.

"Again. Stay with me, baby, just breathe."

God, I love him even more at this moment. His voice is calming me, and as we gain altitude and even out, I begin to calm.

"I'm okay," I whisper.

"Can I get you something?" The tall, leggy, blond flight attendant is at our side. I didn't notice how attractive she was before. "I can fix you some breakfast, if you like."

I shake my head adamantly. "Just water, please."

"Water for both of us, please."

We sip on the cool water, Luke's eyes still trained on my face, and I flush just a bit.

"So, whose plane is this?" I ask.

"Spielberg's." He grins at me.

Holy fuck.

"As in Steven?" I ask.

"The same. He directed the film that just wrapped that I helped produce. We've worked together a few times. I called in a favor." He shrugs.

"I am so out of my league with you." I shake my head.

"What the fuck does that mean?"

My head snaps around at his angry outburst, and my jaw drops at the glare he's sending me.

"I'm sorry . . ." I frown and gaze around the cabin of the plane. This is beyond rich. I know rich. This is *Forbes* 100 list, I-could-buy-a-Third-World-country rich.

"This isn't mine. I borrowed it. I thought you'd like it."

"I do. All of this is wonderful. You are wonderful. You just over-whelm me sometimes, Luke."

"Yeah, well, that seems to be contagious then, because you have completely beguiled me."

I'm feeling vulnerable and scared and excited and in love, and I just need to be in his arms. So I unbuckle my belt and fling one leg over his lap and straddle him. His eyebrows rise in surprise, and he grabs my curvy ass in his hands. I love that he's tall enough that even in this po-sition we're practically at eye level. I grip his smooth face in my hands and lean in and kiss him like my life depends on it.

I feel his hands run up and down my back, and I grind my center against him.

"Fuck, baby, you make me crazy."

"Hmm . . ." I nibble at the corner of his mouth and open my eyes to find his blue gaze on me. "I want you. Make me forget where we are."

He takes control of the kiss, gripping my hair in his hands and holding my face to his, kissing me like he hasn't touched me in days.

As if we didn't make love just this morning.

He reaches between us and unbuckles his seat belt and lifts me easily, his hands planted firmly on my ass to hold me. I wrap my legs around his lean waist and tangle his hair in my hands, leaning my arms on his shoulders.

"Where are we going?" I murmur.

"Bedroom." Bedroom? On a plane?

"What's wrong with the chair we were in?" I lean down and bite his earlobe.

"I'm not giving the flight attendant a fucking show."

"Oh." I forgot. This is what he does to me. He makes me forget. And it's so hot!

He carries me to the rear of the plane and through a door into a small room with a double bed. It has beautiful, inviting linens and pillows in shades of browns and greens.

"Airplane sex!" I straighten in his arms and hold his face in my hands. "I've never had airplane sex."

He grins wide and kisses my chin. "Me neither."

I run my fingers lightly through his soft blond hair and gaze into his sky-blue eyes and can't help but wonder what I did to deserve this beautiful man.

"You are so beautiful." He frowns at my change of pace and just stands there in the middle of the room with me draped around him, not putting me down.

He shakes his head and plants a kiss on my collarbone. "I'm nothing special."

"Oh, honey." I wrap myself around him and hold on tight. "You are beautiful, inside and out," I whisper in his ear.

"Naked, now," he growls and sets me down.

I can't help but laugh, as suddenly we are just a tangle of clothes being flung off and flown about the room, both of us eager to get naked and touch each other.

When the last piece of clothing is shed, Luke grabs for me, pulling me to him in a passionate embrace, but instead of pushing us down onto the bed, he's cornered me against the wall, leaning his heavy torso and hips against me, his rigid erection pushing against my belly.

He slides his hands down my arms, links his fingers in mine and pulls our hands up above my head, pinning me in place. His gloriously soft mouth is on my neck, sweeping up and down. He captures both of my wrists in one hand and glides the other down my arm and to my breast to worry my nipple between his fingers.

"Fuck, Luke."

"God, you're so beautiful. I love how your breast feels in my hand."

I bow my body off the wall, my hands still pinned above me, in need.

"Hush, baby." His hand leisurely travels down to my hip and around to my ass where he rubs it softly, then slaps it. Hard.

"Ah!" I feel his grin in my neck, and I bite my lip. How does his slapping my ass turn me on so much? It's fucking sexy as hell.

"Again," I whisper.

"Oh, baby." He kisses my chin and the corners of my mouth, nibbling along my jaw. "You want it rough?"

"Only with you." And it's the truth. Only he can touch me the way he does and make my skin sing the way it does. It's intoxicating.

"Damn right." He slaps me again and hitches my leg up around his thigh, but he's too tall to rub his cock against my center.

"Lift me," I beg.

"Oh, I will. Patience, beautiful." That glorious hand of his slips behind me again, over my now warm ass, and down between my folds. He slips a finger inside me and moves it in a circular motion, sending me spiraling in sensation.

"Luke! Please!" I'm pulling my wrists against his hand to no avail. I want to touch him! I want him inside me!

"What do you want, baby?" He croons to me as he assaults my pussy in the most delicious way.

"You. Please." I whisper this against his neck.

"You'll have me. Be patient, my love. I'm making you forget, remember?"

"I don't remember my own fucking name right now."

He laughs and kisses me sweetly. "I'm going to let go of your hands now. Put them on your head."

"What?" He's not making any sense.

"Just put them on your head."

"I want to touch you." I pout, and he bites my lower lip.

"Not yet. Trust me."

He releases my hands, and I lower them to my head, weaving my fingers together and leaning my head back on the wall.

"Good. Don't move your hands, baby."

"Okay," I whisper.

He continues to kiss my face and neck, gently bites my earlobe and then heads south.

And I know exactly what he's going to do.

"Fuck." I look down at him as he kisses his way down to my breasts, pulling the nipples into his mouth. My breathing is ragged and blood is rushing though my body on hyperdrive.

I've never been so turned on in my life.

"Easy, baby. I've got you."

As he kneels on the floor, he hitches my right leg around his shoulder and wraps his arms around me, supporting me on his forearms and gripping my ass in his large hands.

"I'm going to fall."

"I won't let you fall." He kisses my belly piercing and then places three sweet kisses on my tattoo.

Without thinking, I lower a hand and run my fingers through his hair, but he jerks his head away and glares at me.

"On. Your. Head."

Oh.

"I want to touch you."

"Later. Come on, baby, play along."

"Okay." My hand goes back on my head, and without hesitation, his lips wrap around my clitoris, and he sucks.

Holy fucking shit!

"Fuck!" My hips push against his mouth, and he pulls back slightly to move down to my lips where he kisses me intimately, running his tongue up and down and around me, teasing me. He nibbles gently and then buries his tongue inside me while inhaling my scent.

I can't take my eyes off of him. Seeing his mouth on me is the most erotic thing I've ever witnessed.

His hands are kneading my ass. His right hand, still supporting my weight, slides closer to my center. He dips his littlest finger in my wet core and flexes it and pulls it out, and as his mouth resumes its delicious torture, he slips that little finger right . . . there.

His molten blue eyes are looking up at my face. I'm so overwhelmed with sensation it's weakening. That finger is moving slowly in and out, and the feeling is unimaginable. It makes me feel just a little dirty and wanton and oh so hot.

His presses his nose on my clitoris, and it's all over. He's pushing all my buttons—literally—and I fall apart, shuddering and pulsating, coming over and over. It just doesn't seem like it'll ever stop.

He pulls his pinkie out of me and kisses up my pubis, my belly, over my breasts and, finally, my lips. He's pinned me against the wall again with his body, because without him, I would collapse onto the floor.

"Please," I mewl, not recognizing my own voice.

"Anything, baby."

"Fuck me."

His gaze finds mine, and it darkens. "I just did," he murmurs against my mouth, brushing his lips back and forth. He grips my hands in his again and holds them over my head.

"Fuck me on that bed." I kiss him. "Please."

He holds me against his chest and twirls us across the short floor to the bed. He tears the duvet away from the sheets and guides me down onto it.

"On your stomach, baby."

I roll over flat on my stomach, and he's suddenly covering me, his hard cock pressing against my buttocks, his chest hair tickling my back. He kisses the very center of my neck and follows my spine down, paying extra attention to the tattoo in the center of my back.

"Why does it say Love Deeply?" he asks.

"What?"

"Why this tattoo?"

I have to blink and pull some brain cells back together to answer his question.

"Because that's what I always wanted, to love and be loved deeply."

He nuzzles the tattoo with his nose. "You are, Nat."

"I know."

I feel his smile as he resumes his journey down my back. He kisses my butt, one cheek at a time, and then sweeps his lips across the tattoo on my right thigh, under my buttock.

"And this one? Why does it say Happiness Is A Journey?"

"Because it was a long journey to travel for me to be happy again."

"Oh, baby." He parts my legs with his own and runs a finger from my anus down to my clitoris, making me angle my behind off the bed and into the air.

"Ah, Luke."

He grips my hips and slides into me, burying himself inside me as far as he can.

It's glorious. I feel full and happy and sexy and so loved.

He slaps the cheek that was ignored when he had me pinned against the wall and starts to move in and out of me, slamming into me hard, over and over.

I grip the sheets in my fists and cry out as I feel the familiar pull of the muscles around his cock and my legs clench. He grips my hips, almost painfully, as he slams into me once more and comes violently, erupting inside me.

# twenty-three

I'm standing on the deck of our gloriously beautiful hut, pointing my camera down at the water, snapping photos of the brightly colored fish. I take about a dozen photos, then look up and snap some shots of the island. It's almost sunset, and I can't wait to get some photos of the palm tree silhouettes in the sunset light.

"Hey, baby." Luke wraps his arms around me from behind and buries his nose in my neck. "How are you?"

"I think I'm going to be a little sore tomorrow, but I'm good. I forgot how exhausting snorkeling is." I smile and turn to face him.

He simply takes my breath away.

He's shirtless, wearing only black shorts that hang off his hips in that sexy way, showing off the muscles that form that V that runs down and disappears in the fabric. He's caught some sun while we've been here, turning his skin golden. My mouth goes dry every time I look at him.

And because I can, I raise my lens and snap his photo. He smiles shyly, and I take another.

"I love taking your picture."

"I've noticed. You've had that thing pointed at me more than anything else in the three days we've been here."

"That's not true." I laugh, and he takes the camera out of my hands, and suddenly I become the subject. "Hey! I'm on the wrong side of that lens."

"Turnabout is fair play, baby. Give me that sweet smile."

I lean back on the railing and pose for him playfully, cocking one hip to the side and planting my hand on my sarong-covered curve.

"We have to come here often," he murmurs as he continues to snap photos of me.

"Why?"

"Because I love watching you walk around all day in a bikini. I get to see your tattoos."

I smile and turn away from him. My left side is exposed to him, and I raise my left arm up next to my face, looking back at him through the crook of my elbow. "Take a photo of this tat, and you can look at it any time you want."

"God, you're good at this." He snaps away, his eyes shining with humor and lust, and I smile at him.

"Okay, hold on." I take off the sarong and let it fall to the floor of the deck and watch his eyes dilate. I love how he enjoys my body. My earlier insecurities have long vanished. I turn my back to him and pull my hair over my shoulder. My hands are out to my sides, resting on the railing. I know that from this view, he can see the tattoos on my back and my upper thigh. "There you go."

I hear my camera snapping to life, and Luke's breathing has changed.

"Finished with those?" I ask.

"Yes," he whispers.

I turn back to face him and jump up on the rail, sitting.

"Careful!"

"I'm fine. I won't fall in." I scoot so I'm sitting at an angle and pull my right foot up to rest on the railing. My tattoo is exposed. "Snap away."

He zooms in on my foot and presses the shutter about ten times.

"I hate to disappoint you," I mutter drily, "but the last tattoo will have to just remain our little secret."

His eyes darken as he steps back and takes more photos of me.

"So no one else has seen these tattoos?" he asks, the camera still up at his face.

"Most of them."

"What does that mean?" He lowers the camera and glares at me.

Crap.

"The one on my pubis is the newest one, and no one but you and the artist have seen it. The one on my back can sometimes be seen when I'm wearing a certain style of top or dress, but no one's ever asked me what it means. In fact, no one but you knows what any of them mean."

"And your side and leg?" he asks.

I shrug. "I wasn't a virgin when I met you."

He frowns and looks down, and I'm desperate to lift this mood.

"Hey." I hop off the rail and close the gap between us. "The past is over, Luke. For both of us."

"I know." He swallows and looks at me with those blue eyes. "It just makes me a little crazy that other men have touched you."

"Honey"—I smile and run my fingers down his face—"your touch is the only one that's ever mattered. You've introduced me to feelings I didn't know existed. Don't worry about before. You are all I see. Besides"—I take the camera back from him and put the lens cap back on—"you, my love, were certainly no virgin, either."

"How do you know? Maybe I was." He chuckles.

"There is no way that you can be as good as you are in bed and be a virgin."

"Oh? How good am I?" He winks at me and pulls me into his arms, running his hands down my mostly naked back.

"Hmm . . . you're fair."

He laughs as he bends down and places feather-soft kisses at the side of my mouth. "Fair, huh?"

"Yeah, I endure it. For your sake."

"You just endure it?" He continues to move those skilled, soft lips across my jaw and over to my ear.

"It's a real hardship, but somehow I find the willpower."

He chuckles and cups my face gently in his hands, sweeping his lips over mine, back and forth lightly, then sinks down into me and kisses me deeply but still softly. Lovingly. Like we have all day. I hold on to his hips, lacing my middle fingers through the belt loops, half of my hands on the fabric and half on his bare skin.

God, my man can kiss.

He pulls back and, still holding my face, gazes into my eyes.

"Wow," I murmur, and his face lights up with humor.

"Did you endure that okay?"

"You are really good at that."

"So are you. Did you bring a dress?"

I blink at the change of subject. "Yeah, why?"

"I have something planned for dinner."

"Oh. I was going to take sunset pictures."

"You still can. Bring the camera along."

"Okay. When are we leaving?"

"In a half hour."

"Where are we going?" I ask.

"It's a surprise, birthday girl." He smiles and runs his thumb across my lower lip.

"My birthday is over."

"This is your birthday vacation, so you're still the birthday girl." He kisses me chastely, then links my hand with his and leads me inside.

Our hut, although hut is really the wrong word for it, is absolutely breathtaking. It's really a bungalow over the water. No little hotel hut would be sufficient for my man.

Our space is large, sporting two bedrooms, a large common area and two bathrooms. The bigger of the two bathrooms has a two-person tub that sits right out in the open on a deck, with open views of the ocean. In fact, most of the rooms are open to the outside air with beautiful floaty curtains to pull for a little privacy. The floors are dark wood, but there are glass openings in most of the rooms so you can look down at the fish below.

The furnishings are plush, expensive and inviting. The master bed is large with soft white sheets, duvet and pillows. The common area has plenty of color: oranges, yellows and reds. It's truly beautiful.

"Have you been here before?" I ask as I pull out my dress and heels.

"No, first time. You won't need the heels."

"Oh, okay. Flip-flops?"

"Yeah."

"Are we going somewhere in the sand?"

He smiles and winks.

Okay, not gonna tell me. "Are you going to change?"

He pulls on a white short-sleeved button-down shirt and leaves it unbuttoned. "There, all changed."

I laugh and reach behind me to pull the strings on my bikini, letting it fall in my hands. Looking down, I do the same to the bottoms. I walk naked to the dresser and reach in for a thong.

"No underwear."

I turn and gape at him. His eyes are smoldering.

"But . . ."

"No. Underwear."

Geez. He's so bossy. And I like it. Weird.

"Okay." I pull the black tank dress over my head and smooth it in place and slip my feet in my black flip-flops. I run my brush through my hair vigorously, then tie it in a simple braid down the left side so it rests over my left breast. I brush on a light coat of mascara and turn to find Luke watching me, his expression unreadable.

"I'm ready."

He shakes his head as if pulling his thoughts together and smiles at me tenderly. "Let's go."

"SO WHAT HAS been your favorite part of our trip so far?" I ask Luke as I take a bite of my steak.

He's surprised me with dinner, in the water on a private tiny island. The resort boated us over, where the small table was already set with our meals and drinks, the table and chairs sitting in the shallow, perfectly clear water on pure white sand.

This almost rivals the vineyard on the romance scale.

"Snorkeling today was fun." He takes a sip of wine and shrugs. "My favorite part is being here with you."

I shake my head and smile. "Charming."

He laughs and continues with his meal. "How about you? Favorite part?"

"I also enjoyed the snorkeling today. The manta rays were incredible. But I really enjoyed exploring the town yesterday, too. Thank you again for the anklet."

"It's beautiful on you."

"What are we doing tomorrow?" I ask. I'm moving my feet around in the water, back and forth. It feels good between my toes.

"I seem to remember you saying something about spending a whole day in bed."

"Oh." My eyes go wide.

"Tomorrow is the halfway mark of the trip. Seems like a good time." He raises an eyebrow at me, and I grin.

"Skinny-dipping! We can scare the fish."

"And our neighbors." He smirks.

"Nah, the back of our room is secluded. I already checked."

He looks up at me, startled, and then breaks out into laughter. I smile smugly back at him and drink my wine.

"This is beautiful." I look out over the water and sigh. The sun is starting to set, and we've finished our meal. "Do you mind if I snap some pictures?"

"Go ahead, baby." He pours himself another glass of wine and sits back to watch me. I sling my camera strap around my neck—I wouldn't want to drop it in the water—and stand up, wading through the shallow water. It's warm around my ankles, the sand is soft, and the light is perfect.

I take about a hundred shots, of the water, the trees and of the tiny island itself. It's something out of a tropical island calendar. Then I turn the lens to my relaxed boyfriend and take a few shots without him seeing me. He's looking down at his wine, his expression thoughtful. He glances up at me and gives me that sexy half smile, and he's perfection. Open white shirt, black shorts, blond hair and golden skin, sitting casually at a romantic table set for two with a single red rose in a vase.

The sight is devastating.

Suddenly, he stands and walks toward me through the water and takes the camera from me. He wraps his arm around me and pulls me to his side, turning the lens toward us and snaps a picture of the two of us together.

For the past three days when we were out, if I had my camera with me, he would ask someone to take a photo of the two of us together.

Yes, we are capturing lots of memories, and it makes me smile.

He places the strap back around my neck and kisses my forehead.

"Thank you for dinner," I say. "It was delicious, and romantic."

"My pleasure."

"When are we being picked up?" I run my hands up and down his chest, under his open shirt.

"In about twenty minutes."

"Okay, let's go for a walk around the island. It's small. It should only take about ten minutes."

"Let's go." He links his fingers through mine, and we set off, wading through the ankle-deep water.

When we make it back to the table, our ride to the hut is pulling up. We board the small boat and set off across the darkening water.

I WAKE TO the sun across my face and no covers over my naked body. Luke's face is between my legs.

"Holy shit!" I come up off the bed, bracing myself on my elbows, and gaze in pure shock at Luke tilting my hips up so he can bury his face in my pussy, licking and teasing my clit.

"Good morning, baby," he whispers against my core and blows on that most sensitive spot.

"Oh my God," is all I can say as I collapse back down on the bed. I feel his grin, and he slips two fingers inside me, making a *come here* motion and light erupts through me.

Holy fuck.

I bear down and come violently as he continues to suck on my clit and rock those fingers around inside me, my muscles shuddering around him. Finally, he kisses my tattoo gently and works his magic all the way up my torso until he's lying next to me, brushing my hair off my face.

"Good morning," I murmur. "Not a bad way to wake up."

"I'm glad you approve." He kisses me, and I taste myself on him, and it ignites my libido all over again. Surprising him, I grip his shoulders and push him back on the bed, lying on top of him and resting my pulsating sex on his hard cock. Playing his game, I link my fingers in his and push our hands up to the sides of his head and hold him down.

"What are you going to do with me?" He grins, his eyes shining with desire. I roll my hips on him, and he exhales sharply.

"Well"—I bend down and bite his neck softly, then lave it with my tongue—"after that fantastic wake-up call, I think I'll fuck you."

"Is that right?" He pushes against my hands, but I hold him down with all my might. We both know he could easily break my hold, but he plays along. "I'm not stopping you, baby."

I lean forward until I feel the tip of his cock against my lips and then I sink down on him until he's completely buried in me.

"Fuck," he whispers between clenched teeth.

"You feel so good."

I start to rock, slow and shallow, back and forth, taunting and teasing him. With each downward motion, I clench my muscles around him, then let go as I rock back up. I gently sweep my lips across his and tease the tip of his nose with mine.

Just when I think he's ready to come, I stop and loosen my muscles.

"Oh, you are such a tease. I should spank you."

"I have your hands," I reply and start to rock again.

"So you do." His eyes close, and he bites his lip as I increase the tempo, and the pleasure is just too much. I let go of his hands and sit up, riding him fast and hard.

"Grab on to the bed frame." I love being the boss, and his eyes dilate even more. He complies.

Suddenly, I roll off him and grip him in my hand, and take him deep into my mouth, sucking hard.

"Holy fuck!" He grasps my head, but I pull out of his grasp and glare at him.

"On. The. Bed. Frame."

He smiles and complies, and I resume the sweet torture, licking my sweetness off him, moving my hands up and down the hardness, and he erupts in my mouth.

As he calms, I kiss my way up his body, reveling in his sculpted stomach, teasing his belly button with my teeth. I run my fingertips up his sides, and he squirms and laughs. I kiss his neck, his chin and finally place a chaste kiss on his mouth.

"Turnabout is fair play," I whisper his words from yesterday back to him, and he groans.

"Jesus, Nat, you're going to kill me."

"Ah, but what a way to go."

He laughs and kisses me tenderly, then abruptly stands up and pulls me with him, throwing me over his naked shoulder.

"I have the best view of your ass right now, my love." I give it a little slap, and he returns the favor on my ass. "Where are we going?"

"Skinny-dipping!" He jogs—*jogs!*—with me over his shoulder out to the deck and down the steps that lead to the water, and just tosses me right in.

I hit the warm surface with a loud splash and come up sputtering. It's not too deep, only about six feet, and as I push the wet hair off my face, I see Luke dive in headfirst. He gracefully swims to me, and I can't help but admire the way his back muscles move.

"Hi." I smile shyly when he surfaces before me and wrap my arms and legs around him.

"Hi." He grins and plants his hands on my waist, then throws me through the air to land back in the water.

Oh, we're going to play! Naked!

I squeal when I surface and splash him, and he splashes me back with a laugh.

He swims for me again, and I try to quickly escape, but he catches me and tosses me again.

"Are you trying to drown me?"

"Maybe I want to do some mouth-to-mouth."

"You don't have to kill me to do that! I'm a sure bet." I giggle and splash him again, enjoying the way his naked body looks in the clear water, reflecting in his perfectly blue eyes.

"God, you look beautiful right now," he says.

"I was just thinking the same thing." I swim to him and wrap myself around him again.

"I enjoy playing with you," he says and kisses my nose.

"Me, too. In and out of bed." I smile sassily, and he bites his lip.

"I have to say, this morning was a first for me."

"A good first, or a bad first?" I run my fingers through his wet hair, loving the way our naked bodies feel twined together in the warm Pacific.

"Definitely good, although I have to admit I prefer being in control."

"Well, variety is the spice of life. I like to surprise you every once in a while." I kiss his chin, and he chuckles.

"No complaints here, baby."

"Hmm . . . good."

He lifts my hips and surprises me by slipping inside me.

I lean my forehead against his as he stills, filling me. "I love you," I say.

"Oh, baby, I love you, too. Let's frighten the fish."

# twenty-four

It's our last morning in our tropical paradise, and I purposely wake extra early to make sure I'm up before Luke. He's done so much for me this week—hell, this month—and I just have to do something special for him before we go back home to reality. Not that reality is all that bad. It's just been bliss to have him all to myself this week.

After our Naked Day, as it will forever be known in my head, Luke surprised me with a shark-feeding trip, which before this vacation I would have assumed would include me as the menu but turned out to be one of the most exhilarating experiences of my life. I'll never forget standing in waist-deep warm water with dozens of docile sharks floating around us to take the food from our hands.

Yesterday was spent getting romantic spa treatments for two. I've been to the spa more in the past two weeks than I have in the past two years.

I'm not complaining.

But today is our last day. I poke my head back in the bedroom to make sure he's still sleeping and then go wait on the steps leading to the water below the bungalow for our breakfast to be delivered by canoe. I set the food and coffee on a tray and go into the bedroom.

After placing the delicious-smelling foods on the ottoman at the end of the bed, I climb up Luke's body and kiss his lips.

"Luke, honey, wake up." I nibble his lips and kiss over to his neck as he shifts beneath me.

"Mornin'," he mumbles.

"Good morning, love. Wake up. I have something for you."

He runs his hand down my back and frowns. "Hard to make love when you're dressed, baby."

I laugh as he opens those sexy blue eyes. "That's not what I have for you." I get up off him and walk to the end of the bed as he sits up, the sheet pooling in his lap, and runs his hands over his face and through his hair. His morning stubble is impossibly sexy.

"Breakfast!" I set the tray on the bed between us and pull the silver dome lid off the plate. There are large helpings of pancakes, bacon, eggs and fruit. On the side is a carafe of coffee and two mugs.

"Did you order this?" he asks.

"Yeah, I thought I'd feed you for once."

He smiles and cups my face in his hand. "Thank you, baby."

"You're welcome. I hope you're hungry." I hold a strawberry up to his mouth, and he takes a bite, then I pop the rest in my own mouth.

"Starving," he says, his lust-filled eyes on mine.

"Later," I whisper.

"You're no fun." He pouts as he pours himself some coffee, and I laugh.

"That's not what you said last night." Thoughts of making love in the bathtub that sits out on the patio flood my mind, and I bite my lip.

"No, no complaints last night."

"What time are we leaving?" I ask.

"Not until this evening. Why?"

"Do we have any special plans today?" I eat a bite of pancake and groan. "God, that's good."

"Damn, I love to watch you eat, baby. No, I thought we'd wing it today. Did you have something in mind?"

I shrug and take another bite of pancake.

"What is it?"

"Nothing. We can do whatever you want." I avoid his gaze, suddenly shy. I don't want to go anywhere today. I just want to be with him, and I don't know why I'm suddenly so shy about speaking up and telling him so. It's silly.

"Natalie." His voice is stern, and I catch his gaze. "What's wrong?"

"Nothing's wrong. I was just thinking . . ." I put my fork down and bite my lip. "I just want to stay here, until we have to go to the airport. I want to be alone, for as long as we can, here in our tropical bubble." The last few words are a whisper, and I glance up at him to see his reaction.

He's smiling sweetly. "Why does that make you shy?"

I shrug again and look down. "I don't know. I thought you might want to go have some grand adventure before we leave, but I just want you."

"Baby, look at me." I do as he asks without hesitating and am so relieved to see his beautiful smile. "Spending the day alone with you in this beautiful tropical paradise sounds perfect to me."

"Okay." I smile at him, relieved, and continue to dig into my pancakes.

We finish our breakfast, and while Luke is in the shower, room-service-in-a-canoe comes to take away the dirty dishes and linens. The man is quite large and is talkative while he gathers the things into a box to put on the canoe.

"Your husband is a very lucky man." He smiles at me, and I smile, but inside something doesn't feel right.

What an inappropriate thing to say. I don't correct his misunderstanding about my marital status and simply say, "Thank you."

"How long have you been married?"

"Um, not long." Why is this creeping me out? I learned long ago to trust my instincts, so I cross the room so I'm standing behind a large couch, near the bathroom door.

"Oh, that's nice." He wanders over to the couch and picks at some pretend lint on the arm of the orange fabric. My heart speeds up as fear takes hold. He's trying to move closer to me, and now his eyes are predatory. "I've noticed you this week. You're very beautiful."

"I think you'd better go now." I move around the other side of the couch away from him, but he's following me, and my heart is in my throat.

"Why?"

"Because I don't want you here. My husband will be out any

minute, and I'm not interested. Get the fuck out or I'll have you fired."

"You can't do that. My uncle owns this resort." He laughs and starts to come at me faster.

"Luke!" I scream, but before the word is out of my mouth, the large man is thrown from behind and slammed into a wall. Luke, his breath heaving and his face contorted in rage, is gripping on to his throat. He punches him in the face, twice, and blood spurts out of the man's nose, and he screams like a girl.

I'm quite sure no one has dared lay a hand on him before.

"I'm going to make sure you don't ever try to touch another woman at this resort again, you fucker." Luke's voice is cold and calm, his eyes glacial, and this is a very angry side to him I've never seen before.

"Are you okay, baby?" He doesn't look at me as he speaks, doesn't take his eyes off of him.

"I'm fine." My voice is stronger than I feel, and I'm glad.

"Call the main desk and tell them to call the cops. Tell them what happened."

I do as he asks and within minutes a motorboat pulls up at our bungalow with management and police, and a man who must be the asshole's uncle.

The police take control of the situation and relieve Luke of his charge. Luke then races to me and enfolds me in his arms. I must be too shocked to do more than stare wide-eyed at what's happening around us.

"Are you okay?" His hands are running up and down my back, soothing me.

"Yes, I'm okay. He didn't touch me. He was just really creepy, and I know he would have if you weren't here. He felt off the minute he came in here, so I moved behind the couch close to the bathroom in case he tried anything, and he did." I shiver, and Luke pulls me tighter to him.

The uncle is yelling for the police to arrest him. It seems this isn't the first time this has happened. The Asshole is crying and blubbering, but no one cares.

As I watch what's happening around me, the fear is replaced with pure rage. I pull out of Luke's arms and walk over to The Asshole being handcuffed by the police. He's crying down at me, weak and afraid, and before I know what I'm doing, I jerk my knee up, right between his legs and bring him to his knees.

My chest is heaving, and there is sudden silence all around us.

"I am not a victim." My voice is hard and controlled and loud because I want him to hear every word. "And you are nothing but a piece of shit."

"Did you see what she did to me? I want to press charges!" The whiny Asshole is wailing, but his uncle raises his hand, silencing him.

"I didn't see anything that you didn't deserve. Get him out of this bungalow."

He's escorted out, and the owner apologizes profusely, offering comps and refunds and anything else I can possibly imagine. I'm sure he's praying we won't go to the press, which we won't anyway.

Luke wouldn't have it.

I turn and look at Luke, whose eyes are hooded, his face hard. He tells the manager that we will still be leaving today.

"We will press charges, but I don't want this to go to the press, either," Luke murmurs, and my heart stops.

Oh my God. This could make things really bad for him if it hits the tabloids. I suddenly feel so guilty. I leave Luke to handle the rest of the business alone and go into the master bedroom to start packing.

Luke comes in the room as I'm finishing with the underwear drawer. He walks straight to me and pulls me into his strong arms, rocking me back and forth, kissing my forehead. "Are you really okay?"

"I'm so sorry."

"For what?" He pulls back and frowns down at me. "You didn't do anything wrong."

"This could be really bad for you if the tabloids catch wind of it."

"Trust me, they won't. Neither the resort nor I want that. But that's not what's important. You are, baby. Did he hurt you?"

"No, I told you, he didn't touch me. But it felt good to knee him in the balls." I smile, and Luke pulls me back to him.

"I was so scared when I came out of the bathroom and heard you scream. I saw that bastard lunge for you, and I honestly don't remember much after that. I just had to make sure he didn't touch you." He's running his thumb down my cheek, and I kiss his palm.

"Thank you."

"I will always protect you, baby. That's what I'm here for. That's what I want to do."

"I know, and it's one of the reasons why I love you. I don't know why I'm not freaking out." I shrug and grin. "I guess I just felt strong, and I knew that you were here, and that he couldn't hurt me." I run my hands through his hair. "Are you okay?"

"As long as you're okay, yes, I'm okay. God, I love how strong you are, baby. It was quite a sight watching you take him to his knees."

"You might want to remember that, in case you ever get out of line." I press my body up against his and smile up at him.

"Oh yeah? You think you can take me?" He rubs his nose across mine, and I sigh.

"Probably not, but the wrestling around part would be fun."

He laughs and smiles tenderly at me. And now, for his other present.

"So, before we were so rudely interrupted, I was going to give you a present when you got out of the shower."

His eyebrows fly up. "You got me a present?"

"Sort of, yes." I'm wearing a bathing suit cover-up that is quite conservative, in black. It's a hoodie style that zips up the front and covers me from my knees to my neck.

I step back out of Luke's grasp and begin pulling the zipper slowly down, keeping the fabric closed. When the zipper is completely undone, I shrug the fabric off my shoulders so it pools at my feet.

Luke gasps, and his eyes widen, finding mine, and his face breaks out into a face-splitting grin. I plant my hands on my naked hips and cock my head. "Do you like my outfit?"

He walks to me and runs his fingers under my pearls and kisses me in that tender way he has, and I feel my knees go weak.

"Baby, you know I love this outfit. There is nothing like looking at you wearing nothing but these pearls."

"I love the way you look at me," I whisper.

Luke's eyes skim hungrily down my body, and when his gaze returns to mine he kisses me tenderly.

"I don't want to fuck you today, Natalie," he whispers against my lips.

Oh. "You don't?" I whisper back and roll my head back, as his lips wander down my neck.

"No."

"I love your whispery voice."

He grins. "I know."

"What do you want to do?"

"I want to make slow, sweet love to you." His fingertips are just barely touching me, brushing up and down my back, sending shivers through me, and his lips mirror them on my neck. It's sensation gone mad.

"That sounds lovely."

He lifts me in his arms, and I wrap my fingers in his hair as my lips find his in a soft kiss. He gently lowers me onto the bed and covers me with his body, his legs between mine. He glides his right hand up my left arm and links our fingers, but instead of holding them above my head, he simply rests them on the bed next to my head.

This isn't about restraining me, or playing with me. This is about him showing me how much he loves me, and it fills me with so much strength and reassurance and tenderness.

He runs the fingers of his left hand through the hair by my face as he continues to kiss me, softly, gently, patiently. I rest the bottoms of my feet on his calves, rubbing up and down, caressing him, as I thrum the fingertips of my free hand up and down his strong back.

I can feel his hardness against me, but he makes no move to sink inside me. Not yet.

"You are so beautiful," he murmurs against my lips.

"You make me feel beautiful," I whisper to him, and he groans.

He plants tiny kisses at the side of my mouth. I weave my fingers into his hair and gently caress him.

"I love your hair. It feels so good in my fingers."

"I figured that," he whispers, and I feel him smile against my neck. "You always have your hands in it."

"Don't ever cut it short, please." I love hearing his whispery voice.

"Okay." He kisses my earlobe and tickles it with his teeth. "You have amazing skin, so smooth and soft. And you always smell so good."

His words are seductive. His hand is still moving in my hair, and my body is humming.

My hips start to move beneath him, and I feel his grin at my throat. "You know what you do to me."

"You do the same to me, baby." He flexes his hips, pushing his cock against my wet center. The tip slides against my clitoris, and I gasp.

"I want you."

"I know. I want you, too."

I love the whispers, the soft sighs and gasps. This is the quietest our lovemaking has ever been, and it's no less intoxicating.

Oh so slowly he begins to fill me, one delightful inch at a time, until he's buried as far as he can go. He fills me up, physically, emotionally, and I feel tears roll from the sides of my eyes.

This sweet, protective, kind, sexy man loves me. And I love him, oh so much.

"Don't cry, baby." His whispered voice is rough with emotion, and he starts to slowly move, in and out of me. My legs hitch up higher around his hips, taking him in even deeper, and as he hits that most sensitive spot, I feel sparks begin to fly through me.

"Oh, I'm gonna come, my love."

"Yes," he whispers in my ear, and I am lost, my orgasm consuming me, but I barely make a sound, caught up in our quiet lovemaking.

Luke stills, pushes into me one last time and empties himself into me, whispering my name.

# twenty-five

I've decided that being back in the real world does not suck.

We've been home from our romantic Tahitian getaway for a week, and we have fallen into a comfortable routine of work, flirty texts throughout the workday, hitting the gym or yoga together and alternating between his place and mine at night.

Tonight, we're staying at my place, and we're having dinner with Jules.

"That is not how you cook pasta!" Jules looks beautiful, as usual, as she glares at my boyfriend, and I smirk.

"How the hell do you do it?" Luke is thoroughly frustrated with her, and I'm sitting back with a glass of wine, enjoying the show.

"You have to put the salt in the water before it comes to a boil. Everyone knows that."

"You know what, you do it. I'm going to make out with my girlfriend." He leaves Jules to finish dinner and comes around the breakfast bar to kiss me.

"Is she being mean to you?" I ask and caress his face.

"No, she just doesn't know how to cook and won't listen."

"I can hear, you know." Jules glares at us, and we laugh.

I love spending evenings with these two. They both mean the world to me, and I love it that they get along so well.

"So, Luke, when does your new movie come out?" Jules is stirring the pasta.

"This Friday," he responds and takes a sip of wine.

"What?" I exclaim. I had no idea! Why doesn't he tell me these things?

"Um, I have a movie coming out on Friday."

I stare at him, dumbfounded.

Jules looks back and forth between us and then mutters, "Oops."

"Why didn't you say something?" My feelings are so hurt.

"It didn't occur to me." He frowns and shrugs.

"You have a major motion picture about to be released for millions of people to see, and it didn't occur to you to mention it to your girlfriend?" I turn and face him on my stool.

What the hell?

"I just did some of the production. I'm not starring in it or anything."

"I don't care, Luke. This is a big deal. Are you going to the premiere?"

"No, absolutely not." He shakes his head and runs his hand through his hair.

"Why? You should go. You're a part of it."

"No." He swallows hard. "I don't do that anymore."

"Either way, you should have told me. You never talk to me about your work, and you know all about mine." This is something that's been bothering me, and I'm glad Jules brought it up.

"What does a producer do, anyway?" Jules asks as she drains the pasta and starts layering lasagna in a glass dish.

"It depends on the producer. There are a lot of different roles. Some are on set during the entire production and run things there. Some work behind the scenes, securing money from a studio or wooing actors and directors. There are a lot of things to do, and there are usually a few producers doing different jobs."

"Okay, so what do you do, specifically?" I ask, sincerely interested.

"I've been doing the behind-the-scenes, preproduction stuff so I can work from here. Sometimes I have to make a trip to LA or New York for a brief meeting, but that's rare these days. Pretty much everything can be done on the phone or by e-mail. So, I talk to actors and directors, and sometimes sit in on conference calls to get money secured for a project." He's talking with his hands, so animated and enthusiastic, and it occurs to me that he really loves what he does. I smile at him and kiss his cheek.

"I'm proud of you."

"Why?"

"Because you're doing something you love, and you're good at it."

"How do you know?"

"I wouldn't be with someone who sucks." I respond sassily, and he laughs.

"So, how much money did you have to secure for the movie coming out on Friday? And who's in it anyway?" Jules slips the lasagna in the oven and leans across the counter, listening attentively.

"It's called *Rough Shot* with Channing Tatum. It's an action movie, lots of stunts and stuff blowing up, so it was high-budget. About a hundred million."

Jules and I look at each other and then back at Luke.

"I'm sorry, did you say a hundred million dollars?" My voice is very shrill. It's disturbing. Almost as disturbing as my boyfriend being responsible for raising a hundred million dollars.

"Yeah." He smiles shyly. "The action/adventure movies are always high-budget, because there's a lot of cinematography involved, CGI, and a lot of other stuff that I don't really understand but know it's expensive."

I swallow. Wow.

"So, this is a big-box-office movie then."

"Yeah, it's expected to bring in about a hundred and fifty million this weekend." He shrugs again, but I see the pride in his eyes.

"So, here's where I get personal, and you can tell me to mind my own fucking business, but I'm curious because money is what I do for a living." Jules' eyes are gleaming with curiosity, and I know exactly what she's going to ask.

"Okay, go ahead." Luke smirks. He knows, too.

"Well, I know how much actors usually get paid for big-budget films, but what about producers?"

"When all is said and done, after royalties and stuff, I'll probably bank about fifteen from this movie."

I narrow my eyes at him and bite my lip, not sure that I understand the words that just came out of his mouth. I look at Jules, and her mouth is opening and closing, also with no sound coming out.

Luke isn't looking at either of us. He's staring down at his wine.

Finally, Jules speaks first. "Please tell me you have a damn good entertainment lawyer and a team of entertainment accountants with excellent reputations. Because if you don't, I know some." She's completely serious.

Luke nods his head. "Yeah, that's all been covered for years."

"Good," she responds.

I just don't know what to say. I knew he was wealthy, but I had no idea.

Finally, Luke looks over at me. "Are you okay?"

"Fine," I whisper.

"You look a little pale." He looks worried.

"I'm okay." I shake myself out of my stare and look to Jules for guidance.

"Nat," she says, "you're no stranger to money."

"No, I'm not."

"Your parents left you, like, twenty million."

Luke blanches.

"I know."

"So, what's wrong?" she asks quietly.

I frown. "Well, I guess it's just a lot to take in." I look at Luke and finally, needing to touch him, grip his hand in mine. "I'm sorry, honey. The money isn't that big of a deal to me, you know that. I guess it's just surprising to hear that my man deals with actors and hundred-million-dollar movies and is friends with Steven Spielberg. It's easy to forget because we're so far removed from that life."

"Nat, I've removed myself on purpose."

"I know."

"Don't freak out on me," he whispers.

"I am not freaking out on you." I smile, finding my equilibrium.

"Um, can I ask one more question?" Jules raises her hand like we're in class, and we laugh.

"Okay."

"Can I have Channing Tatum's number?"

We all bust out in a laughing fit, and I'm relieved to have the tension lifted.

"He's married, Jules."

"Damn it." She frowns. "All the good ones are taken."

"Luke"—I jump off my stool and stand between his thighs, rubbing my hands up and down his arms—"I want to see your movie this weekend."

"You do?" He looks completely shocked.

"Yes. This is what you do. I want to support you. Let's go opening night."

"I told you, I don't do premieres. I'm not going to LA for it." He's shaking his head adamantly.

"No, I mean here. Let's go to opening night here, in Seattle."

Jules jumps up and down in excitement. "I want to go, too! I'm sure I can find a date."

"Let's make a night of it. We'll double-date, go to the movie, maybe dinner. Let's celebrate!"

Luke smiles, a wide, melt-my-panties smile, and for the first time since I met him, he looks genuinely proud and excited about what he does. "You really want to?"

"Absolutely."

"Then I guess we're going. But let's try to go to an out-of-the-way theater. I don't want our night to be ruined because I get recognized and have to stand around signing shit for three hours."

"We'll go to a late show in a suburb after dinner. You can wear a trench coat with a hat and sunglasses." I smirk at him, and he narrows his eyes at me.

"You're such a smart-ass."

"But you love me." I smile sweetly.

"God, get a room." Jules pulls the lasagna out of the oven.

"I'M NERVOUS." I look over at Jules and cringe. "What if I don't like it?"

"Then you lie through your pretty straight teeth and tell him you love it. That's what girlfriends do, no matter what their boyfriends do for a living." She shuffles through my closet, looking for something to wear to the movie tonight.

"Who are you bringing tonight?" I ask as I pull my black dress over my head and step into my black Manolo Blahniks.

"Don't lecture me."

"Uh, okay."

"I'm bringing my boss."

"Holy shit! I didn't think you were seeing him anymore." What the hell?

"We're not really seeing each other."

"Are you sleeping together?"

"No. Definitely not. He's not as bad as I thought he was. Once the embarrassment faded . . . well, he's a pretty nice guy. I figured, why not bring him?" She bites her lip and slips on a pair of my silver earrings.

"I hope you know what you're doing, Jules."

"I'm not sure that I do, but it's just one night. Please, be cool, okay?"

"I am the epitome of cool. I'm offended you'd say otherwise. And here I was going to spring for dinner tonight, too."

She smiles at me as the doorbell rings.

"One of our guys is here." I head for the door, ready to go. "I'll get it."

I jog down the stairs and open the door to find a huge bouquet of red roses staring me in the face.

"Well, hello."

Luke pokes his head out from behind them and smiles at me. "Hey, gorgeous, these are for you."

"Thank you, my love." I bury my nose in them and sniff as he comes inside and closes the door behind him. He looks fantastic in a blue button-down shirt that matches his eyes and a pair of khaki pants.

"You look handsome," I murmur and kiss his lips softly.

"You are breathtaking." He runs his fingertips down my face, and I blush.

"Come on, I'll put these in water, and then I get to go see my boyfriend's movie tonight."

Luke laughs. "You do? That's cool."

"I know. He's very famous, but I can't tell you who he is because we are private people." I nod sagely at him, my eyes wide.

"Are you sure I can't get it out of you?" He wraps his arms around my middle as I arrange the flowers in a vase.

"Nope, my lips are sealed."

"Damn, and here I was hoping to get to take you out tonight." He nuzzles my neck, and I sigh.

"Well, I could probably go out with you later, after my other date."

Luke tickles my ribs, and I squeal. "Like hell. You're mine, baby. Get used to it."

I turn in his arms and run my hands through his hair, smiling up at him. "You are the only one I'll ever want, my love."

His eyes soften, and he gives me that kiss that makes me all gooey. "Ditto, baby."

"Oh my God, do you two ever stop?" Jules rolls her eyes as she comes in the room, and Luke smiles smugly and kisses my cheek.

"Nope."

"Gag. Nate just texted, he'll be here in a few—"

Just then the doorbell rings.

"He'll be here right now. I'll get it." She smiles and saunters to the front door.

"Who's the guy?" Luke asks.

"A guy she works with," I respond, and Luke's eyebrows shoot up. "Really?"

"Yeah. Could be interesting."

"Come on in and meet them." Jules walks into the kitchen ahead of a very attractive man wearing dark jeans and a black long-sleeved button-down shirt. He's tall like Luke, with broad shoulders and slender hips. He has long dark, dark hair pulled back in a short ponytail at the nape of his neck, gray eyes and a nice, square jaw. Yes, he's swoon-worthy, like Jules said before. He also has kind eyes, and he can't take them off of Jules' face as she introduces him to us.

He's smitten.

"Nate, this is my roommate, Natalie, and her boyfriend, Luke Williams."

Nate shakes both our hands and smiles at Luke. "It's a pleasure. I can't say I was a fan of the movies you acted in years ago, but I do love the ones you produce now. I've been waiting for *Rough Shot* to come out for months." He smiles at us both and then steps back to drop his arm around Jules' shoulders.

"Here's hoping you like it." Luke seems relaxed, and I breathe an internal sigh of relief.

"Shall we go? I'm starving."

"Let's go." Luke takes my hand, and we all climb into his Mercedes SUV, me in the front with Luke, and Jules and Nate in the back.

"Where would you like to eat?" Luke asks us.

I turn my head to answer and see Nate kiss Jules' hand. Just friends, my ass. I'll drill her later.

"How about that little Mexican place you took me to last week?" I suggest. "It's quiet, and they have delicious margaritas."

Both Jules and Nate nod in agreement.

"Mexican it is." Luke picks up my hand and kisses my knuckles, and I smile shyly at him.

The restaurant is relatively slow for a Friday night. The owners know Luke, so they escort us to a private booth near the back where we won't be noticed.

After chips and salsa have been delivered and we've all ordered, we sit back to sip margaritas and get to know Nate.

"So, Nate, what is it that you do?" Luke asks.

"I work at the same investment firm as Julianne," he responds and smiles down at Jules.

My eyebrows climb into my hairline, and I meet Jules' gaze with my own.

Julianne? No one calls her that.

Jules narrows her eyes at me, telepathically telling me to shut up.

"How long have you been doing that?" Luke asks, oblivious to our silent conversation.

"About eight years."

We make small talk for the better part of our meal. Nate is polite, attentive, and clearly completely taken with Jules.

And it's completely mutual.

Luke lays his hand on my thigh and squeezes, and I link my fingers through his.

"Do you sail?" Nate asks out of the blue.

"I've been a few times, but I haven't in a while," Luke says. "You?"

"Yes, actually, I have a catamaran docked in Seattle. Would you two like to join us one afternoon for a tour around the sound?"

Luke looks down at me to get my take, and I nod and smile, catching Jules' slight nod.

"Sounds fun," Luke replies.

The check arrives, but I pluck it off the table before anyone else can.

"You're not paying for this." Luke digs for his wallet but I hold the check away from him.

"Yes, I am. We're celebrating your movie premiere, so I get to pay."

"Fuck no, give me that check."

"Mine." I hold it against my chest as I pull my card out of my wallet.

"Goddammit, Nat . . ."

I pull his face down to mine and kiss him, long and slow. When I pull back, we're both out of breath. "Let me do this. I'm proud of you, damn it."

"I can't argue with you when you do that," he mutters and looks disgusted, but I see the gleam of humor in his impossibly blue eyes, and I smile smugly as I pass the check and my card to the waitress.

Nate watches our exchange with curiosity and then breaks out in a wide grin.

"Dude, you've got it bad," he says to Luke.

"You have no idea," Luke grumbles.

# twenty-six

"**F**our for *Rough Shot*, please." I pass my card through to the ticket girl at the movie theater and smile at her. We're quite early, but we want to get seats in the back so we can be inconspicuous and leave after everyone else when it's over.

"This is the last damn time you pay for me to go anywhere," Luke grumbles behind me.

Jules and Nate laugh at him, and I just smile serenely.

We buy two extra-large tubs of popcorn and buckets of soda to share and find our seats. Even though we're more than thirty minutes early, I'm surprised to see a handful of people already seated in the theater.

We climb up to the very top row of the stadium-style seats and sit in the middle, Jules and I between the boys.

Luke runs both his hands down his thighs and takes a deep breath.

"Are you nervous?" I whisper in his ear.

He smiles down at me and kisses my forehead. "A little."

"Do you watch your movies?" I ask.

"Yeah, but I usually wait until after opening weekend to see what audiences are saying. Opening weekend is nerve-racking, and usually busy."

"I'm glad we're here. It's exciting."

He laughs and takes a handful of popcorn out of the tub. "Me, too. I hope you like it."

"I'm gonna love it."

The theater fills up quickly, and finally the lights dim and the previews start.

I'm shocked to see that two of the five movies previewed are billed as being produced by Luke E. Williams. I look up at him, stunned, and he smiles shyly down at me. I shake my head and push some popcorn in his mouth, making him laugh.

I'm excited as *Rough Shot* begins and want to stand up and cheer when Luke's name flashes on the screen during the opening credits. Instead, I kiss him soundly and give him a ridiculously proud smile.

It's hard to tell, but I think he actually blushes.

The movie is fantastic. When a mostly naked Channing Tatum walks across the screen, Jules and I look at each other and start laughing. We can't resist. Luke throws popcorn at me in disgust.

It's a fast-paced two-hour film that keeps you on the edge of your seat until the end to find out "whodunit." There is indeed lots of action and stuff blowing up. There is also an intense love scene between Channing and his co-star, and I can't help but watch it in a very clinical way, knowing that Channing is married in real life, wondering how his wife deals with scenes like these.

I'm also incredibly happy that Luke has chosen to assume a different role in the movie business.

One particularly bloody scene makes both Jules and I squirm in our seats.

"Oh God, really?" I clasp my hand over my mouth as I realize I said that out loud, and both Nate and Luke laugh at us.

As the closing credits roll, I can't stop smiling. I do clap, inconspicuously, when Luke's name appears again, and he grins at me. We wait until all the other customers have left and the lights come up to leave the theater. As we stand, I wrap my arms around Luke and hold him tight, burying my face in his chest and inhaling his sexy Luke scent. I lean my head back and look up into his shining blue eyes.

"I loved it. I'm so proud of you. We are doing this for every movie. I want a schedule."

He runs his fingers down my face and smiles sweetly. "I'll get you one." He kisses me gently.

"Um, Nat? This is a double date. Stop making out with your su-per-cool, famous boyfriend, please."

I laugh and glance back at Jules. "I'm just appreciating his art," I say primly.

"Appreciate it in private. Come on, let's go." Jules and Nate walk ahead of us out of the theater. I move to follow, but Luke holds my el-bow, keeping me back.

I turn back to him, and he kisses me again, passionately this time, lovingly. He pulls back and leans his forehead against mine.

"What is it?" I ask.

"Thank you for tonight. I love you, baby."

"I love you, too."

WE ALL DECIDE to continue the celebration and go out for drinks. We end up near our place at the Celtic Swell, and I have to smile as I re-member the first time Luke and I had drinks together here. It feels like a lifetime ago.

The bar is pretty busy with locals, and no one is really paying atten-tion to us as we snag a booth near the back.

"They make a pretty good margarita here," Luke comments and smiles down at me. He remembers, too!

I grin and nod, and we all decide to continue with margaritas.

Luke orders mine just the way I like it.

"So Nate"—I take a sip of my margarita. Delicious—"What did you think of the movie?"

"It was excellent, as I knew it would be. You?"

"Obviously, I'm biased, but I really liked it. Except that really bloody part."

"Yeah, what the hell is it with boys and blood?" Jules squishes up her nose prettily.

"I am man. I like blood." Nate beats his fist on his chest, and we break out into laughter.

"Mostly naked Channing Tatum is always pleasing on the eyes." I catch Jules' eye, and we wink at each other.

Luke nudges me with his elbow as Nate glares down at Jules, and I giggle.

"I do believe you have a hit on your hands, sir." I kiss Luke's smooth cheek, and he gives me his sexy half grin. Swoon!

"I'm glad you all liked it."

"What did you think of it?" Jules asks.

"I'm happy with how it turned out. I think the cast and crew did a good job, and the movie was entertaining. The audience seemed to like it."

I know I have a stupid grin on my face as he talks, but I can't help it.

"What?" he asks me.

"I just think you're cool." I shrug.

"You're pretty cool, too."

"Oh, I know." I take a sip of my drink and wink at Nate, who laughs at us.

"What are you working on now?" I ask.

"I've just started talking with a studio about another Marvel comic movie that will come out next summer. The movie I wrapped before Tahiti is a romantic comedy with Anne Hathaway that will release in the spring."

Hearing him talk about his work is just so . . . *sexy*. I run my fingertips up and down his thigh as he talks. He grips my hand and brings it to his mouth, kissing my knuckles, then lays our hands in his lap.

"Before I forget"—Luke takes a big sip of his drink—"My dad is throwing a big surprise anniversary party for my mom next Saturday night. Jules, you and your family are all welcome to come."

I smile at him, delighted that he wants my family at his parents' party.

"Oh, how fun! I'll let them know. Is it formal?" Jules asks.

"Yeah, Dad's going all-out. It's their thirty-fifth anniversary."

"Wow." I take a sip of my drink. Thirty-five years.

"What?" Luke gazes down at me, and I swallow.

"That's just a long time." I shrug.

"My parents have been married for forty years," Jules adds.

"Are your parents still together, Nate?" I ask.

"No, my dad raised me. He's always been a bachelor."

"Can I help out with the party?" I ask Luke.

He smiles down at me warmly and kisses my forehead. "No, I think Dad and Sam have it covered. Just come with me."

"So I'm just a piece of arm candy, is that it?" I frown as if I'm offended, and Luke laughs.

"Oh, you're much more than arm candy, baby." He kisses me gently, and Jules makes gagging sounds as Nate laughs.

"We'd better go while we can still pull them apart," Jules says and waves at the waitress for the check.

I WAKE SATURDAY morning to an empty bed. I sit up and stretch, the soft white sheet sliding down my naked torso and pooling in my lap. I listen to Luke's house, trying to decipher if I can tell where he might be, but all is quiet.

I run my hands over my face and then notice the Starbucks to-go mug and red rose on the night table, along with a note.

Oh, he does spoil me.

I take a sip of the coffee. It's still hot, so it hasn't been here long. I sniff the beautiful rose and open the note.

*Working this morning. In the office downstairs. I love you.—Luke*

Office? I don't remember seeing an office. There was one room downstairs that he said was storage on my initial tour. I wonder if that's it.

And, if so, why did he say it was storage?

I shrug and drink more coffee in his beautiful big bed. It's raining today, and his large windows are covered in drops, making the choppy water on the sound look blurry.

I pull on the blue button-down shirt Luke wore last night and go look for him.

Sure enough, when I get downstairs and head down the hall, the room Luke said was for storage is open, and I can hear him talking on the phone.

"Yes, I saw the numbers this morning. It's great news. I'm glad you're happy with it. No, we'll wait for Monday's numbers before we make that decision. Okay, we'll talk then." He hangs up as I walk in the room.

"So, not so much for storage." I look around his office and can't help but feel like I'm in a movie of my own.

This is where he keeps his movie memorabilia. The movie posters from his *Nightwalker* movies, with him on them, are framed and on the walls. There are awards and certificates, photos of him with celebrities and important people scattered throughout the room. He looks impossibly young in most of the photos.

I gaze back down at my man, sitting at his impressive desk. He's leaning back, wearing a white T-shirt and jeans, watching me apprehensively.

"What?" I ask and tilt my head to the side.

"Are you mad?"

"That you lied about this room?"

"Yes."

"No."

"Oh." His eyebrows rise, and he looks a bit thrown off-kilter.

"I know why you did. Any more surprises around here?" I ask as I come around his desk.

"No."

"Good."

Luke scoots back, and I sit on the desk in front of him, bracing my feet on the arms of his chair as he scoots in close and wraps his arms around my waist and buries his face in my belly.

I push my hands in his hair and lean down to kiss his head.

"You smell good," I murmur. "Did you shower without me?"

"Yeah, I got up early. The morning after a release is always busy. Plus, I had to get you coffee."

I smile against his head. "Thank you for the coffee."

"You're welcome."

His phone rings. He sits back and answers it, keeping one arm around my waist.

"Williams." His voice is short and business-like, and I smile down at him.

"Hey, Channing, thanks for calling me back, man. Just wanted to let you know that I saw the film last night. You did a fantastic job." He listens for a moment and then laughs. "I know. I'm glad you survived it. How is your beautiful wife? Good. Hey, I have another project I'm looking at for next year. Can I send you the script? It's pretty good." Luke nuzzles my belly again, and I can barely hear Channing—Channing freaking Tatum!—speaking on the other end.

"Okay, I'll shoot it over next week. Enjoy your weekend, you deserve it. Bye."

"He sounded happy," I murmur.

"He should, the numbers are good this morning."

"Did I mention last night how very proud of you I am?"

"You did. I especially liked hearing it when you were naked." He flashes me a wolfish grin, and I laugh.

"I liked that, too."

"In fact"—he cups my ass in his hands and pulls me more tightly against him—"you didn't get permission to wear this shirt."

"Gosh, I have to stop doing this."

"I know. You'd think by now you'd learn what happens when you wear my shirts."

"But I like your shirts." I pout down at him.

"I like doing this." He slowly unfastens each button, and I shrug out of the soft shirt, letting it fall onto the desk behind me.

He inhales sharply, his eyes level with my breasts, and he runs those beautiful blue eyes over all of me, like he's eating me alive with his gaze.

"Sweet mother of God, you're so beautiful." He leans in and rubs the tip of his nose against my right nipple, back and forth and around in a circle, and it puckers as he watches. "I love how your gorgeous body responds to me."

He pays the same attention to the left nipple, and I moan softly.

He's sitting in that chair, fully clothed, and I'm about to come unglued from just his nose.

Unbelievable.

He looks up at me as he takes a nipple in his mouth and suckles, then licks and kisses his way across my chest to the other side and does the same. His hands are caressing and kneading my ass as he kisses down my torso.

"Lean back on your hands, baby."

I do as he asks, and he kisses my belly piercing. "So fucking sexy. How long have you had this?"

"I got it on my eighteenth birthday."

"It's hot." He kisses it again and nibbles his way down to my tattoo.

He abruptly scoots me to the edge of the desk, making me lean back even farther on my elbows, exposing me to him. He places a chaste kiss on the dark letters. "Don't lie back. I want you to watch."

Fuck. That is maybe the sexiest thing he's ever said to me.

"Okay." My voice is heavy with need, and he grins up at me, his blue eyes molten.

He leans down and, with just the tip of his tongue, licks me from my clit down through my folds and back up again, and then settles his mouth right over my clit, rolling his tongue over and over it, and then suckling gently.

I throw my head back and moan his name loudly and then bring my head up to keep watching him.

It's so fucking hot when his mouth is on me.

He glides one hand around from my ass, over my thigh and slides a finger inside me.

I buck up off the desk, my feet still planted on the arms of his chair, but he holds me tightly against his mouth. His tongue slides back and forth over my clitoris, and that finger is working magic inside me. His deep blue eyes are on mine as I explode, loudly.

He runs kisses up and down my thighs and pulls his finger out of me.

"God, you taste good. I want you all the time, Nat. I never get enough of you."

"Inside me. Now." I'm panting, and I need him.

He stands and pulls his jeans down around his thighs. "Wrap your legs around me, baby."

He fills me as I wrap around him, leaning down to kiss me, cupping my right cheek in one hand and gripping on to the end of the desk with the other, as he pushes into me relentlessly.

"Oh God." My hands are on his ass, pulling him harder. I feel my orgasm already working its way through me.

"Come for me, beautiful." He whispers in my ear, and that sexy whispery voice sends me over the edge into another amazing climax that has me digging my heels into his buttocks.

"Christ, Nat." He shudders as he comes inside me, raining kisses on my face, pushing his hands into my hair.

"I recommend desk sex," I murmur and grin lazily up at him.

He laughs and pulls me up in a sitting position. "Yes, let's do this more often."

# twenty-seven

"**H**ey, Natalie! Thanks for meeting me here, rather than having me pick these up at your place."

I smile at Brad and give him a swift hug. We are meeting at Starbucks so I can give him his finished photos to add to his portfolio before he goes on some auditions this afternoon.

We sit at a table with our drinks as he pages through them.

"Wow, you're really good."

"I had a good subject." I wink at him and take a sip of my coffee. The days are getting cooler and rainier as fall approaches, and I'm thankful for the warm mocha.

Brad smiles shyly and continues to look through his photos. "You make me look good. When can I schedule another shoot?"

"Well, Brad, that could be an issue." I grimace and think of Luke. Hell, Luke wouldn't even like it if he knew I was having coffee with Brad.

"Oh?" He raises an eyebrow.

"My boyfriend doesn't like for me to shoot single men on my own. It's mainly a safety issue for him." I shrug and smile apologetically.

"I'd never hurt you, Nat." Brad frowns, and I feel like shit.

"I know that. Maybe I could arrange for Jules to be there, too, so we aren't alone. Luke would probably be okay with that."

"That's fine. You just do great work. I'm sorry if I was too forward before. You're beautiful, and I'd be stupid not to try, but I understand that you're not on the market. It's cool. I'll talk with him if you want." Brad looks so sincere, and I pat his shoulder.

"Thanks. We'll figure it out."

"Natalie?"

I glance up into familiar blue eyes, and my heart sinks into my stomach. "Hello, Samantha."

"I thought that was you." Her eyes shine shrewdly as she looks Brad over, then back at me and I want to shrink. Fuck! Of all the people to see me here with Brad!

"Will we be seeing you Saturday night at Mom and Dad's party?" she asks, a fake smile on her pretty face.

"Yes, Luke and I will be there."

"I'll see you then." She saunters out of the coffeehouse, and I groan, hanging my head in my hands.

"Who was she?"

"Luke's sister."

"She sure doesn't like you."

I look up at him and chuckle. "No, she doesn't."

"Why?"

"Long story. I'm glad you like your shots. I'll let you know when I've had a chance to talk to Jules and Luke about setting up another appointment."

"Okay, cool. Hey, I mean it, I'll talk to Luke if it will help and let him know that I'm not into you like that."

"I'll keep that in mind. Thanks for the coffee."

"My pleasure."

SHIT.

How in the hell am I going to explain to Luke about meeting up with Brad today? I know Sam will say something to him, and I pray she hasn't called him before I get home to tell him myself. Luke's really possessive where Brad is concerned, and I know I should have run it by him ahead of time, but it just seemed silly to have to ask permission to meet with a client in a public place.

I think I'm going to be in trouble. Maybe I can distract him with sex.

"Honey, I'm home!" I let myself into the house, using the key he gave me when we returned home from Tahiti.

"In the office," he calls back.

I set my handbag on the couch and carry two large, heavy shopping bags back to his office.

He greets me with a warm smile and then he raises his eyebrows in surprise when he sees the bags. "What's in there?"

"I did a little something for your parents' anniversary." I smile at him, nervous.

"You did?" He grins, delighted with me. "What is it?"

"Well, I had some help from your dad this week." I begin pulling out frames. There are eight of them. "I asked him for photos of just him and your mom every five years they've been married, beginning with their wedding photo."

Pulling the last of the frames out, I arrange them on Luke's desk. His eyes skim over them and then settle on the last one.

"I made their wedding photo and this one I took at my birthday party the biggest two, and the others can be arranged around them."

He picks up the photo I took at the party, and he stares at it for a long time. They had been posing for me, all stiff smiles and bodies, and Luke had made a joke about something, sending us all into giggles. In this photo, Lucy is laughing into the camera, and Neil is smiling down at her, his face close to hers, and the love moving between them is touching.

It's my favorite photo of the day.

"You're so talented, baby. They're going to love these. My mom will hang them in the family room." He sets the frame on the desk and pulls me to him, kissing me in that soft way he does that makes me all weak in the knees.

"I hope they like them."

"You're so sweet. You didn't have to do this. I already put both our names on the gift I got them."

"I know." I hug him tight and bury my face in his chest. "But I wanted to do something nice for them. I've grown very fond of your parents. I put both our names on this, too."

I feel him smile against my head.

"What did you get them, anyway?"

"We"—he stresses the word, and I smile—"got them a second honeymoon in the south of France."

"Of course we did." I laugh and kiss his sternum.

"Is that funny?"

"No." I pull back and look up at his impossibly handsome face. He didn't shave this morning, and I rub my hand down his cheek, enjoying the roughness. "I love how generous you are."

He shrugs and looks uncomfortable. "They deserve it."

"Yes, they do."

"Have you decided what you're wearing Saturday?" he asks as I gather the frames back into their bags.

"Yeah, I picked something up the other day when Jules and I took Stacy shopping. Thank you again for including Jules' family. They're excited to go."

"My parents really enjoyed themselves with Jules' family. They'll be happy to have them there."

"Do you have lots of work today?" I ask, steeling myself to tell him about Brad.

"No, I'm done. You?"

"I just so happen to have a clear calendar for the rest of the day."

"Hmm . . . what can we do with a whole day off in the rain?" He raises a finger to his lips and pretends to be thinking really hard, and I laugh, but then remember that there is somewhere I need to be, and my mood shifts. Brad and meeting with Sam are the furthest thing from my mind.

"Actually, I'm sorry to burst your bubble, but I do have to run an errand." I look down at my hands and then back at him, biting my lip.

"Okay. Do you want company?"

"You don't have to go if you don't want to."

"I always want to be with you. Where are you going?" He looks concerned, leaning back on his desk, his arms crossed over his chest.

"The cemetery." I shrug nervously.

"Why?"

"I only go twice a year. On my birthday, which I missed this year because my incredibly sexy boyfriend whisked me away to a tropical paradise." I grin sassily at him, and he grins back. "And on their birthday."

"Their birthday?" he asks, confused.

I nod. "They shared a birthday, exactly three years apart. They always made a big deal of it, with a big party or a fun trip somewhere. They always made sure to include me, and so I want to always remember it for them." The last few words are a whisper.

He crosses to me and kisses my forehead. "Let's go."

MELANCHOLY SETTLES OVER me as we get closer to the cemetery. We took my car since I know where to go in the large graveyard, and I just needed something to occupy my mind.

Luke will most likely drive home.

"I'm sorry, honey, but this might turn into a sad day for me. I don't dwell on this often, but I'm usually not good company after I've been here."

He kisses my fingers gently and sighs heavily. "I wish you never had to go through this, Nat. It's something I can't fix for you, and I would do anything if I could."

"I know," I whisper.

I park on the single-lane-paved driveway a few rows back from my parents' large headstone. After getting out of the car, I reach in the back seat for two bouquets of flowers, lilies for my dad and sunflowers for my mom. They were her favorite.

I walk over to where they rest. Luke walks just a couple paces behind me, giving me space. He always knows what to do to comfort me. I'll have to thank him later.

This section of the cemetery sits up on a hill with a great view of downtown, the Space Needle, and the sound. I gaze around me, taking in their view, and then turn back to the large, black marble headstone.

I kneel before it, not caring about the wet ground, and brush leaves and grass off the base, cleaning it up, keeping myself busy and my eyes averted from their names and dates of birth and death. I place the flowers beneath their names and then sit back on my heels and look up.

CONNER is written in big, bold letters across the top, their names and dates are below. Written in script below that is: *I am my beloved's and my beloved is mine.*

I lean forward and place my palms flat on the smooth, cold marble over each of their precious names and close my eyes, letting the memories flood my mind.

Luke kneels next to me and places his hand on the center of my back.

"Talk about them, baby." His voice is rough, and he's rubbing my back gently.

I don't look at him. I just keep my eyes closed and my hands on the stone, but I find myself talking.

"My mom loved to bake. We would bake cookies every weekend, even when I was in college. She was pretty, and she hugged me all the time." The tears are flowing now, running unchecked and unheeded down my face, mixing with the rain falling around us.

"She had an MBA from Stanford, but rather than leave me in day care, she chose to stay home and raise me herself. And she always told me that it was the best thing she ever did and that she was so thankful for the opportunity to care for me and my dad.

"She was so smart and funny, and she was my best friend," I whisper and brush the tears off my cheeks before returning my hand to the marble.

"My dad was funny, too, but in more of a dry way. He was crazy about my mom. The sun rose and set with her as far as he was concerned. He spoiled her incessantly, which is one of the things that reminds me of him when I think of you." I smile to myself.

"No matter how hectic his job got, he always came home to us, every night. He was a ruthless businessman, but he was the gentlest man I'd ever known. And when it was time to defend his daughter, he was voracious and tenacious, and there was no stopping him.

"They were the center of my world." I hang my head in my hands now, rocking back and forth, letting the grief settle over me. Luke wraps his arms around me and settles me against his chest, rocking me, murmuring words I don't understand against the top of my head. He kisses me and tells me he's sorry.

Finally, when there are no more tears left, I wipe my nose on my sleeve and look at the black stone, again reading their names and dates and the inscription below.

"They would have also been married thirty-five years this year."

He gasps and kisses my head again.

"They tried to conceive me for seven years. They tried everything, but it never worked, so they gave up and resigned themselves to the idea of not having kids at all, or maybe adopting later. My mom got a partnership at a firm, and their lives were taking a very non-child-conducive path.

"And then, suddenly, in the eighth year, she got pregnant. She almost lost me at five months and endured many months of bed rest, but here I am, safe and sound."

"Thank God," Luke whispers.

"I miss them." I begin to weep again.

"I know, baby."

We kneel there, on the wet ground with the rain falling on us, for a long time. It feels like hours, but it might only be minutes. Finally, Luke stands and lifts me into his arms, cradling me against his chest and takes me to the car. He buckles me into my seat and kisses my forehead. As he walks to the driver's side, I raise my knees and wrap my arms around them, pulling myself into a ball, and cry all the way home.

Luke carries me inside and up to his bedroom. I'm not crying anymore, but I'm exhausted, my eyes hurt, and I'm just sad.

He sets me gently on the side of the bed and takes my shoes off for me.

"Stand up, baby." I comply, and he takes my dirty jeans off. "Arms up," he says and pulls my shirt over my head.

He takes my bra off and grips my shoulders in his hands, guiding me back down to the bed. He walks to a dresser and pulls out a white T-shirt, moves back to me and slips it over my head. He strips out of his own dirty clothes and grabs a fresh T-shirt and pajama pants.

Luke pulls the covers on the bed back and lifts me into it.

"It's the middle of the day," I protest, but he kisses my forehead and runs his fingers down my cheek.

"Take a nap. You're wrung out, baby. I'm going to grab my laptop and sit with you, okay?"

"Thank you." I grip his hand and bring it to my face, nuzzling his palm. "Thank you for today. I love you so much. I don't know what I would do without you." I feel the tears start again, and I'm mortified.

"Hey, hush, baby." He's kissing my forehead and cheek, rubbing his free hand soothingly up and down my back. "Nothing's going to happen to me. Go to sleep. I'll be right back."

He pulls out his phone and turns it off and does the same to mine, pulls the covers around my shoulders and walks out of the room.

A few minutes later, he's back with a large bottle of water and his laptop.

He crawls onto the bed next to me, and I turn so I'm facing him. Lifting his hand, he brushes my hair back with his fingers and smiles at me softly.

"I love you, beautiful girl. Get some sleep. I'll wake you in a few hours."

"Okay," I whisper, and close my eyes, enjoying the rhythmic caresses of Luke's fingers in my hair, and drift to sleep.

# twenty-eight

Tonight is Luke's parents' party, and I couldn't be more excited. I'm putting the finishing touches on my makeup—I'm getting pretty good at this!—while Luke is dressing in my bedroom. Jules keeps coming in and out of the room to borrow something, nag me about something, or just chatter because she is also nervous.

I love her.

I hear Luke laugh, and I walk out into the bedroom. He's on the phone, and at the sight of me, his eyes darken and get glassy, and I give a satisfied nod.

Mission accomplished.

I'm wearing a black dress that hangs off one shoulder. There are rhinestones along the high waist, and it falls to my red Louboutin-clad feet. I'm wearing my hair up, thanks to Jules' handiwork, and my pearls.

I feel sophisticated and sexy.

"Okay, Dad, I have to go. We'll see you at the club. Just tell her you're taking her out for dinner. Okay, bye." He hangs up and crosses to me.

He's so handsome in his black suit and white shirt with black tie. His blond hair is in some sort of order, but I'm sure I'll make a mess of it before long.

He rakes his gaze over my dress and hair and runs his fingertip under my pearls against my skin. "You are the most beautiful woman I've ever seen." He kisses me, in that way that makes me swoon, and I run my hands down his smooth cheeks.

"Thank you. You clean up pretty well yourself, handsome. Are you going to be okay tonight with all the people there?"

"Yeah, I'll be okay. I'm an actor, remember? I can play the part for one night."

"I don't want you to be uncomfortable." He doesn't fool me. I can see the nervousness in his eyes and the way he keeps fidgeting with his tie.

"I'll know most everyone there. My parents wouldn't invite a bunch of strangers, so it should be cool." He kisses my forehead, and his lips turn up on one side. "Are you worried about me?"

"Of course I am. I love you."

His eyes soften. "I love you, too."

"Hey, Nat, can I borrow . . . Oh God. We don't have time for this." Jules shakes her head in disgust and stomps into my closet, coming out wearing a pair of my earrings. "Can I borrow these earrings?"

"Yes." I laugh. "That dress is to die for."

"I know, right?" She flashes a Cheshire cat grin and turns in a slow circle, showing off her strapless red dress. She's stunning in red.

"Are you bringing Nate tonight?" I ask.

"No way, not introducing him to family." Jules shakes her head adamantly, and I let it go. She's still not talking much about Nate.

"Okay." I shrug and smile. "Want to ride with us?"

"No, Isaac and Stacy are picking me up. I'll see you there."

"Ready, baby?" Luke asks me.

"Let's go."

THE ANNIVERSARY PARTY is being held at a country club in Bellevue that Luke's family belongs to. The ballroom has been decorated beautifully, with colorful flower centerpieces, twinkling lights and candles. There is a two-person wooden bench sitting near the entrance, along with black markers, for everyone to sign in lieu of a guestbook. Neil will place it by Lucy's favorite flower garden at home.

"Luke, this is gorgeous. Samantha and your father did a great job. Your mom is going to be beside herself."

Luke smiles widely. "She'll love it. Come on, let me introduce you to some people."

He snatches two glasses of champagne from a waiter and hands one to me as we begin mingling about the room. I am excited to see Gail and Steven have already arrived, and I hug them both.

"Oh my goodness, you both look so wonderful!" Gail is simply stunning with her short blond hair styled around her face, and she's wearing a beautiful royal-blue evening gown. Steven is dapper as can be in a black suit and tie. I couldn't be more proud of them.

"Darling, you are breathtaking." Gail hugs me close, her eyes shining with love and happiness.

"Thank you for coming, both of you. My parents will be delighted to see you." Luke shakes Steven's hand and kisses Gail on the cheek.

"Thank you for inviting us. You look so handsome, dear."

"Happy to be here," Steven responds and winks at Luke.

Huh? I look up at Luke, wondering what that wink was about, but Luke's face gives nothing away.

The room is filling quickly with people, and Luke sticks close to my side, his hand on my back, introducing me to his family and friends.

Finally, in a moment alone, he hands me a fresh glass of champagne and whispers in my ear, "You are unbelievably gorgeous tonight. And you are charming everyone in this room."

His smile is possessive and loving, and I warm at his words.

"You're the charming one. Are you having fun?"

"Yeah, I'm excited to see my mom's reaction. In fact"—he looks at his watch—"time to get everyone seated."

He has a word with the band leader who then announces, "Ladies and gentlemen, please find your seats. The guests of honor will be arriving shortly."

Luke and I are seated at the head table with his parents, Samantha and her date and Luke's brother, Mark.

"Luke, Natalie, this is my date, Paul," Samantha says.

Luke shakes his hand while giving him a speculative stare, and I smile to myself.

Overprotective brother.

"Hey, beautiful." Mark flashes me that signature Williams grin and pulls me into a hug. "Good to see you're still putting up with my brother's shit. When you've had enough of him, give me a call." He winks down at me, and I can't help but laugh.

"Stop fondling my girlfriend. Find your own." Luke pulls me out of Mark's grasp as Mark grins at him.

Yes, these Williams men are charmers.

Luke takes my hand and kisses my fingers as he guides me to my seat between him and Mark.

Suddenly, the ballroom doors swing open, and the room erupts into applause. Neil is smiling lovingly down at his bride as Lucy's mouth drops, and she looks around the large room, realizing that she recognizes everyone here.

She turns to Neil with a shocked smile, and he dips her way down low and kisses her tenderly. I can't hear what he says to her, but I'm quite sure he says, "Happy anniversary, my love."

I can't stop smiling.

Lucy is wearing a beautiful black evening dress, and Neil is in a black suit and red tie. They look young and happy and still very much in love.

As they make their way through the crowd to our table, they stop to shake hands and give hugs to other guests.

I turn to Luke and grin up at him. "They look so happy. I'm so happy for them."

"Me, too." He kisses my forehead, and I decide to be the bigger person here, to try to make things right with his sister.

"Samantha." I lean around Luke toward his sister to get her attention. "This is a great party. You did a fantastic job."

She looks stunned for a moment, then plasters the fake smile on her face, and my heart sinks. No smoothing things over tonight. "Thanks, Natalie."

I look up at Luke and shrug. He shakes his head ruefully, and we turn our attention back to his parents.

Lucy hugs me tightly on her way to her seat. "Oh, Natalie, this is amazing!"

"I'm so happy that you're surprised and happy, Lucy. Happy anniversary."

"Thank you." She kisses my cheek and then enfolds Luke into a hug.

"Hello, dear." Neil sweeps me up in a hug, all smiles. "Were you able to finish the project you were working on?"

"Yes, and I'll have it with me tomorrow at brunch." We are hosting brunch at Luke's house tomorrow morning to give his parents their gifts and have a private family celebration.

"Perfect. Thank you." He smiles at me kindly and moves on around the table.

"My parents love you," Luke murmurs in my ear.

"It's mutual."

We take our seats, and Neil stands, tapping his water glass with his spoon, and the room hushes. Someone hands him a microphone.

"I want to thank you all for coming tonight and extend a special thank you to my lovely daughter, Samantha, for being my partner in crime these past few months. It's been daunting keeping this little secret from my beautiful bride." He smiles down at her, and she blushes prettily. "I am a very lucky man. As of tomorrow, I have had the honor of spending every day with the best person I've ever known for thirty-five years. Luce, you are my best friend, the love of my life, and I would do it again every single day. Thank you for putting up with my shenanigans, for our three gorgeous children, and for teaching me how to cook a steak."

As we all laugh, Lucy wipes a tear from the corner of her eye and grins at her husband.

"Happy anniversary, my love. Here's to thirty-five more." Lucy stands amongst the applause, and Neil kisses her soundly.

The band starts to play a bluesy tune, and a delicious dinner is served.

"So, Natalie, how was Tahiti?" Lucy smiles warmly across the table at me.

"Warm, romantic, and completely perfect," I respond with a wink. "I didn't want to come home."

Luke kisses my fingers. "We'll go back."

The band begins to play *At Last* by Etta James, and Neil stands. "I believe this is our song, beautiful."

He takes her hand, and we all watch as he moves her effortlessly across the dance floor. They are gazing at each other as though they're the only two in the room.

"Your parents are so in love," I murmur to Luke.

"Yeah, it gets a bit gross for a kid to watch." He shakes his head, but his eyes are full of humor. "Shall we join them?"

"Sure."

As he leads me out to the dance floor, I see other couples, including Jules' parents, get up to dance to the sweet song. Luke pulls me into his arms, and we glide around the floor.

"I love dancing with you." I run my fingers down his cheek, and his blue eyes light up.

"We should do it more often then."

"Yes, we should." I smile up at him, and his eyes are suddenly so serious. What's wrong? Is he still nervous about the crowd?

"Nat, I . . ."

Jules sweeps by on the arm of one of Luke's cousins. "Definitely glad I came stag," she mumbles to me as she passes, smiles and shrugs, then gives us a finger wave, clearly enjoying her night.

"You were saying?" I ask Luke.

He exhales and pulls me tightly against him, nuzzles my ear with his nose, and whispers, "I love you."

The evening moves quickly, and magically. Luke keeps me tucked close to his side all night, glaring at anyone who dares ask me to dance, and I can't help but laugh at my possessive man.

No one asks for an autograph, and Luke poses politely for the photographer Samantha hired for the occasion, knowing the photos will be the property of the family.

"There you are!" I turn at Stacy's excited voice and hug her tightly.

"Well, hello, pretty girl! I told you when we bought it that that dress is a knockout." I stand back and admire her beautiful white off-the-shoulder dress. It fits her body perfectly, and she glows with happiness.

"Thank you. Yours is stunning, too."

Isaac pulls me into a hug. "Hey, brat. Thanks for helping Stacy find that dress. It's torture. I have two more weeks before I can touch her, and I think I'm going to die."

We all laugh at his pained expression, and I pat his cheek. "Poor boy. I think Sophie's worth it."

"Yeah." His face transforms into a sweet smile. "She is. Hey, dance with me?"

I look up at Luke, and he shrugs and turns to Stacy. "Do me the honor, beautiful?"

Stacy blushes bright red and takes his hand as he leads her onto the floor. I know how she feels. He's a heartthrob.

Isaac isn't too bad himself. He's tall and toned and tan, with dark blond hair and killer brown eyes. I had a crush on him for years.

"Are you having fun?" I ask him.

"Yeah, Stacy is especially, so I can't complain. Luke's a good guy. I wasn't so sure about him at first, but I like him."

"What brought that on?"

"Dad and I had a conversation with him the other day."

"What?" Why didn't I know about this?

"Yeah, you were working, and he invited all of us guys out for lunch." He shrugs and smiles like he's hiding something. I know Isaac. The man is like Fort Knox. If there's a secret, he won't spill it.

"Oh. He didn't mention it."

"Didn't he?" He shrugs again, like it's no big deal. "Well, my point is, I like him."

"Wow, am I getting the big-brother stamp of approval?" I widen my eyes and drop my jaw sarcastically.

"As long as he minds his manners, yes."

"I like it when he doesn't mind his manners." I wink at him and laugh as he cringes.

"TMI. Jesus, I don't want to know that. Are you happy?" He peers down at me, serious now, and I can't help but feel loved.

"I am. He's a good man, Isaac. He loves me. It's not about what he does for a living, or what I've done in my past, or how much money either of us has. It's about who I am when I'm with him." I shrug, a bit embarrassed. "He makes me feel special."

"Ah, Nat. You are special, honey. I'm just glad you finally figured it out. It's a pleasure watching you fall in love." He winks down at me. "Now, before I get too mushy, can you babysit one of these nights? I need some serious alone time with my wife."

I laugh. "Sure, shall we say in two weeks?"

"Oh God, yes. Thank you."

AS THE EVENING draws to a close, Luke pulls me out on the dance floor for one final dance. My feet are killing me, but I can't refuse him. I love swaying in his arms.

I realize that the band is playing Norah Jones' *Come Away With Me*, and I turn my startled gaze up to his. He's smiling down at me tenderly.

"I do believe this is our song. You look as beautiful tonight as you did that night, in the vineyard, in these pearls. You take my breath away, Natalie Grace Conner."

Oh.

I feel the tears in my eyes as I gaze up at him. I run my fingers through his soft blond hair. "You sure know how to sweep a girl off her feet, Luke Edward Williams."

His eyes skim over my face as he moves me about the room. I swear, we're the only two here, and I don't care who's watching us.

He leans down and gently presses his cheek to mine. "Thank you," he whispers.

"For what?" I whisper back.

"For being mine."

WHEN WE REACH Luke's house, he leads me inside and shuts the front door. He tugs my hand gently, pulling me into his arms.

"You were wonderful tonight. You charmed everyone," he murmurs in my hair.

"I had a great time. Your family is wonderful." I nuzzle his chest and inhale his sexy Luke scent.

"Are you sure you're okay with us having the family here in the morning for brunch?"

"Of course. I'll even help you cook."

He chuckles. "Thank you for your service."

"It's a good cause. Let's go to bed." I pull away, but he stops me, his eyes suddenly serious.

"Not yet."

"Are you okay?"

"I'm more than okay. I have something to show you."

"Oh, okay."

He takes my hand in his and leads me through the room. He stops by the sound system and fires up his iPod, and something bluesy and slow starts to pour out of the speakers. He leads us to the deck, opens the French door, and flips a switch, and I gasp.

The deck has been transformed into soft and romantic. Bouquets of red roses with tiny white pearls tucked in the petals cover every surface. There are twinkling white lights strung back and forth, high along the ceiling of the space, and a small table is sitting by the love seat with a bucket of ice and champagne and two glasses.

I twirl and gaze up at him, my eyes wide. "When did you do this?"

"I had it done earlier while we were getting ready for the party at your house."

"Luke, it's magical." I turn to take in the beautiful space, breathless. He's so romantic.

He wraps his arms around me from behind and buries his face in my neck. "Do you like it?"

"I love it. Thank you."

"Come, sit." He leads me to the love seat, and we sit. My dress floats around my legs as I sit, and it feels soft against my skin. I smile to myself, remembering that I'm not wearing any underwear. Luke will enjoy that when he finds out.

He pours us each a glass of champagne, clinks his glass to mine, and I take a sip.

"It's nice tonight. It's not even very cold." I lean my head back against the cushion and close my eyes, listening to the water that we can't see in the darkness. Luke lifts my feet into his lap, and I turn my head so I can watch him.

He removes my shoes and starts to rub.

"Oh, sweet mother of God, I love you."

He laughs. "Feet hurt?"

"A little. Those shoes are worth it."

"Yes, they are. Did I mention that you look beautiful tonight?"

"Once or twice." I wink at him and sigh as his thumb pushes down on the arch of my foot. "You're good with your hands."

"I'm glad you approve."

"I could get used to this, you know. All these flowers and foot rubs and champagne and you, my handsome boyfriend."

He frowns, and my heart stills for just a moment. What did I say wrong?

"Hey." I pull my feet out of his lap and move toward him, lying across his lap. He wraps his arms around me, holding me to his chest, and I cup his face in my hand. "What is it?"

His eyes are on mine, intensely blue and serious, and I know that something important is on his mind.

"Talk to me, baby." I continue to caress his face, and he turns his head to press a kiss in my palm.

"I don't think I want to be your boyfriend anymore."

What?

I still and narrow my eyes at him. "Okay, I'll get my things." I move to get up, but he tightens his hold on me, clenching his jaw and his eyes closed tightly.

"No, that's not what I mean. I'm not breaking up with you."

"What are you doing?" I whisper.

"I'm fucking this up." He opens his eyes, and I see fear, and longing, and love.

What's this?

"I've wanted to do this all night, but I couldn't find the right time, and I'm glad I didn't because it should be here, while we're alone." He swallows and takes a deep breath. "Natalie, since I've known you, my world has changed. I found something with you that I didn't know I was missing, but that I wanted very much. You are such a beautiful woman, inside and out. You beguile me. I can't keep my hands off of you. You are so sexy and fun and smart. Your sassy mouth makes me crazy." He smiles down at me and runs his fingertip along my lower lip.

I'm speechless, which is good because he doesn't seem to be finished.

"I can't ever imagine my life without you. You are the center of my world, Nat. I want to love you, protect you, fight with you, make babies with you and spoil the shit out of you for the rest of my life."

He takes a deep breath and pulls a small Tiffany-blue box out of his pants pocket. I feel my eyes go wide, my heart rate spike and my breath catch.

My eyes search his as he holds the tiny box in his beautiful hand.

"Natalie, be my wife. Marry me."

# twenty-nine

Oh. My. God.

My eyes are locked on his face, and all the breath leaves my body.

Marry him! *Marry him?*

It's so soon. We've only known each other, what, less than two months? Two incredible months.

His worried eyes are gazing deeply into mine, blue to green, and I know in my heart that the answer is yes. After everything we've been through these past two months, everything we've shared, I can't imagine life without him either.

And I don't have to.

He wants to marry me!

"Baby, you're killing me here." Luke moves to open the little blue box, but I put my hand over his, stopping him. He turns startled eyes back to mine, but I smile reassuringly.

"I just have a couple things to say." I am now giddy and jumping up and down on the inside, my heart in my throat, but I'm amazingly calm on the outside.

"Go ahead," he murmurs and still looks a bit scared and uncertain.

"When I see my future, Luke, I see you. I see *you*, not your money or what you do for a living, or who you know. I love and respect you for the kind, giving, loving man you are. I want what my parents had, what your parents share. I would be honored to be your wife, give you children, and make a life with you."

As I speak, tears run unchecked down my face. Luke's eyes soften, and his arms tighten around me.

"Is that a yes?" he whispers, and I giggle tearfully.

"Yes."

"Thank God." He brushes his lips across mine softly, and I cup his cheek in my hand.

"You had me worried there for a minute," he whispers against my lips.

Oh, I love whispery Luke.

I just love Luke.

"You surprised the hell out of me. I think I forgot to breathe."

"Can I show you this now?" He holds the ring box up and grins down at me.

"By all means."

He sits me up on the small couch and kneels in front of me. Oh my. Seeing my sexy man, disheveled blond hair, bright blue eyes, in a black suit with the tie loosened, kneeling before me, holding a little blue ring box, is an image I'll hold in my head forever.

"When I saw this, I knew it was yours. I've had it since the day I bought your pearls."

I gasp, my eyes widening. He's wanted to marry me since the night at the vineyard!

"I didn't think you were ready then." He chuckles as I shake my head.

He opens the box, and cradled in the velvet is diamond perfection. The center stone is princess cut and large, but not crazy big. It's nestled in platinum, with two lines of smaller diamonds on either side that twist around each other to meet at the center stone.

Tears prick my eyes again as he takes it out of the box, places it on my left hand and kisses it there.

"Thank you. It's perfect."

"Like you." He leans up and kisses me, passionately, and I wrap my arms around him, pulling him to me.

He gathers my long skirt in his hands and pushes it up around my thighs, skimming his hands along my thighs and up under the skirt to grip my hips.

"Jesus, I love this new habit you have of not wearing any underwear." I smile against his lips. "We're writing that into the vows. No underwear for you."

I let out a belly laugh, and then gasp as he pulls my hips forward and pushes me back against the soft cushions of the love seat.

He pulls in a shaky breath as he gazes down at me, exposed to him from the waist down, my black skirt hiked up, in my pearls.

"Do you have any idea how beautiful you look right now?"

"You make me feel beautiful."

He sits back on his heels and pushes one finger inside me, his eyes locked on my center, watching his hand. "You are the most beautiful woman I've ever met in my life, baby."

I moan as he continues to torture me with that finger. My breath hitches, and I start to pant. Jesus, what he does to me with just one finger.

"Luke, I want you."

"Oh, trust me, you'll have me." He pulls his now wet finger out of me and sucks on it. "You taste good."

He bends down and pushes my thighs wide with his palms, spreading my labia in the process. I grip the cushions of the couch, preparing for the incredible invasion of his mouth, and buck my hips when his mouth covers me, his tongue pushing between my lips.

"Oh my God!" My hands dive into his hair, my hips circling. He grips my ass, tilting my pelvis higher, and he continues to make me wild with that talented mouth. He rubs the tip of his nose against my clit, and I give in to my orgasm, convulsing and shuddering, calling out his name.

He nibbles my inner thighs as my body calms.

"Holy shit, you're good at that," I pant and run my fingers through his shaggy blond hair.

"Mmm, I'm glad you approve, baby. Stand up for me." He rises gracefully and takes his suit jacket, tie and shirt off, discarding them on the floor of the deck.

"After what you just did to me, my legs are jelly. I don't think I can stand."

He takes my hands and pulls me into a standing position and wraps my arms around his bare shoulders. "Just hang on to me."

"Happily," I murmur in his neck as his hands glide to my back, unzipping my dress. I lower my right arm so he can pull my dress off, and he lets it billow to my feet.

"God, no bra either? It's a good thing I didn't know this earlier. I would have locked us in a bathroom at the club and kept you naked all night." His hands smooth down my back to my bottom.

"You're not naked."

"Oh, did you want me to be naked, too?" he asks innocently, and I bite his collarbone.

"Get. Naked."

"Demanding little thing, aren't you?"

"Why aren't you naked?"

His hands roam from my bottom, up my back and begin taking the pins out of my hair, letting it fall around me.

"I love your hair," he murmurs and watches it fall, one strand at a time.

"I love your hair, too." I push my fingers through it, and he smiles.

"I know."

When my hair is loose, he takes my hands in his and kisses them, one knuckle at a time, his eyes on mine. He steps away from me, and the cool night air swirls around me, sending a shiver through me, making my nipples pucker.

"I love your body. I love that you're curvy, yet strong and fit." His eyes glide greedily up and down my curves.

"I'm glad." I smile shyly. "You're still not naked."

He raises an eyebrow. "Impatient?"

"I want my fiancé to make love to me," I whisper, and his eyes dilate.

"Say it again," he whispers.

"Make love to me," I whisper back.

"No, the other part."

A small smile spreads across my lips. "My fiancé."

"God, you said yes." He swallows, his eyes round, and then he smiles, a heartbreaking, wide, joyous smile, and I fall in love with him all over again.

I nod and glance down at my beautiful ring. I can't wait to get a ring on his finger, too.

"Did you think I'd say no?"

"No, I just . . ." He runs a hand through his hair. "I was just really nervous."

I close the distance between us and kiss his lips softly. "You have no reason to be nervous with me. You've had my heart for quite some time. Now, my gorgeous fiancé, please take me to bed and make love to me."

He sweeps me up in his arms and carries me to his bedroom, kissing me softly the whole way.

"HEY, BEAUTIFUL, WAKE up." Luke nibbles my earlobe, and I turn sleepily to face him.

"You kept me up really late," I murmur, not opening my eyes. I hear him chuckle.

"I'm sorry. But we have to get up and start getting brunch ready." He kisses my cheek and then my nose.

My eyes flutter open, and I palm his cheek in my left hand, and my ring catches the morning light. I smile brightly at him, and he grins and kisses me softly.

"Let's stay in bed all day and make love."

"As good as that sounds"—he pulls back and rolls away—"everyone will be here in about two hours, and we have stuff to do. Coffee's on the night table for you. Go ahead and grab a shower, and I'll meet you in the kitchen."

"I love you."

He flashes a cocky grin at me. "I love you, too. Get up. I'll see you downstairs."

He leaves the room, and I sit in the bed for a minute and grin stupidly, gazing at my ring. I finally shake myself and grab my coffee, making a beeline for the shower.

"OKAY, WHAT CAN I do?" I ask as I stroll into the kitchen.

Luke is at the stove, a white kitchen towel slung over his left shoulder. He's wearing a white linen button-down shirt with faded blue jeans and bare feet.

Yum.

"Here, cut up some fruit." He pulls melons, strawberries, grapes and peaches out of the fridge, and I grab a cutting board and sharp knife and get started with my task.

"So, Isaac mentioned last night that you took the guys out for lunch the other day." I grab a cantaloupe and cut it in half, pull the seeds out and begin cutting it into wedges.

"He did?" Luke frowns slightly and mixes some pancake batter.

"Yeah, that's all he would say, other than he likes you, as long as you mind your manners. I told him I prefer it when you don't." I smirk and begin pulling stems off the strawberries.

"I wanted to ask them all if it was okay if I asked you to marry me."

I twirl at his words, my mouth gaping open. He shrugs and pours the batter on a griddle on the stove top.

"Why?"

"Because they're your family. They love you and protect you, and it's tradition." He takes a sip of coffee and eyes me speculatively.

Wow.

"What did they say?"

"I proposed, didn't I?"

"What if they'd said no?"

He laughs and shakes his head. "I would have asked anyway."

He flips the pancakes, and I wander over to him with a strawberry, holding it up to this lips.

"Here." He takes a bite, and I slip the rest of it in my mouth. "Mmm, that's good."

I lick my thumb, and he takes my wrist in his hand and licks my forefinger. "I love watching you eat."

Desire flashes, fast and hot, through me.

"Yeah?"

"Yeah."

I wander back to the fruit and pluck a grape from the stem. When I turn, Luke has taken the pancakes off the griddle and turned it off.

I do like the way he thinks.

I rub the grape across my lips, then pop it in my mouth and chew slowly.

"Want some?" I hold a grape out for him. He slowly closes the space between us and takes the grape out of my fingers with his lips.

"I like this game," he whispers, and I grin. He lifts me up onto the counter so my feet are dangling, steps between my legs, and puts another strawberry against my lips. I grip it in my teeth and then lean down so he can take a bite from my lips and kiss him at the same time.

He tastes of strawberries and Luke, and I moan against his mouth.

"God, you're so sexy."

I pull my green shirt over my head and throw it on the floor, then my bra follows it. Grabbing another strawberry, I look in his eyes, bite my lip, and swirl the red fruit around my nipples, making them pucker. Luke's quick intake of breath and tightening of his fingers on my ass tell me he likes the sight before him.

I pull the strawberry up my chest, against my skin, over my chin and push it into my mouth, enjoying the sweet juiciness of the fruit.

He doesn't move. He just watches me, his hands gripping my jean-clad bottom, me naked from the waist up, and I set about seducing my sexy fiancé.

I push a chunk of cantaloupe in Luke's mouth and lean down and kiss him, sucking the juice into my own mouth.

"You're making me crazy," he whispers against my mouth.

"That's the point," I whisper back.

He suddenly lifts me, and I wrap my legs around him as he twirls and rushes over to the dining table. He sets me down on it and pulls my jeans over my hips as I raise them and down my legs, taking my underwear with them.

He pulls his shirt over his head, not bothering with the buttons and pushes his soft blue jeans down around his thighs.

"I can't get enough of you." He covers me with his torso, his hands in my hair and face buried in my neck, kissing and suckling my sensitive skin.

"I don't want you to get enough of me." I wrap my legs around his hips, and he slides inside me, all the way to root of his cock, and I clench around him.

He grips my right hand in his left one and pulls it above my head and begins to move, in and out of me, at a steady pace.

"It makes me so hard to watch you eat. Your sweet mouth is the sexiest aphrodisiac I've ever seen." His lips find mine, and I'm lost in his words, in his body moving so gracefully and surely above mine.

I run my hand down his back to his tight ass and hold on tight as he increases the pace.

"Oh God," I moan.

"Look at me," he growls, and my eyes meet his. "I want to watch you come."

Fuck.

And that's all it takes to send me over the edge. He slams into me twice, then stills and bites his lip as he erupts inside me.

"God, Nat, you're going to kill me." He kisses me gently, then pulls out of me, helping me up off the hard table.

"I can't help it that you have a food fetish." I slap his naked ass and collect my clothes on the way to the bathroom to clean up and get dressed.

When I join him in the kitchen, he's fully dressed and has more pancakes cooking on the griddle.

I kiss his cheek and resume cutting up the fruit.

"I have to go to LA next week." Luke flips his pancakes and turns to me.

"Why?" I finish stemming the strawberries and move on to the peaches.

"I have a meeting that I need to be there for in person. I should only be gone one night."

"Oh, okay." I frown. This will be the first night we've spent apart since our magical night at the vineyard.

"Come with me," he suggests.

"I can't. I'm still catching up with clients from our vacation. I'm booked solid next week." I toss a pit in the garbage and grab another peach.

"It's just one night," he murmurs, and I realize he's standing behind me.

I'm suddenly feeling vulnerable, and I don't know why. It's just one night! Surely I can get through one night without him.

I turn and smile brightly, not wanting him to see my insecurity. "It'll be fine. What day are you leaving?"

"Early morning Wednesday. I'll be home Thursday around noon."

"That's a long meeting." I raise my eyebrows.

"I'm going to pack a few meetings in there, since I'll be there anyway. Are you sure you'll be okay?"

"Of course. I love you, but I think I can survive without you for one night. Jules and I'll have a girls' night."

"Okay." He kisses my nose and returns to his pancakes and slips some bacon into the oven.

"What are we going to do about all the flowers outside?" I ask, changing the subject.

"What do you mean?"

"Don't you want to eat out on the deck?"

"No, we'll eat in here. We can bring them in if you like."

I walk over to the glass door and gaze out at my beautiful flowers, trying to shake my melancholy mood now that I know Luke will be leaving overnight next week.

"They're beautiful. I don't know where we'll put them all."

"Leave them for now, and we'll figure it out later."

"Okay." I set the large dining room table for six, pour orange juice and coffee into carafes and set them on the table as the doorbell rings.

"I'll get it." Luke flashes me a smile, and I relax a bit, excited to see his parents and give them their gifts.

"Hello, darling." Lucy kisses Luke's cheek and comes into the great room. Neil and Mark follow with Samantha bringing up the rear.

They've obviously spent a lot of time in Luke's home. They're comfortable moving around the space, and I stand back for a moment, enjoying the view of Luke with his family.

My family now.

"Everyone, I'd like to introduce you to my beautiful fiancée, Natalie."

I laugh as Luke joins me and kisses my hand.

"Yes," I say drily, "we've met."

"Oh, Natalie, I'm so excited that you're going to be a part of our family." Lucy hugs me tight, and I blink back the sudden tears that threaten.

"Thank you."

"And here I thought you'd choose the right brother." Mark shakes his head ruefully and pretends to pout.

"I did." I laugh at his stricken face and give him a quick hug. "Don't pout. We'll find you a good girl."

Mark laughs and heads for the kitchen to steal a piece of bacon. "No need. I'm good."

"Stay away from that bacon!" Luke bellows.

Neil hugs me and cups my face in his hands, his kind eyes happy. "Are you happy, sweet girl?"

"Yes, thank you."

"Good."

Luke's parents are both so generous and welcoming. Samantha, however, rolls her eyes and pours herself a cup of coffee.

"So." Her eyes gleam with malice, and she glances at Luke, then back at me, and I brace myself for what's about to come out of her snarky mouth.

"Who was that delicious-looking man you were with the other day in the coffee shop?"

## thirty

I frown, then the blood leaves my face, and I turn to Luke. His eyebrows are raised almost to his hairline. The room stills.

"I met with a client to give him some work he purchased." My eyes don't leave Luke's, but his face changes, and gone is my carefree, happy man. He knows exactly who I'm talking about, and he's pissed.

Fuck.

I forgot to tell him about meeting with Brad because it was the same day that we went to the cemetery.

"What's his name?" Sam asks and takes a sip of coffee.

"Brad," I murmur, watching Luke as he exhales and hangs his head. "I forgot to tell you because we went to the cemetery that day." My voice is low and thin.

Samantha frowns for a moment and swallows, and she almost looks guilty.

Luke stares at me, his eyes ice cold, and I feel tears threaten. "Don't be mad. I just gave him his photos, and he asked if he could make another appointment, but I told him you wouldn't like it. He offered to call you himself and talk to you to let you know that he's not interested in me like that. It was nothing."

"Why didn't you say something when you got home?"

"I really forgot. It was nothing."

"It didn't seem like nothing when you smiled at him and rubbed your hand all over his shoulder." Samantha shrugs smugly, and I gasp.

"Sam." Lucy's voice is sharp and loud.

Luke's eyes don't leave my face, and I shake my head.

I pin Sam with a glare and ball my hands into fists. How dare she?

"What the fuck is wrong with you?" My voice is shaking in rage.

"What did I do?" She widens her eyes innocently.

"I met with a client. I patted his shoulder when he expressed nervousness about talking with my protective boyfriend about the possibility of having a chaperoned photo shoot with me. We were in a fucking public place having a conversation.

"Is this how it's always going to be, Samantha? You questioning my motives with your brother for the next sixty years? Do you have any idea how much money I'm worth without Luke? I don't need his money or his contacts. When my parents died, I inherited over twenty million dollars."

Sam blanches, and I hear Lucy gasp, but I keep going.

"Your brother is famous. Get over it. I wouldn't love him any less if he flipped burgers for a living, if that's where his passion was. You seem to be the only one hung up on who he is.

"I am marrying him, Sam. I'm in it for the long haul. I'd prefer to have a friendly relationship with you. I think that if you gave me half a chance, you'd like me.

"But I will not continue to be disrespected by you. I don't deserve it."

"I don't trust you," she spits out through clenched teeth.

"I don't trust you either, so I guess we're even." I look at Luke to see what he's thinking. His hands are in his pockets, and he's gazing at me thoughtfully. "Do you want me to go?"

"No, don't go!" Lucy comes toward me, glaring at her daughter. "Samantha, you're being ridiculous."

I continue to look at Luke. He hasn't answered me. Neil and Mark are both also glaring at Samantha.

"Well?" I raise my eyebrow at him.

"No, this is your home," he says quietly, and his eyes warm. Oh, thank God.

"Sam," he says quietly and walks around the table to her. She's still glaring at me, but he turns her chin so she's looking in his eyes. Lucy grips my hand in hers, and I smile thinly at her. I'm shaking like crazy.

"Stop this. I am marrying Natalie. I'm in love with her, Sam. She's nothing like anyone from my past. You have got to knock the chip off your shoulder and move on. I have."

He runs his hands through his hair and looks over at me, then turns his attention back to her. "If you don't trust her, trust me. Give her a fighting chance. She hasn't done anything to you."

Sam shakes her head and closes her eyes, and she suddenly looks tired. "I can't bear to see you hurt again."

"*You* are hurting me, Sam."

She gasps as though he's hit her. "What?"

"When you hurt her, you hurt me. Stop. This is our home, and if you can't respect her in it, you're not welcome here."

Holy shit. He's defending me to his sister, and I just want to wrap myself around him and kiss him, but I stay where I am, riveted.

I look around the room, at Lucy, Neil and Mark, and decide this has gone on long enough.

"I'm hungry." My voice is calm and light. "Let's have brunch. I think Mark's about to eat all the bacon by himself."

Lucy smiles at me and squeezes my hand as we head to the kitchen to place the food on the table. Mark and Neil help us get everything settled, and I watch out of the corner of my eye as Luke murmurs something to Sam. He hugs her gently and joins me in the kitchen.

"I'm sorry." I hug him around his middle and breathe in his scent.

"Don't be. You didn't do anything wrong. I'm sorry for Sam."

I shake my head. "Let's eat."

"Okay."

We enjoy our delicious meal, and the mood lifts considerably. I'm relieved that the conversation isn't forced or uncomfortable after my altercation with Sam. She continues to eye me speculatively from across the table, but she's no longer glaring at me, so I figure we've leaped one hurdle.

"Natalie, let me see that ring." Lucy leans toward me, and I show off my beautiful ring, a silly grin plastered on my face.

Lucy smiles at her son. "I did such a good job raising you."

Luke laughs, and I nod. "That you did. He has good taste."

Luke kisses my hand and smiles at me, his eyes soft and loving.

After breakfast, we clear the table. Lucy, Sam and I clean up the mess and join the men in the living room with fresh coffee.

"Presents!" I jump up and down and clap my hands, excited to give Luke's parents their gifts. Everyone laughs at me, and I grin. "I love giving presents."

"You didn't have to get us anything at all," Neil informs me.

"You only celebrate your thirty-fifth anniversary once." I decide to give this olive branch thing another try and turn to Sam. "Will you please help me bring their gift in from the other room?"

Her eyes widen in surprise, but then she shrugs good-naturedly. "Okay."

I smile and lead her down to Luke's office, where the large box sits on his desk.

"Holy shit, that's a big box."

I laugh. "I know. I had a hell of a time wrapping this sucker. Here, you take that side and I'll take this one."

We lift it together—it's really not that heavy, just awkward—and carry it out to the living room.

"What did you do, buy them furniture?" Mark asks drily.

I stick my tongue out at him, and Sam and I set the box on the floor in front of Neil and Lucy.

"Open it." I sit next to Luke on the couch, and he drapes an arm around my shoulders.

They attack the box from opposite sides, tearing the paper and pulling the lid off.

"Oh my." Lucy's hand covers her mouth as she gazes at the contents. She begins pulling the black, framed photos out of the box, one by one, and Neil takes them from her, arranging them on the floor. At the bottom of the box are the two larger frames of their wedding day and at my birthday party.

"These are wonderful," Lucy says as they hold the image from the party in front of them and gaze at it. "Natalie, you're very talented."

I blush, delighted that they like their present. "Thank you."

Luke kisses my hand. "There's more."

"What?" Neil frowns, not privy to this part of the present, and I giggle.

"We're sending you on a second honeymoon to the south of France. It's all paid for, you can go whenever you like."

Their mouths drop, and Lucy looks back at their photos and starts to cry.

"Geez, Mom, what's wrong?" Mark awkwardly pats her back, clearly uncomfortable with a woman in tears.

"I'm a bit overwhelmed, I guess. First, last night's party, then my son is giving me a beautiful daughter-in-law, and now we're going to France. It's a lot to take in in such a short time."

Neil kisses her forehead and hands her a handkerchief. I didn't know men still carried those.

I freshen everyone's coffee, and we sit and chat about weddings for the better part of an hour.

"Have you set a date?" Lucy asks.

"No." I chuckle and look at Luke. "He asked me twelve hours ago."

"Winter weddings are lovely."

"I'm going to need help. Also . . ." I frown and peer at Luke, and he runs his hand over my back.

"What's wrong?"

"I don't want the paparazzi to get wind of it."

"Do you want a big wedding?" Neil asks.

"No, just family and close friends." I shrug. "I've never really thought about it."

"Every girl thinks about her wedding. It scares us men to death." Mark smirks.

I shake my head. "I'd never planned to get married. This wasn't even on my radar."

"I have an idea," Sam says softly. "What about a destination wedding? You can fly everyone somewhere and have a small wedding somewhere lovely, like Tahiti or something."

The idea takes hold in my brain, and I smile. I look over at Luke, and he's smiling at me.

"What do you think?" I ask him.

"I'm the man. You just tell me when and where to show up and what I'm supposed to wear, and I'll be there."

I grin at Sam. "I like that idea. Let's talk about it some more later."

Sam smiles at me—*smiles at me!*—and I have visions of Luke and I getting married on a white sandy beach with crystal-clear blue water surrounding us.

"SO WHAT ARE your plans for tomorrow night with Jules?"

Luke and I are snuggled up on the couch. It's Tuesday night, and he leaves for his trip tomorrow, which I've been trying very hard to not dwell on. I don't want him to go.

"I think we're going to be in the studio."

Luke raises his eyebrows and looks down at me. "Why?"

"She wants me to do some photos for her." I shrug. "I'm not sure why. She already has quite a collection."

"What do you mean?"

"You must not read *Playboy*."

"Not since I was a randy teenager. Why?" He looks perplexed as I turn on the couch to face him, then realization dawns, and his eyes go wide.

"You're kidding."

"Nope. She posed for them in college." I laugh as I think back on that time. "She's the person I practiced on the most to get good at what I do. She did some work for *Playboy* for about a year, and then abruptly stopped. She said she was over it, and it was time to move on."

"Wow."

"Do not go on the Internet and try to find naked pictures of Jules." I narrow my eyes at him and cross my arms over my chest.

Luke laughs. "No, thanks. She's beautiful, but I've grown to feel very brotherly toward her. I do not want to see her naked."

"I'm glad to hear it."

"No, there's only one woman I want to see naked."

"Oh?" I ask innocently. "Who could that lucky woman be?"

"Just this gorgeous brunette I know. She's all curves and has the sexiest tattoos I've ever seen in my life." He pulls me onto his lap, so my knees are straddling his hips. I'm dressed in one of his T-shirts and my panties because we've been watching TV before bed.

"Do I know her?" I ask.

"I don't know. She always steals my shirts, and she's wearing a very fetching ring on her left hand." He pulls the shirt over my head and nuzzles a nipple with his nose.

"I think I know who you're talking about," I whisper and close my eyes as he sends chills down my back with that nose.

"You do?"

"Hmm . . . she's hopelessly in love with you." I grind my center over his erection, reveling in the feel of his jeans against me.

"Fuck, baby, I can feel how hot and wet you are through my damn jeans." His hands are on my hips, and he's pushing up against me.

"I want you." I kiss his lips. "Now."

He slides me back to his knees, opens his jeans and shimmies them down around his hips. His large hands cup my ass and lift me over him, shifts my panties to the side, then lowers me down onto him.

"Oh God! Luke, you feel so good." I begin to circle my hips, riding him, looking down into his molten blue eyes. His mouth is open, his breathing coming hard and fast.

He sucks a nipple hard in his mouth, and I cry out. My nipples have been extra sensitive lately.

"Gentle," I pant, and he releases the nipple from his lips and lightly runs his tongue over it.

"Okay?" he asks.

"Oh yes, more than okay."

He stands in one fluid motion, me still wrapped around him and without breaking our precious contact. He lays me down across the length of the couch and covers my body with his. He lifts my left leg, pressing it against my chest and over his shoulder, spreading me wide and begins to hammer into me.

"Luke," I cry out as sensation rolls through me. My hips are moving against his, and he's gazing down at me with such possession, such feral need, I come fiercely.

"Yes." He lets go of my leg and pulls out of me abruptly, flipping me onto my stomach. He pulls my ass in the air and slams his cock back inside me, slapping my ass in the process.

"Holy shit!" I squeal and grip the cushions in my fists.

He reaches down and grips my hair in a strong hand and pulls back, just enough to tug, and grips my hip with his other hand, pulling me back hard and fast on his hard cock.

I love it when he fucks me.

His breath is coming hard and fast. "Come again."

"I can't." If I come again now, I'll pass the hell out.

"Come. Again." He pulls harder on my hair and slaps my ass again, and I can't stop it. My muscles tense and shudder in the most intense orgasm I think I've ever had. I scream incoherently, pounding my fist on the couch as my body bucks back against Luke, and he roars my name as he explodes.

"Fuck me." He pulls out of me and pulls me to him, kissing my face, my cheeks, nose, eyes, cupping my face in his hands. "Are you okay?"

"Of course." I frown, not understanding. "Why wouldn't I be?"

"I've never been that rough with you. Jesus, Nat, you devastate me. I forget myself with you." His hands run down my back, soothing me.

"Honey, I like rough sex with you. You know that. I trust you completely. I'm fine." I smile at him. "You can slap my ass anytime. It's fucking hot."

Luke laughs, still catching his breath, and crushes me to him. "God, I love you."

thirty-one

I haven't slept all night. My stomach has been churning, and I feel slightly queasy. I know it's because Luke is leaving this morning, and it makes me nervous. I'll worry about him until he's home safely. I hate that he's flying.

It's not like he can drive to LA for the day.

The green glow from the alarm clock says it's five a.m. Luke will want to get up and get ready for his eight a.m. flight, so I start waking him up.

I love waking him up.

I kiss his cheek and run my fingers through his hair. "Wake up, my love."

"Humph."

"Come on," I reply, laughing at him. "Wake up. You have to get ready to go."

He turns to me and wraps me in his arms, burying his face in my neck.

"Go back to sleep," he murmurs.

Oh, I love being in his strong arms.

"If we go back to sleep, you'll miss your flight." I kiss his lips and continue running my fingers through his hair.

"I wish you were coming with me."

"You'll be home tomorrow."

"I don't like leaving you."

I smile, and my heart gives a little lurch. "I'll be okay."

"Will you drive me to the airport?"

"Of course."

He sighs, his eyes serious as they take in my face.

"Are you okay?" I rub his rough cheek with my hand.

"I miss you already."

"Oh, you have it bad, Mr. Williams."

Luke laughs and rolls me onto my back. He runs his knuckles down my cheek and kisses me in that gentle way he has that makes me all gooey. "Yes, I'm afraid I do."

"I do, too," I whisper.

"I'm glad to hear it."

He sweeps his nose down mine as I raise my legs up and around his waist. We're still naked from last night's lovemaking. He shifts so his hard cock is lying against my folds and rocks gently back and forth.

I know this will be much different from the way he fucked me on the couch last night. This will be slow and sweet.

He's kissing me tenderly, his eyes open and on mine. He pulls his hips back, and then slides inside me oh so slowly.

"Luke," I sigh against his mouth.

"I love you," he whispers.

He doesn't increase the tempo, he just continues a steady, slow rhythm, in and out, cupping my face in his hands, and it's so beautiful I can't stop the tears from falling out of the corners of my eyes.

"Don't cry, baby." He brushes the tears away with his fingertips and rubs my nose with his again.

"I love you so much," I whisper back to him. "Please, be safe."

His eyes widen, and I know he can see the vulnerability in my eyes, and he finally understands my fear about this trip.

"Oh, baby." He closes his eyes tightly and buries his head in my neck. I wrap my arms around him, holding him to me, as he gradually increases the tempo and pressure inside me, and I come, pulsating around him, as he empties himself into me.

"THEY'RE GOING TO be calling your flight. You'd better get through security." Luke's wearing a baseball cap and glasses in hopes that he won't get recognized in the airport. He looks hot.

He always looks hot.

"Have fun with Jules tonight." He pulls me to him and kisses me long and slow.

"Be good." I raise an eyebrow at him, and he laughs.

"I'll see you tomorrow. I'll call you when I get to the hotel." He kisses me again, then rests his lips on my forehead and takes a deep breath, like he really doesn't want to let me go.

"Okay. Safe travels, my love." I run my hands down his chest and step back and watch him walk toward security and his terminal.

"NATALIE?" JULES CALLS as I open the front door to my house. I have hardly been here all week.

"Yeah, it's me." I really don't feel well, and I don't think it has anything to do with Luke's trip.

"Did Luke leave this morning?"

I walk into the kitchen. Jules is buttering a bagel, and as the aroma hits my nose, it turns my stomach.

"Oh shit." I run for the hall bathroom and throw up, barely making it in time.

"Hey, are you okay?" She's standing in the doorway, watching me. Jules is one of the only people in the world I would let stand there and watch me hurl.

"I think I must have the flu. I've been feeling queasy all morning. I thought it was nerves, but apparently not."

My stomach convulses again, and I grip on to the toilet as I violently retch.

Jules disappears and comes back with a glass of water for rinsing my mouth and cool washcloth. She sets the glass on the sink and presses the cloth to my neck, and I moan.

"Thank you."

"Let's get you upstairs and in bed. Lie down for a while and see if your stomach settles."

"Okay."

Jules follows me upstairs. I don't feel too bad, just intensely nause-ated. I hate throwing up.

My phone pings in my pocket as I climb on the bed. It's a text from Luke.

*About to take off. No one recognized me. I miss you already, beautiful.*

I smile and hit reply.

*I miss you, too. Be safe. I want you home in one piece, please.*

And, I have to barf again. I run for my bathroom and stay there for the next thirty minutes. Jules is hovering with wet rags and water and makes me shove a towel under my knees.

"I think we should go to the ER."

"No, I'm fine." I retch some more.

"Yes, I can see that you're in top form," Jules replies drily.

"Don't be a bitch."

"Nat, I'm worried. You can't stop throwing up."

"I don't have anything left to throw up."

"Yet you're still dry heaving. This isn't normal, even for the flu. You don't have a fever."

My abs are starting to ache as I continue to heave over the toilet.

"Nat, don't make me call my mother."

"She'll side with me," I reply.

"Fine, I'll call Luke."

"No, he can't do anything from LA anyway."

More heaving. God, there's nothing left in me! What is wrong with me?

"Okay, Nat . . . get in the goddamn car. Here's a bucket." Jules shoves a big plastic bowl under my face and helps me to my feet. "An hour of uncontrollable barfing is too much. You're probably dehydrated."

She helps me into the car and takes me to a nearby hospital emer-gency room. Surprisingly, it's fairly quiet, and I'm processed through triage and into a room quickly. I'm thankful that Jules is with me to give them my personal information. I can't stop heaving long enough to form a sentence.

I manage to give a urine sample and change into a hospital gown.

"Natalie, I'm Mo. I'll be your nurse today. Put this pill under your tongue. It's called Zofran, and it'll help the nausea." I gratefully accept the medicine from the kind, petite nurse and take a deep breath.

"Let's get another set of vitals." Mo smiles and takes my temperature, blood pressure and heart rate.

"Everything is normal. That's a good sign. Dr. Anderson will be here in a few moments."

"Thank you." Jules pulls a chair up next to me, and my phone starts to ring. It's Luke.

"Hello?"

"Hey, baby, I'm at the hotel. Everything okay?"

"Yes, everything's fine. I'm just hanging out with Jules."

Jules' eyes go round, and she mouths, *What the fuck are you doing?* I brush her off.

"Okay, good. I'm heading back out to my first meeting. I'll text you when I can."

"All right, have a good meeting. I love you."

"I love you, too." I hear the smile in his voice as he hangs up.

"Natalie . . ."

"Stop. He can't do anything from LA. There's no need to worry him. He'll be home tomorrow anyway."

"He should know that you're in the emergency room."

God, she's stubborn.

"That pill they gave me is helping with the puking. They'll probably just send me home."

"Knock, knock." A small blond woman pokes her head through the door. "I'm Dr. Anderson. I hear you're not feeling well, Natalie."

"I've been throwing up for about the last hour and a half."

"Has it been steady, or does it come and go?"

"Steady. Couldn't breathe until the nurse gave me that anti-nausea pill."

"Any other symptoms like diarrhea, fever, abdominal pain?" She is jotting down notes in my chart as we talk.

"No, just the vomiting. I was a little nauseous early this morning, but I thought it was just nerves. Then the vomiting started."

"Okay, well, it sounds like we've got that stabilized." She pushes on the skin on my hands and looks in my mouth and nose. "You're pretty well dehydrated, so I want to start an IV and get some fluids going. We'll take some blood and run your urine and see what we see, okay?" She smiles down at me kindly.

"Okay. Will I be able to go home today?"

"Most likely. Let's get some test results, and I'll be back in a little while."

"See?" I say to Jules after the doctor leaves. "I've probably just got the flu."

Nurse Mo bustles back into the room and starts my IV.

"Oh, no, I'm outta here!" Jules jumps up and runs out of the room.

I smirk at Mo. "She hates needles the way most of us hate spiders."

Mo laughs, draws some blood and bustles back out again, leaving me with Jules.

"How are you feeling?" she asks.

"Better. Still a tiny bit queasy, but I don't feel like I'm going to throw up anymore."

"Good. You were starting to scare me."

We sit in companionable silence for a while, both of us checking our phones and watching a bit of TV. We wait a really long time, about two hours, before we see the doctor again.

"I'm sorry for the wait. I had a few blood tests that I wanted to run, and they can take a little time." She pulls a chair up next to me, and it looks like she's settling in for a long chat.

Shit, what's wrong with me?

"I have some good news and some news that could go either way, depending on how you choose to look at it."

"Okay. I'll take the good news first, please."

"You're very healthy. All of your vitals are normal, and your labs all came back completely fine."

"Good."

"Except, and here's the other news, you're pregnant."

I hear Jules gasp beside me, but I don't understand.

"What did you say?"

"You're pregnant."

"No, that's impossible." I shake my head adamantly. There must be some mistake.

"Oh?" The doctor raises an eyebrow. "Why is that?"

"I'm on the Pill. I never, ever miss a pill. Never. I'm The Pill Nazi."

"The Pill can be very effective at preventing pregnancy, but just like all birth control, it can fail."

"No, if I take it the right way, which I do, I won't get pregnant."

I see Jules pick up her phone and start tapping the screen voraciously while the doctor smiles patiently at me and pats my leg.

"Natalie, the Pill is ninety-nine percent effective when taken correctly. There is a one percent chance that it can fail, and it seems that you are that one percent."

"What?!" The world starts to fall away from beneath me.

"She's right, Nat." Jules shoves her phone in my face. "Never mind that you have an educated MD right here telling you this, but WebMD concurs. Ninety-nine percent effective."

"I take it this is bad news?" Dr. Anderson asks.

I look at Jules, and she looks as shocked as I feel. "I don't know."

The doctor looks at my ring and smiles broadly. "Maybe it's just a shock. We ran both your urine and blood to confirm. I'd like to do an ultrasound to determine how far along you are."

Nurse Mo steps out of the room and returns with a little ultrasound machine on wheels. Instead of putting a probe on my flat belly, the doctor has me put my feet in the stirrups so she can use a vaginal probe.

"The baby is too small to see with the external probe," she explains.

Baby? *Oh. God.*

The nurse turns out the light, and we all look at the screen of the machine. Suddenly, there is a little black circle, about the size of a quarter, and inside is a flutter.

"There we are!" Dr. Anderson smiles. "I'd say you're at about six weeks along."

Jules grabs my hand, and we stare at the screen in awe.

"Is that the heart?" I ask, pointing to the fluttering on the screen.

"Yep. It's hard to make out much more on this machine, but the black area is the amniotic fluid, and that flutter is the heart. You're nausea and vomiting is something we call hyperemesis gravidarum. It's morning sickness times a hundred. You'll probably be pretty nauseated during this pregnancy, so I'll prescribe you some anti-nausea meds to use at home. They won't affect the baby. Also, stop the Pill immediately, start taking some prenatal vitamins with folic acid and make an appointment with your OB doctor in the next four weeks."

She hits a button on the machine, and a photo of the ultrasound prints out.

"Here, something for you to show off." She winks at me. "We're going to keep you for a while, push another bag of fluids and make sure your vomiting is under control, and then you can go home."

"Okay."

She leaves, and Jules and I just stare at each other.

"Are you okay?" she asks.

"No." I feel numb.

"I love your ring. The picture you texted me Saturday night didn't do it justice."

"Thanks."

"Okay, let's talk about this rationally." Jules takes my hand in hers and looks me in the eye. "He loves you."

"He'll think I'm trying to trap him."

She laughs—*laughs*—and squeezes my hand. "Natalie, that won't even cross his mind."

"His family will think that."

"Who gives a fuck?"

"He just barely proposed."

"Now you're just babbling. Natalie, look at me."

"It's too soon." My eyes fill as they find hers. Thank God she's here with me. "We just met. We're still learning each other, Jules. We've been engaged for less than a week. It's too soon."

The tears come in earnest as my phone rings again. I send it straight to voice mail.

"Nat, you have to talk to him."

"I'm not telling him this over the phone."

"No, he'll worry if you don't answer the phone, silly." My phone rings again, but I'm crying too hard now to answer it.

"You answer. Tell him I'm in the bathroom or something."

"Natalie's phone," Jules answers. "No, sorry, Luke, she's in the bathroom. Want me to have her call you back? Uh huh. Oh, okay, I'll tell her. Bye."

"Well?" I ask when she hangs up.

"He's going into another meeting, but he'll call you later."

"Good." I let my head fall against the bed. "Oh God, what am I going to do?"

"What are you talking about? You and Luke are going to be parents." Jules takes my hand again. "Nat, you'll be awesome parents."

"It's too soon," I whisper and put both hands over my face and weep.

# thirty-two

My crying jag subsides, and I take a deep breath as Nurse Mo returns to change my IV bag.

How am I going to tell Luke that I'm pregnant? I know he wants kids, and so do I, but not yet. We're not even married yet. I couldn't bear it if he thought I was trying to trap him into something he doesn't want.

Jules turns on the TV and flips through channels, pausing when she finds a nightly entertainment gossip show.

"We spotted Luke Williams out today."

Holy shit!

"He was having a romantic lunch with Vanessa Horn, one of his former co-stars from the *Nightwalker* movies. Has Luke finally come out of hiding to rekindle his romance with the lovely Vanessa? They were engaged to be married for over a year before their split early last year. We smell love in the air! We will be sure to keep you updated on Luke and Vanessa as we get more details."

There is a series of photos rolling across the screen, taken today. I recognize the black T-shirt and jeans he wore on the plane. He and the beautiful blond Vanessa are indeed leaving a restaurant, his arm is around her shoulders, and he's smiling down at her, his nose pressed against her ear. Then there's a photo of him wrapping his arms around her shoulders and pulling her in for a kiss. The camera is angled badly, so I can't actually see the lip-lock, but it's obvious that's what they're doing. In the next photo, she's getting into a car, and he's holding the door for her. In the last photo, he's getting into the driver's side of that same car.

"Holy fuck, he's cheating on me."

"We don't know that."

"I just saw it with my own eyes!"

"Nat, it's the fucking paparazzi. They make everything up."

"Pictures don't lie. I know that better than anyone. You saw the way he was touching her and looking at her. He kissed her."

The jealousy running through me is primal. My heart is hammering. I'm breathing hard, and I feel my face heat. If I didn't have anti-nausea meds on board, I'd be hurling again.

"Natalie," Jules murmurs and takes my hand. "I'm sure it's not what you think."

I shake my head and give in to the tears. "It's over."

"No, Natalie. No. Talk to him about it tomorrow."

"There's nothing to talk about." I shake my head again, unable to believe what I just saw. "I can't trust him. I can't live this celebrity life with him."

"You're being silly."

"Shut up! You're supposed to be on my side! You're *my* goddamn friend, not his. He's fucking around on me! I just saw proof, so show some fucking loyalty, Jules."

"I'm sorry." She starts to cry, too, and I feel like a shit.

"Come here." I scoot over, and she crawls up onto the bed with me, holding me to her as we weep. "What am I going to do?"

"Take some time. You've just found out you're pregnant after being violently ill. You're not thinking straight. Take some time." She's stroking my hair, and I am so thankful for her.

"Okay."

My phone pings, and it's a text from Luke.

*Almost done with today's meetings, baby. Will call you tonight. Love you.*

"Fucker." I throw the phone down and don't bother to answer, but the floodgates open to more tears. About five minutes later, there's another text.

*I haven't heard from you all day. I miss you. You okay?*

"Nat, you have to talk to him."

"No." I turn the phone off and throw it in my handbag.

A few minutes later, Dr. Anderson returns with my prescriptions and discharge instructions. "You're free to go, Natalie. Good luck."

I'm going to need it.

Jules drives us to the pharmacy and then home. I'm loaded down with medication and vitamins.

When we get home, I go up to my room and crawl onto the bed, curl into a ball and weep like I haven't since my parents died. I feel like my world is literally falling apart, and essentially, it is. I can't be with Luke. He'll make up excuses for what I saw today, but he can't change it. He had his hands on that woman, in an intimate way. He used to be engaged to her, and he lied to me when he told me he never spoke to his former fiancée.

I press my hand to my belly. Oh God, and what am I supposed to do about the baby? Be a single parent? I guess I can do that. I don't see a choice. But the thought of it tears my heart out.

I fall asleep in the middle of my bed, sobbing and mourning the best relationship I've ever had, the loss of the one person I saw myself spending the rest of my life with.

"WAKE UP, NAT." I startle awake at Luke's voice.

"What are you doing here?"

His eyes are worried, and he's leaning over me, his face pale. "I couldn't reach you all day, and I was worried so I came home. Why didn't you tell me you were sick?"

"Who told you I'm sick?" I sit up and scoot back out of his grasp, and he frowns, confused.

"Jules said you'd been sick today, and she took you to the ER. Baby, you don't look very good."

"Yeah, I'm probably contagious. You should go home." I wrap my arms around myself, and I just can't look him in the face.

"Natalie, what's wrong?"

"I just don't feel good."

"Bullshit, look at me. Where's your ring?" His eyes are on my left hand.

"In my jewelry box."

"Why isn't it on your finger?" His voice is rising, and he's starting to look desperate, and I'm still sad and pissed and hormonal, and I know this is not going to go well.

"Luke, I think you should go home."

"No. Tell me what's wrong."

I can't stop the tears as they fall down my face. Luke reaches for me, but I pull back.

"Let me touch you."

"No." I shake my head. "I just want you to go home."

Luke pushes his hands through his hair in frustration. "Nat, let me help. Talk to me."

"You've done enough."

"What does that mean?"

"Just go home!" I shout.

"No!" he shouts back.

I hang my head in my hands and hate myself for crying in front of him. "Just go," I whisper.

"You're scaring the shit out of me. What is wrong?"

"I saw you." I raise my face and look him square in the eye. "I saw you with Vanessa outside of a restaurant in LA. I saw you with your arm around her and your nose against her fucking ear, your mouth was on hers, and you got into a car with her."

He frowns and swallows.

"Now get the fuck out."

"Natalie, that was a lunch meeting for a movie I'm asking her to do. There were three other people there. Did you see them in the photos, too?"

"I don't care."

"I'm not lying to you."

"I know what I saw."

"You saw exactly what the motherfucking paparazzi wanted you to see! I told you from the beginning, you need to talk to *me*, Natalie."

I'm shaking my head adamantly. "You lied to me when you told me that you don't speak to your ex-fiancée. You wig out on me about Brad, ask me to respect your feelings when it comes to working with men, but you don't give me a heads-up that you're going to be meeting with a woman you not only used to fuck but were supposed to marry? According to those photos, you more than talk to her. Did you fuck her in that car?"

"Jesus Christ, no! Is that what you think?"

"Just go. I can't trust you, and I don't want you here."

"You're making this more than what it is. I'm telling you, it was a business meeting."

"Okay. I still don't want you here."

"Fuck, Nat." He stands up and paces around my room, looking everywhere, running his hands through his hair. "Why won't you believe me?"

"You lied to me, and that's a line I can't deal with you crossing."

"I didn't lie!" he shouts. "I haven't spoken to her until this week when I asked her to do the fucking movie!"

Oh, why won't he just go? My tears are coming again.

"Baby, don't cry. I promise, I'm not lying to you about this." He steps toward me, but I hold my hand up, stopping him.

"You need to know what seeing that did to me. You didn't look like colleagues, Luke. You had your hands on her, and the look on your face was the one you give me when you smile at me." He swallows, and I continue. "You effectively ripped my heart out and stomped it to dust with just one look. Now, I'm upset and hurt and hormonal, and I can't deal with you tonight. I need you to give me some space, and I need it now because I just can't look at you anymore."

"Natalie, we've both done things we regret. Fuck, your whole body is a road map to your mistakes."

I blink at him. Did he seriously just say that to me?

"I guess this will just be an experience that I'll add to my road map.

Now get out of my house before I call the police."

"I love you." He's looking me square in the eyes, his blue eyes bright with fear. "This is not over. I'll give you some time, but goddamn it, Nat, this is not over."

He leaves my room and slams the door behind him. A few seconds later, I hear the front door slam, too, and then I hear his car—the Lexus?—peel out of the driveway.

I lie back on the bed, too exhausted to cry or, ironically, sleep.

"I didn't tell him about the baby," I say as Jules walks into my room.

"I figured. Did he deny it?"

"He says it was a business lunch about a movie he's asking her to do." My voice is monotone.

"He could be telling the truth."

I glare at her, and she continues. "Natalie, if you hadn't just gotten the news about the baby five seconds before we saw the show, would you be reacting the same way?"

"Yes."

"I don't think so." Jules climbs on the bed with me but doesn't touch me. "Honey, I think today has just been an emotional roller coaster for you."

"That's the truth." I sigh and throw an arm over my face. "We hurt each other really bad tonight."

"I heard."

I glare over at her again, and she shrugs. "My room is fifteen feet away, and you were yelling."

"What do you think?" I ask, because I love her, and she loves me, and she'll tell me the truth.

"Do you want me to tell you the truth or do the best-friend-loyalty thing?"

"Um, both."

"Okay." She takes a deep breath and looks down at me. "Luke is the best thing that ever happened to you. I don't believe he was cheating on you today. I think that he needs to remember to be more careful of how he behaves, especially in public, because the fucking paparazzi will twist just about anything into a good story. But he's been away from all of that for years now, and I can understand why he let his guard down."

She pauses and gazes at me intently. "Natalie, he loves you. He had tears in his eyes when he stormed out of here. He knows he fucked up. Not only that"—she raises her hand to stop me from speaking—"you have to think about the baby, too. I'm not saying to stay with him for the sake of the baby, but I am saying that he needs to know, and you need to remember that you're incredibly hormonal."

I'm trying to process everything she's saying. She's right. I am probably blowing this way out of proportion.

"I don't want him to think I'm trying to trap him into being with me because of the baby," I whisper.

"Honey, why would he think that? You didn't do it on purpose."

"I'm scared."

"It's going to be okay." She wraps me in her arms and hugs me tight.

BY THE NEXT morning I'm starting to feel a little foolish. It's amazing what a night of sleep, some anti-nausea meds and a good cry will do.

Now, how do I make it right?

I take a long shower and frown at my puffy eyes in the mirror as I get ready for the day. I look horrible. I dress in some jeans and a sweater and pull my ring out of my jewelry box and put it back on my hand.

We have a lot of talking to do, but we'll get through this.

Jules is in the kitchen when I go downstairs. "You look horrible."

"Thanks. I feel a little better."

"Good. Going over there?"

"Yeah."

"Good."

"Okay, I guess I'll go."

"Everything is going to be fine."

"Thank you. For everything, Jules."

"I love you. Now go get your man." We grin at each other, and I leave the house, on foot. I'm going to walk to his place, get a little exercise and fresh air. He doesn't live too far away from me.

As I walk I think about all the ways he's shown me over the last two months that he loves me. The coffees, the massages, how he's always so concerned about how I'm feeling or what I'm thinking. Even his possessiveness is loving. And the flowers! All the hundreds of flowers.

Not to mention my birthday and taking me to Tahiti. Holding me on the plane. The way he held me at the cemetery.

My God, he loves me so much. And I threw it all back at him last night.

I have to apologize. I have to make it right.

I walk faster and make it to his house in less than fifteen minutes. I decide to knock on the door rather than use my key, because I'm not sure how I'll be received, but he doesn't answer. I ring the bell over and over, but still no answer.

Weird.

I let myself in with my key and wander through the house, calling his name. He's nowhere to be found. I go upstairs, and he's not there either. His bed looks like it hasn't been slept in since he and I left yesterday morning to take him to the airport.

Shit. Where is he?

I pull my phone out of my pocket and call him. It rings and rings and then goes to voice mail.

"Hey, it's me. I'm at your place, but you're not here. Please call me. I'm worried." I can't help but feel a little hypocritical after he came to me last night because he was worried and I threw him out.

I send him a text as well, in case he doesn't check his messages, and wander downstairs.

I go out onto the deck and sniff my flowers. They've stayed remarkably fresh-looking thanks to the cool, early fall weather. I sit on our love seat and can't help but remember Saturday night after Luke's parents' anniversary party when he proposed.

I look down at my ring and grin.

Where is he?

I try calling him again, but it goes to voice mail.

Suddenly, the doorbell rings, and I go to answer it. It's Samantha.

"Thank God you're here." She hugs me, and I automatically hug her back in shock.

"What's wrong?"

"I've been trying to find you. I don't know your phone number. I was just at your house, and Jules said you'd come here."

"What's wrong?" I repeat.

"It's Luke. Nat, he's been in an accident. We have to go to the hospital."

Oh, dear God, no!

# thirty-three

"What happened?" I'm sitting in the passenger seat of Samantha's SUV, and she's driving like a bat out of hell. I brace myself against the dashboard as she makes a sharp right turn.

"I don't know the details. Dad called me about a half hour ago and said that he got a call from Harbor View Hospital to let him know that Luke is there. They had to wait for him to wake up to ask him who to call."

Her voice catches on a sob, and I instinctively grab her hand. Who cares if she hates me? I'm all she has right now.

"So he is awake?" The tears are rolling down my face unheeded. I just need to get to him, to hold him and make sure he's alive.

"He was. I guess he keeps coming in and out. Mom, Dad and Mark are already there. I don't know why none of us has your number. Well, I know why I don't, but no one else does either, but Luke told me where you live once, so I went to your place, and that's when Jules told me you'd gone to Luke's."

"Thank you for looking for me. I had no idea." God, drive faster!

"Natalie, I'm so sorry for everything." We're both sobbing now. "I didn't realize until Saturday morning how much you mean to each other, and I was just looking out for him. That bitch Vanessa did a number on him, and I just couldn't bear it if anyone hurt him like that again. But I can see the way you look at each other, you really love each other."

"I know. Don't worry about it, Sam. Just get us to him, please." Oh

God, what will I do if I lose him? After all the horrible things I said to him?

What if he never sees his baby?

No, I mustn't think like that. He's fine.

Please let him be fine!

Samantha finds parking and scrolls through her text messages as we run into the huge Seattle medical plaza to find the text from her father instructing us where to go.

We hold hands in the longest elevator ride of my life. Finally, we find his room. Neil and Lucy are standing outside the door, talking with a doctor. Lucy comes to us immediately when she sees us hurrying down the corridor.

"He's going to be okay."

Oh, thank Christ.

"What happened? Can I see him?" I can't control the tears streaming down my face, and I just want to push her aside and run to my love.

"Yes, you can see him. They have him sedated." Lucy holds one of our hands in each of hers. "We could have lost him."

I look down at her and see the circles under her blue eyes, her pale skin. I hug her close.

"What happened?" I ask again.

"He was in a car accident very early this morning, around two a.m. A drunk driver sideswiped him and sent him into the median on Interstate 5." Lucy wipes the tears under her eyes, and I feel like retching.

It was after I sent him away. Oh, this is all my fault!

"Why was he out at that time?" Samantha asks.

"We got in a fight," I whisper. "This is my fault. Oh God, I'm so sorry."

"No, sweetie, no." Lucy folds me in her arms and rocks me. "It's not your fault."

"Nat, you go see him. I'll stay here with Mom." Sam pats my shoulder reassuringly, and I walk into Luke's room.

My world stops moving.

He's lying so still in the hospital bed. There's a bandage above his left eye and a large bruise on his cheek. He's in a hospital gown very much like the one I wore yesterday. There is a clamp on his index finger, a blood pressure cuff on his arm and an IV in the crook of his elbow. His left wrist is bandaged tightly.

I walk over to the side of his bed and grip his right hand in mine, then sink down in the chair and begin to weep.

"Please, baby, wake up. I need to hear your voice." I'm stroking his hand and staring him in the face, willing him to wake up.

Neil walks in the room and pats my shoulder. "They gave him some medicine to help him sleep."

"Are there internal injuries?" I ask.

"No, he has some bruised ribs and a sprained wrist, and he got knocked around a bit, but he's very lucky. If the car had spun in the other direction, he would have gone over the bridge."

I gasp and rest my cheek against Luke's shoulder. "I'm so sorry."

"Natalie, it's not your fault, honey. Couples fight."

I look up at Neil in surprise.

"Lucy told me that you'd fought and that that's probably why Luke was out so late." He smiles kindly and pats my shoulder again.

"I could have lost him," I whisper.

"He's going to be fine. He'll just need some TLC for a few weeks. I'm going to take Lucy and the kids down to the cafeteria for some breakfast. Take your time."

"I'm not leaving him."

"I'm not asking you to."

A pretty blond nurse bustles in and checks Luke's vital signs and smiles at me. "He's doing really well. Are you Natalie?"

"Yes," I respond, surprised.

"He was asking for you this morning when he regained consciousness. He'll be glad to see you when he wakes up." She winks at me and leaves the room, and Luke and I are alone.

"Oh, honey." I lean up and run my fingers through his soft blond hair. I hate seeing Luke like this, broken and vulnerable in this sterile bed. He's so strong and steady. This is not him. It's not right.

And I know that everyone says it's not, but I can't help but feel that it's my fault that he's here.

My phone rings, and it's Jules.

"Hello," I whisper, so I don't wake Luke.

"What the hell is going on?"

I can tell she's in a panic, and I start talking, low and fast. "Luke was in an accident after he left our place last night. We're at Harbor View. He's okay, just beat up, but they have him sedated."

"I'm on my way."

"Thanks, Jules."

I sit at Luke's side all morning as people come and go. His parents and siblings come in to hug me, and they take turns sitting vigil with me. Jules comes, bringing me a coffee and to also sit with me for a while.

The nurse and doctor both bustle in and out, reading machines and taking notes.

"How long will he sleep?" I ask the doctor.

"We gave him the medicine about six hours ago now, so he should wake up soon."

"Can I snuggle next to him?" I look at the doctor, pleading with my eyes.

"His left wrist is sprained, and a couple ribs also on the left side are bruised. Stick to his right side, and you'll be fine, but be gentle."

"Thank you."

I gingerly wriggle up next to his right side and kiss his stubbly cheek. I rest my head on his shoulder and run my fingers through his hair and down his face.

Oh, I love him so.

"I love you so much," I whisper to him. "I'm so sorry for the way I acted. I'm so sorry."

I continue to croon to him, laying my head on his shoulder and resting my hand over his heart. I stay very still so as not to move him and jostle him.

I wake to Luke's lips on my forehead. I lift my head and find his beautiful blue eyes gazing down at me.

"Oh God, Luke." The tears start again, but they're tears of relief. He's awake!

"Hush, baby, I'm okay."

I adjust myself so he can wrap his right arm around my shoulders, and I run my fingers through his hair. "I'm so sorry. For everything."

He kisses my forehead again. "I'm sorry too." He brushes his fingers through my hair, and I kiss his jaw.

"How do you feel?"

"Sore. Relieved that you're here."

"Sam found me this morning."

"She did?"

"Yeah, your parents called her, and she found me at your place."

His eyebrows shoot up. "My place?"

"I went there this morning to apologize, but you weren't home, so I was waiting for you there. Jules told her I was there." As I remember those horrible moments of not knowing if he was dead or alive, I shudder.

"Are you cold?" he asks.

"No, I'm worried about you. Why were you out so late?"

"I couldn't go home. You weren't there. You wouldn't let me stay with you, so I just decided to drive."

I close my eyes and shake my head, ashamed of how I spoke to him last night.

"Yesterday was rough," I whisper.

"Yes, it was. Will you tell me about it?"

I sit up, and he frowns. "First, let me get the doctor so he can examine you, and once we get you taken care of, if you still want to talk, we will."

"Don't leave me." He holds on to me tightly, clenching his eyes shut.

"Never again," I tell him, and his eyes open quickly, finding mine. "Never," I repeat.

I reach over and push the red nurse-call button.

"How can I help you?" a disembodied voice asks.

"Luke is awake," I respond, still stroking Luke's hair.

"Someone will be right in."

"Hello, Mr. Williams." The doctor smiles at Luke and, seeing me curled up at his side, winks at me. "I have good news for you. We're going to kick you out of here tomorrow. You're banged up pretty good, but nothing is broken, and according to the CT scan, you don't have any internal injuries. You are a very lucky man."

"Thank you. Can I eat?"

"Are you hungry?" I ask him.

"Starving."

"Sure, you can eat. Start with something light. No steaks today."

I get up off the bed so the doctor can examine Luke. Taking advantage of the time, I call Jules and ask her to bring Luke a light sandwich and cup of soup from our favorite deli, and then I call Luke's mom, using the number she gave me earlier, to let them know that Luke is awake and being released tomorrow.

They promise to visit later this evening.

The doctor finishes up as I hang up the phone.

"Jules is bringing you some dinner." I take his right hand in mine and bring it up to my cheek.

"You should go home and eat, get some rest."

"I'm not leaving until you do."

I expect a bit of an argument, but he smiles shyly and caresses my cheek. "Okay. Will you tell me about yesterday?"

"Persistent, aren't you?"

"I want to know what happened."

"Maybe we should talk about this tomorrow, after we're home."

"Talk to me, baby." His face is somber and a little sad, and I close my eyes. Should I tell him about the baby while he's here in the hospital, or should I wait?

I open my eyes, and he's still patiently watching me, and I know that he deserves to know the truth.

I take a deep breath. "I wasn't feeling well yesterday morning before you left, but I thought it was just nerves because you were flying, and I was scared."

I grip his hand in mine, and he squeezes gently. "I wish you'd told me."

"I didn't want to worry you. When I got back to my place, I got violently sick. I spent a good hour throwing up, even when there wasn't anything left to throw up." I squish up my nose in disgust. "Sexy, huh?"

"Keep talking," he responds.

"Jules made me go to the ER when the vomiting showed no signs of stopping."

"Why didn't one of you call me?"

"You were in meetings all day, and there was nothing you could do from LA."

"I could have caught the next flight out."

"I just wanted to see what the doctor said. I thought for sure I had the flu, and they would tell me to drink juice and sleep it off." I shrug.

"What did they tell you?"

I bite my lip and shut my eyes for just a moment. "Well, I'm healthy."

"But?"

Here goes nothing.

"I'm six weeks pregnant," I whisper.

I'm looking down at our hands. The room is silent.

Finally, after what feels like hours, he whispers, "Look at me."

I shake my head no.

"Look at me, baby."

"I didn't do it on purpose."

"Look at my face, Natalie."

I slowly look up at him, and he is gazing at me with love and wonder and a little confusion. But he's not mad.

"You're not angry?" I ask.

"Why would I be angry?"

"Because it's too soon." I shake my head and close my eyes. "It's just too soon."

"I'm not angry. But, Nat, didn't you say that you were on birth control?"

"I was. I'm OCD when it comes to taking my pill, but the doctor said that, just like all birth control methods, it can fail, and clearly, it did."

I look up into his gorgeous face and take a deep breath, steadying myself to finish the story.

"So, the doctor told me I was pregnant and did an ultrasound to see how far along I am. I have a picture. I'll show you in a minute."

"Okay," he whispers.

"After the doctor left, Jules was flipping through channels on the TV in the room and stopped on an evening gossip show, and that's when I saw you." I try to release his hand so I can stand and pace, but he holds on tight.

"Don't go. Finish the story."

"My world fell apart. I hated seeing those pictures, more than I've hated anything in my life. I hated the way you were looking at her . . ." My voice cracks, and I clear my throat.

"Nat, it was nothing."

"I know, but it didn't look like nothing, and then I learned that you'd been engaged to her, and I was hormonal and scared and sick, and I just wanted to be in your arms."

"Come up here."

I lie back down next to him, and he cradles me close to him.

"When I couldn't reach you yesterday, it made me crazy. I couldn't concentrate in any of my meetings. It's not like you to not respond or answer your phone."

"At first I didn't know what to say, and then I was mad at you."

"I caught a late flight back to Seattle and went straight to your place, and you know the rest."

"I'm sorry for the things I said."

"Me, too."

"Luke, I don't want you anywhere near that woman. I don't want you to work with her."

"I called her after I left your place last night and told her that I was going with someone else for the movie. I won't talk to her again. I'm sorry I hurt you. I wasn't holding her when we left the restaurant. I certainly didn't kiss her. I probably hugged her goodbye, but it didn't mean anything. I don't even remember what I was doing, but the rags always twist things to look the way they want them to. I was probably thinking about calling you."

"So," Luke says, and I tilt my head back so I can see his eyes, "we're having a baby."

He smiles, widely, and just looks so . . . *proud of himself.*

"Looks that way."

"I guess we'd better get married sooner rather than later."

"Luke, I don't want you to feel like you have to marry me just because I'm pregnant . . ."

"Stop right there. I asked you to marry me before we knew you were pregnant."

"I know, but . . ."

"No buts. Natalie, I love you so much. I want children with you. This is a wonderful thing. It is soon, sooner than I would have preferred, but a baby is never a bad thing. You're going to be a fantastic mom."

I didn't know I could cry so much in one day. More tears flow. I'm relieved and happy and so in love with this beautiful man.

He leans down and rubs his nose across mine and kisses me in that gentle way that makes me swoon. "I love you, baby."

"I love you, too."

"Oh God, Natalie, the poor man has almost been killed. Must you maul him?" Jules breezes in with a bag full of food. She shakes her head in exasperation.

"Don't be a brat, Jules." I sit up and start unloading Luke's food for him. My stomach grumbles, and I'm pleased to see that she brought some for me, too.

"We're having a baby." Luke gives Jules a wide smile.

"I know. I'm so happy for you guys." Jules walks to him and plants a kiss on his cheek, smiling at both of us.

"Lips off my man, Montgomery."

"Jesus, you're so selfish."

WE'VE BEEN HOME for a week, and Luke has mostly recovered from his injuries. There will be no visits to the gym for a few more weeks, but the bruises have faded.

"The moving van is here."

"You are not lifting anything. Don't even think about it. Your wrist is still healing." He hasn't even lifted me lately, and I'm missing it.

"Well, that makes two of us."

"I didn't hurt my wrist." I raise an eyebrow at him as he crosses the great room to me.

"I do love your sassy mouth." He slaps my bottom, and I squeal, before he moves his hand around to settle on my belly. "There is no lifting for the beautiful woman I knocked up."

I laugh and caress his handsome face. "Are you sure about me moving in here?"

"Of course. We're getting married in two months anyway. It makes sense." He stiffens and frowns down at me. "Don't you want to?"

"I want to be wherever you are. It doesn't make sense for us to move in with Jules." I smirk. "Jules can live in the house as long as she pleases, and I'll still use the studio for work."

"But?" He raises an eyebrow.

"But I think that as our family grows, we might need more bedrooms."

His face softens, and he kisses me gently on the forehead. "I'll buy you any house you want."

"I want to stay here for now. We'll keep our options open."

"Okay." He kisses me again before the moving guys ring the doorbell and start unloading boxes and a few pieces of furniture. I left the majority of everything at the other house for Jules. All of the boxes go up into a spare bedroom, so I can sort through them at my own pace. The unloading doesn't take long.

"Do you need to work this afternoon?" I ask Luke after the men leave.

"No, you?"

"Nope." I walk toward the stairway and start ascending the stairs toward our bedroom.

"What in the world should we do to occupy our time on a rainy Thursday afternoon?" Luke murmurs in my ear at the top of the stairs.

"Hmm . . . we could read," I suggest.

"Nah, I've been doing a lot of that lately." He nibbles my neck and wraps his hands around my waist, spreading his palm over my belly.

"We could watch a movie."

"I'm not in the mood."

We finally make it to the bedroom, and I turn in his arms, kissing him softly while I run my fingers down his cheek.

"I'm all out of ideas," I whisper.

"That's okay," he whispers back. "I have a few ideas of my own."

# *epilogue*

"**H**oly shit."

I'm standing in a beautiful bungalow in Tahiti, in front of a full-length mirror, and I don't even recognize the woman staring back at me.

I love my wedding dress. It's long and billowy. It's white chiffon with a beaded bodice and spaghetti straps, and the skirt falls from the empire waist all the way to the ground. I won't be wearing shoes today. My makeup is classic and simple, perfect for a beach wedding, and my hair is curled into an intricate bun behind my left ear with a red rose pinned to it.

I'm wearing my pearls.

"You are stunning." Jules kisses my cheek, and I smile at her nervously. She is also stunning in her simple pink chiffon gown.

I look around the bungalow and smile in happiness and warmth and love. I am surrounded by beautiful women. Luke's mom, Lucy, and Jules' mom, Gail, have their heads together in a corner. They both look lovely in their pretty pink dresses.

Samantha and Stacy are cooing over little Sophie, who is simply adorable in a soft pink dress with a pink headband.

Jules is, of course, my maid of honor, and Stacy and Sam are my bridesmaids. Sam and I buried the hatchet after Luke's accident, and we have become good friends. She did most of the legwork on planning this fantastic wedding.

"Are you nervous?" Stacy asks.

"I wasn't until I put this dress on. Now I'm a little nervous." I smile and look back in the mirror. Holy shit, I'm getting married!

Neil walks through the door and smiles widely when he sees all of us. "I've been sent in here to give you this." He hands me a wrapped box with a card attached and kisses my cheek. "It's almost time."

"Are the boys ready?" I ask.

"Yes, and your soon-to-be husband is a nervous wreck. He is ready to make you his wife."

I laugh and kiss Neil's cheek. "Here, take this back to him." I hand him a wrapped box, also with a note. "And tell him I'll meet him in a few. I'll be the one in white."

I walk into the bedroom to open the gift in private. My man does enjoy spoiling me. As if renting out this entire beautiful resort for our family and friends to enjoy for a whole week and our beautiful wedding weren't enough, he's given me little gifts every day.

I'm crazy about him.

Luke has written on the envelope of the card, *Open the box first, then read this.*

He's so bossy.

I unwrap the beautiful white paper, and there is a small Tiffany-blue box. Inside, nestled in the satin, is a pair of amazing diamond earrings. They are soft pink princess-cut diamonds with teardrop diamonds dangling from them. They take my breath away.

I open the card and sit on the side of the bed.

*My Love,*

*When you read this, you will be minutes away from becoming my wife. I can't express to you how honored I am that you are mine. I am ready to love you for the rest of my life, as your husband.*

*I love you, with all that I am.*

*—Luke*

Well, isn't he a charmer?

NATALIE DECIDED THAT returning to Tahiti with our family and friends was where she wanted to get married, so I've flown everyone here and booked the resort for the week, just for our affair. I hope it's everything she ever dreamed it would be.

I button my white shirt and check my reflection in the mirror of the master bedroom of my parents' bungalow. Nat wanted the guys to wear khaki pants with white shirts for the ceremony, so that's what we're wearing.

She's the boss.

My hair is a mess, as usual, and it doesn't make sense to fix it, because Nat's fingers will be in it as soon as she sees me.

I smile as I think of my bride. I am one lucky son of a bitch. Natalie is, without a doubt, the sexiest woman I've ever seen, all long dark hair, beautiful green eyes, and smoking-hot curvy body. But her heart is what caught me. Her gracious, loving nature, and sassy mouth are what I can't ever imagine living without.

And I don't have to.

"Hey, Williams, stop mooning over yourself and get in here for a celebratory shot!" Jules' brother Isaac calls from the main room of the bungalow.

All the guys are here: My brother, Mark; Jules'—and Nat's—brothers, Isaac, Caleb, Matt and Will; and their father, Steven. My dad raises his glass as he hands me mine in a toast.

"To my son and Natalie. Thank God she said yes."

"Here, here!"

Everyone slams down the shot, and the room erupts once again in chaos, men yelling lewd jokes and throwing insults.

It does not calm my nerves.

I'm not at all nervous about marrying my girl. I'm just ready for it to be over already.

"Dad, I need you to take something over to Natalie." I hand my dad a small blue Tiffany box.

"No problem, I need to check in with your mother anyway. Are you about ready?" He smiles and pats my back.

"Yes, I've been ready. Let's get this show on the road." My dad laughs as he heads over to the bridal suite, and Isaac approaches me with another shot.

"No, man, I need a clear head for this." I wave off the shot and look out the door toward Nat's bungalow.

"This isn't for you, moron, it's for me." He grins and slugs back the tequila and winces. "Fuck, that's good. Are you ready for this?"

"Everyone keeps asking me that. Yes, I'm ready. I'm past ready."

"You're good for her, you know."

I look over into Isaac's face, shocked. All of Natalie's family have always been welcoming and friendly with me, but I know the brothers have had reservations, and as a brother myself, I can't blame them.

"How so?"

Isaac shrugs and looks back over at the other guys, then back to me. "She's opened up more, laughs more. Hell, I don't know, man. She's just happy. I've known her for a long time, and I don't remember ever seeing her smile this much."

"I'm glad." I nod and smile to myself.

"But if you hurt her, or that baby," Isaac continues, and I know what he's going to say, "I'll fucking kill you."

"No need. I'm not going to hurt her." I hold my hand out to shake his, and he takes it, then pulls me into a guy hug.

"Welcome to the family, bro."

"The girls are ready." My dad stalks back into the room with a wrapped gift in his hand. I told her not to get me anything. She and the baby are everything I need. "This is for you."

I walk into the bedroom to open the gift, and the note, alone, wondering if she likes the pink diamond earrings I sent over. Everything in this wedding is pink, and she should have pink diamonds, too.

*Luke,*

*I know you said that Baby and I are all you need today, but I couldn't help but get you a gift. I chose this particular gift because it symbolizes how precious time is. I am grateful for the time you give me, and for the many years we are about to spend together, as a family, and as lovers. You are what I was waiting for, Luke, and I can't believe that in a few short hours you will be truly mine, as I am yours.*

*Thank you for picking me to share this life with.*

*Love,*

*Nat*

*P.S. I can't wait to kiss you.*

And she calls me charming. God, I love that woman.

Inside the white box is a platinum Omega watch with a black face. On the inside is an inscription, which makes me grin. Nat is big on inscriptions. That sexy body of hers is full of them.

*You are my now, always, forever.—Nat*

Well, hell.

I fasten the watch on my left wrist and stomp back into the main room. "Let's go. No more waiting around."

Without waiting for an answer from anyone, I walk down the wooden boardwalk to the sandy beach where the ceremony will be held. The resort did a great job getting set up with white chairs, a small arbor with red roses, and candles lit and scattered over the sand, giving the beach a soft glow. It's almost sunset, and I know Nat would think the lighting is perfect.

I shake hands and wave at some of our fifty or so guests who have flown here for the week-long celebration and make my way up to the arbor with Isaac and Mark right behind me. The front row is reserved for our parents, and I made sure to have the resort place lilies and sunflowers on two of the chairs in honor of Natalie's parents.

Where is she? I see the girls, all in pink dresses. I'm relieved that my sister, Sam, and Nat have become friends and gotten to know each other better since I proposed. Sam happily helped plan this wedding.

Our mothers are escorted to their seats, and my heart starts to beat a little faster. Jesus, I can't stand the suspense. I need to see her.

Where the fuck is she?

Finally Jules, Sam and Stacy make their way toward us and take their places, and the music changes. Natalie and Jules' father come into view, and the rest of the world just falls away. Her beautiful dark hair has been curled and pulled into a loose bun behind her left ear with a rose tucked in it. Her dress is long and billowy, with a beaded top and spaghetti straps, and she's holding a large bouquet of red roses with the pearls inside. Her new diamonds sparkle at her ears, and, thank God, she's wearing our pearls.

I feel the grin spread across my face as I stare into her gorgeous green eyes, and my heart calms. This is it.

"Who gives this woman to this man?" the pastor asks.

"On behalf of her parents, I do," Steven responds, and places Nat's hand in mine.

Every time I touch her, I feel the hit to my gut. Every single time. I'm drawn to her in ways I never knew possible, and I will never grow tired of the feeling I get when she's near me.

"You are stunning," I whisper to her and grin as she smiles shyly and looks up at me through her long dark lashes.

"You're pretty beautiful yourself," she whispers back.

She can call me beautiful any damn time.

"Welcome, friends and family," the pastor begins. He says a quick prayer and moves right into the ring ceremony.

"With this ring, I thee wed," Natalie says, her eyes on mine, in her soft, sweet voice, and places my ring on my finger.

"With this ring, I thee wed," I respond and push the wedding band onto her small finger, next to her engagement ring.

The rest of the ceremony is relatively short. We decided against the unity candle ceremony and live music, wanting to focus solely on our vows to one another. We wrote our vows together, last week before we left for Tahiti.

We laughed, argued, and Nat cried, but we eventually came up with what we both want to say. Instead of each of us saying the vows in their entirety, we will say them together, alternating the lines.

"And now, Luke and Natalie will recite their vows together." The pastor steps back, and I take both of Natalie's small hands in mine, rubbing my thumbs over her knuckles.

"Are you ready?" I whisper and take a deep breath.

"Yes," she whispers back, her sassy smile in place. God, that smile does things to me.

I clear my throat, and as I look deeply into her eyes, we begin.

"I vow to love you."

"I vow to love you," she responds, her voice strong.

"To respect you."

"To be your best friend."

"To read aloud to you." I run my knuckle down her smooth cheek and see her eyes start to well up.

"To lead a charmed life."

"To write you love letters."

"To laugh at your jokes." She winks at me, and I grin.

"To always make the coffee, or have it delivered."

"To help you cook."

"To always believe that your newest haircut is the best you've ever had." I tuck a strand of her soft hair behind her ear.

"To be patient."

"To always support your hopes and dreams."

"To not overshadow you with my fame," she says, and I can't help but laugh with everyone else.

"To be your biggest fan," I respond. God, I love her.

"To wake you every morning."

"To wake *you* every morning. You are not a morning person."

"To kiss you every night."

"To hold your hand."

"To always remember where I left my keys and phone."

"To cherish you." I take another deep breath.

"To believe in you."

"To believe in us."

"To never give up." She clenches my hands in hers more tightly.

"To never, *ever* give up."

"To forsake all others and be true to you."

"To work every day toward being the man you deserve."

"To work every day toward being the woman you deserve." We both have tears in our eyes now.

"Do you vow to be my wife?"

"I do. Do you vow to be my husband?"

"I do." Fuck, yes, I do.

"It is my pleasure to present Mr. and Mrs. Luke Williams. You may kiss your bride."

I cup her beautiful face in my hands, and she runs her fingers through my hair, gazing up at me with such love, such trust, it takes my breath away. I slowly lean down and brush my nose down hers and sweep my lips over hers in the way I know she loves. She sighs against me as I slide my arms around her, pulling her more tightly against me, and cup the small baby bump between us in my hands.

Our guests are applauding, our mothers dabbing at their tears. I rest my forehead against hers as she runs her fingers down my cheek.

"I love you," I whisper.

"I love you, too. Let's go dance."

The End

The With Me In Seattle Series continues with Jules and Nate's story in FIGHT WITH ME. It is available now.

Also, don't forget about Isaac and Stacy's story in UNDER THE MISTLETOE WITH ME, a novella also available now! Here is a sneak peek:

# Under the Mistletoe *with me*
## SNEAK PEEK

## *one*

"I'm just glad you didn't have a game today and can actually enjoy Thanksgiving dinner with us." My mother-in-law, Gail, smiles over at her son Will, who is currently stuffing his face full of mashed potatoes.

"Me, too, Mom. God, this is good."

"That's a lot of carbs for a man in training," Isaac mutters next to me. I run my palm up and down my husband's thigh and grin up at him. He loves giving his brother a hard time.

"Dude, it's Thanksgiving," Will replies.

"So the carbs don't count?" Isaac asks.

"Exactly." Will grins and takes another bite of his potatoes. I am surrounded by a room full of loving, funny people. The Montgomery gene pool is impressive. But more than being, well, gorgeous, they are welcoming and good-hearted, and I'm proud and lucky to be a part of them.

Sophie, our four-month-old daughter, squirms in my arms.

"Here, babe, let me take her." Isaac pulls our baby girl into his arms and lays her on his broad shoulder. She settles in and falls back to sleep, her face pressed against his neck. I can't blame her. It's one my favorite places to be, too. "You eat, honey."

We are all gathered at Luke and Natalie's house for the holiday. The loving couple have been married for about two months now, and I couldn't be happier for them. Natalie isn't a sister by blood, but she's been a part of this family for years. She and Jules', the youngest and only girl of the Montgomery clan, are the best of friends. With the addition of Luke's parents, Lucy and Neil, and two siblings, Samantha and Mark, along with my parents as well, this house is overflowing with bodies, loud with voices and laughter, and is a little too warm.

There is nowhere I'd rather be.

"Stace, how is your blog going?" Jules asks next to me.

"It's going well, thanks. I really love it."

"She's being modest," Isaac cuts in with a grin. "It's going great. She's got over two thousand followers, and her reviews have been picked up by some publishers to add to book covers."

He smiles down at me and kisses my forehead, his blue eyes shining with pride. God, I love him.

"What kind of books are you reviewing?" Natalie asks.

"Romance novels," I reply with a smile.

"The dirty kind?" Will asks hopefully, earning a smack in the arm from Luke's sister, Samantha. "What?"

"Don't be a perv," she mutters, glaring at him.

"Actually, all kinds, but yes, the erotic novels are pretty hot right now," I respond and wink at him.

"Oh! Have you read those books that everyone's been talking about?" Samantha asks. "You know, the ones where the guy ties her up and spanks her and is all kinds of naughty?"

I feel my ears burn as I blush. The guys all roll their eyes, but Matt, Isaac's younger brother, clears his throat and won't look anyone in the eye.

Interesting.

"Yes, I've read them, Sam."

"I could use some of those," Jules whispers in my ear. "I've hit a dry spell."

"I'll e-mail you a list," I whisper back, and we giggle.

"What are you whispering about?" Isaac asks, pulling my hand up to kiss my knuckles.

"Just books," I reply.

"Okay, gimme the baby." Natalie stands and walks around the table, her arms open, and scoops Sophie up off of Isaac's shoulder, nuzzling her. "Hi, precious. I missed you."

My gaze finds Luke. He's watching his wife, his blue eyes full of love and contentment. Natalie is pregnant herself.

"Anytime you want practice with middle-of-the-night feedings, you're welcome to it," Isaac tells her.

I roll my eyes and smack his arm. "Quit trying to give my baby away."

He winks at me and takes a bite of his turkey. "I'm just kidding."

"You know I'd keep her in a heartbeat," Natalie responds with a happy smile and kisses Sophie's cheek, making her giggle.

Isaac's phone rings in his pocket. He checks the display and scoots his chair back. "I'll be right back."

I wonder who it could be. Surely not work on Thanksgiving. I shrug it off and finish my dinner, and then help clear the table and clean the kitchen. With all of us chipping in, the chores are done quickly, and we all settle in with glasses of wine or coffee to chat and recover from the delicious Thanksgiving meal.

Finally, Isaac returns from his phone call, a frown on his handsome face.

"Who was that?" I ask.

"It was nothing." He shakes his head and walks to the kitchen to pull a beer out of the fridge before sitting next to me on the couch.

"It was some*one*," I respond.

He shakes his head again and takes a pull from his beer. "Don't worry about it."

I frown up at him. This is new. It's not that we have to share every little detail about who we talk to, but we usually do. He's never been evasive before.

Before I can argue with him, he takes my hand in his and links our fingers, bringing them up to his lips. "Just drop it."

He grins down at me and winks, then strikes up a conversation with Will about his football season with the Seahawks, effectively closing the subject. With a full belly, and a warm fire blazing not far away, I settle in next to my firm husband, rest my head on his muscular shoulder, and watch the activity around me.

"Stacy, here are the photos we took last week of Sophie." Natalie hands me a thumb drive. "I think you'll like them."

"Oh, I know I'll love them! Thanks again for doing it. I'll order Christmas cards next week." I grin at her as she takes a seat across from me with Jules.

Jules and Nat have their heads together, as usual, cooing over a sleeping Sophie. I smile at the three of them. Three beautiful girls. I pull my phone out of my pocket and snap a photo of them.

Sam sits next to them and kisses Sophie's head, and I snap another photo.

All of our parents are settled around the dining room table with coffee, chatting about grandkids and Christmas plans.

Will and Isaac ramble on about football, with Matt, their other brother, and Luke chiming in here and there. Mark saunters in from the kitchen, passes Luke another beer and joins them. The only one missing is Caleb, who is off on some SEAL mission.

I hope he'll be home for Christmas.

"You okay?" Isaac whispers.

"Mmm."

He grins down at me and kisses my hair. My eyes are heavy. I let my eyelids fall and listen to the conversations around me.

"I'll be back in a minute." Isaac catches my chin in his fingers and kisses me softly. I never get tired of his lips. My man can kiss. He moves away from me and lowers me onto the couch so my head is on the armrest, and I feel him walk away from me.

Will, Luke and Mark are enthralled in football talk, passionately arguing about the offensive line.

Suddenly, my eyes blink open, and I wonder how long I've slept. I didn't mean to drift off.

Our moms have left their husbands at the table and joined the rest of us girls in the living room. My mom cradles Sophie in her arms, earning a frown from Jules.

"I never get to hold her. Between Natalie and you guys, I never get her."

"Don't whine," Natalie mutters.

"Shut up," Jules responds, and I giggle. They are so funny, even when they bicker.

"Stace, I'm glad the blog is going well," Luke's mom, Lucy, says with a smile.

"Thanks, me, too. I just need something to do while I'm home with Sophie. Don't get me wrong, I'm not bored, but I just . . ." How do I explain that I need something, just for me, without sounding selfish?

"I get it," Lucy responds.

"So, let's talk strategy, girls." Jules rubs her hands together and perches at the edge of the couch with a large stack of newspaper ads. "Black Friday." She grins excitedly and bounces on the cushion, her pretty blond hair bouncing with her. She licks her finger and grabs the ad on top, flipping through it.

"I'm not going at four a.m. this time," Natalie informs her, while she rubs her tiny baby bump. "This little one won't let me out of bed that early."

"I can't do that early either," I chime in.

"I'm doing my shopping online." Sam waves us off and rolls her eyes. "I refuse to get into a fistfight over a scarf."

"You're no fun." Jules pouts.

"I'm in, if we leave around seven. I can have Sophie fed and be ready myself."

"Okay, Nat and I will pick you up then."

"Gonna spend all my money, baby?" Luke murmurs into Nat's ear as she climbs into his lap. He wraps his arms around her and holds her close, and I can't help but grin at them. They are so in love.

"Yep. All of it. We'll be homeless when I'm done."

"It's okay, we'll go live with Jules."

"Oh, hell, no." Jules shakes her head and laughs. "We'll save enough money for you to cover the mortgage."

"Oh, good," he replies drily.

"Well, some of us *are* on a budget," I inform them with a chuckle. "So go easy on me."

"It's gonna be so fun!" Jules claps her hands as Sophie begins to fuss in my mom's arms.

"We should probably head home," I murmur and stand, stretching my arms up over my head. "Will, where are Isaac and Matt?"

"I think they're on the deck," Will responds, and then returns to his football conversation with the boys.

What is it with men and football?

I walk over to the patio door and open it quietly. I hear my husband's deep voice say, "I just don't know what to do about her."

"Well, bro . . ." Matt begins, but stops when he sees me in the doorway. He offers me a smile. "Hey, Stace."

"Hey." I step out on the deck and smile at Isaac, but my stomach is in knots as I remember the mysterious phone call at dinner, and now this. "What's going on?"

Isaac shakes his head and shrugs nonchalantly. "Nothing."

"Uh huh." I eye him, knowing he's keeping something from me, but then I hear Sophie cry inside. "We should go. Soph is ready for bed."

"Okay, let's go."

Made in the USA
Middletown, DE
18 January 2019